Farm N‹

by

Donduce Ritchie

To Neil,
Thank you so much for coming,
and hope you enjoy the book!
Best Wishes,

Donduce Ritchie
10/11/19

I would like dedicate this book to Suzie, and to thank Suzie, my Wife, for all her love, help and support without which this book would not have been possible. Thank you Honey, Love you xxx

Chapter 1

"Fuck off

noooooooooooooooooooooo!!!!!" mumbled Beauty as the alarm went off at stupid o'clock. She disappeared even further under the duvet and cuddled up even more tightly to her husband Donduce.

Chapter 2

After an outstretched hand turned the alarm to snooze several times, a muffled "Oh shit, we had better get up Honey" from Donduce came from under the duvet, and very slowly two bodies emerged.

"What time is it my Angel?" asked a very sleepy Beauty as her head appeared from under the folds.

Donduce looked at his watch; "It is 7:30am, my Babsey, and, shit, guess what we are doing later on this morning".

Beauty rubbed her eyes, looked puzzled for a few moments, and then her eyes opened wide; "Oh My God! You are going to tell me the secret of the 'Old Empty Barn' later on aren't you. All the press and media have been camped out for a while there; it's quite a famous story. When are we going?".

"I think as soon as we have got up and got ready", said Donduce. "We don't want the press on the farm estate any longer than we have to. I just wanted to leave it until enough of the media got here so that we get as much coverage as possible".

The Old Empty barn was a building on the Estate of where Donduce and Beauty lived, and for some reason there was always a sort of mist which could be seen over it.

The whole site was a farm called EE-I-O; the site itself was vast, however the barn was located quite near to the main entrance. Donduce had had an idea of how to make quite a lot of money out of a 'secret' about the barn, however he was worried.

The secret he was going to disclose to Beauty and then afterwards the press was one he had made up, and with publicity and advanced bookings for his announcement the plan had gone very well. What worried Donduce was the real secret of the old empty barn, which he would tell Beauty in the fullness of time was a horrific and ghastly one.

The locals, in the nearby village of the same name new of the farm very well; they didn't know about the secret, but they did know of the history of the barn. It had been there for centuries and indeed had a chequered and mysterious past. The locals also had mixed views about the farm; and indeed Donduce and Beauty, the Farmer and his beautiful Wife; some for good reasons, however a lot for bad; more on that later.

Donduce and Beauty climbed out of bed and started their usual morning routine; into the bathroom scuttled Beauty, whilst Donduce made the bed; as he walked around it laying the duvet back all perfect, he trod on the squeaky floorboard again and swore to himself "Fucking thing, I am seriously going to have a look at that, it pissed me off every bloody morning".

He finished the bed, took his dressing gown off and got dressed.

"Just going to the kitchen to start in there", he called out to Beauty, "See you in a bit".

"Ok, my Lovey, won't be long" called Beauty from the shower, "Love You".

Donduce called "Love you" back and went into the kitchen to empty the dishwasher first, then it was all the usual stuff; emptying the bin, and cleaning all the pots containing tea, coffee, sugar etc finishing with the kettle. Then it was cleaning the toaster, bread bin and last but not least, the microwave.

Beauty would be out of the shower soon and when they had their usual cuddle and passionate kiss, it would be his turn to hit the bathroom whilst Beauty did the polishing in the lounge. Last of all Donduce would clean the bathroom after he had finished, and then the joys of hoovering: great.

"I wonder if Beauty want's me to walk those bloody Danes later. If she does it will have to be after the barn event." thought Donduce as he had a quick drink whilst he waited for Beauty to emerge.

After about five minutes there were signs of life coming from the bedroom. Donduce went in, and Beauty was sitting on the stool by the dressing table waiting for Donduce to dry her long dark beautiful hair. It was part of their deep unique religion that neither of them cut their hair; Beauty's was down to just below her bum, and Donduce's was just below his waist. His beard was also very long too and stretched down to his belt line. He dried her hair and gave her a loving kiss on her forehead.

"All done, my Lovey", he said and then added, "I was thinking when I was in the kitchen about walking those bloody Danes later, but it won't be at the normal time because of the empty barn event. What do you think?" he asked with a giggle in his voice due to the reference of 'bloody'.

Beauty let out a giggle: "Those Danes are *lovely*. I know you think they are huge but they make us so much money with our breeding program my gorgeous Hubby. I was going to say to walk them round the usual way just round the farmhouse and the field bit, but you have reminded me it clashes with the barn. Could you radio one of the farmhands to do it. They will go mad if they aren't walked at the usual time? Pretty Please?!"

"Ok, good idea", replied Donduce. "They go bloody mad even when I do walk them at the usual time" he added, and they both broke into fits of giggles.

"Right then" said Donduce, "My turn in the bathroom my Lovey".

"Right then" said Beauty, "My turn for polishing and then doing your beautiful hair, my Babsey".

After Donduce and Beauty had done all of their usual bits; they made sure each other's hair was brushed, and especially Beauty's who always had her hair flopping right over her face. Beauty was very particular about this. Where possible Beauty preferred that only her Hubby saw her face and so was Donduce. Beauty's real name was Suzie, but nobody ever called her that; Donduce nicknamed her 'The Beauty' or 'Beauty' because she was beautiful and all the staff on the farm addressed her as 'Beauty' on Donduce's orders. Donduce's real name *was* Donduce. An unusual name but so be it; more on that later as well.

The other insistence that Beauty had was that she never ever spoke to people; she hated them and her Hubby was the only living person that she spoke too. This came about from events many years before but more on that as well, later.

Once this hair ritual was completed, Donduce picked up the front door keys and then said to Beauty "Ok, here we go my Babsey; are you ready to meet the masses, the thronging crowds; the paparatsy; the tv cameras and the roving reporters?"

"Fuck off am I" replied Beauty, "When this is finished, we or rather you can tell them to sod off please, my Babsey".

"I'll take that as a 'no' then shall I?" laughed Donduce as they went out the front door.

After Donduce had locked it, they walked across their front yard area, past the garages and through the entrance gates located in a gap in the very tall tree line that hid the main farm house area making it private and secluded from the rest of the immediate farm complex. Once through the gates they were walking along the main entrance road, which ran from the main road, called 'Akks Lane' to one of the junctions on the farm estate. A left turn off 'Main Entrance Road' took them past several fields.

"Why the fuck didn't we take the car, my Babsey?" asked Beauty who was thinking about her poor feet. "We are going to have to walk bloody back don't forget".

"Shit", said Donduce, "I never thought of that, and, bollocks, the car keys are in the fucking farmhouse. We are only just out of our front gate. Shall we go back and get the jeep, my Lovey?"

"Yes, please my Babsey", said Beauty; the smile abruptly returning to her pretty little face or rather what you could see of it.

They turned and walked back into the yard; Beauty waited while Donduce popped in and got the car keys. He returned and pressed a remote device which operated one of the automatic electric garage doors. It sprang into action, revealing their jeep: a four by four and was purple in colour. It was in fact the only vehicle on the farm estate to be this colour as all farm vehicles had the livery of the official State that the farm actually was; brown with a gold stripe horizontally down the middle.

Now came another ritual. Donduce opened the passenger side of the jeep first, and Beauty flicked her beautiful hair back, and folded it so that it wouldn't touch the jeeps floor. Once Beauty was in, they kissed passionately, door shut, and Donduce went round to his side and did the same thing.

"Here we go again, take two", laughed Donduce, "I had forgotten about the sodding walk, especially coming back as well; well done you, my Angel".

"That's quite alright, my Babsey", said Beauty with a giggle, "Considering I didn't want to fucking go anyway".

They both burst into fits of laughter and Donduce started the engine. They were soon out of the yard, and heading up the 'Main Entrance Road'.

After about two minutes, Donduce signalled right and they turned into a farm track. It was a lovely sunny morning; you could see for quite a distance but during the winter sometimes this track looked rather desolate. It had an earthy surface, not tarmac: fences lined either side of the road as it divided two large fields in a large hockey stick shape; with the road entrance at the curved end. As one approached the straight part after it bared round to the left, the field on the right was occupied by sheep, and before that horses; on the left between the track and the Main Entrance Road, cows. The track was a dead end and at the end was the old empty barn. In front was a wide area where there was more than enough room to turn a vehicle round.

Donduce and Suzie got to the bend, and as Donduce turned the corner, he said "Oh shit, My Babsey, look at that lot! No wonder you didn't want all the fuss."

"Oh fuck, no, I hate them, my Babsey, let's go back" said Beauty but then added, "I do want to know the secret though; obviously you deal with them and then we will go. Is that ok Sweetheart?"

"Of course it is my Babsey, don't worry, just stay next to me", replied Donduce.

"Too fucking right I will, my Honey, I don't want those contaminating shits even near me" she said with a giggle.

In the distance was a crowd of the people who had been camping out waiting for the big event. Lorries, with satellite dishes were there, and loads of tents.

"I can't believe that so many people can fit into an area like that, they are crammed in like sardines", said Donduce as they got nearer.

"I know", replied Beauty, and added "And how the fuck are we going to fit in amongst that lot, plus even reach the stupid sodding barn, my Babsey?"

"Don't worry, just leave it to me, my Lovey" said Donduce.

They got within roughly fifty yards of the assembled throng when Donduce said"

"Oh Blimey, there's Mac Hassle. He looks very flustered; he's spotted us and he's coming my Babsey. Don't panic".

Mac Hassle was the chief farm foreman and anything that happened on the farm state principality was reported to him, and then to the state, being Donduce. Donduce *was* the State.

"Ok, my Sweetheart", said Beauty nervously and observed the impending encounter. Mac Hassle had spotted the jeep and walked over signalling to Donduce to wind the window down. Donduce duly did that and Mac Hassle bent down so that his head was level with Donduce's.

"Morning King Donduce" and looked at Beauty "Morning Queen Beauty Ma'am", he said, "Fine morning for all this shit isn't it. The head of the press organisation is waiting to greet you with some sort of presentation, so please could you follow me and I will introduce you".

"Thank you Mac Hassle" replied Donduce; Beauty smiled, "Give us two minutes to get out of the Royal Jeep and we will be there".

"Ok Sir. Private security followed you up and they are currently milling around the crowd. We have also done a code one, and lastly, your radio message regarding the Royal Danes has already been acted on. Now, considering this lot is from outside the Royal Principality, can we please speed up proceedings and loose them at the first opportunity, Sir?"

"No problem Mac Hassle", said Donduce.

He wound the window up, and they kissed passionately while Mac Hassle hurried off.

Donduce and Beauty got out of the car and performed their usual hair ritual. Then hand in hand, they walked the fifty yards or so towards the throng. A man wearing a very posh suit was talking to Mac Hassle who had already got to the front of the crowd, and as Donduce and Beauty got nearer, he looked up and almost stood to attention. He smiled and with a gesture to Mac Hassle to follow him, they both started to walk towards them.

"Don't worry, my Babsey", said Donduce, squeezing Beauty's hand, "Just leave this to me" he added.

"Ok, my Lovey", Beauty replied, and then said in a quiet whisper "Good Luck Honey".

Donduce and Beauty, Mac Hassle and the smartly dressed man met.

Mac Hassle was the first one to speak:

"King Donduce, Queen Beauty, may I introduce Adam Westerly, he is the Director of the 'EE-I-O Herald' and is the co-ordinator of the media gathering that has been here for this great announcement".

Adam Westerly bowed twice and shook Donduce's hand.

"King Donduce, it is a pleasure as always", he said "My Queen Beauty Ma'am a pleasure" he added. Beauty smiled and thought "Fuck off you pompous Bastard".

Adam Westerly continued "Before you make your announcement, I would be honoured if you would accept a presentation box of newspaper articles of happenings on the farm that you sent us over the years for you to keep as a souvenir, and maybe at a later date give us permission to publish in our future new publication 'EE-I-O' the early years".

"Thank you very much", said Donduce and thought "I can't remember this guy's fucking name already, I will just be polite. Donduce continued "The Queen and I would love to accept such a wonderful surprise and we will have many happy hours reading all the events over the years that have happened on our Estate".

"Thank you", said Adam, and he gave Donduce a leather bound box. Donduce took it, they shook hands, and then Adam was handed a microphone from one of the members of the media. He thrust it in Donduce's hand and said:

"All yours Sir!"

8

"Oh, Fuck!" thought Donduce.

"Oh, FUCK!!" thought Beauty.

Donduce composed himself, and gripping Beauty's hand, Beauty squeezed his very tightly to say "Good luck and I love you", Donduce held the microphone to his mouth and said:

"Good morning, as you are all aware, everyone, including my beautiful Beauty want to know the secret of the VERY OLD, VERY ANCIENT, EMPTY BARN. Well, what I am about to tell you all is as follows", he paused, and then said "I am going to take Beauty into the barn and tell her first, and then come back with her and make an announcement to the world's press".

With that, Donduce led his beloved Beauty into the very old very ancient Old empty barn. It was old and made of flint. The walls were cold, and the wind had a chill in it as it blew through the open doorway. The mist that was over the barn suddenly started to form inside as Donduce and Beauty stood there. They could still hear the chatter of the press outside, and there was an air of anticipation all around.

"Right then my darling Babsey", he said, "This is for your ears only and it goes no further than between you and I. The secret that I am about to tell you goes like this: the whole point of the secret was in two parts, the first, was to make money by selling the story to the media, who don't yet know that they will never know, and they have all paid to come on our land, so we have made quite a bit, very legitimately. The next part of the secret is quite simply the answer to the mystery that I made up. It is this: the secret story of the very old and ancient old empty barn: There was nothing in it!! It was empty. The real secret of the old empty barn I will tell you at some point but in private on our own".

"Ok my Babsey" replied Beauty and then asked "This secret about here, is it exciting or nasty or what my Lovey".

"Can't tell you now my Babsey" replied Donduce, and added "And especially not *here*".

They had a major hug and had just started to giggling over the 'nothing in it' secret when Donduce noticed the outline of a shape on the back wall of the barn. It was the figure of a man.

"Fucking hell my Babsey" said Donduce, "We've got to get out NOW!"

"What's the matter, my Babsey?" asked a very startled Beauty as Donduce led her very quickly towards the barn's door frame.

"I will tell you when we get back to the jeep" replied Donduce. "Try to act calm though whilst we face the press, my Lovey".

"Act fucking calm, after you reacted to something and virtually dragged me out, my Babsey? Are you fucking kidding?"

"Sorry my Babsey", said Donduce and added "Leave this to me".

Donduce and Beauty left the barn and went out to face the media. Donduce raised his arm and called for quiet. "There is only ever going to be one other person who will ever know the secret of the old empty barn, apart from me, and that is Beauty. Thank you all for coming, and Goodbye".

The media started packing up their equipment, and Donduce and Beauty made their way back to the jeep armed with the leather box containing the old newspaper cuttings.

"I wonder what happenings from the past are in there, my Lovey", said Donduce, "We will have to have a look when we get a moment".

"I can't wait", replied Beauty, "Shit, all the adventures that we have had over the years, there must be hundreds of them, my Babsey".

They arrived at the jeep and Donduce opened Beauty's door. She flicked her hair back and folded it in readiness to sit down. Once perched, they kissed passionately and then Donduce shut her door; walked round the front of the jeep and got in, placing the leather bound box on the back seat.

Donduce started the engine and as he did he said to Beauty:

"Right my Babsey. When I was hugging you in that barn I saw the outline of the figure of a man standing against the back wall; a ghost. Don't panic too much but it involves the real secret of the barn. I had to get you out fast for our own protection, but more about that later my Angel"

"Don't panic too much, my Babsey? A fucking ghost? Get us out fast for our own protection? Fucking hell!! I'm fucking glad we're back in the fucking jeep! Oh my fucking god, my Lovey."

"I thought you might say something like that", replied Donduce then added:

"Why don't we drive up to the barn and just look at it. We haven't really seen it for a while on our own. It would be nice to see it up close. We will be safe in the jeep, my Babsey".

"Are you fucking kidding, my Babsey?" exclaimed Beauty, "I never want to fucking go near it again!"

Beauty paused for a minute and then said: "Ok, my Lovey, I suppose I'm sort of intruigued now.", and then added "Can we go home after that because after all of what happened I'm a bit pissed off with looking at the fucking thing".

"Right then", said Donduce laughing, "We will just simply turn round outside it and then go back. We have got to anyway because the track isn't wide enough here to turn round, my Lovey"

They pulled forward and drove up to where the old empty barn was. At the end, the track took on the shape of an oval and the barn was located at one end. As they turned, they could see it must have been 15th or 16th century. It was made of flint and had little slits in the walls.

"Those slits are part of the secret, I will have to research the details of it though, as my memory is a bit foggy. I just wondered if the barn was a strong hold for archers many years ago, my Lovey", said Donduce as they sat in the jeep and peered up at it.

"I have no idea, my Babsey", replied Beauty and added "I don't remember from the history of our farm anything about battles; maybe look it up sometime when we get the chance, now come on then, chop chop!"

"Of course, my Lovey", giggled Donduce.

They headed off back down the hockey stick shaped farm track, and were very soon back on Main Entrance Road. Donduce signalled left, and very soon after that they pulled into their front yard and were back home. Donduce reversed the jeep back into the garage and cut the engine. He leaned over to Beauty and they kissed passionately.

"Home at last my Lovey", he said, "Next thing on the agenda is that fucking floorboard. I am going to get some tools out of here, take a section of carpet up and fix that pissing squeak once and for all. Is that Ok my Babsey" he asked.

"Yes, of course it is", said Beauty. "That squeaky floor board is really pissing me off too, my Babsey", she added.

Donduce got out of the jeep and walked round as usual to Beauty's door. He opened it and she got out. She flicked her beautiful hair forward, and, after Donduce had done the same he went over to the back of the garage and picked up the handle of a large toolbox.

"This will come in very useful for that fucking floorboard my Sweetheart", he said. "Wow, my Honey", she replied, "I haven't seen that for a while". He extended the handle so that the toolbox took on the shape of a small wheeled suitcase. He opened it and put the leather box inside so that it would be one less item to carry. Then they linked arms and walked arm in arm to the front door. Donduce got his keys out, after having shut the garage door with the remote.

They were soon inside and Donduce locked the front door. "Where shall we put this box my Lovey? How about the lounge for now?" he asked.

"Yes, I will put it in the sideboard draw for now so we know where it is, my Babsey" replied Beauty "Then I had better attend to our cats. They will need feeding; I should have done it this morning but with all of this on my mind I completely forgot about it, sorry Babsey".

"Fucking hell, so did I! Honey", replied Donduce. "I will take the toolbox to the bedroom and start squeak curing".

Chapter 3

Donduce and Beauty had two cats: tortoise shell females called Molly and Lucky. Molly they had had from a kitten, and Lucky had been a stray found on the farm by one of the farmhands soon after the purchase of Molly. The morning routine did involve feeding them and letting them out of Donduce's office; but, due to the event; it had been overlooked.

Donduce headed into the bedroom with the toolbox. He pushed with his foot where he thought the floorboard was and that fucking annoying squeak happened again.

"I'll fix you, you bastard", thought Donduce to himself and opened the toolbox.

"Oh shit", he thought, "That fucking box is in here, I'll go and give it to my Babsey". He pulled it out and set off to the kitchen where Beauty was preparing the cat food.

He was about half way when Beauty was calling him and she sounded rather worried:

"Babsey, are you there? Please hurry, something's up Babsey?!!"

Donduce broke into a run and flew into the kitchen. He rushed over to Beauty; she had a knife in one hand and a sachet of cat food in the other. He gave her a big cuddle; Beauty's arms were up in the air as she had her hands full and didn't want to cover her Husband in cat food.

"What's the matter, my Lovey Honey", he asked "Are you alright?"

"Babsey, I just heard the Communications machine, Mac Hassle wants you on a 'Code One' NOW!" she said worriedly.

"Ok, don't panic my Babsey" replied Donduce, "What the fuck does he want I wonder".

Donduce and Beauty released their cuddle and he went into the lounge where a large communications device was sitting by the settee. It was a large multichannel receiver that picked up every industrial and Royal control room on the Royal Estate.

13

He pressed 'One' which was the Communications Centre and said"

"Donduce receiving 'Code One'. Come in Mac Hassle".

Immediately came the reply:

"Mac Hassle here Sir, we have received two messages. The first is that two lions have escaped from the Royal Sanctuary and are on the loose, the second is that an ELK is laying down on the cattle grid to the north of the Main Entrance Road, just before the prohibited zone. What is your command Sir?"

Donduce pressed the button on the receiver. Beauty had heard this message and had come running in from the kitchen.

"Donduce here. Message received. Firstly, when did the lions escape?"

"Mac Hassle. They were reported missing roughly an hour ago. Sanctuary Wardens found a massive hole in their fence area. Command please Sir"

"Donduce here. Right, the Sanctuary is about two hundred miles south of this area. This part of the Royal Estate should be safe for a couple of days. Send a 'Code Two' to staff and issue them with suitable equipment ready for an encounter. We will deal with...what was it again?"

"Mac Hassle. An ELK on the cattle grid Sir".

"Donduce. An ELK?"

"Mac Hassle. Yes Sir, an ELK".

"Donduce. What sort of ELK?"

"Mac Hassle. With all due respect, I don't know Sir, just an ELK, and it is stopping Estate transportation coming onto the farm. We don't need an ELK interrupting exports Sir"

"Donduce. Ok. Where did the ELK come from, and how do you know it's an ELK?"

"Mac Hassle. With all due respect, all I have been told to inform you by the security services is that an ELK is lying on the cattle grid and about the lions. Security has not had the time to ascertain that it is an ELK, but Sir, it is lying on the cattle grid Sir".

"Donduce. When you say 'lying', is it alive?"

"Mac Hassle. No idea Sir, but again, with all due respect, who is going to find a dead ELK around these parts and place it on the cattle grid?"

"Donduce. Point taken. We will deal with the 'ELK' from this end, and 'State Security Code Two' issued from Donduce immediate effect regarding the lions.

"Mac Hassle. Thank you".

"Donduce. Thank you.

Donduce pressed a button and the receiver went silent.

"Fucking hell!! Lions! An ELK or something similar! Shit Babsey! Cattle grid Immo! Now! Babsey! Fuck!" exclaimed Donduce.

"Ditto, my Babsey and Fuck!" exclaimed Beauty.

"We'll have to get the sodding jeep out again, my Babsey, fuck. Come on, let's get out there" said Donduce.

"Oh, what a pissing pain in the arse", said Beauty then added: "We can't leave the ELK or whatever it is there, but then how are we going to move it? My Babsey?"

"Don't panic, we will try and guide it back here. It could live in the grassy meadow behind the coalbunker area", replied Donduce; then he added "We could call that ELKY's meadow, eh my Babsey?"

"Lovely my Babsey", said Beauty, "But we need an ELK first!"

Donduce and Beauty burst into fits of giggles then they kissed passionately and Beauty eventually put the cat food down with the knife she had still been holding. They headed to the front door and the communication device went off again.

"For fuck's sake, what now?" shouted Donduce in the direction of the machine.

"God knows, fucking Mac Hassle again, come on my Babsey, we had better get it".

They went back into the lounge, and Donduce pressed the button again.

"Donduce answering 'Code One' *again*."

"Mac Hassle here."

Donduce frowned and gritted his teeth.

"Donduce. I know it's you Mac Hassle; what's up now?"

"Mac Hassle. Sorry but I forgot to tell you about the gorilla."

"Donduce. About the WHAT?"

"Mac Hassle. Gorilla Sir".

"Donduce. Ok, what gorilla?"

"Mac Hassle. We have also had a report that a gorilla escaped from the sanctuary as well".

"Donduce. How long has it been missing?"

"Mac Hassle. About three months"

Donduce and Beauty stared at each other: "Three fucking months" they said in unison.

"Donduce. Three months?"

"Mac Hassle. Yes, Sir."

"Donduce. Why the hell has this report taken so long?"

"Mac Hassle. They have only just discovered it was missing Sir. It wasn't in an enclosed area, it was in the rain forest".

"Donduce. So how do they know it *is* missing then?"

"Mac Hassle. All the gorillas are tagged with a transmitter, and this one is out of range, and so not in the area it is supposed to be".

"Donduce. Can't the communications centre pick up the signal?"

"Mac Hassle. They have Sir."

Donduce said to Beauty "Fucking hell, we could spend the rest of the day with this conversation; talk about hard to talk to, my Babsey".

"Tell me about it, my Lovey" said Beauty.

Donduce composed himself and said:

"Donduce. According to the signal, where is the gorilla now?"

"Mac Hassle. In this area Sir"

"Donduce. *Exactly where* in this area?"

"Mac Hassle. Don't know Sir, the signal keeps breaking up, but it's within 30 miles of the Royal Estate"

"Donduce. Ok, approved 'code 2' usual routine".

"Mac Hassle. OK Sir, thank you".

The machine went dead.

"Fucking hell Babsey, I was expecting the fucking gorilla to be outside the fucking front door at this rate, my Babsey" said Donduce".

"It still might well be my Babsey" said Beauty, and added "Let's get on and recover this fucking ELK, and while we are at it we'll invite the fucking gorilla in for coffee".

They kissed passionately and then went out of the front door to start the ELK rescue.

Donduce locked it behind them and said to Beauty, "Fancy a quick wander up to the meadow just to check that it is suitable, my Lovey?"

"Ok my Babsey", said Beauty and added "It's big enough I am sure".

They walked hand in hand across the front yard the other way and went through a gate which led to a path that went round the back of the farm to the back yard. Having arrived at this point, the coalbunker on the other side came into view.

"Oh shit!" said Donduce looking rather annoyed, "The coalbunker hatches are open! That's unusual for the coal man; must have been in a hurry. I will shut them when we get back my Lovey".

"Oh Babsey, sod the meadow; it will be suitable" said Beauty, "Let's go and find this ELK. It is holding up everything on Main Entrance Road, my Babsey"

"No problem my Sweetheart", replied Donduce. They turned back and went to the garage. Donduce pressed the remote again and the door sprang into action. Very soon they had done their ritual, and where heading once more out of the front yard. Donduce signalled left and they started up Main Entrance Road.

"There's not much about, my Babsey", said Donduce "If the ELK is still there you would have thought there would be some sort of traffic jam".

"I know, my Babsey, or maybe they are just driving around the ELK or something", said Beauty.

Donduce laughed "I doubt that, my Sweetheart, the ELK won't have suddenly got used to traffic! He'll be standing there with a set of temporary traffic lights next!"

They both laughed as they went past the farm track on the right where they had been earlier. In the distance there came into view a silvery patch in the road.

"There it is, the cattle grid and there's no sign of an ELK my Babsey, shit" said Donduce.

"Bollocks, Honey" replied Beauty and then added "Let's go up a bit further and see if it is wandering about anywhere".

"Ok my Sweetheart", replied Donduce and they continued over the cattle grid.

Beyond that was the main entrance which had a big ranch style sign over it with 'EE-I-O' printed on the main road side being Akks Lane. It was brown and had two big poles either side of the road supporting it. Either side of the sign was a thick tree line which was the boundary of the Estate and the trees extended well into the distance. Akks Lane wasn't visible until you actually turned out onto Akks Lane.

Donduce and Beauty were looking out each side of the jeep, across the fields that finished at the tree line. There was no sign of the ELK anywhere.

"It must have wandered off my Babsey" said Donduce. "We had better turn round by the sign and head back."

"Ok my Sweetheart" replied Beauty and added "I would like to know where it has gone though. One thing is for sure: it's not dead, just on the loose which is worrying".

"Yes, my Babsey" chuckled Donduce, "It is probably sitting outside the communications building annoying Mac Hassle with ELK shit. That's a point; let's check the cattle grid for ELK shit. That will confirm it *was* actually there".

"Good idea, my Babsey", replied Beauty and added "I hope we find some, and if we do then we have acquired our very own ELK; how exciting is that!".

"I can't fucking wait, my Babsey" groaned Donduce and then said "If you think I am going to walk a fucking ELK along with the fucking Danes, think again my Sweetheart".

"You'll love it", teased Beauty.

"Babsey!" replied Donduce, laughing.

They had got to the sign and turned round. Heading back the other way the cattle grid got nearer. About ten yards from it Donduce pulled up to the left onto the grassy border that lined both sides of the road and stopped the jeep. Donduce got out and let Beauty out.

"This is going to be interesting my Babsey", he said as they walked the last few yards to it.

"I'll say, and I can't wait" replied Beauty eagerly.

There didn't appear to be any sign of ELK shit anywhere. Donduce and Beauty had expected a pile but all that was visible was the silvery grid lines that crossed the road.

"Hang on a minute my Babsey", said Donduce "Stand on this and look down."

Beauty had been standing on the grassy bank just before the grid. "Sorry I didn't stand on the grid with you my Babsey" she said, "I was just scared that there wasn't going to be any."

"Well my Sweetheart, don't be scared anymore. Come on here and look down".

Beauty stood on the cattle grid with her Husband and looked down. There was a sort of pit underneath the grid with holes in it that looked as if they had been made by rats. Scattered all over the bottom of this pit were small piles of what looked like horse manure.

"That, my Babsey, is definitely shit from a large animal. Yes, I would safely guarantee that an ELK *has* been here" declared Donduce.

"Brilliant!, brilliant!, brilliant!, my Babsey" exclaimed a very excited Beauty. "Now all we have to do is fine the fucking thing".

Donduce looked up and down the main entrance road and across the visible parts of the field.

"I was looking for, believe it or not, an ELK shit trail, my Babsey, but there doesn't appear to be any more lying about nearby" said Donduce.

"I don't suppose the ELK comes here from the cover of the boundary trees to use the cattle grid as it's own personal toilet, my Babsey?"

Donduce laughed "No, my Sweetheart, the ELK will not be house trained or should I say cattle grid trained. It will shit on the move. This though goes to prove that it has sat on this grid more than once.

What I will do is to get a farmhand to watch from close by and radio through when he gets a sighting. The chances are that the ELK *will* be back. Meanwhile, let's go back as I want to finally sort out that fucking floorboard my Babsey", said Donduce.

"Ok, brilliant", said Beauty. "Good idea to get someone to keep watch, they are going to be here for ages. Anyway, you do the floorboard, and I will finally get round to feeding the cats before they start helping themselves; that packed of cat food I had in my hand: I didn't even have time to open it when Mac Hassle fucking interrupted, my Babsey" she added.

"Right then my Babsey, to the jeep and home" declared Donduce.

"Yes please my Angel and I love you", said Beauty.

"I love you too my Babsey" replied Donduce, and they kissed passionately.

They returned to the jeep; performed their ritual and then set off back to the farmhouse. On the way Donduce and Beauty scoured the road and surrounding area for more signs of ELK shit but didn't see any, no even on the concrete outside the buildings that lined the road near the farmhouse. Donduce pulled into their front yard area and activated the remote. Once in the garage, he turned the engine off, and they kissed again passionately.

"Right then, to the fucking floorboard my Babsey", said Donduce with a giggle.

"Right then, to the fucking cat food, my Lovey", replied Beauty also with a giggle.

Donduce got out of the jeep and walked round to Beauty's side. He opened her door. When she got out they both flicked their hair back, and, hand in hand returned to the front door.

Once inside Donduce set the alarm, and then Donduce said:

"Bollocks, Babsey, I haven't shut the fucking coal bunker".

"Oh shit, Honey" replied Beauty and then added "Why don't you radio Mac Hassle and get a farmhand to do it? That will save you having to go out again and the pissing hatches on it are heavy".

"Oh God, and talk to Mac fucking Hassle again? My Babsey" said Donduce, "I suppose it would save me some time".

They went into the lounge and Donduce pressed the button.

"Donduce. Hello Mac Hassle, could you get someone to the farmhouse coalbunker please. The coal man forgot to shut it?"

"Mac Hassle. Hello Sir?"

Donduce raised his eyes to the ceiling for the third time that morning.

"Donduce. Did you get that request?"

"Mac Hassle. Yes Sir.

"Donduce. About the coal bunker"

"Mac Hassle. Yes Sir."

"Donduce. Is someone coming?"

"Mac Hassle. Yes Sir."

"Donduce. When?"

"Mac Hassle. Now Sir, they are on their way. Coal bunker hatches. Coal man or someone left them open. What do you want them to do again Sir?"

"Fucking hell" thought Donduce.

"Donduce. Shut the hatches.

"Mac Hassle. Lock them or just shut Sir?"

"Donduce. Shut and locked."

"Mac Hassle. Padlock or bolted as well?"

"Fucking fucking hell" thought Donduce.

"Donduce. Padlocked and bolted"

"Mac Hassle. Has the man I sent got the keys?"

"Donduce. How the hell should I know; you sent him!"

"Mac Hassle. I haven't given him any keys."

"Donduce. Well radio him to return to you and give them to him"

"Mac Hassle. Ok Sir, will do".

Donduce pressed the button again. He looked at Beauty who was so red in the face trying to supress hysterics burst out laughing.

"Fucking hell", said Donduce, "In that time I could have fucking done it myself my Babsey".

"Oh, shit! Honey" said Beauty "That was hysterical. Right, to the cats" she announced.

"Time to murder Mac Hassle, my Babsey said Donduce and added "I'll use his fucking head to fix that pissing floor board".

They kissed passionately and then Beauty headed to the kitchen, whilst Donduce went to the bedroom where the toolbox was, still parked where the squeaky floorboard was.

"Right you bastard, time to kill your fucking squeak", Donduce thought to himself. He pressed on the floor again to make sure he had got the right area and low and behold, it squeaked. He reached into the toolbox and produced a sharp knife with which he proceeded to cut a small square out of the carpet. The intension being to remove the offending board and then replace it with a new piece of wood which they had plenty of in the second garage.

He removed the piece of carpet and revealed the board or rather part of it. He pressed it again and that part squeaked. He was just about to cut another part of carpet up to access the whole of the offending board when he noticed there was a small gap of about five millimetres between it and the board next to it. Also he felt a small draft coming up from the gap. "That's strange" he thought, "The foundations should be sealed. I know there is a bit of space under the floor boards but not that much". He got a torch out of the box and shone it into the gap. "Fucking hell" he exclaimed out loud, "That looks a long a long way down".

Quickly he cut enough carpet up to reveal the whole of the board and using the nail pulling end of a hammer, he managed to take up the whole of the floorboard. He felt quite a draft now and shone his torch back down the hole.

"FUCKING HELL!! He yelled, "There's another room down there! We've got a fucking basement!"

Donduce shone the torch round the area that the gap allowed. It was a fairly big room and there was a table and four chairs just visible in the middle of the room.

He turned the torch off and hurried into the kitchen, where Beauty had fed the cats and was watching as they were having a bit of a run around on the kitchen floor.

"Babsey, you are not going to believe this, but there is what appears to be a basement under the bedroom".

"Fucking WHAT? Shit! A basement?" exclaimed Beauty, and then said "Let's have a look!"

They returned to the bedroom and Donduce turned the torch on.

"Look down there my Babsey and tell me what you see" said Donduce.

Beauty took the torch and shone it down the gap.

"Fucking hell, it *is* a basement! We never knew *that* existed did we, my Lovey?"

"News to me too, my Babsey" said Donduce and then he said "Where the fuck is the entrance to it I wonder? What I will do is get some wood and make a trap door in this floor. Then, we can lower a ladder down there and have an explore. There must be an entrance to it; obviously a door, but where the fuck does it lead to? All of the doors in the farmhouse are accounted for My Babsey".

"Ok, good idea, my Babsey" said Beauty "Shit, this is exciting, and I can't think of where the entrance to it is either".

"Right then my Babsey", said Donduce, "I am going to get some wood from the storage garage number 2, and construct a trap door, if only temporary so that we can get down there and investigate. Good idea, my Angel?"

"Yes, brilliant, my Lovey" said Beauty. "Whilst you are doing that I'm going to start the washing and all of the usual chores. Any idea what you would like for lunch my Babsey?"

"No idea, my Babsey" said Donduce. "Maybe I will be inspired after this lot, my Lovey. What have you got in mind Sweetheart?"

"Don't know yet, my Babsey", Beauty replied; "Possibly roast Mac Hassle".

"With all the trimmings, veg etc", asked Donduce giggling.

"Don't you mean boots etc?" giggled Beauty.

"No, too tough", said Donduce laughing.

They kissed passionately, and then Beauty disappeared off to the kitchen, whilst Donduce picked up the garage remote from it's shelf in the hall, disabled the alarm and unlocked the front door. Once outside he pointed the remote at the garage complex and pressed button two. The same garage door situation started. The door next to the jeep woke up and hummed into action. In this garage they stored lots of household back ups: new skirting boards; DIY stuff and pieces of new wood, which Donduce was after. Choosing what he wanted, plus other bits, he put the items into a big holdall which he used for such a task and after locking up, returned to the bedroom.

Firstly, he took a marker pen from the toolbox, and with a ruler drew a line on the carpet eventually drawing an oblong shape. Then, after cutting away the carpet that he had already started with the exposed hole, he pulled up the relevant pieces of floorboard in the square. With an electric saw, he cut to size pieces of new floor board, so it ended up with a perfectly formed oblong hole with the floorboards up to each side; and, no squeak. Then came a wooden frame around the hole and finishing up with a strong lid; handle that folded flat and hinges. The trap door was complete. After popping out to the garage again for a ladder, he returned and with the trap door folded back so it was flat on the floor open, he stood over the space with his legs astride the hole and gently lowered the ladder until it touched the bottom. The hard bit was extending the ladder and clipping it downwards because most people extend ladders upwards.

The job now complete, he tidied the toolbox away and put it for now against the wall in the bedroom.

Donduce walked back into the kitchen and found Beauty folding up some washing that she had just got out of the tumble dryer. She saw him come and wrapped her loving arms around him.

"Oohh my Babsey I missed you, any luck?" she asked.

"All done, and can't wait for you to assist, my Babsey, would now be ok?" he asked with a smile.

"Let's go, my Sweetheart and I can't wait" replied Beauty very excitedly.

Hand in hand, they walked back to the bedroom and Beauty saw the new trap door and the ladder sticking up out of it.

"WOW!! Babsey, you've done brilliant my Angel, and so quick, well done you!!" she said and they kissed passionately.

"Right then, my Babsey, I'll go down first; I've got the flashlights in the toolbox; should have got them out, hang on" said Donduce.

He went over to it, took them out and returned.

"I love you my Angel" said Beauty "When you said: You were going down there first, you want me to go down *that ladder* into there as well, my Babsey? You're having a fucking laugh! Please couldn't I stay up here and watch you down there my Babsey, Plleeeaasseee?" whimpered Beauty.

"Ok my Babsey", said Donduce, "*I'll* go down and shout up to you what I find. Deal?"

"Yes please my Babsey" said Beauty happily and gave her Husband a big kiss and cuddle. "Good Luck and be careful" she added.

Donduce picked up a torch and stood astride the hatch, then he sat with his legs dangling in the hole and put his feet on the ladder. Gripping the top, he looked up at Beauty and said:

"Won't be long my Babsey, don't worry".

Beauty leant over and kissed her Husband on the forehead. "Be careful, I love you and good luck" she said".

"Ok my Sweetheart", he replied "Love you too".

Donduce climbed down the ladder and after only a few seconds his feet touched the bottom. He let go of the ladder, turned his torch on and shone it around.

Donduce surveyed the scene down there: the walls were dampish and made of a sort of dirty concrete like material. In the middle of an otherwise bare room was an old table and chairs either side. No drawers or anything, just a table and nothing on it. Donduce shone the torch very slowly around the room again, and low and behold there were two doors at each end of this room. After getting his bearings He said to himself: "Neither door leads back inside the farmhouse area, so, where would each one lead to? Were they blocked up from the other side?".

There was only one way to find out. He walked around the table to the 'left hand door', tried it, but it was locked, bollocks. He knew then that the door would have to be broken down anyway and replaced, and there weren't any mysterious keys unused on the farmhouse set, not unless the bedroom door key matched; unlikely. Donduce crossed the room and tried the other door.

"Fucking hell" he thought to himself, as unexpectedly, it did open, with a creek, and revealed a passageway!

"Are you Ok down there, My Babsey?" called Beauty, who was kneeling on all fours watching her Husband from the safety of the bedroom. She was looking into the hatchway; she could see her Husband from time to time and glimpsed what was there when the torch been lit it up.

"Yeah, my Lovey, we've got a fucking passageway down here my Babsey" he replied. "I have found two doorways" he continued. "One is stuck shut locked, which is on one side of the room, and the other I have just opened, and behind it is a passageway. Fuck knows where it goes to, but I am going to shine the torch down it. I won't be long. Don't worry my Lovey".

"FUCKING HELL!" Beauty replied. "Be careful and come back quickly, I love you" she added.

Donduce shone his torch into it but could see no end. He thought to himself that it certainly didn't lead back up to daylight, so he proceeded forward very slowly. It was pitch black and the passageway had a downhill slope to it, so he was in fact going deeper and deeper underground. It seemed like he had been walking slowly through the passageway for ages, and as he shone the torch around it, he noticed that the walls were made of the sort of stone cladding you find on old railway stations. The floor, was still made of sort of stone, like the basement and the passageway itself was built quite strongly, it definitely was designed to be there and was not just something someone had done for fun. There also was this strange smell, not as bad as the stench that had been under the sink, but an odour of something, and it was getting nearer. Donduce likened it to a stench of rotting leaves, like a compost heap. Cracks were now appearing in the slightly arched ceiling, quite large, and holes were there too. Bits of brick were lying on the floor where they had fallen from the roof, leaving the holes and apart from the smell, which by now was all round him, a sense of dampness. Donduce rubbed his hand along the wall, and shone his torch to see what if anything was on his hand. There was, a dampish, brownish green powdery substance; Donduce sniffed it; his eyes widened with shock "ELK SHIT!!?? Down here?? NO, NO, NO!!! he shouted to himself "That bloody ELK cannot be, CAN-not-be down here, NO. NO. NO!". After he had got over that shock he thought again: "Of course the ELK can't be down here, he's around somewhere, but not down here. Stupid bastard I am, he can't get through a closed door from a basement that has no entrance".

Donduce shone his torch on the floor and there was loads of 'it' everywhere. He shone his torch up into one of the holes in the ceiling, and, he saw, about 15ft up, a glint of daylight. He then shone his torch into the rest of the passageway, and still couldn't see an end, but, suddenly, he realized he *knew* exactly where he was!!

"Oh fuck, I think I know what has gone on here" he thought and went back to the basement. He arrived and went over to the patch of square light shining through the hatchway.

"Hi Babsey", he called, "Are you there?"

"Hi Honey, I missed you, you ok, everything ok?" replied Beauty, sticking her head through the hatch. "Fuck, what is that all over your trousers and shoes; that looks like manure Oh shit, you don't think the ELK is down there do you?"

"The thought had crossed my mind, my Angel, however the door was shut and so impossible for him to enter that passageway" said Donduce, he continued: "Although I didn't get to the end of it, I have a hunch about something".

"Come on up then and tell me all about it, chop chop, my Babsey", said Beauty smiling.

"Coming up, my Babsey" said Donduce and he climbed back up the ladder.

Donduce said to Beauty, "I've got to take you down to the front gate of the farm, my Babsey, because, like I said, I have a hunch about something. Also, I'll get some more tools, and get the other door in the basement open, because that *must* lead to where the entrance to the basement actually is; there's no other way to get in, and the passageway must lead to somewhere, but as yet, I don't know, but I think I do know in which direction. We will do all of that this afternoon; you mentioned lunch earlier; how about me taking you out to the 'Dane and Freckles'?"

"Superb, on yes please my Babsey", replied Beauty, happily and added "I can't wait to find out what your hunch is all about.

"You'll find out soon enough, my Babsey", replied Donduce with a smile.

Beauty and Donduce had a quick wash, and performed their rituals.

"I am looking forward to this my Babsey" said Beauty as Donduce locked the front door for the third time that morning.

"So am I my Lovey", replied Donduce. "I do like the 'Dane and Freckles', but the landlord in my view is a fucking self opinionated wanker, and as thick as pig shit", he added with a giggle.

"You like him then!" said Beauty and they both laughed. Donduce performed the usual task with the remote; and with the usual rituals they got into the jeep.

Donduce drove out of the front gate and turned left onto Main Entrance Road.

"Still keep your eyes peeled for ELK shit, my Babsey", said Donduce, "You never know, it could have come back since we have been at home".

"That's true, my Lovey", replied Beauty and they both started looking around the road and surrounding area.

They went past the farm track turning and then over the cattle grid, but there was not a sign of the ELK anywhere. Up to the main entrance sign and then Donduce slowed down. He signalled left and they were on AKKS Lane.

This road, in effect just took the driver round a very large field, for on the other side was EE-I-O village, and, their favourite lunchtime, evening, anytime, all the time tavern, the 'Dane & Freckles'.

It was a very friendly little tavern and Beauty, and Donduce enjoyed going there a lot. The pub had an old English feel to it, and the smell of the big log fire at one end really added to the atmosphere. The food was really nice as well, but not nearly as nice as that prepared by Beauty, although they did eat there on nights when Beauty wanted the night off.

After having left the entrance to the farm the road curved round to the right and went for roughly three miles. A lamp post on the left hand side heralded the start of the village, and about a mile after that was the 'Dane and Freckles' on the left hand side.

They pulled into the car park and Donduce switched off the engine.

"Queen Beauty, my Babsey", said Donduce, "We have arrived. I will let you out and then we will go and partake in a nice cold beer or two and some food. Does this meet with your royal requirements?" he asked.

"Oh, King Donduce, my Lovey", replied Beauty, "Oh, yes, it does meet with the Queen's requirements. Yes, please would you assist me with disembarkation from the royal jeep so that we can have just such liquid refreshment, and thank you", Beauty added. They leaned over to one another and kissed passionately.

Donduce got out and went round to Beauty's side and let her out. After their rituals with their hair, they kissed again. Then, hand in hand, they went into the main entrance of the pub. It led to a corridor with a door at the end on the right, which was the main bar. It was quite large and had an open fire at one end; the bar stretched along the right hand wall, and in the middle were groups of tables and chairs. Donduce and Beauty went over to it and Yvonne, the manageress was serving a man.

"That will be £10.50 please Sir, thank you" as she took the money. She went over to the till and brought his change back.

"Thank you, and your food will follow in due course".

"Thanks", said the man and walked over to where a lady was sitting.

Yvonne came over.

"Hello Sir, Madam, nice to see you, the usual?" she asked.

"Yes please, Yvonne, nice to see you again too. Keeping well?" asked Donduce politely. He couldn't give a flying fuck really; nor could Beauty.

"Oh, not bad", replied Yvonne as she filled two pint glasses, "Can't grumble" she went on "Well I suppose I could grumble but it wouldn't make any difference but maybe it would but then again I would be grumbling about something else wouldn't I so, on the whole, no, I can't grumble" she finished.

"Fucking hell" thought Donduce, "If you don't shut the fuck up, I'll be fucking grumbling".

"Never mind," he said as Yvonne placed the beers on the bar, "We're ok, thank you".

"Oh, sorry, I didn't ask!" said Yvonne as she took the tenner that Donduce had just got out of his wallet, "You are both ok then?" she asked.

"Yes, fine thanks and even better when we are on the outside of this beer, thanks" he said as Yvonne handed him their change.

"Waffle fucking waffle, my Babsey" said Beauty as they walked over with their beers to a settee style set up next to the fire.

"I know, my Babsey", said Donduce as they sat down.

Donduce put his loving arm round his Wifey Babsey's shoulders. "When we go back", he said, "I want to show you something which, if it is there, I have never noticed, but, if I am right, I know exactly where the end of the passageway leads to!" Beauty could hardly speak with excitement.

"Where?" she asked, "Please tell me, where? My Angel.

"Ok, my Babsey", said Donduce. "You know we went to the cattle grid to look for ELK shit earlier?"

"Of course I do", replied Beauty, "I hope we find the ELK, sorry carry on, my Honey".

"Well, my Sweetheart" continued Donduce rather excitedly, "when I was in the passageway, I saw all the ELK shit down the walls that had come from a gap in the ceiling. I could also smell an aroma resembling burning wood, or certainly it reminded me of an old bonfire that had gone out. I think, that quite possibly, the passageway comes right under the fireplace that we are sitting next to here!"

Beauty looked absolutely stunned and shocked.

"Fuck me, my Babsey", she said.

"Yes please, my Lovey, but not in here." replied Donduce giggling.

"But why would the passageway lead to here, my Babsey?" asked Beauty.

"That, is what I want to find out, my Babsey" replied Donduce. "Like I said, I have got this hunch, but I need to take you somewhere when we get back, well, on the way back anyway. Is that ok, my Sweetheart?"

"Of course it is my Babsey", replied Beauty, and added "Right then, one more beer and some food and then we will go 'hunch curing', my Babsey".

"Ok my Lovey", said Donduce. He took their now empty glasses in his hand and asked "Usual for lunch, my Honey?"

"Yes please my gorgeous Husband, chop chop!" said Beauty laughing.

"I'll give you fucking chop chop, my Sweetheart", replied Donduce and with that he headed to the bar.

Yvonne saw him coming and walked up to where Donduce had arrived.

"Same again Sir?" she asked.

"Yes please" replied Donduce giving her the empties, "Please can I order some food?"

"Of course, Sir, what would you like?" asked Yvonne, fetching a pad and a pen.

"Fucking hell, this is a bit dated; where's the fucking computer gone?" thought Donduce.

"Sorry about the pad, Sir" said Yvonne; she had seen the strange look on Donduce's face peering at the pad.

She continued "We are having a new computer system put in and the idiots have taken the other one away before installation. So, it's back to old fashioned writing things down which makes me grumpy because too much writing makes my wrist go funny and seize up and holds me up from running the bar and serving customers which makes them grumpy because they don't like waiting and the kitchen staff don't like it because they keep losing the orders because there's not really anywhere in the kitchen to put the orders apart from on the area that when the food is cooked it is placed for either me or Paul, he's the manager, to collect for the customers and some customers get the wrong orders or their lunch is late which makes them grumpy and start complaining to me which makes me even more grumpy and I have to start apologising to them and say that when the new computer system arrives things will get back to normal once they have shown us how to use it and we have got to be trained in that which is going to hold us up even more but I am sure it will all work out in the end".

"Fucking hell", thought Donduce, "Is she finished now?"

"Crumbs", said Donduce, "Ok, I am sure it will be fine in the end. Please could I have one cod and chips with mushy peas and a side dish of bread and butter, and one eight ounce rump steak with salad but no onions please".

"Thank you Sir", replied Yvonne. "How would you like your steak done?"

"Rare, please." Donduce replied.

"Ok Sir, would you like to pay now, or when you leave?" she asked.

"Now, please", replied Donduce.

"Ok, that will be £15.49 then please" replied Yvonne.

Donduce produced his bank card for a laugh.

"There you are", he said.

"Thank you Sir" replied Yvonne, "I will just stick it in the machine. Oh shit! We haven't got it have we. Bloody men taking the bloody machine reducing me to use a bloody pad making me bloody late. Sorry. Do you mind paying cash Sir?"

"Sorry, I forgot too" lied Donduce and got a twenty from his wallet. There you are".

"Thank you", said Yvonne and went to the till. She came back with Donduce's change and said:

"We will bring your food over when it's ready Sir".

"Thank you" said Donduce, "Please could I have the bank card back?"

"Oh shit, sorry" said Yvonne "It's still in my bloody hand".

"No problem" said Donduce, and taking it, he put it back in his wallet, picked up their drinks, and went back to Beauty who was looking pained.

"Fucking hell, Babsey" she said "I thought you were going to be there all year. What was all that about, Honey?"

Donduce told her and she pissed herself laughing, "Oh my God, she doesn't half rabbit some incesant crap. I'm glad I wasn't there!"

"I wish that I hadn't of been there; I would have poured the fucking beers myself my Babsey".

They kissed and started slurping. Behind the bar, Yvonne was explaining to another customer the saga of the computer system. The customer was listening patiently through gritted teeth and Donduce and Beauty could unfortunately hear it all.

"She's doing my fucking head in, my Babsey", said Donduce, and added "And I am starving, how about you, Honey?"

"Likewise my Babsey", replied Beauty. "Shall we go to the kitchen and cook it ourselves?" she giggled.

"And bump into her husband, oh, his name's Paul, by the way, I don't think so, My Babsey".

"Ok my Sweetheart, not such a good idea. Paul. How nice." replied Beauty.

Yvonne had disappeared from the bar, and about ten minutes later they heard a thud as the kitchen doors, which were out of view round the corner closed. Yvonne came into view with two plates and came over to their table.

"Sorry about the delay" she said. "Right, one spaghetti bolognaise, and one chicken in blackberry sauce". She looked expectantly at Donduce and then at Beauty waiting to be informed as to who was having what.

"Sorry Yvonne, you have brought the wrong order", said Donduce. "We ordered the fish and the steak".

"The fish and the steak?" said Yvonne looking startled.

"The fish and the steak." confirmed Donduce.

"Who ordered the fish and the steak then?" asked Yvonne.

"We did", replied Donduce.

"So who ordered the spag bol and the chicken then?" asked Yvonne.

"I have no idea" replied Donduce, trying not to laugh. "Maybe the customer you served just before us, but I would hurry because their order is getting cold".

"True" she said, "I'll be back with yours in a minute".

"Excuse me", said a loud voice towards the middle of the bar. A man was waiving vigorously at Yvonne, "I think that is ours", he shouted.

"How do you know?" asked Yvonne as she approached their table.

"I think I know what Spaghetti Bolognaise looks like", replied the man.

"Did you order it then?" asked Yvonne.

"Of course I bloody ordered it; you wouldn't be carrying it if I hadn't would you and now it's getting cold".

"I'll go and stick it in the bloody microwave then shall I?" said Yvonne.

"No, otherwise it will be another ten years before we get it", replied the man looking at his wife for support.

She looked suitably grumpy as Yvonne placed their lunch on the table.

"Enjoy", she said as she walked away. "Yours is coming, don't worry" she called to Donduce and Beauty.

"Thank you" called Donduce.

Soon afterwards the noise of the kitchen doors thudded, and Yvonne appeared from round the corner and arrived at their table.

"Sorry about all that" she said, "One steak and one cod and chips".

"Thank you" said Donduce, "I am having the steak and my wife is having the cod".

Yvonne put the plates down in front of them.

"Would you like any sauces?" she asked.

"No thanks" replied Donduce, and added "Thanks for putting up with all the problems".

"Oh, that's ok" she replied, "I'm used to all that; I'm married to a problem, anyway, enjoy".

She left and disappeared back to the bar, where quite a queue had formed.

"Married to a problem, my Babsey" said Donduce as he munched his steak, "Obviously those two aren't happy. How's your fish?"

"Really nice, Honey" replied Beauty, with a couple of chips in her hand, and added "Like you said, I don't think much of this 'Paul' if Yvonne is upset".

"Their problem, Honey" replied Donduce.

The bar had returned to some degree of normality, and after a few more wrong food deliveries, Yvonne resumed serving. She had got rid of the queue and was a bit happier now.

Donduce finished his plate more or less at the same time that Beauty finished hers. He had a slurp and said:

"Nearly time to go and do the 'hunch curing, my Babsey".

"Ok, my Honey" she said, "I cannot wait, but can we have one more beer before we go?" Donduce smiled, gave his beautiful Wifey a kiss and massive hug and said "Of course we can, my Babsey, I will go and get a refill.

"Don't get stuck again for fuck's sake Honey" laughed Beauty as Donduce picked up the glasses.

"Don't worry, my Babsey, I won't" replied Donduce with a giggle.

He walked over to the bar, however Yvonne had already seen him coming and had their drinks already on the bar.

"These are on me for all the problems Sir" she said as Donduce arrived, and added "With our compliments".

"That's very kind of you Yvonne" he said, "If it will cheer you up at all, lunch was delicious and thanks again".

"No problem Sir" she said.

"Please", came a voice from down the bar.

"Got to go" said Yvonne, "See you soon".

Donduce picked up the drinks and went back to Beauty.

"Shit, that was quick, Honey", she said "No rabbiting?"

"No, my Babsey" said Donduce as he put the drinks on the table and sat down again, "These are free for all the problems we have had".

"That's nice, and also to be expected for royalty", said Beauty with a giggle.

"Absolutely, Queen Beauty, I would expect nothing less" replied Donduce giggling.

After a suitable time to digest lunch and finish their beer, Donduce said "Come on then, my Babsey, time to go and start 'hunch curing'".

"Ok my Angel" she replied and added "Can't wait".

They left the glasses on the table and walked over to the door that marked the exit. "See you next time", called Yvonne from the bar.

"Ok and thanks again", replied Donduce.

They walked back down the corridor, out the front and got to the jeep.

"That was a nice lunch, my Babsey" said Donduce as he opened the passenger door.

"Really funny and lovely, and thank you my Babsey" replied Beauty, and once she was in they kissed passionately.

"That's quite alright, my Queen and my Babsey" said Donduce.

He shut Beauty's door and got in himself.

"Ok, my Babsey, here we go" said Donduce.

"I love you and I can't wait", replied Beauty eagerly.

Donduce started the engine. They left the 'Dane and Freckles' car park and turned right. Very soon they had reached the lamp post which signalled the end of the village; the road bent round to the left and soon, the large perimeter tree line of the farm came into view on the right hand side. The perimeter boundary tree line didn't run parallel with the road: it was at an angle and when the road bent away from it, land started that was basically just trees and grass. It was really the start of EE-I-O but not the populated part.

The farm sign came into view; from the road it looked very impressive: the gold letters spelt 'EE-I-O Estate' in gold, and at night was lit by a large neon strip light. A large gap in the trees, indeed, but a large entrance.

Donduce signalled right at their farm sign, and then parked up about ten yards before the cattle grid.

"Follow me", he said, "Hunch busting time!"

He and his beautiful Wifey walked about 5 yards up the long driveway, and then Donduce stopped. "Yes, just as I thought", he said to Beauty, "Look!"

"What at?" asked Beauty, "I can't see anything unusual".

She looked puzzled and was looking everywhere.

"In the driveway, just there my Babsey, what can you see?" he said.

Beauty looked and then said "Oh, you mean that cattle grid, to stop the animals wandering off?"

"Exactly", said Donduce.

"I hate to say this, my darling", replied Beauty, "but what of it – its just a cattle grid, and not only that we were here earlier, and yes there was ELK shit under it."

"I know", said her husband, "However, I know that is the ELK sat down there, and I know there are holes under it where the droppings have fallen into the passageway. That is how if you remember that I knew where I was down there and the passageway continues on. Come and stand on the grid and look directly ahead, and tell me what you see!"

Beauty held her husband's hand and did exactly that. They both looked directly out, straight ahead, and then Beauty said: "Babsey, directly in front of us, but in the distance on the other side of that massive field, just visible through the boundary fields is the roof of the pub we have just come from, sticking up over the hedge that surrounds the field".

"Exactly" said her Hubby, "You know I said in the pub that when I was in the passageway earlier, I could smell something, apart from the ELK shit which reminded me of old burning wood or coal. I'll bet that the passageway comes up right under the fire in the pub, and you said why would a passageway link the pub with our farm, well, let's stand on the cattle grid again and we'll take a closer look".

"Ok, my Babsey" replied Beauty and added "What are we going to see that is different from this morning, my Babsey?"

"Let's just Look, my Lovey" Donduce replied.

Chapter 4

Hand in hand Donduce and Beauty walked over to the cattle grid and looked down again into the shallow pit where there were still bits of ELK shit at the bottom.

"Babsey, can you see round the sides at the bottom?" asked Donduce.

"Yes, my Honey" she replied, "It looks like very old sort of brick work."

"That confirms my hunch, my Lovey." Said Donduce. "This did not start out as a cattle grid. This started out and continued for many years as an air vent for the passageway or tunnel from the farm."

"Wow, my Babsey", said Beauty but added "I still have to ask the question as I did at lunchtime, why would there be a tunnel linking us to the Dane and Freckles, my Babsey?"

"Babsey", said Donduce, giving his gorgeous Wifey a cuddle and a big kiss, "Smuggling!!!". Probably years ago, the hops were grown on the farm, fermented, and then transported to the pub. It's just a hunch, but we will have to go the whole length of it and prove ourselves right".

"Do you fancy doing this expedition this afternoon, my Babsey?" asked Donduce.

"Too fucking right, my Honey, I can't wait; not only that but the walk will wear lunch off."

"Good, and to the jeep we go", replied Donduce.

Donduce and Beauty left the cattle grid and arrived at the jeep. They kissed passionately and after the usual rituals, got in and headed back to the farm.

Donduce parked the jeep in the garage, and then they walked hand in hand to the front door. Once in, Donduce locked it, then set the alarm, and then they both went into the bedroom.

They had left the trap door open and Donduce held Beauty in his arms, he asked:

"Are you ok to make your first descent, my Babsey?"

"Yes, my Sweetheart" she replied and added "As long as I am with you or near, I'll be ok, now chop chop, let's get this passageway mystery sorted out".

"I will go down first, and then you follow. I am just going to get the flashlight out of the toolbox first though, my Angel" said Donduce.

"Ok my Angel", said Beauty.

Donduce retrieved the flash light and the electric saw from the toolbox and returned. They kissed passionately, and then, after another 'ok' to each other, Donduce eagerly descended the staircase. Once at the bottom, he called:

"Ok down, you next my Babsey".

He watched as Beauty stood astride the ladder. He could only see the lower half of her gorgeous body, but, the very brave girl that she is, as she got her footing with a lot of encouragement from her husband, Beauty descended the ladder and arrived in the basement.

"Fucking hell, that was scarey, my Babsey" she said, "I'm here!"

"Well fucking done" said Donduce and they kissed passionately. Once Beauty had got her breath back and had a look at her new surroundings, she said:

"Fuck, I can see those chairs now, they are really old, my Babsey, this is exciting".

"I know, my Lovey. Right then", said Donduce "The other door: let's see what is behind that!"

Donduce tried the door again, but it was locked. He banged on it, and it felt very solid, not like there was a space behind it or anything.

"There's only one thing to do here, my Babsey", he said, "Saw through the top hinge, then the bottom one, and the door should just come off". With the electric saw, Donduce started on the top hinge. He got about half way through it when an almighty loud creaking noise started as if something major was going to give way.

"What was that?" asked Beauty, looking suddenly very alarmed.

"I don't know", replied her Husband "But something I think is behind the door, leaning against it, and we will soon see once we have sawn through them hinges. I think the door will just come off. Stand behind me, My Babsey, it will be safer".

Standing now to the side of the stuck door, Beauty stood behind her husband as he cut through the hinge. Then, it happened. A massive creak, an incredible sound of splintering wood and then Donduce and Beauty, got out of the way very fast as, with a massive creak, a splintering of wood noise and what sounded like thunder, the basement door shot off it's hinges across the basement floor, closely followed by tons and tons of coal, and very black looking ELK. It took several seconds for the dust to settle, and before Donduce or Beauty had a chance to say or do anything, the ELK got up, shook itself and started kicking the shit out of the table, which did have the chairs around it, but was now in the middle of the pile of coal. Then, the ELK, bored with that, started to try and trot around the basement, but for the lack of space stopped it from going very far.

"Bloody hell", yelled Donduce, "Babsey, climb back up the ladder, I will follow you, natter in a minute". Without further adoo, they both climbed back up the ladder, through the trapdoor, and into the relative safety of the bedroom. Once there, they sat down on the bed and collected their thoughts.

"Well", said Donduce, "We know now that we do indeed have an ELK and the coal bunker used to be the entrance to the basement my Babsey".

"Yes, my gorgeous Hubby", replied Beauty, "But that poor ELK, and the coal, what are we going to do now? We haven't got anywhere to put the coal now either!"

"Nothing's ever a problem my Sweetheart", said her loving Hubby with a smile. "The first thing to do is to get cleared up, as we are both covered in soot, and the second is to get hold of Farmhand Mac Stupid. He will be able to clear all of this up".

"HIM!???" exclaimed Beauty, "OH FUCKING HELL, OOHH GOD! I can't stand that man: he is a total fucking idiot".

"I know my Babsey" said Donduce, "But he does a thorough job when he puts his mind to it".

"Ok, my Sweetheart, I suppose he does make me laugh because he *is* so stupid".

Farmhand Mac Stupid was one of the farmhands but was rather deaf, took everything you told him literally, and he had a really annoying habit of stating the bleeding obvious. His real name was

Richard, but most on the farm called him Rick. Beauty had spoken to him on a couple of occasions; the first was when he was with another farmhand who had had an accident, or at least wasn't feeling well, and looked terrible. Mac Stupid suggested the hospital, and Beauty had asked what it was i.e. his medical complaint. He had replied that it was a rather large building consisting of lots of doctors and nurses. They had operating theatres there and they try to cure you.

"I FUCKING KNOW THAT!" she had shouted,

"Well why did you ask then if you already knew then?" he replied.

"I wasn't asking what a fucking hospital was", she had yelled, "I was asking what the matter was with the man – his illness".

"We won't know until we get him to a hospital" he said.

They kissed passionately and then Donduce and Beauty washed and got changed. "That feels better, my Babsey" said Donduce "I feel fresh again. Right then, I will go into the lounge and radio Mac Hassle to find out where Mac Stupid is lurking.

They went into the lounge and Donduce pressed the button.

"Donduce. Mac Hassle, do you know the whereabouts of farmhand Mac Stupid?"

"Mac Hassle. Hello Sir."

"Oh fuck, not again, please be normal for fucking once" thought Donduce.

"Donduce. Mac Hassle, did you get that?"

"Mac Hassle. Yes Sir."

"Donduce. Do you know where he is?"

"Mac Hassle. Yes Sir."

"Donduce. Where is he then?"

"Mac Hassle. Who, Mac Stupid?"

"Donduce. YES!!!!"

"Mac Hassle. He is in the cow field near the barn doing a head count stock take, Sir."

"Donduce. Is he still there?"

"Mac Hassle. Yes as far as I know?"

"Donduce. Ok thank you. Out".

Donduce looked at Beauty and they both burst into hysterics. "Fucking hell, my Babsey, I don't know who's worse, Mac Hassle or Mac Stupid" said Donduce wiping his eyes.

"I know my Lovey", replied Beauty rubbing her eyes and added "I suppose we are going to get the jeep out again, aren't we?" she finished with a giggle.

"'Fraid so, my Angel" replied Donduce "Come on".

Donduce had pressed the button again to stand by. They left the lounge and were very soon back in the jeep for what seemed like the millionth time.

"Are you ready my Babsey?" asked Donduce with a giggle.

"No" replied Beauty.

"Are you ready my Lovey?" asked Beauty with a giggle.

"No" replied Donduce".

They both burst out laughing, and then they kissed passionately. Then, Donduce started the engine and they drove once more out of the front yard, through the gate and onto Main Entrance Road.

The field in question was located on the left hand side of the farm track they went up to go to the old empty barn, soon, Donduce had signalled right and they started looking for Mac Stupid. They drove down the track still looking and went round the left hand bend where the barn came into view.

"There he is, my Babsey, just parked on the left. See the tractor, and he's standing staring at it. Not much of a head count going on" Said Donduce.

"I don't know what he's fucking doing either my Babsey" replied Beauty and added "I'm not sure he does either."

Donduce parked up about twenty yards from the tractor, and after a passionate kiss Donduce said to his Wifey "Don't worry, stay there, I'll go".

Donduce gave her another hug and a kiss and Beauty said:

"Good luck, my Babsey".

"Thanks Honey" replied Donduce and added "I think I'll need it."

Donduce got out of the jeep and went over to Mac Stupid.

"Are you busy?" he asked. Farmhand Mac Stupid looked over;

"What?" he said, Donduce repeated

"Are you busy?",

"What?" he said, and then added, "I'm busy".

"Are you counting the herd of cows?" asked Donduce.

"Heard of cows?" he replied, "Course I've bleeding heard of cows! Have you come out here to ask me that?"

"No", said Donduce. "Are you counting the cow herd?"

"The cow heard what? Why would I want to know what a cow is listening to eh?"

Donduce chose to ignore this question. "We need you to clear out our basement, we have tons of coal and an ELK down there".

"Bloody stupid place to keep them, if you ask me", he said.

"We didn't, they fell down there from the coal bunker", replied Donduce.

"You kept an ELK in the coal bunker? Should have bleeding coal in it not ELKS, call yourself a farmer? You'll be calling yourself a brain surgeon next", he said.

"I will", replied Donduce, "And you'll be my first patient! Now, please would you drive your tractor back to the farmhouse and help us" commanded Donduce.

Beauty had got out of the car because she couldn't resist the inevitable conversation that her gorgeous husband was having with this fucking idiot. Donduce, whilst talking had noticed that Beauty was standing a few yards behind him to his left. Beauty listened to the rest.

"No", He said.

"Pardon?" replied Donduce.

"No", He said.

"What do you mean, 'No'?" asked Donduce.

"What do you mean, what do I mean", he said, "No, usually means 'No', and it's the opposite of 'Yes', in any standard dictionary. I said No because I mean 'No'".

"Why not?" Donduce asked.

"No, because the bleeding tractor hasn't got any petrol in it, that's why 'No'", he said.

"How did you get the tractor here then?" asked Donduce.

43

"I bleeding drove it here, didn't I?, How else would I get it here, by bleeding helicopter?" he said.

"You said it didn't have any fuel though" said Donduce.

"It bleeding did then, but it ran out. Why else do you think I am standing here like an idiot. I want a lift back, but you walked here so your no use".

Donduce returned back to where his beautiful Wifey was standing and said "Run!"

They both did, just to get away from him, and kept looking back to see if Farmhand Mac Stupid was following – he wasn't.

They both climbed very quickly back inside the jeep and Donduce immediately turned the ignition. He pulled out onto the track and was just driving past the tractor when Mac Stupid stepped out in front of them. Donduce swerved round him and raced to the barn.

"Fucking nut case, I nearly ran the cunt over!, my Babsey" exclaimed Donduce.

"Fucking wish you fucking had, my Lovey" replied Beauty, recovering from the unpleasant occurrence. They turned by the barn and then Donduce said

"Oh fuck, Honey, we have got to drive past that idiot again".

"Oh fuck, my Babsey, yes", replied Beauty. "Just drive quickly and hope he doesn't do that again, Honey".

"Ok my Sweetheart" said Donduce and they started back towards the tractor. Mac Stupid was sitting in it, talking on his radio.

"That's good, my Babsey", said Donduce, "He's probably organising someone to get him some fuel".

"Good, my Angel", said Beauty, "At least he won't be jumping in front of us."

"Not unless he leaps out of his cab, my Babsey" laughed Donduce.

"And bounces off the bonnet, my Lovey" laughed Beauty.

They finally got back to the farm house and Donduce reversed the jeep back into the garage.

"Right then, my Babsey, passageway time" said Donduce.

"Right then, my Honey, passageway time", replied Beauty, and they kissed passionately.

After they had performed the rituals of getting out of the jeep and their hair, they walked towards the front door.

"Oh fuck, my Babsey, I have just had a very worrying thought" said Donduce.

"What's that, my Babsey?" asked Beauty: she sounded concerned.

"We still have a locked coal bunker, coal in the basement, and a loose ELK. I forgot to shut the passageway door" said Donduce.

"Shit, my Honey" replied Beauty, and added "What happens now?"

Donduce opened the front door. Once they were in, and Donduce had reset the alarms, he said:

"Ok here's the plan. The coalbunker hatches are shut, and we have an ELK loose in the basement and also possibly in the tunnel passageway. Mac Stupid hasn't arrived yet, so I vote that we go down to the basement, see if the ELK is still there, if not, then we come back, get supplies for our journey into the passageway to find the ELK, and by that time, Mac Stupid will have cleared the coal from this end."

"That sounds good to me, my Lovey" replied Beauty.

Donduce and Beauty went straight to the bedroom and the hatchway.

"I hope the poor thing isn't still in the basement, my Babsey", said Beauty as she looked at the hatchway. "I can't hear anything."

"That sounds ominous, my Lovey" said Donduce and added "If the ELK was down there, we would certainly hear him. It's dark and he would be knocking into the table and chairs as we speak, that is, if he hasn't already eaten them".

Donduce got the flash light switched on and stood on the ladder.

"You ok to go down, my Babsey?" he asked.

"You try and fucking stop me, my Lovey" she replied eagerly.

Donduce climbed down and stood on the basement floor.

"Babsey", said Donduce.

"You alright, my Babsey", said Beauty who was about to climb down the ladder.

"Yes, fine, my Babsey" said Donduce, "Where the coal, and by the way there's no ELK, right. Where the coal has come from the bunker it has revealed that there is light coming from the gaps in the hatches although they are shut. You can actually see much more down here."

It was now a bit lighter as the daylight was coming from the bunker hatch. Coal and bits of wood were everywhere, but because Donduce had forgotten to shut the passageway door, of course there was no sign of the ELK, as there wasn't any place for it to go but into the tunnel.

"Oh Christ", continued Donduce "I did forget to shut the door to the passageway, the ELK has gone down there, it must have".

"Babsey, won't it get bored and just come back?" asked Beauty as she arrived at the bottom of the ladder and gave her husband a cuddle.

"It can't" said her husband, cuddling her back

"The passageway Isn't wide enough for it to turn round. It is going to have to be coaxed back in reverse. However, there *is* another way".

"How?" asked Beauty intrigued.

"Simple", said her husband, "If it's ok with you, we will go down the passageway, after getting some supplies, until we find the ELK, and then carry on going, leading it forward until in theory, we can lead it out the other end".

"Good idea Hun", said Beauty "But what if the other end is blocked off?"

"Well", said her husband, "Considering that this end just had the creaky door which opened, the chances are that maybe the other end will too. Come on, let's go back up and get the supplies we need for the journey".

They climbed back up the ladder and were soon back in the bedroom.

"You ok, my Babsey" asked Donduce as they sat down on the bed after their ascent.

"Yes, my Lovey" she replied, and they kissed passionately.

"Let's go, my Babsey and grab a couple of beers from the fridge" said Donduce, he continued: "Sit down in the lounge and have five minutes break, have a cuddle, then we pick up some supplies in ruck sacks and head off".

"Ok, my Sweetheart" replied Beauty and added "That sounds brilliant. I will get the ruck sacks, actually, where *are* the ruck sacks, my Honey?" she asked.

"In here, my Babsey, in the wardrobe, I'll get them" said Donduce.

After he had retrieved two ruck sacks from one of the two built in wardrobes they had in the bedroom, they went into the kitchen and got beers from the fridge. Then they headed into the lounge and sat down.

"It really has been quite a day", said Donduce, as he hugged his gorgeous Wifey and had a slurp. "What with discovering where the actual entrance to the basement finally is, meeting and then loosing the ELK, and seeing Farmhand Mac Stupid, we need a break".

"We do, my Honey", said Beauty, "And I absolutely love our cuddles like this my Angel".

"Me too, and I love you my Babsey", said Donduce, giving his Wifey a big hug and a kiss.

"Oh my God, my Babsey" said Donduce as he had a slurp, "I was going to suggest radioing Mac Hassle and asking him if Mac Stupid was on his way, but I really can't be fucking bothered talking to him *again.*"

"Me neither my Lovey" replied Beauty having a slurp and added "That administration office; I'm fucking glad it's not in here!"

"Me too! My Babsey" replied Donduce and added "That would mean Mac Hassle would be in the building with us! Fuck that!".

"Oh, sod that, my Angel" laughed Beauty.

About five hundred yards past the farmhouse was the administration office that the main foreman, Farmhand Mac Hassle worked. He was in charge of the main workforce on the farm; obviously, Donduce was the boss along with his secretary Beauty. Donduce was known as Donduce to the workers, and his Wifey was affectionately known as 'The Beauty'.

The workforce consisted of many hundreds of farmhands and they all lived and worked within the farm perimeter; Farmer

Donduce employed all of them and paid their wages, which also consisted of free housing, healthcare, and virtually anything they needed. No actual money existed on the farm as a credit card system had always been in operation. Every month each farmhand's allowance was put on the card, and that enabled them to buy what they needed up to a certain limit depending on how much they earned. They were paid for their skills and also by the hour. Any money that wasn't spent was paid into the State Farm Account so it was there if they needed it. It was also there if the State Farm needed it too and as a result, everyone were happy. Everything that was ever needed was on the farm was run by Donduce or Donduce, and Beauty or 'The Beauty' with maximum efficiency. The Beauty was brilliant at helping her Hubby out with anything, and she had another incredible talent; she could always sense trouble; she knew if there was unhappiness anywhere on the farm, and would always tell her husband if there was a problem.

If something did happen, and the person concerned was unhappy with the way the farm was run, he was evicted there and then, but then, Donduce and his gorgeous Wifey Beauty would have to think of the last time that had happened; certainly many many years before. The farm was also completely self sufficient, and it's sole trade was to sell anything to the community outside the front gates. Farm produce, and any other product you could think of, whether it be cars, aeroplanes, meat, clothes, you name it, the farm produced it. Everything in the local village of EE-I-O was made on the farm, and the village was made up of people who worked as delivery drivers, but who 'didn't like farm life!'

Of course, the farm had it's own bank; it literally catered for every aspect of everyday living, all run by Donduce, and with the everlasting help of Beauty.

On virtually a daily basis, a massive empty delivery lorry would arrive at the farm, and go to the Farm Output Area; a huge building, about a mile up the main Farm driveway. It loaded up and then left for its destination, wherever that was.

Then there was the communications centre, that operated very like the emergency number, for any health problems; The Farm of course had it's own security and Police Force, and Donduce and

Beauty was extremely uncannily brilliant at knowing if there was an argument against the farm rules, which like anywhere had to be obeyed, and by every farm hand without exception; no farmhand wanted to hear that they had to 'cross the cattle grid', as that meant the end of their residency on the farm. Only Donduce and his Beautiful Wifey Beauty left the farm boundary across the cattle grid and out the main entrance and they did that whenever they wanted to.

Donduce and his Wifey the beautiful Beauty finished their drinks. Then, they both decided it was time to re-enter the passageway and see if they could retrieve the ELK, or at least find it. After filling up rucksacks with provisions from the fridge, and armed with flashlights, they went into the bedroom, down the trap door and into the basement.

"Here we go my Babsey" said Donduce, "You ok".

"Yes, and this is going to be brilliant!" said Beauty, and clutching very tightly to her husband's hand, waited until he had made sure that the door could be closed again at some point.

"Right, my Babsey" said Donduce. "The door is ok, but we will obviously leave it open until we get back, and hopefully with the ELK".

"Ok, my Honey" replied Beauty and added excitedly "Let's go."

Donduce opened 'the door' which creaked again. He shone the light down the pitch black arched shaped void, and checking the floor to make sure that the ELK wasn't right there, said "Come on, as you quite rightly said let's go".

They started walking, and listened out intently for an ELK noise or something ELK-ish, nothing. On they went and after about five minutes, light could be seen in shafts, coming from the ceiling. Once under the rays, Donduce said "Above us is the cattle grid or air vent and the main entrance. I haven't been any further, so It's now unknown".

"Ok, my Honey", said his gorgeous Wifey "I am right with you".

They started walking and on the slight downhill inclined floor. Ten minutes, half an hour, an hour, still nothing, and no sign of the ELK.

"Well my Babsey, one thing is for sure; this doesn't come up in the Dane and Freckles like I thought, we must be miles past it by now, I wonder where it *does* finish?"

"No idea, my Angel", said Beauty, "Let's keep going though, it's a shame it doesn't' go to the 'Dane and Freckles' however it's got to end somewhere, but where?"

"We will find out my Babsey" said Donduce and added "Patience."

The passageway did not seem to have an end but it must do. Donduce and The Beauty, his Beauty had been following the passageway for what seemed like hours when Donduce suddenly stopped, and his beautiful Bride, Beauty, who wasn't expecting him to stop quite so suddenly nearly fell over.

"What's up?" she asked, "Can you hear something Babsey?"

"I can't hear nothing, but I can smell something very familiar! It takes me back to well, years ago." Said Donduce.

"Something familiar?" repeated Beauty. She took a large sniff and said. "I get the sense of cold, damp, mist, and a slight burning sensation on my lips, my Lovey".

"Exactly", replied her husband, "The Sea!!!".

They both looked at each other, and then started walking much more quickly down the passageway. The smell got stronger by the minute and then, sure enough, they could see an archway of daylight ahead. By now they could hear the sea, pounding the shore or that's what they thought it was, but, it sounded echoey.

"If that *is* the sea", said Beauty, "It sounds like it's coming from inside a room – it's weird".

"I know", said Donduce, "We are going to find out right now".

They got to the archway, which had no door and it was just ragged all round, like the stone had been worn away after centuries of being pounded by something. They came out of the passageway and found themselves at the back of quite a large cave!! They were not at sea level, about two feet above and on a terraced looking bit, but sand was at the base, and they could see the sea just outside the entrance; it was like being in a huge creature's mouth, looking out.

"Look!" said Beauty and pointed to a spot roughly half way between them and the entrance, "On the sand".

Donduce looked and then gave his Wifey a huge kiss and cuddle, "The ELK!"

"The poor thing", said Beauty, "We must rescue it, but I need your permission my Lovey, of course".

"Oh, you have my permission, my Babsey, oh yes. We have got to get that ELK back to the farm right now".

"It's not in trouble with you is it Babsey?" asked Beauty, a worried look appearing across her beautiful pretty face.

"No, Lovey my Babsey, far, far from it", Donduce was thinking furiously about something; something odd but very daunting.

"We haven't brought any rope have we?" said Donduce, "Could you use that animal knack of yours to coax it back my Honey?"

Beauty was well known for her, and her husband's love of animals, but it was she who could somehow talk to them and communicate with them, even only to make them feel wanted and at ease.

"I'll give it a go", she said and with her husband walked down to the sand. It was quite soft, and powdery and you could see little clouds of it flying off their shoes as they made their way over to the ELK. It was lying down, facing directly out of the cave with it's back to them.

"Give it a wide berth, and approach from the front", whispered Beauty, so with a nod from her husband, they crossed to the edge of the cave, by the rocks and got to a point where they were level with it's head. Nothing. A bit further forward, Nothing; the ELK was still staring straight ahead. They got about 30 feet further on and then stopped again. The ELK suddenly moved it's head and looked straight at them.

"Oh my God", whispered Beauty, "It's now or never, keep still my Honey".

"What happens if it gets up and runs off again?" said Donduce. Suddenly, and without warning, the ELK suddenly stood up, and came, walking slowly straight towards a shocked Donduce and Beauty.

"Just keep really still, Honey", whispered Beauty, and her husband nodded.

The ELK then did something totally amazing: it arrived right beside Beauty, Beauty and nuzzled it's nose up and down her arm; the arm that wasn't wrapped around her husband. Then it licked Donduce, and then walked slowly past, and towards the passageway entrance. Stopping, briefly, it looked back around to the farmer and his wife, then back at the entrance, and then back at them.

"The ELK is saying, let's go back", whispered Donduce, squeezing his wifey tightly.

"I know, bless it, come on then", said Beauty.

As they started to follow the ELK, it saw them coming, and started walking itself. They all stepped up into the entrance and started the long journey back to the basement.

"That is no ordinary ELK", said Donduce. His voice now echoed in the stoney confines of the passageway.

"When we get to bed tonight, I want to tell you what I have been thinking, but I want to say it out of the ELK's earshot". Donduce made it sound like the ELK could understand what they were saying, and Beauty nodded.

"Yes, OK", she said "I have got strange vibes about that ELK, nothing bad, but there's more to it than meets the eye".

"One thing is for sure", said Donduce, "When we get back, we will lead the ELK up out of the coal bunker, I am sure that Mac Stupid has cleared and opened it now, a it can now live in that piece of uncut grass area just behind. There is plenty of greenery for it to eat, and I will order the farmhands to build a shelter for it to sleep in".

"Brilliant", said Beauty.

They had got quite a long way on the now upward slope of the passageway and, every so often, Mac Donduce would shine his torch up ahead. Sure enough they could see the ELK, plodding along, and could just hear it's hooves clip clopping on the stone floor. How come the ELK wasn't afraid of the passageway? Why was it so calm, and why had it been staring straight out to sea, and not looking round the cave?

Although the Farmer and his Wife had been technically 'out' for most of the afternoon, Donduce knew that the farm would be running in it's usual strictly efficient way. It was run solely, and owned solely by the State, or Donduce, and with the unfailing brilliance of his gorgeous Wifey Beauty who was his very efficient and effective secretary. Beauty could always sense when something was not right and would then immediately tell her husband. Nothing on the farm was done without State Authority and it all ran like clockwork.

All the farmers did their jobs and then went home to their various houses for a relax, and all the farmhands lived and worked on the farm. They could leave anytime they wanted to, but there was no point: they had everything they wanted, and there was only one farm. To leave meant having to start from scratch all over again, as the Farm State provided literally everything. Also, they were under the Farm Contract which they signed when they left school, and were given their guaranteed for life job; it was just far too beneficial to leave and all the workers were more than happy in their chosen careers.

Obviously, like anywhere, there were arguments, but these were quickly resolved by passifying and calming the situation.

Even unions were not needed, or even thought about, as they were all happy in their work. They knew their job, they knew their wage and they knew their rules of the farm.

It was so well run, in fact, that there was never a need for a meeting of any kind; if a problem occurred, then Donduce would be informed by Farmhand Mac Hassle, and Mac Donduce would sort the problem. Mac Hassle would then pass it on to whoever it was who had the problem, job done.

Donduce and his beautiful Wifey were getting closer to the basement door now and on the way, he had been nattering about their plans for the following day.

"Tomorrow, my Babsey", he said, "We will go for lunch at the Dane and Freckles in the village. Then, we will walk round the village, because we haven't done that for as long as I can remember. It will be nice to look round and I would like to get you something to say I love you".

"Awww Babsey, thank you and yes please", said Beauty eagerly".

They finally arrived at the door, made sure that the ELK was in the basement and then closed it. The ELK was there and was standing by the coalbunker shaft. They went up the ladder, through the trap door and were back in the bedroom. After a quick check around, they closed the trap door and then Donduce and his beautiful Wifey Beauty then went outside to the coalbunker and opened the hinges. Right on cue (Good!!) the ELK plodded up and out, into the back yard. They walked to the back field that Mac Donduce had said about and the ELK, settled by a sort of bush, and started chomping vigorously at it – the ELK must have been starving.

"Well, the ELK's OK now", said Mac Donduce, "Only one more place to attend to before we turn in, eh, my Babsey?"

"That's right", said Beauty, "The communications building".

She smiled, and hand in hand, they left the meadow field, back across the yard, and across the main entrance road.

Opposite the farmhouse, and still within the sacred area, was the communications building. It was about half the size again (1 ½) times the size of the old empty barn, but much more modern. It had been rebuilt a few times as, over the years technology had improved, and the building now housed the vast telephone exchange, intercom system, and security technology. Donduce ran this entire operation with the help of his beautiful Wifey, and it was a task that he did love doing, so did his Wifey. Very similar to checking the answering machine, and other things as well, and once they had been there for about an hour, they left and went back to the farmhouse.

It was now dark outside, and the entrance lights either side of the main entrance road had come on. If you were to look up the road, the lights, like pure white street lights stretched as far as the eye could see.

Back in the kitchen, Farmer Donduce and his Wifey Beauty were enjoying a beer before bedtime.

"What a day was that my Honey", said Beauty, "I am exhausted. I am very glad that we found the ELK, and what a fabulous little cave by the sea!"

"Yes I know", said Donduce "We will have to go back there soon and have an exploration. Come on, let's natter in bed.

Soon, they were both tucked up and, after giving his gorgeous Wifey a loving kiss Donduce took a slurp of his beer and said:

"That ELK is no ordinary ELK, my Beauty",

"What makes you say that?" asked Beauty, a very intrigued and puzzled look came across her pretty face. It was almost as if she knew that something was strange herself, but she wanted to know what her Hubby's opinion was.

"Well, my Beauty", her Hubby began "If it wasn't for the ELK, we wouldn't have discovered the real entrance to the basement, or the passageway, or the cave, or the fact that the passageway runs directly in line with the main road. If it hadn't of sat on the official cattle grid, I wouldn't have known where I was in relation to the farm. It is as if the ELK were showing us it all, but for what reason? ELKS are a type of deer, and don't possess any interest in their surroundings apart from 'Mrs ELKS' and food supplies. It was definitely deliberately leading us all over the place, my Beauty".

"Yes, my Honey", replied Beauty. She sat up in bed and reached for her beer, took a slurp and then said "Babsey, you know my way with animals; it's like they can communicate with me somehow; I can sense what they want or what they are thinking. Am I allowed to spend more time really getting to know the ELK and see what I can get from it?"

"I was going to suggest it anyway, my Beauty", Hubby Mac-Donduce replied. "I was also thinking about when the ELK was in the cave, and he was staring straight out to sea. It was either looking at something or waiting for something, but I really don't know at the moment".

"it's strange, isn't it, my Lovey", said Beauty, "the ELK wandered, in the first place from the massive wildlife reserve, beyond the mountains, to the North, and has been in the area ever since".

"Oh, I know where you mean", said her Husband, "That wildlife sanctuary is located at the base of them mountains but on the other side. We call that area 'The Ark'. Beauty took another slurp from her beer and then picked up a weird looking electrical device from the bedside table. It was known as the 'Box' and was a remote unit directly linked to the communications or 'coms' building.

"All's O.K.", she reported, and put it down again.

"Is everything as it should be on the network?" asked her husband.

"Yes, not much going on there, but there hasn't been anything that we needed to know. Is there anything, my Honey?"

"Not that I can think of that I need to know; nothing on the list but if I do, then I will make a note to remind you next time we visit the coms building my Lovey", said her Hubby.

Donduce and Beauty never 'went to', or 'popped into', or 'arrived at' 'the comms' building. They always 'visited' it.

In the very far distance, they could hear the roar of a jet tacking off from the freight airport. These jets delivered farm products all over the world and the farm only allowed it's own jets to take off and land. This was largely because there was so many flights to cater for, there was no more 'air-space' left for other commercial jets. Donduce and Beauty had a fleet of private jets that were for their own use only, and indeed were based on a strictly confidential part of the airport. These flights, and the farm-produce flights were strictly the only flights that took place, and they went anywhere off the farm that they was required; anywhere in the world.

"Tomorrow, like I said, we will go to the village for a look-round. I will buy you something nice, and then we will go to the 'Dane & Freckles' for a beer", announced Mac-Donduce. "I want to see what the 'vibe' is like there, because I have a few things on my mind about it!".

"OK, love to and yippee, goody", chuckled his now very excited Beauty. "What's on your mind Babsey?"

Her husband took a slurp from his beer and said "I would like to, or rather, we are going to visit a lot of the local shops, such as the butchers, greengrocers etc. to find out how their trade is going. Of course, the farm, being the only one here, supplies the village with everything, but, crucially, unlike our fabulous 'community', they are subjected to competition, and, us being the supplier, are subjected to it too. It is all to do width the pricing, and companies undercutting each other to get a sale, which of course, with our way of life, just doesn't exist, as we produce literally anything, and so therefore have no need to buy or import goods. In the village, there are goods sold by other traders and possibly cheaper than ours, but maybe not of the same quality; your don't have our farm guarantee on them. As you know, my Beauty, there have been many people who have left the farm for different reasons, and live in the village, which of course, they find a struggle as they don't have the fantastic security of life that they have here. So, every so often, a visit to the village is a good exercise in public relations for us, and an opportunity for a day out. On our farm, competition doesn't exist because the farm produces everything itself, and the employees buy everything and anything they need here; it is one of the stipulations of the 'State Farm Contract', or 'S.F.C' or contract; another being that no employee whatsoever must trespass on the designated farmhouse area". Her husband stopped talking at this point and had another slurp.

"I can see what you mean my Honey", said Beauty, confidently, "I bet those ex-farmhands wish they'd never left and were back here".

"Well, considering that they were lucky enough to be born on the farm and have not known anything else, they probably find it a struggle, so do the families, but then, it was their choice to go, my lovey".

"Just like emigrating to another country I suppose", said Beauty.

"Absolutely spot on right, my Babsey" her husband replied.

They finished their drinks and turned off the bedside lights. It was strange to think that only about two or three from the bed was the 'new' trap door, leading directly to the basement. All them years they had been in the farmhouse, and they had never known of it's existence....or had they?

It was pitch dark as they cuddled up for the night, but after about 15 minutes th Beauty became aware of a faint glow of light around the gap between the bedroom door frame and the door: Beauty nudged her Husband and told him.

"Something has tripped the auto-light by the kitchen back door", he said, "I'll go and check; stay there".

"Not on your life", said Beauty "I'm coming too".

They both got up and opened the bedroom door. Sure enough, the light was coming from the halogen security lamp positioned above the door, on the outside and it lit up the area of the yard, the coalbunker and a bit beyond. The kitchen light was off, and - Donduce peered out of the window; his hands cupped round his eyes to enable him to see better. "I can't see anything at all my Beauty,.....OH, MY ....GOD", said Donduce, "Those escaped tigers are walking around the backyard! There's two of them actually in the yard and one by the coal bunker in the gap leading to the ELK's meadow".

"Oh my God, Babsey, the ELK! What on earth are we going to do?"

"No problem, my Lovey, don't worry", said her Husband in his usual very calming but very commanding voice, "Watch".

Her Husband flipped open a control panel to the right of the back door. It revealed a control panel, which looked rather like a calculator, but mounted on the wall. He put a code in and then pressed a button. All of a sudden, there were several sounds of gun-shots and loud voices could be heard, and as Donduce and Beauty peered out of the window, the tigers were immediately startled and bounded off round the corner of the kitchen in the direction of the main entrance road. Donduce then pressed another button, and the gunshots were heard, but a lot further away and in the direction the tigers was heading. Her husband then got onto a radio-thing that always sat on the kitchen window ledge. "Network one", he said, smiling and blowing Beauty a kiss.

"Yes, DD?" said a voice after a beep.

"Tigers on loose on main drag, please deal immediately, Thank you" the radio bleeped.

"OK DD, will deal, out". The radio went dead.

"Sorted my Beauty", said her husband as he put the radio back and caressed Beauty in his arms.

"So, what happened there then my Honey?" asked Beauty curiously. They sat down at the breakfast bar, after her husband had got a couple of beers out of the fridge.

"That control panel on the wall is like a burglar alarm, well, it is, but it also contains, because this place has every species of animal there is, due to the nature of the farm and the 'Ark', a multifunctional scarer, to warn off unwanted predators. It also acts as a caller in case we lose someone or something" explained Donduce. "Tigers hate the sound of gunshots, so it scares them off, and there are loud speakers all round the farm to control the animals when we need to".

"OK," said Beauty. "But why didn't we use it then when we lost ELKY?"

"ELKY!!" laughed her husband. "I like that name, why didn't we use it? Firstly, because ELKY usually finds us, and nextly, because your vibe was OK. I know you very well my lovey, and if an animal is in distress, you get agitated; in ELKY's case, you 'knew' things would be OK, and as a result I also knew not to worry 'unduly'".

Beauty smiled; she loved her Husband so much, and she knew that he knew her better than she herself did; it wes all part of the T.C.R.D. that she received every second of her life. "OK, then, my lovey", she said, in her mind, wondering what the response would be to her next question. "What would you record into the control panel to summon ELKY then, another ELK?"

"No, my Beauty", said her husband with a smile, "Your gorgeous voice".

"Awwwww Babsey, that's beautiful, thank you Honey. Talking of ELKY, we had better go and check on it", said Beauty.

"Him", said Donduce, "ELKY is a him".

They left the kitchen and, crossing the yard, walked past the coalbunker into the small meadow to the rear. Sure enough, ELKY was lying down under the bush he had been chomping on, and was asleep with his head leaning on his front forelegs. Even in that position he was a good four foot tall.

Knowing ELKY was safe, Donduce & Beauty returned to the farmhouse and were very soon back in bed and recounting the evenings happenings. All's well that ends well my Babsey", said Donduce, as he settled down with Beauty in his arms. "Tomorrow, we will go to the village and pick ukp the vibe and the mood of it".

"OK, my Honey", said Beauty sleepily, and turning the light off, they both said "I love you sweetheart nite nite", and went to sleep.

As Donduce was in charge of the entire farm State and its rules and regulations, it was he, and his gorgeous secretarial Wifey Mrs Mac-Beauty who ran the whole 'business'. It was Beauty's talents with animals and indeed every creature that existed that looked after everything, and with her help, the boss -Donduce looked after her and the 'business'.

Donduce and Beauty had originally been born on the farm, but quite a few miles away from where they lived now, at the helm. Due to various circumstances many many years before they had had to leave the farm, but had met in the Dane and Freckles on what they had always thought was a set-up, by someone, or something. Suffice to say that they had returned, and were now solely in charge. Indeed, they were the only two people in the farm's entire existence who had ever left the farm and returned.

They loved to go to the 'Dane and Freckles', as it brought back fond memories of their first real encounter, and the start of their beautiful and perfect life together.

Donduce had the radio and with his Wifey, Beauty, operated the comms room. Every dwelling on the State had an intercom system, , so that they could get into contact directly if there was a problem. There was also a phone exchange too, and everything was paid for through the employee's wages. The wage amount was determined by what job they did, and the higher the quality the job, the higher the salary, and consequently, the higher the allowance paid to them by the State, minus of course, deductions, such as State duty and services.

-Donduce had always run the farm in this completely efficient way, and the State contract was final and binding. Whichever career was chosen, it was the State who was the Employer and so therefore, the Boss.

It was the dead of night. Donduce and Beauty were in bed fast asleep. There was not a sound from anywhere.

The Elk got up and gave itself a shake. Then after carefully checking all round the little meadow, found the pathway that lead off into the forests that started at this point, just at the end of the meadow, and started plodding down it.

At the same time, Beauty, fast asleep, hugged her husband even more tightly. Only about two hours to go and it would be morning. On the horizon, the sky had taken on a pale blue colour as dawn was approaching. Where was ELKY going? Would he be back? If yes, when? What would Beauty do or say if the Elk wasn't there in the morning? It was fast approaching now, morning, and, although neither of them had to be up particularly early, Donduce always set the alarm for 5 a.m., which is when the two family cats needed feeding.

Suddenly and totally unexpectedly the alarm clock went off!! It was 7 a.m., and was supposed to go off at six, but Donduce had put it forward instead of back by mistake. Not only that, but although Beauty had reminded her husband about the hour, there was really no need to set it , for Donduce automatically woke at 6 a.m. to feed the cats.

Reaching out from under the duvet (sounds familiar this, Babsey!) he pressed the snooze button and cuddled up once more to Beauty, who was still asleep.

This routine was repeated for about 3 or 4 goes, and by the fourth, they were both awake.

"Good morning my Angel", said Donduce, as he kissed Beauty, "are you ok?" he asked.

"NO", grunted Beauty, and disappeared back under the duvet. She was, really, and was thinking that it was another beautiful day, pleasing her husband and promoting the values and views of her husband in running the farm. She loved these values and views, and also because she was devoted to him, and whatever he said was law.

Beauty re-emerged from the duvet and kissed her husband.

"We're going to the village today my Honey, I can't wait", she said, happily.

"We certainly are", said her husband and got out of bed. He went to the kitchen and got two beers out of the fridge returning a few moments later. "There you are my Lovey", he said, "Enjoy".

They sat up in bed slurping, and when they had finished, Beauty went into the bathroom to have a shower, and her husband went into the kitchen, fed the cats and checked out the remote comms unit that he had picked up from the bedside table.

When they were all ready, they picked up their keys and went out of the front door. This was the side of the Farmhouse that was nearest the main entrance and were walking across the tarmac driveway to the garages opposite.

"Oh my God", exclaimed Beauty suddenly, "We haven't checked ELKY. We must make sure he's ok before we go".

"Well done you, my lovey", said Donduce, "I had actually forgotten about him, come on".

Donduce had designed the farmhouse into two parts: the front and the back. This made it so that Farmhands who came to do maintenance on the actual farmhouse could only get to the back where the yard was; coal bunker and various other bits, which left the front only accessible by Donduce and Beauty. Consequently, there was no back gate and so the only was to get to the back, was by going back through the front door. This they did and were soon walking past the coalbunker and into the meadow. They rounded the corner, and sure enough the ELK was awake and standing up, eating the same bush that he had started on the day before. ELKY turned his head and looked straight at Beauty. She smiled and walked over, with her hand out. Her Hubby followed behind just as ELKY nuzzled Beauty's arm, and when Donduce got next to him, ELKY gave him a lick on his nose. The Farmer patted the ELK'S nose and then it turned back and carried on eating.

"Well, HE seems happy enough", said Donduce, "Come on then my lovey, Village time".

"Oh, he's so sweet", said Beauty, I am so glad he's ok, I had a weird dream last night that he had disappeared and I was worried. Yes, village time".

They had returned through the farmhouse and were walking once again across the driveway. With the pressing of a remote, the steel garage door buzzed into action, and, as it rolled itself up into the roof, the jeep was revealed. There was not a mark on it since the Moose had sat on it, and next to the jeep was the Astra.

"We will go in the jeep, just in case we get loads of shopping", said -Donduce as he unlocked it with another remote. "When we get there, we'll go the cash machine and drew some out to keep us going, since we're off the farm".

-Donduce and his beautiful wifey Mrs Beauty were the only two on the vast farm State who carried cash, or had direct access to a bank other then the State bank. This was because the Farm State's own credit cards were not accepted off the Farm premises, and there was good reason for this.

They had got into the jeep, made sure that the tank was full, and started off. Out of the garage, onto the front driveway which swept round to the lift, through the gap in a large hedge, which kept the front of the farmhouse out of sight and then left onto the main entrance road. Five hundred yards later, they went over the cattle grid and then out onto the curved road, known as 'AKKS Lane' which lead to the village.

"It's a lovely morning, my Honey", said Beauty, sitting happily in the passenger seat, we will be there soon, and walking round the shops – I can't wait".

"Nor me, Babsey my lovey", said Donduce, "I wonder what today has in store for us."

They had followed 'AKKS Lane' round on a slow left-curved bend, and were now nearing the village that was actually located on the other side of the massive field between it, and the farm. A car park came up on the left hand side, and there were quite a few already parked there. They pulled up to a machine and after a buzzing noise and a lot of clattering, a ticket came out of it's mouth, and after Donduce had taken it and passed it to Beauty to look after, a barrier lifted and they drove; found a space and parked up.

They got out and Beauty's husband locked the Jeep. "I wonder how today will turn out", he said thoughtfully.

"I don't know, my lovey", replied Beauty, wrapping her arm around him tightly. "but I am looking forward to it".

Her beautiful long flowing hair caught the slight breeze as - Donduce gave her a kiss and wrapped his loving arm around her. "You look beautiful", he said. His own hair caught the breeze too, but with his hair down to just below his waist, and Beauty's hair down to virtually the back of her knees, her's was much longer. Beauty was wearing her sheepskin hippy coat, and her husband was wearing a black jacket made of leather. Their tattoos of their names were just visible as the cuffs of the jackets they deliberately kept back so they was visible. Both had lots of tattoos and just further up their arms were tattoos of the 'Farm Emblem', which they was very proud of.

As Beauty's hair blew in the breeze you could see how many earrings she had, the same as her husband, 21; eleven in her right, and 10 in her left ears respectively.

They had walked, arm in arm across the car park, and at the other end was a road that ran past the car park. They left it, and crossing the road, got to a junction shaped like a cross. They would turn left which was the main high street and at the top of this road was a pedestrian precinct and acted like a continuation of the shops, but without the traffic. At the end of that was a big church, the spire you could just see from the farm entrance. Donduce and Beauty got to the junction cross roads, rounded the corner turning left into the main high street, and, bloody hell, bumped straight into Dad!!

"Hello", he said, and put his arms around his daughter Beauty, and gave her a warm hug; he did the same with Donduce. "You're out early this morning; I've only come out for a stroll to get a paper and some milk; what are your plans?"

"Donduce is taking me shopping", replied Beauty happily, "Then we are going to the 'Dane & Freckles' for lunch, and then probably heading back".

"That's nice", said Dad, "Well, I won't hold you two up; and no doubt you will phone later?"

"Of course", said Donduce and Beauty simultaneously, and then Donduce added, "Come round for a beer, Dad, you are always welcome".

"Thanks", said Dad, "Better get on, and love to the pair of you".

He gave Beauty another hug and a kiss, and affectionately nudged Donduce's arm. "Take care", said Beauty and Donduce together, and after smiling and waving, Mac Dad disappeared round the corner in the direction of the car park .

"I didn't expect to see Dad", said Beauty, "I wonder if we should call him later, my Lovey?" she added, as she wrapped her arm back around her husband.

"Yes, my Babsey, we will, but for now, shopping" said Donduce.

The main high street was quite long, and, crucially, was very old. Every shop building was originally made of stone blocks, like old-style London, but there were several parts of the town that were brickwork where the buildings had been modernised. The high street was very traditional; it comprised of separate shops, for instance, a proper butchers, greengrocers, chemist etc., and the only modern building was the bank, situated about half way up the road.

"OK then, my Babsey, follow me, you will have loads of questions to ask me in the 'Dane & Freckles', but for now, just watch".

"OK, Honey", said Beauty, and a curious puzzled look spread across her beautiful pretty little face.

The first shop they went into was the first one on the left hand side of the road, the side they were on, and, as they went in, a pair of inquisitive eyes were watching them from the other side. It was the butcher's shop they started in.

Laid out in traditional style, with all the various meats and produce on display, and the butcher had a counter at one end where he prepared customer orders, a weighing machine and the till. The butcher was writing something down when Donduce and Beauty walked in, and the bell rang, which caused him to look up, and then appear a bit startled.

"Good morning", he said and sort of smiled; he had something on his mind when he saw Donduce, but hid it well.

"Morning", said Donduce, ignoring the butcher's look of unease, "A large order please if you would".

"Certainly Sir", he replied, "What would you like?"

"Two portions of every product you sell please, except for anything that has come from 'EE-I-OH Farm'. Please then could you deliver my order to 'R and D', EE-I-OH Farm, Akks Road, as soon as you can please?"

"Certainly Sir", replied the butcher, but then said, "I do vaguely recognise you and your lovely wife, don't you come.........."

Donduce interrupted him with a smile and said "How much does the invoice come to?"

The Butcher finished pressing the buttons on his rather ancient calculator, and said, "With everything, nine thousand pounds Sir".

"Thank you", said Donduce, and paid with their credit card. "See you soon", said Donduce as they left the butchers, and as they walked back out the door, the bell rang again.

When they got back into the high street, Beauty said to her Hubby, "Nine grand, just in the butcher's?, this is some shopping trip, my Lovey".

Donduce gave her a kiss and said "I did say that you will have loads of questions when we get to the pub".

The next shop was a hardware store, and, instead of looking round the shelves, Donduce guided Beauty straight to the other end of the floor to where the assistants were standing.

They all wore typical protective grey full length coats and again, looked startled when Donduce and Beauty approached. After the assistant had greeted them and asked how they could help, Donduce asked for exactly the same request; two of every product that the store sold, except for any product that was made on E-I-O Farm. This time the bill came to just under thirty thousand pounds, and again Beauty's Hubby paid by credit card. As they left the shop, the pair of inquisitive eyes were still on the other side of the road, but were watching Donduce and Beauty intently.

Chapter 5

This 'method' of shopping happened in every store they went into, with the exception of the bank; Donduce put a card into the machine inside the building and drew out enough for lunch. Outside, the pair of eyes had moved up the street, but had kept at a suitable distance.

"How much have we spent now my Honey?" asked Beauty, sounding a bit concerned as she had been trying to add all the figures up in her head, but had all but given up.

"Oh, about half a million, so far", replied Donduce, "Don't forget, I bought a couple of them brand new cars from the showroom across the way. Right, next stop, the jeweller's".

"is this for my present?" asked Beauty excitedly.

"It certainly is", replied her loving Husband. "Your present will comprise of two items. The first is something I want to get you, and the second is what you want to get".

"How do you mean?" asked Beauty, really puzzled now.

"Well", said Donduce. "I want to get you something which I know you are going to love, and I also want to get you something that

Is something you will love".

"Wooww", said Beauty, in a tone of voice that resembled someone who loved chocolates, had just been given the keys to a sweetshop.

They went into the jewellers; a smallish shop, but you could tell that the merchandise was of very good quality. Donduce placed exatly the same order again and then said, "I would like to have an item especially made please" to the assistant.

"Of course", said the lady behind the counter. "What did you have in mind?"

"A necklace", said Donduce, "but with the main charm being of this design, in 24 carat gold, encrusted with as many real diamonds as you can fit on", with that, Donduce produced from his pocket a copy of a picture he had drawn for a card celebrating a year of their engagement, only this time it was to be a solid version.

"No problem", said the assistant, "About two weeks, and then pop in to see it for approval?"

"Lovely,OK", said Donduce, then giving his beautiful Wifey a kiss, said "Have you spotted anything you would like Lovey?"

"Yes, Babsey", she said "There is a lovely bracelet in that display cabinet over there. There Isn't no words in the bracelet, but it's solid gold and has a little gold horse dangling from it".

"No problem", said her husband, giving her a kiss, and, turning to the lady said "Yes please".

"Well, with everything that you have bought and ordered, the total comes to", and she discretely showed Donduce the figure. It was just over four hundred thousand pounds.

"Lovely", said Donduce, and paid again, using the credit card. The lady put Beauty's necklace into a special presentation box, and then into a bag.

"Have a really nice rest of day", she said, and smiled with the same unease that every shop owner had showed. Beauty and Donduce left the jewellers and returned to the main high street. They had been into virtually every shop there was, including the pedestrianised part, and after visiting a computer shop, then an electrical one that sold washing machines and every type of appliance you could think of, and doing the same amount of purchasing, and sending it to the specific address, (Are you keeping up, my Lovey? Confused? Yes? Good! read on…) Donduce said "Time for the 'Dane and Freckles' I think, how about you my Lovey?"

Beauty nodded her beautiful head vigorously and said "Awwww,yes please, lead me to it!"

The wind caught her hair again in the breeze as they started walking back down the high street in the direction of the cross roads. She really was a total stunner and her Boss and Hubby Donduce was very very protective of her, and very proud of her, he loved her with all of his heart and soul, always had done and always would. The wind had caught his hair too; as the village or rather small town was on the other side of the big field that 'Akks Road' went round one side of. It was exposed to the elements. The north side of EE-I-O, behind the church was more sheltered as the shops and buildings provided a sort of wind buffer. Mac-Dad lived on the north side in a house paid for by Donduce and Beauty.

As they walked back towards the cross roads, they didn't know that at a discrete distance, that inquisitive pair of eyes was still following them. No one else had noticed, no passer-by, for the owner of the pair of eyes was clever.

"Nearly there", said Donduce, thankfully. They had reached the cross roads, crossed over, and were now walking down the road virtually next to the car park on the other side.

"I can see the 'Dane and Freckles' sign", and Beauty, excitedly, and her pace quickened. Donduce laughed as he also speeded up, and by the time they got to the end of the road and turned left again, they were virtually running. The 'Dane and Freckles' was just about 50 yards up the road, and opposite was the familiar field. Beauty and Donduce went in through the door, and sure enough, their usual place was un-occupied and the fire had been lit. There was virtually no one in there as the 'Dane and Freckles' had only been open about half an hour; one or two people were in already: they just looked up to see who it was and then quickly looked down again, or carried on with their conversation. Donduce and Beauty went up to the bar and Donduce ordered the beers. Beauty never, ever left his side no matter what, and never ever spoke to anyone, only her beautiful Husband. She preferred it that way and so did Donduce. The barman had asked them how they was, and Donduce had said 'very well'; Beauty just smiled. They collapsed into the comfy sofa like chairs by the fire and put their drinks down on the glass table in front of them.

"Well", said Beauty, after she had taken her coat off and given her beautiful long hair a brush, having made sure it was all flowing forwards to stop her sitting on it, although she adored doing that as well, she didn't trust what could have been on a 'public' chair, "That was well-brilliant, and thank you my Honey for the beautiful bracelet you bought for me; it's gorgeous Babsey".

"That's ok", my Lovey, he replied, putting his arm around her shoulders, "That was a brilliant morning".

"How much did we spend my Sweetheart?" asked Beauty, intrigued at the way the mornings shopping had been done.

"Just over one million", said Donduce, cheerfully, "and I am so glad you love your bracelet and the present that's on order too".

"Ok, Babsey", replied Beauty, "I am absolutely dying to know, how come we was buying two of everything that wasn't supplied by our farm, but sending it to somewhere on the farm then Honey? I recognised the farm address".

"Well then my Lovey, it's like this", said Donduce "There is a reason why I spent so much money, on two of everything, two of everything that specifically is not supplied by the farm and it is this Donduce took a slurp of his beer and said:

"Yes, two of everything not produced by the farm are bought by us, and sent to 'R & D', so that they can be checked out to see if they are faulty or not; then, once they have been given the all clear, one of the two of each product bought goes into our own private store, and the other stays at 'R & D' for spare parts, just in case the item goes wrong. It is also a good efficient way of keeping serviceable parts handy, in case a farmhand's appliance develops a fault.

"Ok, Lovey" said Beauty, "I think I understand, although it is definitely your 'department', but we have actually spent one million, wasting, it on research, haven't we then?"

"No, darling, because some of the stock were consumables and so we need to sell on to farmhands, and also the rest, like I say we sell as spare parts back in the village. Don't forget, we produce anything and everything on the farm anyway".

"So Babsey, why buy in stuff made by our competitors then, if we produce our own?"

"One reason is 'R & D", explained her Hubby, "Them other reasons are trade secrets, which I will tell you all about, but in the privacy of our own four walls, and not the 'Dane and Freckles', here".

"Ok, my Darling", said Beauty with a smile. She loved it when he had his business head on. It wasn't just business though, it was the way in which he ran the farm which she loved too. In turn, her Husband loved the way that Beauty had with animals; she could sense when an animal was trying to communicate, and certainly knew when one was poorly.

"Another?" asked Donduce, pointing at his Wifey's empty glass.

"Yes, please Honey", she said smiling, "Just coming'.

Beauty flicked her gorgeously long dark hair back behind her now that she had stood up, and holding her husbands hand, walked over to the bar with him. Mrs Mac-Beauty, or Beauty, as her husband loved to call her, never ever ever left her Husband's side. It just wasn't in her nature to do so, and her` Husband always wanted her literally next to him all the time. It was literally the pure, raw, deep unconditional love they had for each other. Beauty would be right there by his side permanently, and her husband was there looking after her permanently too. -Donduce was always and would always be the one to speak to whoever it was; the barman, farmhand, shop owner or on the phone. Beauty never spoke to anyone, she preferred and insisted that her Husband did that, there was only two people, ok four that she would make a point of communicating with: her beautiful Husband obviously;, her Dad, and her 'In-laws', Donduce's Mum and Dad whom she loved and they loved her.

"Same again?" asked the barman.

"Please" replied Donduce and added "Business good?"

"Not bad", replied the man, uneasily. "The farm produced brand is selling very well, and we have just ordered another lot. There is a guest brand coming in next week, would you like me to send you some?"

"Please", said Donduce, usual address, pay now?"

"OK, or next time you are in will be fine", he said.

"I may as well pay now, because we are always in", laughed the Farmer, he smiled at his Wifey and she giggled.

Donduce paid, and they carried the beers back to the table. "It is so lovely in here Babsey", said Donduce, "Do you remember when we first met in here, all them years ago?"

"I do", said Beauty, reminiscing on them fond memories; then she added "Quite a few years ago now, my Honey".

"Yes Darling", replied her Husband, "Many many".

"After this, we will go back as we have things to do, unless you want to stay a bit longer" said Donduce.

"Yes, my Honey", replied his Beauty, "I do want to stay a bit longer, is that OK?"

"Of course it is", said her Hubby, laughing, "As long as you want my Angel".

Outside the 'Dane and Freckles', the pair of inquisitive eyes was waiting for the pair to come out. The wind was still breezy, and a slight dampness in the air had caused a layer of condensation to cover exposed surfaces, such as the tops of low walls. It was getting towards winter and the days had noticeably been getting shorter, and colder.

Inside the 'Dane and Freckles' more people had come in and low murmer of conversations filled the bar area. The conversations ranged in diversity of subjects and the lace had an air of pleasantness, but also of discontent ranging from money issues to the usual problems associated with life. 04/04/11

"At least we don't have none of that Babsey", said Beauty, happily reclining in the comfy settee style chair with one arm round her husband tightly. (

"I know", said Donduce, "Everyone is happy on the farm. We haven't been to the State Tavern for a while, have we my Lovey? We must go sometime".

"Last time we went there, Farmhand Mac-Stupid was in, remember?", said Beauty.

"Oh God, yes!!" laughed Donduce. "Well", he continued, "I will arrange for him to be bussy one evening, and then we'll go – your thoughts my Babsey?"

"O.K.", laughed Beauty, and then thinking the terrible thought what they might still bump into the obnoxious creature, said rather desperately "OH GOD!!"

"Come on then", chuckled her husband. They had finished their beers and, after getting up, and putting their coats back on, Beauty flicked her hair back, then did her husband's and went over to the door.

"See you soon", said Donduce to the barman who nodded and waved as they went out.

It was noticeably colder as the outside air greeted them and Beauty did up a couple more buttons on her coat. Donduce lit a cigarette, and after putting their arms around each other turned right, back in the direction of the car park. Unbeknown to them, the set of inquisitive eyes had gone, but wasn't far away.

The sky had now developed a greyish colour signifying low cloud, and it was beginning to drizzle quite a bit.

"Come on my Lovey" said Donduce, "We are going to get soaked".

They speeded up, rounded the right hand corner, and the car park was on the opposite side of the road. The owner of the inquisitive pair of eyes was on the opposite side of the car park staring back at them; they didn't notice.

Half way up the road was a gap in a waist high wall which surrounded the car park, and on reaching it, Donduce and Beauty walked through and Donduce spotted the jeep half was across. The owner of the inquisitive pair of eyes started walking at the same speed, out of sight towards the jeep. Donduce got out their car keys and pressed a button. The jeep's alarm beeped to let them know it was unlocked. They had approached the jeep from behind, and at the same time, the owner of the inquisitive pair of eyes got to the jeep from the front. Just as Donduce opened the passenger door to let Beauty get in, the owner of the inquisitive pair of eyes leaped on the roof of the jeep and Sat there, still as anything, like a statue.

"Oh my God my Beauty", yelled Donduce, "We've got a big dog on our jeep!".

"Bloody hell", said Beauty, "I wondered what that big thud was, I thought you had dropped something Honey".

Beauty got back out of the jeep and stood by her husband. "Oh, isn't he gorgeous! Babsey!" she exclaimed.

"About as gorgeous as the bloody dent in the roof that we have got now", said Donduce, but then added "Hold on a minute, my Lovey". He put his hand up towards the dog's neck and found that it didn't have any collar, so consequently no owner or address.

"Well", Donduce said "My Lovey, it appears that it is a stray. Would you like to take it back to the farmhouse and train it to be our guard dog?"

"Wow, yes please", said Beauty, "How the hell are we going to get it off the roof though Hun?".

"One way to find out", replied her Husband, and he opened the hatch back boot lid. Without even a second thought, the dog leapt off the jeep, landed on the tarmac, had a quick scratch and then obediently jumped in; the dog didn't so much as growl. Donduce shut the lid, and then Beauty and Donduce got in themselves.

Donduce started the jeep, and then the dog decided it wanted to see where it was going, so it re-positioned itself with it's back paws tucked under it's bum on the floor of the boot, and It's head resting on top of Beauty's head with it's front paws aside the back of Beauty's seat.

Beauty absolutely cried with laughter; "Oh my God, I can't move", she yelled "Come on Honey, lets get this thing home, now, fast, Immo!!".

"O.K., my Lovey", said Donduce, giggling loudly, "Now are you two going to be O.K.?" Beauty squeaked "Yes, Darling", from somewhere under the dog, and the dog licked it's lips and started panting. It then started to dribble all over Beauty.

"Our nice clean jeep – now look at it", said Donduce, watching as puddles started appearing on the dash board, "Can't you wipe it's mouth?" he asked. "Babsey.....please?".

"What with?", laughed Beauty, "Honey, my handbag with tissues in, is inside my handbag, and I think the dog is sitting on it Honey".

"Bleeding Hell, we need more than poxy tissues, we need a beach towel Babsey" said Donduce, laughing.

"Beach towel? Honey! What else do you think we brought with us? A bucket and spade? We went shopping my sweetheart, not on a holiday to the Riviera".

They were now heading down 'AKKS Road', dog and all, and were nearly up to the farm's main entrance. Donduce signalled right, and they drove up, over the cattle grid, and a bit further up turned right again, through the gap in the tall hedge and into the front driveway. They got out and Donduce let the dog out of the boot.

"Oh crumbs, Honey, I can breathe again" said Beauty as she got out. Her husband put his arms around his Wifey and she did the same to him. They kissed passionately, and then Donduce said "He is rather nice, Babsey, Isn't he?"

"Gorgeous, my sweetheart, and thank you for letting us bring him back."

"No problem", said her husband with a smile, "Let's introduce it to the back yard my Babsey".

The dog, who had been sitting in the middle of the drive way, waiting, stood up as they both called it, and it dutifully followed them out of the gap in the hedge, and into the next right turn which was the back yard. The dog walked around it sniffing intently, by the back door, the coal bunker , paused in the gap that lead to the ELKS meadow, back round the yard and then sat down outside the back door, like a sentry.

"Well", said Beauty, "He has definitely found his home, bless him, Babsey, and it is a him. What shall we call him my darling?"

"As he is going to be our guard dog, my gorgeous Beauty", said her husband, "We'll call him 'Fang'".

"O.K.", said Beauty, "Babsey, 'Fang' it is, and Fang, welcome to the farm.

Fang seemed to understand what Beauty was saying, because he suddenly started wagging his tail.

Fang was very like a large Alsation; brown and white with a brown patch around his right eye. A shortish coat of fur and in remarkably good condition.

"We haven't got any dog-food Babsey, have we?" said Donduce, as he and Beauty opened the back door and went into the kitchen.

"No, sweetheart, we haven't", replied Beauty, a worried look spread over her pretty little face. "Any ideas Babsey?".

"Of course, my Lovey", said her husband. "Lets sit down with a beer, and then drive up to the State Stores and get some there, it won't take long, but first we must go and lock the jeep up".

"O.K. Lovey" said Beauty, happily.

They went back out the kitchen door and round to the front driveway. Donduce shut both the car doors, and then pressed the button on the remote. The jeep beeped to confirm it was locked, and after they checked the meadow, and saw that ELKY had his head buried in his favourite lunch-bush, they returned to the kitchen. Donduce went to the fridge and got a couple of beers out, and then they sat in the lounge and started slurping.

Donduce and Beauty loved their jewellery. As they sat on the Settee with their arms around each other, there was three clearly visible necklaces around each of their necks. One was a crucifix, the second was the farm logo, and the third, another cross. Each of them had a specific meaning to Donduce and his beautiful Wifey, Beauty.

The main entrance road of the farm, which the farmhouse was the first building after the cattlegrid on the right, ran for about half a mile into the farm, and the buildings along it, which included the 'State Administration Building'; 'State Security', and a 'Stores' building, were only accessible by Donduce and Beauty. At the end of the main entrance road was a 'T' junction and along the road that ran at ninety degrees to the entrance road were ten separate roads that ran further into the farm. Down road six, as it was literally called, well, it's full title was 'State Road Six', was the 'State Stores', similar to a supermarket, but much, much bigger, and infront of the building was a massive car park, where the farmhands all parked. This is where - Donduce, and Mrs. Mac-Beauty would be going, but crucially

Donduce always made a 'phone call first. It was to the State Store, and he simply said "'Code One' please". This meant that they were to clear the store and empty the car park. This was to ensure that nobody at all was in or around the building, as Donduce and his beautiful Wifey Mrs. Mac-Beauty could do their shopping alone. Beauty did not like crowds or anyone 'getting too close'.

This system worked very well, and indeed it was used for anywhere on the Estate that Donduce and Beauty needed to go. The State Store was in fact one of five, but was the nearest to them. Five stores, because there was five major areas on the Estate, each one of them vast. They were all connected by road, and of course, the farm State railway.

From the area of the State stores, if you were to look directly south, in other words with your back to the farm house area, you would see the start of the hills, and then the mountains in the distance. There was always a mist that hung over the upper mountain slopes, and even on a clear day, it was never possible to see the peaks. Between the hills and the distant mountains was the wildlife reserve known as 'Noah's'. To drive there, once you had travelled over the hills would take a good day and an overnight stop in one of Donduce's and Beauty's many other private dwellings.

Next to 'State Road Five' was (yes, well done my Lovey); 'State Road Four'. This lead up to a massive plaza , and a massive hall called 'The State Building'. Here, once a year, many thousands of farmhands would gather to listen to music from bands who performed on the Estate. The groups came from all over the farm, and on this day, Donduce and Beauty would watch from the specially constructed area within the building. Then, Donduce would address the crowd and then they would all depart. Of course, this musical festival happened more than once a year, but this particular day was when Donduce and his beautiful Wifey Mrs. Mac-Beauty did attend. There was also another event, which happened in the summer that attracted thousands of people and that took place in the plaza: it was known as 'State Day' and it was very patriotic.

Donduce and Beauty finished their beers, and after a loving kiss, he picked up the 'phone and made the call.

"No problem my Angel", he said, "About 20 minutes and we will go".

"Brilliant", smiled Beauty, and then added "Do we need anything else, whilst we are there, Honey?"

"Not that I can think of", he husband replied, "But I am sure that we will find other things as we walk up and down the aisles sweetheart".

They got up, and after a quick stretch, and a hair comb for both of them, they both looked in the mirror to make sure they looked o.k. for each other. Beauty always wanted to look her best for her husband, and likewise (Awww), Donduce always wanted to look best for his gorgeous Wifey.

He looked away from the mirror; a full length one; and turned to Beauty. The sun's rays were streaming through the lounge window and catching Beauty's earrings making them glisten. They were gold hoops, well, the first four was, and then studs, the same as her husband. Her jewellery glistened too, the two crosses and the farm State symbol. "You look beautiful as always my Babsey", said Donduce, wrapping his loving arms around her, as if to protect her from something (you're giggling my Lovey).

"Thank you my sweetheart", she replied and added "You look pretty stunning yourself, Mr Mac-Donduce".

They kissed again and then left the lounge, went into the kitchen and out of the back door to check to see if Fang were o.k.. He was lying down with his head in his front paws, but as soon as he saw them he got up and almost stood to attention. Beauty laughed and said,

"Do you know what, Honey, I almost expected him to put his paw up then and salute us!!2

"It would have been funny if he did, my Babsey, could you train him to do that?" asked Donduce with a giggle.

"You ARE joking!! Darling!!" laughed Beauty. "Poor Fang is not capable of raising his paw like that; he's a dog, not a human. Talking of paws, we ought really to take him to the 'Vetenary Hospital' at some point and get Farmhand Mac-Darwin to check him over, eh Babsey?"

"Good idea", agreed Donduce.

The State Vetinary Hospital was located down 'State Road One', along with the main 'State Hospital', and also every conceivable medical practise your could ever need. Also located there was the 'Network Centre, Fire Station, Ambulance Station along with a few other buildings as well. This whole massive area was linked with the massive 'Zone Five' area.

Donduce and Beauty had returned to the kitchen, and Donduce picked up the keys to the jeep.

"Just before we go to the stores my Babsey", he said, I have got an idea, which I would like your thoughts on".

"O.K., my sweetheart", said Beauty, curiously, "What's on your mind?"

"We are the 'Royal Couple', 'King and Queen', are we not, it's just that no one actually refers to us like that – yes, my Babsey?"

"Yes, of course", agreed Beauty.

"Well, you know that massive bit of land, just next to the farmhouse, that stretches along the 'Main Entrance Road' for quite a way, before you get to the 'T' junction, my Babsey?"

"Yes, of course I do my sweetheart, what about it, Honey?"

"Well, my gorgeous, beautiful Babsey, why don't we actually build a palace for us, my Babsey?" he said.

"Wow", said Beauty, "That, my sweetheart, sounds fantastic, but I do love this farmhouse, and it would be a shame to leave it".

"Oh, no, my Lovey", replied her Husband, "I don't mean leave here, I mean build a palace that joins onto the farmhouse and makes it one huge building. We could have new stables and a courtyard; ELKY'S meadow would still be there, and the farmhouse would become a sort of annexe. If you wanted too, and I have been thinking about this, we would still live here, but the palace itself would, unbeknown to the population, become the massive headquarters of the State. It would completely centralise all of the State's various departments into one place and we wouldn't have to travel to any other building to monitor State operations; what do you think, my Lovey?"

"A great idea, my Honey", replied Beauty. "What would happen to all of the existing buildings though?"

"Simple, sweetheart, they would become out buildings, like more stables, pig sty area would get bigger (stop giggling, darling, my Babsey), or we could re-locate the despatch area near to the main gate, so that 'outside' delivery lorries collecting exports and bringing in 'R & D' stock wouldn't have to come so far onto State property".

"Whatever you say, it sounds fantastic, Honey. When were you thinking of drawing up the plans and starting?"

"Maybe, my darling, I will start working on a design, when we get back from the stores, of course, we need to do it together; we could stop by the field area on the way back if you would like".

"O.k.", said Beauty. "Now come on, shopping, sweetheart".

They left the kitchen and after checking that Fang and ELKY was o.k.; they was, ELKY was asleep in his meadow, and Fang was virtually asleep in the backyard.

"If any stranger came into the backyard now, looking at the state of Fang, Babsey, he would either have free access to everything or else he or she would get licked to death!!".

Beauty laughed, and then they left the yard and went through the farmhouse to the front door. Locked it behind them and got back in the jeep. -Donduce let his beautiful Wifey Mrs. Mac-Beauty into the passenger side, and after kissing her on the forehead, shut the door and then got in himself. Out of the gap in the hedge they went, but this time, turned right, so the backyard came into sight with the gate that blocked it off from the main state road. Then a big hedge which was the one that finished up encircling ELKY'S meadow and then the big field. It was enormous, and virtually ran the length of the rest of the main entrance road.

"What we need to build as well, my Sweetheart", said Donduce, as they were driving past, "Is to build a massive high fence, ornate, with big railings so that it is visible from the state farm road, so that whoever is walking past can admire it".

"My darling", laughed Beauty, "It's only us what do drive past, there Isn't no one that comes into this area, apart from deliveries Honey".

"True Babsey", laughed Donduce. They reached the end of State farm Road and turned right at the 'T' junction. Then about five hundred yards on the left was 'Farm Road Five' which they turned down. The State Stores loomed up on the left hand side, and, as planned, there was no one in the car park; the whole place was deserted. Donduce pulled straight up to a side entrance and using a special key, unlocked a set of doors.

"Right then, Babsey, we will grab a trolley and see what is here", said Donduce.

"O.K. Boss", said Beauty, happily.

They did and then started pushing round the aisles; the store was set out exactly the same as any other supermarket and had loads of different sections; clothes were on sale as well; and a music selection. Of course, every item in the supermarket was 'Farm State' produced including the music which were by bands famous and not so famous.

"Bloody hell", said Donduce, "We are walking slowly up and down the aisles, my Lovey, we only actually came in for dog-food!!".

"We also need some beers as well Sweetheart", said Beauty, "And whatever else we fancy", she added.

They did get a few extra bits, and then when they had decided they had got enough, went to a special checkout by their private entrance. It looked like one of them metal detector xray scanners you get at airports, but it simply checked the barcodes, and what the item was. Once all the shopping was put through, a receipt came out of the machine at the other end, and it bleeped at you to put your 'State credit card' in. Donduce did so, of course, Donduce and Beauty's cards was limitless, but they still technically paid, even though it was all their property anyway, simply so that Donduce could balance the State accounts every month. He kept a close eye on the profit the farm made and, of course, all profits were put straight back into the State Funds.

Once through the scanner, which was also there to prevent theft and fraud, both practices completely against the 'State Farm Contract', and were punished by the removal of the individual from the Farm State, Donduce and Beauty loaded up the back of the jeep, shut the hatch back, and then locked the set of doors once more.

Once more, Donduce was just about to open the passenger door for Beauty, when he suddenly said "Oh, Babsey, bloody hell, we have forgotten to go the 'Private Area'".

"OH MY GOD, we can't forget that", giggled Beauty, and after they had a hug & kiss, Donduce opened the doors to the store again. Once in, they turned left, and halfway between the toilets and the information and tobacco kiosk was a door sized closed metal shutter: above it a big sign simply said 'Private Area'. Donduce got out a special key and put it in a security lock, located in the wall to the right of the shutter and at about the same height as the screen on a 'hole-in-the-wall' machine. The key went in and Donduce turned it clockwise to a position resembling quarter past on a clock. Then, on reaching this position, a green light underneath lit up and the metal shutter started lifting up. Behind the shutter was a couple of extra rooms of the store, complete with aisles, but crucially sold all Donduce's and Beauty's favourite 'other branded products'. Donduce had remembered that Beauty was running low on her beers, and also her beloved Rum. Once these items were retrieved, Donduce turned the key to half way back, in other words anti-clockwise to a position resembling a quarter-to, and the shutter closed once more. Back through the scanner, and onto Donduce's card. Only Donduce's and Beauty's credit cards accepted 'OBPS', and once scanned, Donduce said "Right, let's try again, Babsey", chuckling.

"I really feel tired now Babsey", said Beauty, as she held her husband's hand as he locked up their private shop entrance.

"Don't worry, my Lovey, we'll soon be back, shopping put away and then we can relax for the evening. It's been a long day, Lovey", said Donduce, as he held the passenger door of the jeep open once more.

They kissed, and Beauty got in. Then Donduce got in himself, after putting the shopping in the boot.

"Homey, homey!!" they both said in unison, and drove out of the car park area, turning right onto 'Farm Road Five', then back to the junction and then left onto 'Main Entrance Road'.

As they were passing the massive field on the left, Beauty said: "Darling, it is a truly massive area, and it has so much potential to be a massive self contained functional Royal Establishment within the farm. We could actually re-organise the Farmhouse layout to make it very soon totally private, but, Sweetheart, how would we get round the problems of maintenance?" Beauty enquired.

"Well", said Donduce, "The whole project, construction, and future maintenance can be a job for the 'Network' my Lovey. The design, and building materials will be our decision, and also the time taken to build. If we finalise the design between us, from start to finish will take about a year, but as bits are finished, it would be just like extending the farm house more and more".

"Brilliant, I really can't wait to start helping you with that", said Beauty, as they turned into the front driveway once more.

Once the shopping was retrieved from the boot, Donduce locked the garage and once they had got indoors, Donduce and Beauty put the shopping down, and Donduce put everything away in the massive walk-in larder pantry room they had, just of the kitchen. The only item that was left out was a packet or rather big bag of dog food. Beauty was in charge of all cooking in the Farmhouse, however they both fed the animals. Beauty opened up one of the kitchen cupboards and got out a large bowl, which she put on the floor. "Honey, we Isn't got no dog bowls in the farmhouse. I knew we should have picked one or two up at the stores, shit".

"Never mind my Lovey", said her husband, "We'll put a couple on the list for next time. Is the one what you're using o.k. for now though?"

"Yes, it will do o.k. my Sweetheart", and Beauty kissed her husband, whilst still holding the bowl, which by now she had put Fang's dinner in, and holding it in mid air. Then, they opened the back door and put the bowl down in front of Fang, who jumped up, and started munching, vigorously.

"Awww, bless him Sweetheart", said Beauty, "He must have been hungry".

"Talking of being hungry", said Donduce as he watched Fang get through his dinner in twenty seconds flat, "What are we having tonight Babsey, my Lovey?"

"Don't know yet my Babsey", said Beauty, looking thoughtful. Beauty was just going to suggest what Donduce might like for his dinner, which Mrs Mac-Beauty also loved, and had just said "What would you like for dinner, my Sweetheart, knowing that her gorgeous husband would come up with the same thought, when a loud voice interrupted what was a nice relaxed moment;

"YOU THERE?" a voice shouted loudly, from just beyond the gate to the back yard.

"OH NO!" exclaimed Donduce and Beauty together, "It's bloody Farmhand Mac-Stupid!"

He was standing at the back gate.

"What the hell does **he** want?" said Beauty, rather annoyed that the otherwise peaceful tranquillity of the farmhouse had been so rudely interrupted.

"I'll go and see what he wants, Babsey, but stand by the back door so you can listen: his conversations are usually about right for his name", said Donduce, and just as he had finished his sentence, Mac-Stupid yelled out "OI! IS THERE ANYONE THERE?"

"Oh God", said Donduce, "Here we go, Babsey!"

Beauty smiled as her Hubby walked over to the farm back gate; Farmhand Mac-Stupid always answered a question with a question, and he was leaning over the gate trying to look in. He jumped noticeably, as Donduce came into view.

"Didn't think you was in mate, but you are aren't you", he said.

Donduce thought to himself as he got there; "I certainly Isn't your bleeding mate, and said "Hello, what's up?"

Donduce was also thinking "Come to think of it, what are you doing at our back gate: it's private?"

"It's my tractor, isn't it", said Mac-stupid.

Donduce thought he would reply in similar sarcasm; "Yes, your tractor certainly **is** a tractor"

"What?" said Farmhand Mac-Stupid. Donduce repeated what he said.

"I know it's a tractor, do you think I am stupid or something, mate?" he asked.

Donduce was trying very hard not to nod his head, "What's wrong with it then?" he asked.

"I didn't say there was anything wrong with it, did I ", came the reply. "There Isn't no bleedin' diesel in it is there".

Donduce frowned. "What, you haven't filled it up since you was at the field with the cows?" he asked.

"No" said Mac-Stupid.

"Why not?" asked Donduce.

"Why not what?" asked Mac-Stupid.

"Why haven't you put diesel in it?" asked Donduce. He thought by now that he would be spending the rest of his life having this conversation.

"It's run out, hasn't it!" said Mac-Stupid. "I can't bleeding drive it to the pumps can I? Or do you expect me to bleeding pick it up and carry it!".

"No", said Donduce, "Use a 'Billy can'".

"What?" said Mac-Stupid.

Meanwhile, Beauty was over hearing this conversation from the safety of the kitchen, and crying with laughter (I'll bet you are giggling my Lovey).

"Use a 'Billy can'" said Donduce, repeating himself.

"Billy can what?, and who the hell is 'Billy'?" asked Mac-Stupid.

"No, a 'Billy can'" said Donduce.

"I couldn't care less what 'Billy' can or can't do, I Isn't never heard of no 'Billy', I need my tractor fixed mate!" said Mac-Stupid.

"No", started Donduce, "Billy Isn't a person, it's......" Mac-Stupid interrupted him.

"He Isn't a person? What is he then, some sort of bleeding creature, something from the sky, a different world, and if he was, he wouldn't know about fixing tractors would he?" said Mac-Stupid.

"A 'Billy can'" replied Donduce, "Is a metal container that you put diesel in at the pump, and then you take to the tractor, fill it with the can, and then drive the tractor to the pump."

Donduce had thought he explained this very well.

"No", said Mac-Stupid.

"Pardon?" said Donduce.

"No", said Mac-Stupid.

"Why not?" asked Donduce, a bit taken aback by this response.

"Cause I Isn't got one, have I?" said Mac-Stupid.

"Well, go to the stores and get one then", said Donduce.

"No", said Mac-Stupid.

"Oh God", thought Donduce, "This is ridiculous", so he said to Mac-Stupid, "Why can't you go and get one then?"

"I Isn't got no transport have I? What do you expect me to do, fly?" he said.

"Well, you got here, didn't you?" said Donduce.

"Obviously", he said, "Otherwise, how would I be standing at your gate?"

"Well", said Donduce, "If you got here, you can go to the stores then can't you?"

"And if the stores Isn't got any, I'm stuck, Isn't I?" he said.

"They will have some, they sell everything", replied Donduce, and then added, "Once you have got one, then you can fill it up and take it back to the tractor".

"Then what?" he asked.

"Then drive the tractor to the garage and fill it up. Also fill up the can, so you won't run out again", replied Donduce.

"Who's running out, out of where?" he said.

"No, the tractor, it won't run out if you keep the can with it!" said Donduce.

"Tractors don't run anywhere, you drive them mate; they will be taking part in bleeding marathons if they could".

Mac-Stupid stopped leaning on the gate and stood up.

Thankfully, he started walking back down the 'Main Farm Road', but then turned his head and shouted "The stores had better have one, or I'll be back". He disappeared into the distance, and Donduce watched him to make sure that he had actually gone. Once out of sight, Donduce left the gate and returned to the kitchen, where Beauty just wrapped her arms around him and said: "Babsey Honey, how on Earth did you manage to keep a straight face through all of that?".

"Oh God my Lovey", said Donduce, "It was hard, to think that a 'Farmhand' had the audacity to lean on a 'Royal State Farm' gate, and hint that he wanted me, the King, to leave you, the Queen, and give him a poxy lift in the 'Royal State Jeep' to get a bleeding petrol can – the flaming cheek of the man".

"Never mind my Angel", said Beauty in her gorgeous comforting voice, "He's gone now".

"That's just it, my Lovey", exclaimed her Hubby, "If the stores don't have and cans, he's coming back!".

"Oh God", said Beauty, "Babsey, do you think he will?"

"I wouldn't put it past him to move in and take up residence Honey!" said Donduce and added "Along with his poxy tractor as well".

Beauty was wiping the tears of laughter away. Donduce got a couple of beers out of the fridge, and they were just about to sit at the breakfast bar, when Donduce peered out of the kitchen window for a minute.

"He's not back already, surely not Babsey – is he?" asked Beauty, suddenly alarmed at her Husband's sudden interest in the back yard.

"No, no my Lovey", he replied, "I have only just noticed that the cow you rescued from the pond has now gone. Did it recover then Babsey?"

"I've no idea Hun", said Beauty, joining him at the window, "I hadn't noticed it had gone either!"

They both looked at each other and said in unison, "How can you possibly miss a cow, they're big enough!".

It was getting dark outside, and quite late.

"Right, my darling", said Donduce, "Put your beer down, then put your coat on, and follow me".

Beauty did so, so did Donduce and, then she asked, "Where are we going Babsey?"

"On an adventure", said Donduce, smiling at Beauty. He loved to surprise her.

"Brilliant, Babsey, but where, and how are we going to get to where I don't know we're going?" said Beauty, with a giggle.

"Well my Honey", said Donduce, "The adventure starts in the garage!".

"Oh, Kay", said Beauty curiously. "By that answer, my darling, I take it we Isn't going by car then?".

"Hmmm", said Donduce, deliberately being unhelpful, "Come on, my Beauty."

They went out of the front door and headed across the driveway to the garage. It was now dark, and the security lights had come on casting shadows on the ground of the hedges and various tubs containing plants and shrubs that gave the front of the farmhouse a bit of colour.

Up to the garage, but this time Donduce lead Beauty to a side door and unlocked it. The door itself was about ¾ of the way down the depth of the garage, and it led to a car spare parts storage area, jump leads, battery chargers and all the sorts of things one would need in an emergency. Of course, if all else failed, they had the 'State Breakdown Service' which operated 24/7, however it only operated within the farm boundaries. If a break-down was to occur outside the farm, there were other ways and means, but, it had never happened yet.

Into the garage they went and Donduce held Beauty's hand and pointed to the far wall of the garage store room.

"Look", he said, "There!".

Beauty followed the direction of his arm, but couldn't see much in the darkness. Then, as her eyes got used to the dimly lit room, she suddenly exclaimed "Bicycles!!".

"Yes, my Babsey", said Donduce, "We are going to cycle to the 'Dane and Freckles' for the evening; fancy it?"

"I fancy something else too!", said Beauty with a smile, "But yes please to that as well".

They got the bikes out; his and hers. The bikes had gold coloured frames with burgundy red writing on them. Beauty and Donduce, respectively.

"Are you O.K. there Honey?", asked her Husband, as Beauty sat astride her bike. "Fine thanks, my darling", she said, "Ready?".

With a nod from her Husband, they rode out of the front drive and onto the 'Main Farm State Road'.

"Don't forget to stand on your pedals when we cross the cattle grid", said Donduce, as it came into view, "Otherwise it will be rather sore on you my Babsey".

"Good point, Honey", said Beauty and stood up. Her hair was blowing out in the breeze and she looked gorgeous. She almost had the same stance on her bike as she did when she rode her beautiful horse around the fields at the back of the farmhouse. Although the main field was going to be developed into the palace, behind it were miles and miles of fields and countryside, which both Beauty and Donduce rode in a lot. Beauty had taught her Hubby to ride many many years before and the stables were up beyond the back yard. Donduce proposed to re-house them in a massive complex right inside the palace grounds. In fact a lot of things was going to be within the grounds, but also, within the palace building. Donduce now stood up on his bike; he was slightly behind Behind Beauty, but once he was over the grid, he caught up. Beauty had slowed down whilst she were waiting. Beauty and Donduce were never more than a foot apart, ever.

They turned out of the main gate and it got noticeably darker. The 'Main Entrance State Road' had been brightly lit by the security lights, but once off the farm it was virtually pitch black. The lights on their bikes really came into their own and lit up 'AKKS Lane' fine. It was a typical country road, on the left, a hedge, and unusually tall trees, hundreds of feet high lined the first part of 'AKKS Lane' before they curved away as 'AKKS Lane' curved to the right. The tall trees marked the farm perimeter and they stretched off into the distance as far as the eye could see. One couldn't see a lot anyway as other trees and hedges masked the farm perimeter ones. On the right was the field that separated the farm from 'EE-I-OH' town. It always seemed that nothing drove up or down 'AKKS Lane' apart from Donduce and Beauty; there was others, like Dad, and of course the delivery lorries.

Donduce and Beauty were now about half way down the lane and were cycling side by side. It was virtually silent, apart from the wind blowing through the trees on the left. On the right, they could see the distant lights of the town just over the far hedge of the field, which itself was plunged into darkness. It wasn't a clear night. There had been low cloud ever since Mac-Stupid had been, and now there was a definite chill in the air.

"This makes a lovely change to cycle to our favourite pub, my Babsey", said Beauty happily, and then she added "After that encounter with Mac-Stupid Babsey, I can quite see why you preferred not to bring the jeep!".

"Exactly my darling", replied Donduce, "Not only that, but I wanted to blow them cobwebs away".

The trees on the left had finished and they were now in the street-lit part of the lane. They went past the car park where they had found 'Fang', that morning, or rather 'Fang' had found them, and very soon the 'Dane and Freckles' appeared on the left. There was a small pub car park to the right of the pub and they left their bikes locked up against a sort of railed terracy bit that was doing It's best to be a beer garden. There was no garden and only about two bench seats were left. There had been more but with wear and tear had got broken and not replaced. Anyway, the car park was not the most picturesque place to sit and relax.

In through the front door they went and straight up to the bar. Someone different was on for the evening shift and there were only about six or seven people in. Beers bought, and they sat down, for the second time that day in their usual spot by the fire.

"Aaaahhh", they sighed simultaneously, as the settee swallowed them up, "That's better, Babsey", said Donduce, and added "You O.K.?", "I always am with you right by my side my Babsey",said Beauty.

"I know I said that we ought to go to the 'State Tavern' sometime, but I really don't like going there, because it is full of people that we just don't have anything in common with or don't like, my Lovey", said Donduce.

"I quite agree Babsey", said Beauty "I hate it – 'The State Tavern', I don't like the regulars, and you know what I am like and how I feel about socialising with 'them'. I much prefer it here as its quiet, friendly and 'they' leave you or rather 'one' alone, even though we are royalty, we are off the Estate my darling".

"In the morning, my Lovey", said Donduce taking another slurp of his beer and reclining further back into the settee; Beauty in turn, sank deeper too into the settee, and rested her beer on Donduce's tummy. He continued, "I will phone up Mac-Dad, and Mac-Sweet, you know, the head of residency on the 'Executive State Zone Five'. I want to know certainly his opinions in our special way of costings for the palace, whether to get in his recommended builders or to use contractors outside the farm perimeter. What I need you to do, is to use your talents when we tour the animals tomorrow. You can usually get the vibe from them as to the general mood of the non-animal population".

Beauty indeed had special powers which had actually been given to her by her Husband many many years before. Her Husband, - Donduce could get a positive response from somebody by putting a question in a special way, and because of Beauty's special love of animals, he had trained her to do the same with them. It had taken many many years of special work, but now, Donduce and Beauty were expert in their views and way of living. Donduce would just have to simply say something to Beauty, and she would understand what he wanted. Although Beauty never ever spoke to humans, apart from her beloved Husband and Dad

She had great communication skills when it came to animals. The nature of the farm found Beauty's skills both essential and invaluable. There was hundreds of thousands of animals, birds and in fact every species of creature that had ever walked the Earth on the farm, and Beauty knew every single one or them, and they loved her. They also loved Donduce for it was him that gave them their home. They loved Beauty because of her uncanny knack of knowing if there were a problem with something. Donduce and Beauty was like that with each other; just one look and they would know something was up. Good or bad and it would be fixed immediately. Donduce and Beauty were unique really, because they never had and never would have an argument; there wasn't anything to argue about and never would be.

"I am looking forward to touring the animals tomorrow, my Sweetheart, said Beauty, dreamily, "all of them, or the 'usual' ones? Babsey?" she added.

"No my Lovey, just the 'usual' ones of the 'link'", said Donduce.

"O.K., my Sweetheart, it will be sorted", said Beauty, almost taking on her official role already. Donduce noticed that straight away and said giggling "Not now, my Lovey, tomorrow!!".

Beauty laughed and said "Oops, sorry Babsey".

They sat snuggled up together and watched for a minute the goings on in the bar. They were sat at the end of the room where the log fire was, roaring away, and could feel the warmth of it. Every so often there was a small whistling sound as the pieces of wood burned and a small thud as the burnt bits dropped down into the hearth. The carpet was a typical buff colour with little blue squares dotted around it. On the left wall opposite the bar were more settee like seats with tables, and above them were framed pictures of the town, both old and new. The bar ran two thirds of the length of the room and went round the corner to the right, at the end of which was the kitchen. If you were to walk into the pub and turn immediately left, you would end up at the flap doors of the

kitchen area. Immediately to the right of the pub entrance and technically opposite the kitchen doors were the toilets. Donduce and Beauty had had another beer and when they had finished, Donduce said:

"My Lovey", he said, "Before we go home, I have got to take you somewhere".

"Oohh, somewhere really exciting, I'll bet", said Beauty, suddenly curious, and then said, "Where? Babsey".

"If I told you where my Lovey, it wouldn't be a surprise now would it Sweetheart" said Donduce chuckling. "Come on".

They stood up, and Donduce helped Beauty on with her coat; it was only a short one, down to her waist as they were using the bikes; her beautiful hair flopped down her back past her coat and rested just below her thighs. Donduce then put his on, and flicked his hair back too, down to his waist. Then, hand in hand, they left the bar and as they did, Donduce said "Goodnight" to the staff.

The cold night air hit them as they got outside and the wind had got up. It was blowing across the field, and causing a few gates to some houses nearby to rattle.

"Follow me", said Donduce, "We Isn't going to get the bikes just yet".

"O.K. Sweetheart", said a puzzled looking Beauty, and wrapping her arm around her Husband, and Donduce did the same with her, they turned left out of the pub entrance and walked past the car park. A bit further on was a left turn and Donduce said "Up here my Babsey".

They turned left and had only walked about ten yards up the road, when Donduce said "Look up the road my Sweetheart, what can you see?"

Beauty looked, and her eyes opened really really wide, "Bloody Hell, my Babsey, OH MY GOD!! It's "A K.F.C. !!" squeaked Beauty, "Oh brilliant! Babsey! Wow!!".

"Come on then my Lovey", laughed Donduce, "What are we waiting for?".

They more or less ran up the road, crossed over and went in. It was about half full, and when Donduce had ordered two portions of chicken bits, two fries and two drinks, they sat down by the window so they could look out and start munching.

"Babsey", said Beauty, with chicken all round her mouth, "How did you know about this place?".

"Well, my Lovey" explained Donduce, "When we was walking back sown the high street this morning, I just noticed it as we turned the corner, but going the other way. We Isn't far from the main high street".

"Wow, what a lovely surprise, my Sweetheart", said Beauty, happily, "Can we come back again sometime?"

"We can come in or get a take away as often as we want, my Lovey", said Donduce, then he added, "After the 'Dane and Freckles' though".

"Of course", laughed Beauty, wiping her mouth and starting on her chips, "We have got to get our priorities right my Honey".

They finished, and after throwing away the empty boxes in a bin by the window, they left and arm in arm started walking back down the road to retrieve the bikes.

"I am getting a bit sick of this bloody wind my Lovey", said Donduce, going back, the wind is going to be against us, so be prepared for a struggle".

"Never mind", said Beauty in her gorgeous, comforting voice, "It won't take us long. I hope".

Donduce and his beautiful Wifey Beauty were now sitting up in bed at home and relaxed. They were supping their beers and reminiscing on the days events: it had been quite eventful and they were both tired, but at the same time really happy, but then again, they always were.

"It seems like five minutes ago since we got up this morning and went shopping my Lovey", Donduce was saying as he took another slurp.

"I know Hun", said Beauty, "and everything was brilliant, and all the animals are O.K. too", she added.

When they had got back, Fang had been waiting for them; he hadn't minded being stuck out in the yard, but Donduce and Beauty had brought him in and he was now contented with his head resting in his paws in the kitchen. ELKY was fine too and was sitting under his favourite bush in the meadow.

The cats were curled up on the end of the bed, and there was a lovely sense of peace around the whole farmhouse.

"I'll set the alarm for 8 my Lovey", said Donduce. "That will give us plenty of time to get ready in the morning and then phone Mac-Sweet. I can also then start drawing up the plans for the palace, and phone Mac-Dad. Then we can do our tour of the animals on the 'link'".

"O.K. my Angel", said Beauty, taking another slurp of beer herself, "I am looking forwards to the animal tour, especially the ones on the 'link', my Lovey".

'The Link' was a unique communication system devised by Donduce, to enable Beauty to find out from the 'vibes' of animals any information they needed to know about problems or general chit chat. The animals on the 'link' were the ones that were specifically fed and looked after and monitored by the farmhands solely. For example, all the herds of various cattle, which were very high in numbers were 'link' animals, as the farmhands rounded them up on horseback using lassoos etc. It took several farmhands to do this and of course, neither Donduce or Beauty had the time. They were called 'Link' animals because these breeds could hear what the farmhands were saying to each other about anything, and obviously when neither

Donduce nor Beauty was around. So, at frequent intervals, Donduce and Beauty would go to a selected field, and Beauty would get the vibe from a loyal, well, they were all loyal, but because of the numbers, a specifically chosen cow, or pig or whatever, and find out the gossip. It worked very well, and this arrangement was private between Beauty, Donduce, and the animals; all of them. Even domestic animals, such as the Farmhand's family pets were on the 'link', as they would be out and about on the streets; or tied up outside the local stores, but could hear conversations from humans. One way, out of several in which Beauty could gain the 'vibe' from these pets was a rather unique system involving sweet wrappers.

The 'State Stores' sold pet treats like sweets and they came with a brownish coloured wrapper, which tasted of dog food. If the particular dog or cat had something on it's mind, it would eat more of these treats, and it's owner would discard the used wrappers in specially designated doggy bins, so, consequently, the more wrappers in each bin, the higher the stress levels of the domestic pets, and because the bins were transparent, when Donduce and Beauty went 'out', as they had done that day, Beauty would be able to tell instantly if there was a problem, so, for that matter could Donduce. When they had gone to the 'Stores' that afternoon, Beauty had done a quick reconnaissance of the bins as they drove through the car park, they were of a 'safe' level and the bins in the 'Store' by the Entrance/Exit were O.K. too. Beauty also possessed the power to actually know which animal had eaten which sweet and how many.

94

So, she was then able to ascertain who the owner was, and then Donduce would instruct the 'Vetenary Hospital' to send out a 'check-out' notice. This was a computer generated form which instructed the pet's owner to bring it in for a check up; it was compulsory. The owner left their pet at the 'Centre' within the 'Hospital', and then Donduce and Beauty would go along, and in a nice, animal friendly room, with no-one around apart from Donduce, Beauty would get the

vibe from the pet, and then be able to discover other vital pieces of information, and Donduce would then decide what action, if any, needed to be taken. So, that was three ways in which the 'Link' worked.

'The Network' was another way for communication. The farmhouse, and the area of the 'Crown' was right by the main entrance, and all of the fields containing the 'link' animals, or the first chain of the 'Link' surrounded the 'State Crown Farmhouse Complex'. So, looking from above, zone one was left most beyond the main entrance road, and zone five was farthest right. 'Zone Five' was also known as the 'Network and Executive Zone', as every resident Farmhand had to have a 'State Capital of at least £1000,000,000.00. The State had calculated about five years previously that the least wealthiest occupant had a State value of 700 million, and so the minimum was raised accordingly. All capital within the State was State owned and the State had the right of access to any capital if required. The dweller however had a very generous allowance per month to spend, and the right to occupy one of the many mansions that existed on 'Executive Row', as it was affectionately known. Also written into the 'State Farm Contract' was compulsory membership of the 'Network'. Failure to perform tasks required of the 'Network', resulted in immediate termination of the contract, and consequently, eviction from the farm. So, residents entitled to dwell in the very affluent area were very loyal to the 'Network' and of course, to the 'Crown'. These residents, and there were several hundred of them had been born and had grown up on the farm, and loved their lifestyle. Every human who resided on the 'Estate' had indeed been born there, and were very happy with whichever zone they had been allocated by the State, which in turn had been decided by their earnings. It was possible to move lets say from zone three to zone four, if their allowances permitted theincrease in rent which the State took.

Farmhand Mac-Sweet was one such resident who was in charge of State construction, and this involved building new dwellings and the repair and maintenance of existing ones. All repairs costs were payable to the Crown State via the dweller's monthly allowance. Any major work was taken in instalments, so that the residents of the 'being repaired' dwelling had enough money to live on.

Farmhand Mac-Sweet was very good at keeping his ear to the ground, and it was also his requirement, under the State Crown Farm Contract or 'S.F.C.' to report any problems what he either had himself, saw or heard, immediately to the Crown. He also had a large group of others, all from the 'Executive Zone', and selected by the 'Crown' to assist him. The network was a bit like the 'Link' but the human equivalent. Unbeknown to the 'Network' however was the 'Link's' requirement to check on them to ensure proper function, well, they WERE farmhands of course.

The 'Crown', of course, were -Donduce, and his beautiful Wifey Mrs Mac-Beauty, or to give her proper 'State title'; Queen Beauty. Her loving husband's official 'State title' was of course, 'King Donduce'. Of course, the King and Queen of 'EE-I-OH', were the official Royal Couple, or family as 'EE-I-OH', like other countries within countries was a 'Royal Principality'.

"It is very close to bedtime", said Beauty, as she stretched out her arms above her head, yawned and then wrapped them around her loving Husband. "I adore you my Babsey", she said with passion, "I really do".

"I adore and love you too my little Sweetheart", said her husband fondly. He wrapped his arms around her too.

"I am looking forwards to tomorrow my Lovey", he said, "I want to get an estimate of how much the palace is going to cost".

"Babsey, considering our unique 'State Farm' set-up, and theway you, alone, manage the whole lot, with such great efficiency and effectiveness, it don't matter, does it Babsey?"

Donduce could sense an alarm in Beauty's voice. Any mention of being short of money sent understandably her feeling, which was genuine, of the need for total security, and she had that guaranteed by her husband, the King. She was totally helpless without him and he completely looked after her, which he loved doing, and Beauty loved him doing it too.

Donduce reassured her that they would never ever be short of money, God no.

"Of course it doesn't matter my Lovey", he reassured her. "I just want to hear what the general consensus of opinion is to us building the palace, my Lovey. Also, I want it totally private, so nobody can disturb us", he added.

"What happens it we get an air of disapproval then my Babsey?" asked Beauty curiously.

"We won't, Hun", re-assured her husband. "Our farmhands love us, and their beautiful way of life in this farm principality. It will just simply test their loyalty to the 'Crown' my darling".

"So, in the event of some 'people' not liking the idea, what happens then, Lovey", asked Beauty again.

"It will be seen as disagreeing with their 'S.F.C.', and will result in their immediate eviction, my Lovey", replied Donduce with a wry smile.

Beauty just looked at him lovingly. She knew exactly what her husband meant, and loved every minute of it. It also reminded her of all the bad times that she had had to endure before she met up with her husband all them years ago, and that great expression came into her mind which she said to her husband "Yes, my Angel, after all them years of sadness, 'what goes around, comes around'"

"Of course, my Lovey", he said lovingly, no more tears, enough is enough, we are O.K. now, and have been for many many years. Come on then my Lovey, one more beer and then bedtime my Lovey?"

"Yes please, my darling", said Beauty, and with that, he got out of bed, walked down the hall, into the kitchen, and opened the fridge. Fang opened one eye, and on seeing who it was, shut it again. Donduce closed the fridge again, and after giving Fang's head a rub, and a low 'rrrr' issued from Fang, as if to say "Yeah, love you too, I'm asleep, sod off", he returned to where Beauty was, sitting up in bed. She looked stunning and her hair was flowing down the duvet. The two cats, who were lying on the end of the bed, were motionless, but it was just possible to see their bodies breathing. "Bottoms up Lovey", said Donduce, as he passed

Beauty a beer and opened one himself, "At this rate, we Isn't never going to get up in the morning".

"Yes we will Lovey", giggled Beauty, and added, "I will get you up to get me my morning beer".

"Now just why does that really not surprise me at all my darling", laughed Donduce, as he got back under the covers. "Ciggy time", he said, and rolled one. "Lovey, what is the time?" he asked. Beauty peered past her husband at the clock on his side of the bed.

"Bloody Hell", she exclaimed, "It's nearly 2:30 a.m.! Lovey, we need to go to sleep Babsey".

"O.K.", said Donduce, and after they had finished their beers, they settled down, with their arms around each other and Donduce turned out the bedside light.

"I love you, Sweetheart, nite nite" said Beauty.

"I love you too, Sweetheart, nite nite" replied Donduce.

All went quiet and peaceful. The bedroom was pitch black and there wasn't a noise to be heard anywhere.

At that moment, ELKY got up and shook himself. He drew himself to his full height, and his antlers glistened in the tiny bit of moonlight that had suddenly appeared from behind an otherwise cloudy sky. He walked around the meadow once, to check that his 'home' was O.K., and, after sniffing the air, rather curiously, he looked directly at Donduce's and Beauty's bedroom, then turned around, and walked to the other end of the meadow to where the path was. Then, looking back one more time, he started walking. ELKY was by now about five minutes away from his meadow and his pace was slow, but precise. He knew exactly where he was going, and this path he liked because it was hidden with tall undergrowth eitherside. He was a very very happy ELK as he had got the loving, mystical and communicative vibe from Donduce and Beauty, and he knew that they would be able to do business, especially with Beauty, who would in turn, communicate what he wanted, in human talk, to Donduce. There was or were several reasons why ELKY had travelled many hundreds of miles from the other game reserve on the farm, but beyond the desert; somehow he had to get Beauty to understand, and then tell her husband. Everything would then be fine once they both knew. Suddenly, ELKY's train of thought disappeared as he thought he heard something. He was still on the pathway, but a good couple of miles away now, and he had to get back before Donduce and Beauty awoke. ELKY stood still, motionless, listening intently. Yes! He could hear feet on the pathway getting louder; they made a dull thudding sound as they approached.

Quickly, ELKY moved silently off the path and into the tree like hedge shrubbery. ELKY was the right colour and blended into the foliage, so was instantly camouflaged. ELKY waited, and then ELKY's eyes opened very wide, the maker of the footsteps noise was visible and coming down the path; ELKY knew who it was, it was the Gorilla!!!!!!!!!! ELKY kept very still, silently watching from the safety of the overgrown bushes and trees. Any noise that ELKY made could startle the gorilla but thankfully there was a breeze blowing and the noise it made rustling the leaves helped to mask any small movements. Also and luckily for ELKY, his scent was carried on the breeze, but away from the gorilla. When ELKY had left his meadow he had detected a strange aroma in the air, and the gorilla had been the cause.

It bounded straight past ELKY and off down the path and disappeared into the darkness. ELKY waited for a few minutes, and after shaking himself, re re-emerged back onto the path. ELKY was worried; he had somewhere he had to be, he had to be back before Donduce & Beauty knew he had been gone, and now he had the added worry that the gorilla was back in the area, and might be about to break back into the farmhouse. That would mean his new Master and Mistress would be distracted from his plight, which they still knew nothing about. Somehow he had to tell them the gorilla was back. He knew how to do this, and that involved Beauty. Right now he had to reach his destination and then head back. He reached into the bushes with his nose and pulled some greenery for a quick snack; when he had finished munching, he shook his head and body, then started cantering slowly up the path; it was going to be a long night.

Beauty had again tossed and turned again in bed, and cuddled up even more tightly to her husband in her sleep. Her subconscious knew there was something not quite right, but she was tired, and rested once more.

Chapter 6

Dawn was breaking over the land. It was to be a clear day, and the horizon began to turn a pale blue. As the sun came up, it's rays cast shadows of the buildings onto the main Farm State Road. There was a film of dew that covered virtually everything and a cold-light of day sleepy air was about the place. The animals in all the fields were quietly munching on the grass, and the distant sound of the sheep in their field could be heard. Bleedin' Doo was crowing in the hen house, and Freckles and Maisy were eating their straw in the stables. Everything was nice and peaceful, and Fang, the incredibly ferocious, feared by everyone, except for Donduce and Beauty, was sound asleep in the kitchen.

The alarm clock went off. A Donduce shaped hand came out from under the duvet and pressed the snooze button, then the hand returned back under the duvet, and then two familiar shapes disappeared even further under the duvet, with a muffled "NO" heard from Beauty's side.

Soon, the realisation of the day ahead entered both of their minds; for Beauty, it was another fantastic day with her husband, and the animal tour, and for Donduce it was another fabulous day with his beloved bride, and start planning the palace, phoning Mac-Sweet.

They both rose together out of the duvet and stretched. Donduce reached over and made sure the alarm clock was off.

"Good morning, my Lovey", he said sleepily, "Sleep O.K.?"

"Good Morning, Sweetheart", Beauty replied, "Yes, I did, but had a bit of a funny night my Lovey".

Donduce put his arm around his loving Wifey, and a concerned tone came to his voice.

"Why Babsey my love", he said, "What's on your mind", he asked.

"I don't know my Angel", said Beauty, "I'm puzzled, I just had this really funny feeling about ELKY, I think he's in some sort of trouble, - I can't quite put my finger on it, but things Isn't right, Babsey".

"Well my Lovey", said Donduce with a lot of reassurance, "Your instincts usually, in fact always turn out to be right. When we get up, after we have fed Fang, we will check on him to make sure he's O.K., Babsey".

"Thanks my darling", said Beauty and they kissed passionately.

"Would you like a beer my Angel", asked her husband. "It's going to be quite a busy day. I said I was phoning Mac-Dad as well, didn't I honey? I can't remember".

"You did Babsey", replied Beauty. "You was phoning him about something to do with the 'Network', but I can't remember what, can you?".

"Yes I can", replied Donduce "I think, my Lovey, it was just simply to keep his ear to the ground in the village about feedback on the palace, and of course, we Isn't told him yet, have we Honey".

"Oh shit, darling, no we Isn't, God, we have been talking about it so much, in my mind; it's half built already" she laughed.

Donduce went out into the kitchen again, and raided the fridge. Whilst he was there, he opened the back door and let Fang out into the yard so he could do his bits. Whilst he was out there, Donduce picked up his bowl and filled it full with the dog food. He put the packet back in the cupboard, and as he was about to shut it, Lucky jumped up on the work surface and meowed at him, rubbing her nose on his hand.

"Bleeding Hell, you want to go out again! Your supposed to be in", then he remembered that both cats **had** been in all night; "Why haven't you been out then, you haven't been out! God, I am losing the plot, confused by a cat". Donduce was chuckling to himself, as he let Lucky out, and Fang in, who started demolishing his breakfast.

Donduce headed back into the bedroom where Beauty was sitting up in bed looking at him as he walked over.

"Bloody Hell my darling, I love you", she said, very emotionally, "I love you too Babsey, my Lovey", replied Donduce. "That was very heartfelt, and beautiful, thank you and Likewise my Lovey".

"Thank you Lovey", she said, "Twice, one for your lovely comments and the other for my beer", she giggled.

Donduce took a slurp. "It was like Piccadilly bleeding Circus in the kitchen just now, my Angel", he said. "We need to install a set of traffic lights for us and the animals. We also need to put a flap in the back door so that Fang can....no". said Donduce, stopping abruptly.

"Darling..", said Beauty, "What's with the sudden 'No'?" she was giggling.

"I was about to say", said Donduce, "that we need to install a flap in the back door so that Fang can come and go as he pleased, and then it dawned on me in mid conversation that the size of the flap wouldn't warrant having a door at all Babsey, so forget that one; the flap would be big enough for us!!".

"If you think, my gorgeous mad husband", said Beauty, "that I am going to start coming in and out via a flap, no. No. NO." said Beauty.

"Well, Honey, actually...." Started Dondude.

"Do you want a....." started Beauty.

"Yes please". Finished Donduce and they both finished up in fits of giggles.

"Moving swiftly on", said Donduce, "We really ought to put a carpet down in this bedroom, a nice fluffy one my Lovey. What do you think?"

"Good idea my Babsey", said Beauty, "Those floor boards are a bit basic. What colour shall we have?"

"Dunno yet, but I will organise that with the 'State' factory. I will give them the dimensions, and then I will fit it. I'll ask Mac-Dad to help me, he will enjoy that, especially cutting it around the trap door to the basement, my Lovey. Talking of basements..." his voice trailed away and they both said it is unison:

"ELKY!!"

"Come on my Lovey", said Donduce, lets put some clothes on and see if he's O.K.".

"O.K. boss", replied Beauty, giving him a kiss, and with that, they both got out of bed and got dressed. Beauty always stood by the mirror first and combed her beautiful long flowing hair first. Then she flicked it back and Donduce combed it log and straight, down to just below her thighs. She would wash it when they got in, but they was going on an ELKY mission first. When she had finished, or rather Donduce had finished she combed his hair, just down below his belt line (had to get that one in my Lovey!!) and then, when they

102

were ready, they went out into the kitchen, opened the back door and out into the back yard.

It was rather chilly outside; the dew was still glistening on the stone yard slabs, but the sun was up and the breeze had subsided a bit. A collection of birds were busy fighting over breakfast at a large bird table and feeder which hung a bit to the right of the back door.

They crossed the yard and walked past the coal bunker to the grassy gap that led to the meadow. Sure enough, ELKY was standing up with his head in his favourite bushy tree having a feed. As soon as he heard Donduce and Beauty approaching, he immediately stopped feeding, looked around and stared at them both intently.

They walked over to him, and this time, he walked over to them.

"Bloody Hell", said Donduce, as ELKY firstly stroked him on the arm with hes nose, Donduce acknowledged him by putting his hand on ELKY's nose and stroking it. "Babsey my Lovey, he hasn't done that before".

"No, my Lovey, he hasn't", said Beauty as ELKY then nuzzled her arm. She too stroked ELKY's nose, but a bit higher up, which was really sweet as it told the ELK her Husband's routine and then hers; it was part of her immense talent with animals and would come in useful in the future.

When she had finished, Beauty said "Something is up, my Lovey", and looked directly into ELKY's eyes.

Donduce was just about to reply, when ELKY pushed Beauty's left arm, causing her to turn slightly left, Donduce was holding her right hand. He deliberately then cantered very close to Beauty, and brushed his silky but hairy nose against her as he walked towards the grassy bit by the coal bunker. He then stopped and looked around, directly at them.

"Come on my Lovey", exclaimed Beauty excitedly, "He wants us to follow him".

"Blimey", said Donduce, "Where to, my Lovey?" he asked.

"Don't know, Babsey" Beauty replied. "We are about to find out".

ELKY cantered slowly towards the grassy bit, and then into the yard. Donduce and Beauty followed, and expected the ELK to go up to the back gate, wanting to go out, but instead, ELKY went straight up to the back door!

"Oh my God", exclaimed Donduce, he wants us to follow him into the kitchen, he Isn't going to fit through the back door frame, my Lovey, what do we do now?"

"I know", said Beauty, thinking furiously, "We go into the kitchen and stand there Babsey. Wherever we stand will cause some reaction from ELKY, he is a very seriously intelligent ELK". She said.

So, leaving ELKY standing by the back door, Donduce and Beauty squeezed past him and did just that. They had their backs to the breakfast bar and were waiting for ELKY to respond.

ELKY did just that. He looked at them and then turned his head so that his nose was pointing towards the fridge.

"The fridge?" said Donduce and (ELKY together) Beauty together (oops!!) Beauty went over to the fridge and opened it. There was the usual stock inside; milk, beers, butter, cheese, and two tins of cat food. Beauty looked back at ELKY, and ELKY looked away, staring straight at Donduce.

"Whatever ELKY wants us to find, is not in the fridge, my Lovey", said Beauty, "It's near you, my Sweetheart!"!

Suddenly, Donduce stared at ELKY, patted him on the nose, and said "Babsey my Lovey", exclaimed Donduce, "It's not what is in the fridge that ELKY is trying to tell us, my Babsey, it **is** the fridge!".

"What do you mean then?" asked Beauty, looking puzzled.

"The fridge, my Lovey, the history of it", explained Donduce, "It was stolen by the gorilla, and he took it up to the loft, didn't he. ELKY is trying to tell us that the gorilla is back, somewhere, my Babsey".

As if to confirm what Donduce had said, ELKY reached forward and licked Donduce on the cheek.

"Well done ELKY", said Donduce and returned to compliment my patting him on the nose.

"Bloody Hell, my Babsey", said Beauty, "I hope he's not back in the loft again, but then again, I Isn't seen no bananas lying on the floor. Anyway my Lovey, how does ELKY know that the gorilla is back anyway?" she added.

"I don't know, my Lovey", said Donduce, "But I am sure he will tell us in his special way, like he has just done with the news that the gorilla is back".

ELKY didn't know where the gorilla was, and he hadn't seen it since the night before. The gorilla was nowhere to be seen when ELKY himself got back from where he went just before dawn. He was worried that the gorilla was indeed back in the loft, but as Beauty had said, there weren't any bananas lying around anywhere. ELKY couldn't vouch for inside the house though, and he looked at Beauty again.

Beauty was looking at ELKY too, and then said to her Hubby. "Come on, my Angel, we had better check that loft, just to make sure".

"No problem, my Sweetheart", said Donduce, and with that, he got the step ladders out of the walk in pantry and they both went into the hallway. He positioned the ladders under the loft hatch, and looked up as he did it.

"It doesn't look disturbed, my Babsey", said Donduce, "and there isn't any gorilla hair on the hatch. I can't actually smell him either, my Babsey", he added.

"To be fair, we didn't smell him before, my Sweetheart", said Beauty, but she added, "Best to check though my Babsey".

Beauty held the ladder and Donduce started climbing. When he got near the top, he looked down at Beauty, smiled and said "Here we go, my Babsey!".

"Good luck, my Sweetheart", said Beauty rather nervously.

Donduce flung the hatch open and stuck his head through the square hole. He looked around for several moments and then said "Coast clear, my Angel, there's no sign of him".

"Thank God for that my Hun", said Beauty, "So I wonder where he is then?".

"I am sure he will be found, my Babsey, don't worry, we will soon know though", Donduce paused and giggled, "We will soon know by the sudden lack of bananas in the larder".

Beauty laughed as Donduce replaced the hatch and climbed back down the ladder. He gave Beauty a kiss and then they returned to the kitchen, putting the ladder back on the way. ELKY was still at the back door, and they went up to him. Beauty patted him on the nose and said:

"Thanks for the info, ELKY, don't worry, the gorilla Isn't in here anywhere".

ELKY licked her on the nose, and then reversed out of the open back door. Then he turned round, shook himself, and started cantering back to his meadow.

"What a clever ELK, my Lovey", said Donduce as they watched him return to his meadow. We have a guard dog and a guard ELK thrown in as well, my Babsey".

"I know my Sweetheart", replied Beauty, "There is still something not quite right with ELKY though, I don't know whether it's because he's worried about the gorilla, or about something else. I did have a bit of a restless night again, my Angel".

"Sorry, my Babsey", said Donduce comfortingly, and then added

"We have got so much to do today as well, phone calls, and that tour of the 'Link' animals, my Babsey. I have got to make a call before we do that anyway, to clear the areas of Farmhands".

"O.K.", Sweetheart", said Beauty, "But right now, lets have a relax with a beer my darling. It has been an eventful morning, and we are not really officially up yet!".

"That's true", said Donduce, and shut the back door. Fang through all of this had sat quietly in the kitchen watching everything that had gone on. He hadn't even flinched when ELKY had come to the back door. Fang really liked ELKY, and were on the same wavelength; Fang had already decided that he was going to protect ELKY too, no matter what, and he hadn't seen the gorilla either; he would certainly have been woken up by it at the very least, but was thankful that the gorilla had not slipped past him and gone in the loft, with him as a guard dog, now, that **would** have been embarrassing!

The 'immediate' animals that Beauty more than Donduce looked after were located to the right, and really all round the outside of the meadow where ELKY lived. If one was to go through the grassy gap as if to see ELKY but then turn right, through the gap in the surrounding hedge, one would arrive in the immediate animal area. This comprised of a large chicken run where Bleedin' Doo the Cockerel lived, next to that, a free run area of pheasants and peacocks, then a goat enclosure, one of which was responsible for getting his head stuck in the post office letter box, but that was all over now. Other enclosures housed various other breading smaller animals, ferrets (thought you might like that one my Lovey), as well. Various other areas bordered all round the meadow, and the only interruption was 'the pathway', although there was gaps in the tall bushes surrounding that to access the animals area. Way beyond all of this were fields containing the larger animals, and these all made up a sort of three sided outside border of the main farm area, the 'Royal State' part. Beyond the fields on the meadow side, the 'Executive Zone 5 State commenced, which is where Donduce and Beauty would be going to see Mac-Sweet, deputy head of the 'Network'. The head was obviously Donduce, but with the backup of Beauty and Mac-Dad.

On the other side of the 'Main Farm State Road', beyond the official 'State' buildings were the cow fields, sheep, pigs etc., and nearer to the perimeter hedge was the lake and pond. Between them and the cattle fields was the 'Old Empty Barn'.

It was to these out lying fields that Donduce and Beauty would be going to later that day, and it was also where Farmhand Mac-Stupid had run out of diesel.

Months before, a farmshop had existed in this immediate animal area, and 'outsiders' from the local town of the same name came to buy produce. It was decided though for 'State' operational reasons by the 'Crown', that all produce was to be sold in the local outlets in the town itself, and this arrangement had proved very successful. This new arrangement ensured as well, that like any private 'State', the only outsiders permitted onto 'State' land was the delivery drivers, and they only went to the 'Import, Export Building', situated as the first building on the left on the 'Main Entrance Road'. It's fair distance from the farmhouse area also ensured peace and quiet for Donduce and Beauty. They was sitting down in the lounge and nattering about what was to be done, and slurping beers.

"When we get ready, or rather afterwards, my Lovey", said Donduce, "I will phone Farmhand Mac-Sweet and arrange for us to go over there for half an hour" he said. "Then, when we get back, I will phone Mac-Hassle and clear the 'Link fields' so that we can do a tour. Then when we have done, **that**, we will see what the time is, and maybe fit in an immediate animal tour. What do you reckon, my Lovey?".

"Sounds great my Lovey", said Beauty happily, "Whatever you say, is fine Babsey", she added.

They both finished their beers and went to the bathroom to have their showers, baths and get ready, once ready Donduce and Beauty did their hair, and were then ready to start the day.

Once sat down, Donduce picked up the phone. "This won't take a minute, my Lovey", he said.

Beauty, her arms wrapped around her loving husband said "O.K., my Babsey".

Beauty hated any contact with a human, even her husband talking to someone else she disliked intensely, but there was some occasions when it had to be done, and this was one of them.

Donduce dialled the number and waited, then said,

"Hello, Farmhand Mac-Sweet?, Hello, it's Donduce; I need to speak to you quite urgently, I am sure it will be O.K. for us to come round please, only for half an hour or so?".

He paused as he waited for the response. Beauty did smile to herself. When Donduce said he was sure it was O.K. to go there, he didn't ask if it was, he told them it was – Wow!!"

Her husband spoke again. "O.K., thank you, that's fine, we will be there shortly". Donduce put the phone down, and Beauty nodded. "I'll get my coat", she said. "Darling", she added,"We won't be there long will we, Honey?"

"Oh, God no, we Isn't stopping my Lovey", said Donduce with an air of reassurance, "Only about twenty minutes tops, come on then, my Angel".

They stood up and embraced; and, after a passionate kiss, went out the front door and Donduce pressed the garage remote control. Once more, the metal door started rolling upwards, slowly revealing their jeep.

"The last time I was in there, Fang was sitting on my head", said Beauty, giggling, then she added; "A bit more freedom for me now, my darling, eh?"

"Absolutely", replied her husband, "You can relax so much on this trip that you can stick your feet in the glove compartment if you want, my Babsey".

Donduce opened the passenger door and Beauty got in, flicking her hair forward as she did. Her husband shut the door and then walked around the front and got in himself. He reached over and kissed his gorgeous Wifey and then started the jeep. They drove out of the front driveway, through the gap in the hedge, and then turned right. Past the massive field, and eventually got to the 'T' junction. Turning right this time, they headed to 'Zone Five Road', which was about three miles away. The landscape was open fields and there was, up ahead, the start of some hills. 'Zone Five' started at the foot of these hills, and many hundreds of the mansions that were in the 'Executive Estate' were built on the slopes. The views were magnificent and each residency covered a large area.

"It is lovely out here, my darling", said Beauty as they got closer, and then she added "That arrangement we made, years ago, certainly still seems to be working, because it actually feels warmer, the closer we got to the Estate, my Sweetheart".

"It will do, my Babsey", replied Donduce, as in the distance, the left turn signpost to the 'Executive Estate' appeared, then Donduce added,"The whole Estate comes complete with it's own 'micro-climate', my Lovey".

They got to the turning and signalled left. Rounding the corner, they went under a large, golden brown coloured sign that stretched across the width of the Road, it said: 'Executive Estate Residents Only'.

The scenery had changed completely and large poplar trees lined each side of the road. Set back, tall hedges and walls marked the boundaries of each mansion and they seemed to go on forever. Donduce signalled right, and turned into another road that started to wind into the hills. More massive houses and they were getting larger. Beauty glimpsed the view as they got higher and said to her husband, "The scenery is stunning up here, my Angel".

"Just wait until we get to Mac-Sweet's house, my Lovey", Donduce replied, "Then you will see the helipad, my Lovey, it's rather large!".

"Bloody Hell, my Sweetheart", exclaimed Beauty "He's got his own helicopter?".

"Yes, he has, my Babsey", said Donduce, "It's easier for him to fly down to the fields than to drive. That is what that square patch of land is for by the 'Old Empty Barn'".

"Why don't we get one my Honey?" asked Beauty, "Then we could fly around the farm instead of using our jeep. In fact we could even fly to the town, my Babsey".

"Well, my darling", said Donduce, as they approached Mac-Sweet's mansion area, "When we build the palace, that is exactly what we are going to do. The only reason why we Isn't got one now is because the helicopter would frighten all the animals, but yes, we are getting one, my Babsey".

"Does Mac-Sweet actually own the helicopter then, my Sweetheart?", asked Beauty.

"No, of course not my Babsey, we do. Everything is 'State' owned, he maintains and runs it out of his allowance. It is faster transport for him though with his work for us on 'Network' business".

They turned lift, and into Mac-Sweet's front drive. Beauty saw straight away the helipad located to the left of his mansion in a big green area. In the middle of the green was a circle of black tarmac, and on it was a largeish helicopter painted brown, but with a gold stripe along the middle with 'EAT' in brown letters on the stripe. "Babsey my Lovey", said Beauty, with a giggle, "What on Earth does 'EAT' mean or stand for? Surely the helicopter doesn't eat carrots?!! (Sorry, my Lovey, had to get that one in; - you're giggling!).

"No, my darling", said Donduce, laughing, "The carrot eating is your department", he said, teasing. "'EAT', stands for 'Estate Ariel Transport', and is the name of the company that makes all our aircraft".

"O.K., my darling", said Beauty, still giggling over the name. She was glad that she left everything to her loving husband.

The driveway was curved and Donduce and Beauty had come in the 'In' end. They pulled up by the front door, and as if by magic, the front door opened and Mac-Sweet stood there expectantly. He was just taller than Donduce at about five foot ten, and had similar hair to Donduce except short. He was quite a stocky man, but wasn't the aggressive type and he was in his late 50's.

"Don't worry, my Babsey", said Donduce, as he was about to get out of the car, "Leave this to me".

"O.K. my Honey", said Beauty and smiled. Her husband got out and walked around to Beauty's side. On the way, he smiled at Mac-Sweet, and said "Good morning".

"Morning", replied Mac-Sweet, and as Donduce opened the passenger door to let Beauty get out, he added, "A pleasure as always, Donduce. Is this official or a social call?".

"A bit of both", replied Donduce. Beauty got out, Donduce locked the jeep, and they walked, hand in hand to the front door. Just to shake Mac-Sweet's hand, Donduce let go of Beauty's but immediately replaced it once the pleasantries were over. Mac-Sweet bowed and said "Ma-am", and Beauty smiled.

"Follow me", said Mac-Sweet and led the way. Inside the door was a large lobby with a big sweeping staircase on the opposite side. The lounge was off tho the right, which is where they went, and from the large picture windows at one end, you could see a massive back garden, and the fields of the 'Estate' rolling off into the distance, a bit closer you could see other mansions of the 'Executive Estate'.

Donduce and Beauty sat on a settee on one side, facing the lounge door, and Mac-Sweet sat in an armchair directly opposite them. They could hear Mrs Mac-Sweet busying herself in the kitchen.

"Now then, Donduce, Sir, what is on your mind? Nothing serious I hope". He looked rather worried and, expectantly waited for the response; all kinds of worries were going through his mind. "I am changing the 'State' system of operations", said Donduce. All official business will not be happening in separate buildings anymore and is to be centralised. A palace is going to be built next to the 'Royal State Farmhouse' and I am going to take sole charge of every aspect of 'State' administration. The purpose of this visit was to inform you of these new developments, and to ask you what was the most cost effective way of construction, whether to employ farmhands on this project or to build it 'myself'.

"Of course Sir, thank you for letting me know of this change, and I will of course leave it to your good self as to any employment decision. As far as costs go I can let you know how much labour would cost, which of course affects allowances. If there are any opportunities that your good self considers appropriate to use employment, I will of course let the farmhands you select that these opportunities are there, I take it they will be subject to the 'EFC'?" asked Mac-Sweet.

"Of course", replied Donduce, "I also require you to gauge the opinion of the farmhand populations as to the popularity of the palace, using the 'Network' of couse", he added.

"Naturally", said Mac-Sweet, "Any confusion or problem with farmhands will be reported directly of course. One question, Sir, does this mean that there will be no more monthly 'Network' meetings in the 'State' building?".

"That's right. All 'State' business will now take place at the palace, which will be private and confidential. Anything that you need to know as part of the 'Network' will be communicated either by phone, or in private meetings such as this. The building of the palace will commence immediately. On to the usual subject now, have you experienced any problems, or have any concerns with anything?", Donduce asked.

All through this conversation, Donduce held Beauty's hand tightly, for reassurance.

"No Sir, nothing to report, everyone is really happy and life is good. There are minor problems, everyone has them, but nothing anywhere near major. 'State' business is really good and 'State' trade with the population is at it's usual brisk pace", Mac-Sweet reported. "One question, Sir, how does or rather how is the privacy of the 'Royal State Palace' going to be affected by noise from the road leading up to the farmhouse?".

"As the palace will be set back from the road", replied Donduce, "We won't hear any noise at all, except for obvious sightseers from the distant 'State' locations who want to see the 'Royal' residence".

Donduce had to be careful how he answered Mac-Sweet's questions, as no farmhand or 'State' resident knew exactly what existed beyond the farmhouse building. The only access was for delivery lorries and for Donduce and Beauty. No farmhand was allowed on or near the 'Main Entrance Road', as far up as the area between the farmhouse and the cattle grid. "No problem, Sir", said Mac-Sweet, and then added "Anything else, Sir?".

"No, that will be all for now, and thank you for your time Mac-Sweet", replied Donduce.

"No problem at all, Sir, your wishes and requirements are my commands", said Mac-Sweet.

"Of course, I expect nothing less", said Donduce, officially.

They all stood up, and Mac-Sweet stood to attention. They shook hands, and Mac-Sweet bowed to Beauty, who smiled.

"Regards to Mrs Mac-Sweet", said Donduce as they walked to the front door. Mac-Sweet nodded as he opened it and said "Of course, thank you".

Donduce and Beauty walked back to the jeep and Beauty's gorgeous husband opened the door for her. As he did, he gave her a loving kiss and whispered "Shhh".

Beauty gave him a very private but knowing look, and he shut the door; walked round to his side, and, after one final wave to Mac-Sweet, who was still standing by the front door, got in.

"Well done you, my Lovey", said Donduce as he got comfortable.

"Did you understand it all, my Babsey?" he asked her, lovingly.

"Sort of, Sweet heart", she said, "But not completely. "Could you?".

She looked at him and smiled, resting her right arm an her husband's knee.

"Explain". Donduce finished her sentence off. "Well Babsey, basically we have just ensured that absolutely everything on the 'State' is now centrally controlled by us alone. We have also ensured total privacy. When the palace is built, there will be a large tall fence surrounding it and no one, apart from us will enter. Outside contractors will build it, to ensure that no 'State' resident ever sees the inside, because I's private. I have also directed Mac-Sweet to spread the word of the construction of the palace through the

'Network'. This action will generate both good opinion and bad, which in turn tests out 'State' loyalty of our residents to the 'Crown', and don't forget my Babsey, disloyalty to the 'Crown' is a breach of the 'SFC', my Babsey".

"Blimey", said Beauty, "What an arrangement, it's fantastic, and I love coming with your on 'State' duties, my Babsey".

"I am so delighted you do my Lovey", replied Donduce, "You must be by my side literally 24/7, no matter what, and that goes back to all them years ago when we met again in the 'Dane and Freckles', my Lovey".

"Oh, my God, what a beautiful day that was, my Angel, and then we returned for good to the 'Farm State' to run it properly", said Beauty happily.

They had now left the 'Executive Estate' and were driving down the road towards the 'Main Entrance Road'.

"The next thing to be done will be to erect large screens to hide the large field from view, my Lovey. Then, I will get contractors in to construct a temporary road running off the 'Main Entrance Road', so that the site construction people can access the back of the field. The screens will also totally block of all 'State' official buildings, so that everyone who did get as far as them buildings will get used to it being blocked off. The whole project will be completed within six months I reckon, my Lovey".

"Wow", said Beauty. "Babsey, have your got any idea what it will look like yet?"

"Yes, my Sweetheart, I have. I will draw it for you, I do hope you like the desigh, and you must love it. If you don't, I will re-design it, as we have both got to love it my Angel", said her husband.

They were already pulling into the front driveway, and Donduce took the remote and pointed it through the jeep windscreen. As if by magic, the garage door began to open.

"Well, my Lovey", said Donduce, as he reversed the jeep back into the garage, "That is the first job of the morning done".

"It certainly is, my Sweetheart", replied Beauty "God, l love you so much", she added passionately.

"I love you too, my Angel", said her husband, as they got out of the jeep, and arm in arm, walked towards the front door. Donduce got his key out and unlocking it, turned to his beautiful Wifey, and gave her a huge hug.

"Guess what happens next, my Lovey", he said, looking deep into her gorgeous brown eyes.

"I don't know, my beautiful Hubby", she replied.

"Well", said Donduce, excitedly, "We are going to do something incredible, my Sweetheart.

"It's the tour of the animals, Isn't it my Babsey", said Beauty, her voice with an air of excitement in it.

"Yes, my Lovey, but in a little while. First of all, I want to show you something", replied her Husband.

"O.K., my Babsey", Beauty replied, "I can't wait, lead on", she added.

Donduce took her hand and led her into the lounge. They had just passed Fang who had stood up to greet them, they had just patted him, and he lay back down on the kitchen floor, happily.

Her Husband shut the lounge door and drew the curtains. No one would have been able to see in anyway, but Donduce wanted to make doubly sure and also to make things more private. Once done, he guided a rather puzzled looking beauty into the middle of the room, and took both of her hands in his. He kissed her on the forehead, and said; "Right, my Beauty. Close your eyes.".

Beauty did, and after a few seconds had an incredibly warm sensation; a sort of tingling that started in her head, and gradually spread right throughout her gorgeous model – like body.

"Wow, Babsey", she exclaimed, "That's really nice". She still had her eyes firmly close and Donduce was still holding her hands.

"That's good", he whispered. "Keep going my Beauty". The warm feeling inside her was getting warmer by the minute and eventually she was tingling all over, with a great imphasis on her hands and upper arms where Donduce was holding her.

A few minutes later, Donduce said: "O.K., my Darling, open your eyes, my Babsey". She did, and blinked a couple of times. Her eyes were O.K. as the lounge had been dimmed with the curtains drawn.

"That was really nice, my Angel", said Beauty and then added curiously, "What did you do Hun?".

"Aah", said Donduce. He drew the curtains and said to Beauty, "Look outside, my Lovey, and tell me what you see".

Beauty did just that and said "Oh my Goodness, there is a thick fog outside that must have come down whilst we were holding hands, my Babsey".

"Let's go out and see, my Lovey", said Donduce. They went out the front door, and sure enough, a fog had descended on the entire farmhouse; you couldn't even see the garage, or indeed the hedge; it was really dense.

"Oh, no, Babsey", exclaimed Beauty, "We can't do an animal tour in this, my Honey, we'll never get there".

"Follow me", said Donduce, and he led Beauty, after shutting the front door again, back into the lounge, and closed the curtains once more.

"What are we going to do now, Sweetheart?", asked Beauty; she was completely confused, and also a bit annoyed that the animal tour was going to be postponed.

"You'll see, my Lovey", said Donduce smiling. "Close your eyes again, my Babsey".

Beauty did just that, and once more the tingling feeling that Beauty had experienced returned. After a few minutes, Donduce said, "O.K., open your eyes again my Babsey". He let go of her hands once more and Beauty rubbed her eyes "That was equally as nice, my Sweetheart, but...."

Before she had time to finish, Donduce said "Look, my Lovey". He opened the curtains once more and Beauty shouted "Oh my God!! Babsey!!, the fog has gone!!".

Donduce led Beauty to the front door, and as they walked out, Fang joined them. Donduce and Beauty stood in the middle of the driveway, and Beauty looked around her in total disbelief. It was a beautiful clear sunny day and not a trace of the thick fog that had been there, no more than 5 minutes previously.

"What on Earth happened there, my Babsey?" asked Beauty. "Come back in and I will tell you my Sweetheart", said Donduce, with an air of satisfaction and pleasure that he had really surprised Beauty.

They all returned back through the front door, and Fang lay back down in the kitchen. This time Donduce and Beauty left the curtains open, and just as they were about to sit down, Donduce said "Beers".

Beauty laughed, he went into the kitchen and returned with two, one he handed to her.

"So, my Sweetheart", taking a slurp of beer, "What did you make of all that then?" asked Donduce, rather excitedly.

"Incredible, my Babsey", Beauty replied. "The warm tingly feeling was beautifully relaxing, and I felt like I was in another world. Then the fog came down, and I must admit I was upset that we wouldn't be able to go on our tour, than we did it again and….Oh, my God, are you telling me my Sweetheart, that what we did, and the fog are related? It was no coincidence? Babsey?".

"That's right, my Lovey" replied Donduce. "Just as you have your talent being able to talk to the animals with your psychic communication skills that we call 'The Vibes', similarly, I can do the same thing with our environment. Basically, we created that fog ourselves, and because we was holding hands, I installed the energy in you as well my Lovey".

"Blimey, that's incredible my Angel", said Beauty, taking several slurps of her beer, "So, say, for instance we need rain for crops, we just simply 'make it happen' Honey!".

"That's right my Lovey", said Donduce, "We literally do control everything on the farm.

"I also thought, my gorgeous Sweetheart", said Beauty, happily, "That Mac-Sweet was so nice and cooperative with you this morning as well; you did speak to him in a very business like manner and with loads of authority; however, he agreed with literally everything you said my Babsey".

"Why do you think I shook his hand when we got there, and then when we left, my darling?" laughed Donduce.

"Out of politeness?" said Beauty, "Babsey, out of politeness?". She started giggling, as she knew that this was not completely the right answer.

"Of course not", laughed Donduce. He was giggling now, and when he had calmed down a bit, he said "Obviously, my Lovey, politeness is the impression that is intended, what I was actually doing was giving him simply some 'pursuasive' and 'agreement' energy my Babsey".

"So", said Beauty, having another slurp, "You can make anyone agree to anything just by shaking their hand, Babsey?".

"Yes, my Darling", said Donduce. "It doesn't have to be a handshake either; it depends on who it is. Just a look in a certain way can do it too, my Sweetheart".

"That is amazing", replied Beauty, and then she suddenly and without warning, burst into hysterical laughter, the tears were streaming down her beautiful pretty little face.

"What on Earth is so funny, my Angel?" asked Donduce, now laughing himself.

"Oh my God my Babsey", said Beauty, wiping the tears away, but still in fits of giggles, "It doesn't work on Mac-Stupid, does it then!!" She burst out laughing, and Donduce erupted into fits of laughter as well.

When they had both composed themselves, Donduce said "That obnoxious creature is a bit of a special case, my Babsey".

"You can say that again", laughed Beauty, "I hate him, my Babsey – Ugh!!".

"Darling", laughed Donduce, "You hate everyone, apart from me and family".

"No, my Babsey, I mean, I really hate him, "I wish he never existed, along with his stupid tractor, his stupid billy can and his stupid diesel, and leaning his stupid self on our bleeding gate.....my Lovey", said Beauty, giggling, but at the same time looking serious.

"I take it then, my Lovey that you hate him", said Donduce.

"YES!!" said Beauty.

"You would prefer him not to be on the farm", said Donduce.

"YES!!" said Beauty, "I want him removed, Immo!! Along with his bloody tractor, my Babsey. If I never ever see that stupid, god-forsaken, disrespectful, large, appaulingly awful idiot again, it would be too soon Babsey", said Beauty, finishing off with a giggle.

"Well, my Lovey", said Donduce, with a comforting tone to his voice, "there is actually a reason why I put up with him and his ways".

"It must be a bloody good one then my Lovey", replied Beauty, "I am all ears!".

"it is basically because we can find out information from the 'harsh' end of the farmhands. It is because his attitude is disrespectful, he is useful to ascertain the state of the 'bad' vibes if there are any; in other words, although he is bad news, he is useful bad news; do you see what I mean, my Lovey?".

"Yes, my Darling, of course I do", said Beauty, seriously, and then added "It's you that has to deal with him after all, but I can't stand anyone upsetting you or making you angry or cross, my Angel.

"Oh, don't worry about that, my Lovey", said Donduce, "If I found him that bad, he would be evicted now!".

They carried on slurping their beers and a few minutes later. Donduce said "I will make a call in a minute and clear all the farmhands from the 'Link' fields, so that er can go on our tour, how about that, my Angel?".

"Brilliant, my Lovey", said Beauty. "I can't wait!".

They finished their beers and then Donduce picked up the phone and dialled a number. Then he paused, blew Beauty a kiss, and then said "Hello, Mac-Hassle? Hello, code one please, farmhands, out". He waited for a minute and then said "Twenty minutes, thank you, out". Donduce put the phone back down on a small table, next to the settee.

"Guess what?" giggled Beauty, "My Babsey, are we, by any chance going to tour the animals on the 'Link' fields in twenty minutes?"

"No, giggled her husband.

"Oh dear, my Lovey", giggled Beauty, happily, "When are we going then Honey?"

"In 18 minutes and 32 seconds my Sweetheart", laughed her Husband and wrapped his arms around her again.

"Babsey, wou know that 'way' you have with people, with the 'handshake' and everything", said Beauty, "Is that restricted to the 'Farm Estate', or can you do it anywhere, my Lovey?".

"You can use it anywhere at all, my Angel", replied her Husband, and then added, "However, due to the nature of our supreme influence on the 'Farm Estate', it is a lot stronger, far more powerful and very effective. It is the same with your effect over the animals my Lovey".

"So, it would work in the Town then my Babsey?" asked Beauty.

"Yes, my Lovey, and it does. Very useful sometimes as well, due to the history of the town don't forget!!", replied Donduce.

"The history of the town?" repeated Beauty, puzzled again, "Why, **has** it got history? A bad one, my Lovey? Tell Me!" she added.

"The inhabitants, the residents, the town population, my Angel", said Donduce, "Don't forget where they all originated from!".

"Where my Lovey, what's the problem with them? Why the bad vibe?" asked Beauty urgently.

"Because, my sweet Angel", explained Donduce, "Don't forget, they are all from here! The Farm Estate! They have all, at some point, been evicted!" he finished.

"Oh yes, of course they have my Darling, I had forgotten", said Beauty.

Donduce looked at his watch. "Twenty minutes have just about gone my Angel", he said. "We will start the tour my Beauty".

"wonderful, my Sweetheart", replied Beauty, "Come on, I can't wait".

After popping into the bedroom to do their hair, Donduce and Beauty put their coats back on, and after checking Fang, who was O.K. went out the front door for the seventh time that morning and with the remote, opened the garage door. Donduceopened the passenger side for Beauty, and said "I love you, my Babsey" as she got in. After shutting her door, he walked around the front of the jeep himself.

It had turned out to be a very nice and bright morning. There was still a chill in the air, and it was cold enough for water vapour to come out of one's mouth when one

breathed out. Donduce and Beauty had got thick clothes on underneath their coats as standing by the fields was going to be chilly.

"Here we go then my Beauty", said Donduce as the jeep sprang into life once more.

"God, do I love you my Babsey", said Beauty as she leaned over and gave her Husband a big kiss.

"I love you too, my precious Angel", said Donduce as they pulled out of the garage.

They left the front drive and turned right, however this time, they only travelled a short distance past the official buildings on the left which were to be redundant and then turned left down a fairly wide farm track. This led at right angles to the 'Main Entrance Road' and up hill slightly. The road was actually shaped like a big 'L', but the other way up ('7'). At the end of the roadl; you started at the bottom of the 'L', was the 'Old Empty Barn', and then coming back was the helipad and then the animal fields. Tallish hedges grew either side of the track, but it was wide enough for on-coming traffic.

The cows in the end field had noticed that the farmhands had all suddenly disappeared; so had the horses next door, and also the sheep next door to them. One of the cows pricked her ears and watched the road. She knew Donduce's and Beauties jeep and 'mooed' in a different pitch to normal. The rest of the herd, heard her and another cow split from the rest. They met up and ambled to the fence ready to meet Donduce and Beauty.

"Look at that! Babsey", said Donduce as they got nearer, those two cows, Honey, are right by the fence. It's as if they are expecting us Babsey".

Beauty was so excited "They are, my Lovey", she said, "They are just beautiful, My Babsey, it's a shame that they can't put the kettle on, or open a beer".

Donduce drove past the cows, and turned the jeep round by 'The Old Empty Barn'. Then, they came back and parked by the cow field, just a few yards from where the cows were standing. Steam came off them as they panted in the cold morning air. Donduce and Beauty got out of the jeep and walked over. They got right up to the two cows, reached out and patted their huge noses; they 'mooed' loudly in appreciation. Then, when Beauty had said "Hello", in a quiet voice and kept her hand on the cow's nose; she was holding Donduce's hand with the other, she stared at and into the animal's eyes for several minutes. Every so often she said "Oh", or "O.K.", and when she had finished, Beauty nodded, and then patted the cow on her head. Beauty did the same with the other cow and when she had finished, and Donduce had patted them as well, the cows turned, as if being summoned, and started trotting back to join the rest of the herd.

"Well, my Babsey, I just love our animal tours", said Beauty, really happily, however, there was a hint of alarm in her voice, and Donduce noticed it straight away.

"But, Babsey", said Donduce, "My Lovey, I am waiting for the problem. What have you found out?. I was waiting for the 'But Babsey', My Lovey", he said.

"Yes, my Lovey", said Beauty, a big hint of alarm in her voice.

"Them two cows, who are our eyes and ears on the 'Link', my Lovey" said Beauty, "They are going to slaughter, My Babsey", she said, her eyes became very moist as she said that, and Donduce immediately hugged her. "Oh no, they aren't", said Donduce; a tone of strong reassurance in his voice, he added "Babsey, my Lovey, I took the precaution of noting down each of their branding numbers, whilst you were doing your thing, and I will simply phone Mac-Hassle and say that these two cows are exempt. They have been very loyal to the 'State Link' and will continue to be. However, all other cattle bred for meat are still part of the food chain and so won't escape, my Lovey Not only that but obviously the slaughtering side of 'State' business we do not see as it is too upsetting for either of us, although of course we have absolute 'State' access to the proceedings if and when it is necessary".

"Oh, thank God, my Angel", said Beauty, looking very relieved, "I would hate to think of their fate".

"Did you find out anything that we needed to know though, my Lovey?", asked her Husband.

"Yes, my Angel, and there are no problems at all. The farmhands are all contented and talk about herd numbers and officially related business such as feeding them and the usual milking procedures; there is nothing that is said which is 'anti-State'. The cows have a good rapport with the horses too, and everything is fine, my Babsey".

"Any mention of Mac-Stupid, my Lovey?" asked Donduce with a smile on his face.

"Yes, Babsey", laughed Beauty. "I asked the cow how Mac-Stupid was with them, and she said 'Oh, you mean that fat idiot who's tractor broke down? He's O.K., harmless", the cow said, "and the whole herd heard him say to the farmhands that he was going to walk to the 'Royal State' and ask King Donduce for a lift to the 'State Stores', after that day when you and the King came and he had a go at you. We all thought it was so funny, because he Isn't got no respect for anyone, not even King Donduce and Queen Beauty. We cows and all of us animals love you so much, because you love us and you come and see us. We are privileged to be the

Specially chosen 'Link' cows and we are totally loyal to the 'State' and you both, the 'Crown'; there is no other way and can be no other way but this beautiful life". So, my Angel, the cows are all happy, Isn't that good, bless them?" Beauty finished.

"That is marvellous, my Sweetheart", replied Donduce, giving her a kiss, "We will move onto the horses now, my Darling, is that O.K.?" asked Donduce.

"Oh, yes please Honey", said Beauty, happily, and then she whispered in Donduce's ear, "They are my favourites, obviously, but I don't want the cows to hear, or feel my 'vibes', as they will get jealous, Darling!!".

"Takes on a whole new meaning to 'a cow herd' don't it Babsey?" laughed Donduce.

"Oh my God Honey", giggled Beauty, "Don't start that again, it reminds me too much of that conversation with......."

Before she had time to finish, Donduce, laughing, interrupted her and finished her sentence for her "HIM! Yes my Babsey, moving swiftly on, my Angel, Horses". He said.

The field that contained the cows was huge, and from the farm track it extended up the hills and at the top, all you could see was the horizon. The fields, the one with the horses as well, next to it, ran parallel in length with the 'State' boundary, and if one was to walk to the brow of the hill and look beyond, after the same distance it was possible to see, on a clear day, the start of 'State Zone One'. This Estate comprised of residents on low incomes, low 'State' allowances, partly due to the nature of their 'State' jobs, and also for residents who had just started out on life's ladder. Depending on how they performed with their chosen careers, and once it was approved by the 'State' they were permitted to move to 'State Zone Two', once they had saved enough money from their 'State' allowance to do so, and once they had proved to the 'State' that they could afford to live in the more affluent area, according to their allowance. Of course, as they progressed through their chosen career, promotion was a possibility, after they had continued to show absolute unconditional loyalty and commitment to the 'Crown State', and

Also that their work and production output was at a very good standard. All farmhands had to work hard to earn their 'State' priviliges. Some chose to live their lives at the same level and were happy which was fine, however some wanted to progress, and it was these farmhands that were notices by the 'State', and in some cases, were appointed to more official roles. This was completely under the control of Donduce, and Beauty's side was to do the same with the animals; a prime example hed just happened when the cows loyalty to the 'State' was rewarded by being spared.

'State Zone One' also came complete with it's 'State Stores', and was very similar in layout (the stores) except the prices were the same as in any other zone, and not cheaper. It was 'State' policy that if an item was un-affordable with a particular 'State' allowance, then it wasn't to be purchased, as 'State Farm Incentive' dictated that this practice gave the individual the drive to earn more money through drive, determination and loyalty, so they would be able to afford more.

This also led to a certain degree, in some parts, of animosity between the 'State zones', jealously between the 'haves' and the 'have nots'. The 'State' encouraged this as it was healthy to promote enthusiasm with the lower classes, to live as the rich classes did. Of course if this jealousy went too far and erupted into feuds between farmhands, that was recognised as a breach of loyalty to the 'State' and also a breach of the 'E.F.C.', which resulted in immediate eviction. This interzone feuding was one of the many tasks of monitoring performed by the 'Network', who, would report it to the 'State' and a decision would be made by Donduce as to the outcome of the problem.

Behind 'State Zone One' and to the right hand side was 'Zone Two', for the farmhands who were better off. These zones were not to be confused with the 'Five Farm Roads', where, a lot of the 'State Official Buildings', where, including the 'State Stores'; in 'State Road Five' that Donduce and Beauty had been to, a dew days before. Of course, these roads sort of formed the 'Royal State Zone', rather like the capital city.

Donduce and Beauty had got back into the jeep and were headed along towards the horses field. As the morning warmed up, the puddles in the farm track left by the early dew had evaporated, and revealed more stones and bits of mud, left by the farmhands boots. There was a grassy sloped bank on the left hand side of the track on the field side, however the other side was flat, and you could see the backs of the admin buildings from there.

The horses had all been silhouetted on the horizon, grazing and like the cows, there was several hundred of them. They were a mixture of breeds, all 'State' raised, and the best of the best were stabled on the 'Royal State Area'. One horse had seen the jeep arrive at the cow field and told another who had already watched as the cows had returned to their herd. The two started to canter down the field in readiness for their 'Royal' visitors.

"Look, Babsey", said Beauty excitedly, as she pointed out of the jeeps window, "Even they know we are coming!".

"My Goodness, my Lovey", replied Donduce, smiling, "We ARE popular today".

Donduce pulled up to where the horses were waiting. Like the cows, their heads could easily reach over the fence which only came up as far as an average stable door. None of the fences were solid, but all the animals knew not to try and break them down.

They got out of the jeep again and walked over. Donduce put his hand up and rubbed the nose of the left hand horse, and Beauty did the same with it's friend. "Hello", she said "You alright?", and gave it an apple from her coat pocket.

"That's where all our apples go Honey', laughed Donduce and watched as Beauty did the same thing as she had done with the cows. After a few minutes, Beauty said "Honey, the general consensus of opinion is that the horses want us to ride them with the farmhands as they round them up to do the new branding and numbers, but, they also are aware of my complete aversion to humans, so, they have decided to let that one rest as I have just decided, with your permission, that we could do the same job, the two of us, on horseback, without the farmhands here, under a cone one situation. Is that O.K., my Angel?",asked Beauty.

"Absolutely fine", said Donduce, "I will allow that. Also my Lovey, could you tell the horses to spread the word that the 'Royal Stable' block for the elite is going to be very much enlarged as it is being re-housed in the palace court yards when it is built. For the record, and for them two horses ears only, due to their absolute loyalty to the 'Link' and to the 'State', they will be the first for promotion to 'Royal' status with all of it's privileges, and two more horses will be selected by the 'State', on the recommendations by these two, for specialised 'Link' duties". Donduce paused for a minute, giggled, and then said "Did you get all of that my Honey?".

"I did, my Angel", laughed Beauty, and as she said that, the two horses licked Donduce and Beauty and moved their heads up and down, as if to nod. "By the looks of it my Sweetheart, so did they", laughed Beauty, she paused and looked at the horse, then smiled and said "Yes, Babsey, message received and understood. They are going to return to the herd now and tell them, they say, take care and see us soon", Beauty added.

"Awww, bless them, that was nice, my Babsey", said Donduce. He looked at his horse and gave it's nose a rub. "You have certainly earned your right to 'Royal' status, so has your friend. I have got your brand numbers, so that is a 'State Crown' promise. See you soon and take care. You finished now my Lovey?" asked Donduce turning to Beauty.

"Oh yes Babsey, I have", said Beauty, taking her Husband's hand in hers. The horses turned, and made their way back up the hill, and back to their friends on the horizon, who were waiting for them and all the horsey gossip.

Donduce and Beauty returned to the jeep again, and he opened the door to let Beauty in. They had a loving kiss before he shut the door and then walked round the front of the jeep again and let himself in.

"This has been great, my Angel", said Donduce, "The final stop being the sheep, I take it?", he asked.

"Yes, my Lovey", said Beauty, and then added "My darling, the sheep are an incredibly useful asset to the 'Link', as they have two information sources, and not just one".

"Go on my Babsey", said Donduce; even he looked curious now.

"Yes, my Lovey", Beauty explained, "The sheep hear things from the shepherd farmhands, my Lovey", she said, "And...."

Beauty waited expecting her husband to guess, and finish off her sentence – nothing.

"Go on, my Babsey", said her Husband, "Who, Honey?"

"Can't you guess my Lovey", laughed Beauty.

"No, Honey, I've got no idea, go on, put me out of my misery, my Babsey, pleeeasse!!", said Donduce.

"The sheepdogs, of course!" laughed Beauty.

"How come? Babsey", asked Donduce, still looking very puzzled.

"Well Honey," Beauty started. "The sheep overhear conversations between the farmhands and they can then pass on any information that has been said, that is either detrimental to the 'State', or against the 'E.F.C.'. The sheepdogs, who are also part of the 'Link', unbeknown to the farmhands, live with the farmhands and therefore have real insider knowledge of what is said both out on the fields or at home. If a farmhand is at home nattering and saying things that are against farm policy or the 'E.F.C.', they then tell one of the sheep, who then tells the head sheep, who tell me, who then tells the 'State'; you!! my Angel, and by the way, I love you my Babsey", said Beauty. (So do I my Lovey, I love you, and Happy Birthday!).

They had now driven past the horses, and, low and behold a couple of the sheep who had been grazing about half way up the field was waiting by the fence as Donduce and Beauty pulled up. Again they got out and went over. The now customary pat on the head took place and Beauty looked into their eyes. After a few minutes Beauty whispered to the sheep "O.K., thanks, brilliant. I will tell Donduce".

He had been standing up, however Beauty had knealt down for this chat, because of the size of the animal. "Babsey, we do have a small problem with lambing. The sheep are all rather upset because one of the ewes gave birth about 3 days ago to a little one, bless him, and none of the sheep have seen it since. The ewe concerned is dreadfully upset because she misses it and wants to bond with her new born. They are all worried about the little lamb's welfare and hope it's O.K., and they want it back. What on Earth are we going to do my Babsey?" said Beauty, suitably very concerned.

"Oh, my God, that is terrible, my Babsey. O.K., ask the sheep the following; firstly, is the little one definitely missing, and, I have to be direct, dead, somewhere and the sheep are too upset to tell us?", asked Donduce.

Beauty crouched down and looked at the sheep again, her hand touching it's nose. "No, my Babsey, the sheep wouldn't hide anything from you, and it has definitely been gone about 3 – 4 days, disappeared, but definitely not anywhere on the farm fields. They have also asked the horses and the cows who Isn't seen it either. They have also asked all the sheepdogs, who have confirmed that none of them farmhands have stolen it, otherwise something like that would have been reported; we all stick together", said Beauty, repeating what the sheep was saying to her.

"Shit, my Lovey", said Donduce, "That is a pain, because my next question was going to be theft, but the sheep have ruled that one out then Hun?".

Beauty looked again at the sheep. "Yes my Babsey, it's definitely not theft".

"I am going to have a big think about that one then, and we have got to get it sorted and the little one back with it's Mum as soon as possible. The longer the little lamb is away from it's Mum, the more vunerable it will be, and the family bond will be damaged my beautiful Angel. How fast can the 'Link' spread the word around the entire 'State' Babsey, and why didn't the horses or the cows tell us?".

Beauty looked at the sheep again. "Right", said Beauty, "Babsey, the answer to the first question is that the word has already spread around an immediate area of 50 miles. This is a reasonable distance that the little lamb **could** have travelled, my Angel. The answer to the second question is purely that the sheep told the horses and the cows not to tell you two as they wanted to tell you themselves".

"O.K. my Sweetheart", said Donduce. "Babsey, tell the sheep that I quite understand that and it's fine. Also tell them that we will get a search underway immediately for the little lamb my Hun".

Beauty did just that and then she said "Babsey, the sheep said to tell you and us "Thank you" and they hope we find it before it's too late".

Beauty gave the sheep a reassuring pat, and so did Donduce, before they returned to the jeep. They stood up and watched as the sheep moved up the hill and joined the others. It was strange because Donduce and Beauty could hear a noticeable increase in the noise of the flock; the two 'Link' sheep were relaying what had been said to the rest of them.

Back in the jeep, and Beauty rested her arm on her Husband's knee. "My Babsey", said Beauty. "You don't think the little lamb is a gonna do you? Do you think it's O.K.? What do you think, my Lovey? Honestly?".

"No, my Lovey, that little lamb is very much alive, and I have a majorley gut feeling that it isn't too far away, my Babsey. It's just a case of locating it. Let's get back to the farmhouse now and go over this mornings developments", said Donduce. "I could do with a beer, my Babsey, how about you?", he asked.

"Too bloody right, Honey", laughed Beauty, "I couldn't agree more!".

They drove back down the farm track and the track bent directly at right angles as it approached the 'Main State Road'. Donduce then signalled right, and they pulled out onto the 'Main State Road' with the large field, designated to be the 'State Crown Palace' opposite. Into their front drive and parked.

"I am going to leave the jeep out now, my Babsey", said Donduce. "Although we have finished touring, you never know, we might need it this afternoon. Right now, let's grab some beers eh Babsey?".

Donduce let himself out, as Beauty said "Awww", and let Beauty out of her side.

"God, I love you so much my beautiful Angel", said Donduce as they walked arm in arm to the front door. "I love you too, my Sweetheart", said Beauty happily.

Once inside they took their coats off, and Donduce hung them back up in the cloakroom cupboard. Then, they went into the kitchen and Fang jumped up and started wagging his tail.

"You O.K.?", laughed Donduce as he returned the greeting by rubbing Fang's ears, "Do you want to stretch your legs?" Donduce opened the back door and Fang sort of half walked and half trotted out into the back yard.

"Poor Fang, he has been inside for most of the morning, Babsey", said Beauty, "I'll bet he was dying to get out for a bit, Hun".

"I'll bet he was too, darling", replied Donduce. Beauty was holding on tight to Donduce's hand as she always did and must always do. It was the totally natural and very loving bond that the couple had. They were literally never more than a foot apart, and even that were quite a distance.

"A sit down now my Babsey and beers in the lounge", said Donduce, firmly.

"O.K., yes please", replied Beauty adding "I love you, my Babsey", and together they went back inside, but leaving the back door open for Fang, Donduce opened the fridge, got two beers out, and they collapsed in a heap together on the settee. It was short lived though because no more than two minutes later, Donduce shot up. "Babsey Babsey, we have got to go NOW!! I know where the lamb is!! Donduce exclaimed.

"Bloody Hell, Babsey", said Beauty, almost spilling her beer, "Where?", she asked, "Where Babsey?" she added excitedly.

"I, for some reason just knew not to put the jeep away, my Darling", said Donduce, "Come on, my Angel, we have got to rush".

Beauty was up out of the settee like a bullet, and with a quick stop by the cloakroom to retrieve their coats, went back out of the front door and into the jeep.

Where on Earth are we going, my Sweetheart", asked Beauty. "The sheep said an area of fifty square miles. Is it going to be far?".

"If my hunch is correct my Darling, relatively speaking, our missing lamb is virtually on the doorstep".

"Oh crumbs, Babsey", said Beauty, "That close, God, I do hope you are right".

They pulled out of the driveway and turned right. A little way up the road the left turn to the fields appeared and Donduce signalled left.

"Honey, we are going back to the 'Link' fields again where the sheep are", said Beauty, she was mystified. "Babsey, the sheep, **and** the rest of the animals stated that the poor little lamb was not in any of the fields not even beyond the brow of the hill".

"That's because our little lamb is not in any of the fields my Sweetheart", said Donduce.

"I am mystified Honey", said Beauty. "it wasn't wandering along the farm track road either. There's nowhere for it **to** be Babsey, no ditches that it could have got stuck in. Is it in a hedge near the border of the 'State' then, Babsey?" she asked.

"No, my Darling, but if I am right, you will soon find out!".

They turned left and headed slowly, this time, just in case the little lamb **was** wandering down the track, but then again, the animals would have spotted it, down the farm track. After what seemed like quite a while, because they were driving slowly, they got to the left hand bend. On they went and drove past the sheep on the right hand side. The two sheep, who they had seen earlier saw the jeep, and said to each other, "The jeeps back! The King and Queen may have news about our little one, let's prepare". They bleated to the others and started wandering down as the jeep drove slowly past.

"They are searching; hail to the King and Queen, making the effort to assist us in our hour of need".

"The sheep know we are here Babsey", said Donduce as he looked over, them two are heading down from the field to the fence".

They drove past, and finally got to the end of the cow field, but still kept going.

"There's nothing else here my Lovey", exclaimed Beauty, as they neared the turn round part of the track as it was actually a 'cul-de-sac'.

They swung round on the loop part of the road and stopped for a minute.

"Now, we are going to head back the way we came, Honey", exclaimed Beauty", an air of disappointment in her voice. She had

131

been really hoping to almost see the missing lamb miraculously appear from somewhere, in front of her.

"No, we're not, my Angel, well not yet anyway. I said the missing little lamb was not in any field, or on the track. So, she's not out here my Babsey. What can you see my Angel?", he asked.

"Just the fields, and obviously the farm track, and just up there, the......" her voice trailed away. Her eyes opened very wide, and Beauty started shaking with excitement.

"OH MY GOD.....The 'Old Empty Barn'!", she said "Babsey, is that little lamb in there?"

"It, my Babsey, is 'hopefully' the only likely place it could be, and, it's sheltered", said Donduce.

"Yes, but Darling", said Beauty, "The wind howls through there; I hate the place because of the fucking secret and it's freezing".

"Babsey", laughed Donduce, "You haven't got a woolly coat my Angel so you would be cold and the sheep doesn't know about the secret".

"Babsey", said Beauty now giggling "Sod the secret and I was going to say about the lamb: Nor has the poor little lamb yet, it's only a baby".

"Well my Lovey", said Donduce, "Let's go and take a look".

Donduce got out and, after letting Beauty out of the passenger side, they walked, hand in hand off the loop part of the farm track and onto a large slightly sloped green area. It was like a small field, but the grass was shorter than the fields as it had virtually worn to the bare Earth. In the middle of this area was the 'Old Empty Barn' and one of the oldest parts of the farm 'State' buildings. The farm 'State' itself wasn't the original site of the farm, that was quite a few miles away, but the barn itself was still many hundreds of years old. The last time Donduce and Beauty had been there was when Donduce revealed to the local media the false secret of the 'Old Empty Barn'; and they had endured the real ghostly experience; all that, as a sort of 'State' publicity exercize, which had been fun to do.

"Wait a minute, my Babsey", said Donduce, "Stop and listen, Sweetheart".

"O.K., Babsey", she said, and they did. After a few moments, Beauty said "Can you hear anything Honey?".

"No, my Sweetheart, I cant", replied Donduce "I was rather hoping that we might hear the little lamb baaing, but nothing".

"Oh God, I hope it is in there Babsey", said Beauty, "Shall we call it?".

"No, my Darling", replied Donduce, "We'll probably frighten the poor little thing".

They walked very slowly and quietly towards the barn; the mist was ever present above it, and got to the door frame. The door itself had rotted away, in fact the whole barn was pretty derelict.

"Here we go, Sweetheart, and try to forget the secret for now", said Donduce in a soft whisper "Let's hope, my Darling". Beauty nodded, and then in they went. Inside the barn was quite dim, and the only sunlight that entered the place came from holes in the high roof and it formed beams of light, which lilt up patches on the stony floor.

"Look, Babsey, my Lovey, over there, in the far corner, I can see a little white lump! It's there!! Brilliant!! Let's go and check it my Honey", exclaimed Donduce, really excited.

"Oh, brilliant Babsey, well done you my Lovey, we have found it, the sheep are going to be so happy", said Beauty, and then a very concerned expression came over her pretty little face.

"It **is** alive, Isn't it my Angel?" Beauty asked her Husband.

"I bloody well hope so, Lovey, replied Donduce. "Approach slowly, and from either side so that it doesn't bolt and run off Then what would we say to the sheep my Darling?".

"Very 'baaah-ed' news for you sheep?" laughed Beauty.

"Moving very swiftly on, and I am not even going to mention 'mint sauce', let's retrieve this lamb my Lovey", said Donduce.

After her had given Beauty a reassuring kiss on her forehead, they split up and walked down to the far left hand corner of the barn towards the 'white lump'. Indeed, it was the lamb, which was O.K. but asleep. Donduce and Beauty had not trouble in reaching it and after seeing that it was just curled up, but breathing, Beauty knelt over it, and gently put her hand on it's head. Most of her long, gorgeous hair flopped forward too, onto the lamb, so for all the world it looked like it had suddenly acquired a blackish brown duvet. Donduce crouched down right next to her and the lamb suddenly twitched and opened its eyes. Looking up at

Beauty and Donduce, it let out a bleat, but did not flinch at all.

"Hello, you", said Beauty in her gorgeous reassuring and loving caring voice, "Everything's O.K. now, you are safe.". Then she asked, "I want to ask how you managed to get in there, your Mum is worried sick".

There was a longish pause and Beauty suddenly said "O.K., it's going to be O.K., we are going to take you home now little one.".

"What did it say?" asked Donduce, eager to know, "Babsey, my Lovey, I am in suspense here!", he added.

"Well, my Lovey", said Beauty "Our little lamb, a 'she', just simply got lost. She said it was when it was dark, and she stood up because her new legs were a little stiff and she wanted to try out this 'walking' business. So, she started, and went from her Mum a short distance, then back, and her trips got longer, until when she turned round to go back again, she couldn't see anything. So, she then started wandering about and found this sort of 'thing' with a gap at the bottom".

Beauty paused as she then explained to Donduce that this 'thing' with the gap was actually the field's fence. Donduce nodded. Beauty continued, "In the farm track, where she was by this time, she found that she didn't know where she was, or how to get back, but luckily was heading to this enclosed thing where she thought she would be warmer. She didn't actually say 'enclosed' she said 'the instincts were right', anyway, that's how she got here, and she hasn't seen any tall, two legged things and she really misses her Mum, please could we show her how to get back now?" finished Beauty with a smile. "Aww, bless her!", said Donduce, really touched by the lamb's adventure story, and relieved that she was in one piece and alive. "Babsey, tell her that we will do better than show her; we'll take her back to Mum and her friends personally," said Donduce. When Beauty told the little lamb by looking into her eyes and touching her head, she let out a little 'baah', and jumped straight into Beauty's arms, licking her face.

"Come on then, you two," laughed Donduce, "Let's go back to the sheep with the good news!".

With the little lamb safely in Beauty's arms, they left the barn, and headed back down to the jeep, where Donduce held the passenger door open for them. Once Beauty was inside, Donduce shut the door and then got in himself. He looked at Beauty, and two faces were looking back at him, a very happy Beauty, who said "I love you, my hero, Babsey.", and a very happy little lamb, who licked Donduce's face and said "Baah", only a little squeaky one. "Aww, bless you both," said Donduce. Just before he started the engine, he looked up and to the right towards the horizon.

"Babsey, my Lovey", he said, "There Isn't one animal on the horizon, I'll bet they know already that there has been a positive result, and all the animals are by the fence along the track, like a bloody welcome home gathering.".

"Knowing them, my Babsey, it's a certaincy", said Beauty, and Donduce finally started the engine and they moved off.

Sure enough, as they rounded the slight right hand bend, as the fields came into proper view, the whole of the fence length was crowded with animals; cows first, then horses, and finally the sheep. As Donduce and Beauty drove slowly past, Beauty started waving at the nodding and mooing and braying animals, and baahing (oops!).

Donduce looked at her, so lovingly and said "My Lovey, this may as well be a 'Royal Parade' drive past, bloody hell. What worries me a bit is, when we get to the sheep, how will we know who Mum **is**, my Babsey?".

Beauty smiled and said, "I love it my darling, it certainly is like a 'Royal Parade', and we've only rescued a lamb. Don't worry though, we will find out who Mum is, the sheep will help us there, my Angel", she added.

The crowds of animals who had lined the length of the fence was several deep, and Donduce wondered just how the little lamb would be reunited with her Mum.

They arrived at the start of the sheep crowd, and as they drove along, the flocks retreated back by about two lengths, and suddenly, Donduce noticed that all the flocks had retreated back by the same distance, two sheep lengths, except for two of the sheep, the two that they had spoken to that morning.

Donduce pulled the jeep up right by the two 'Link' sheep, and emerged to thunderous 'baahing', and in the distance, he could here the mooing and neighing. Donduce waved to the 'crowds' as he went to open Beauty's door, and the flocks erupted once more into thunderous 'baahs'. Beauty kissed her Husband, and held the little lamb tightly as she too waved to the flocks. "Bloody Hell, my Babsey", exclaimed Beauty, "Do we get the same response on 'State' occasions with the humans my Lovey?".

"I don't know, Lovey", laughed Donduce, "I will take notice next time we have one and have a look. I should hope so, the supreme 'State' is the 'Crown', and the residents are supremely loyal. I will enquire with the 'Network' to observe. It is of course a breach of the 'E.F.C.' not to show complete loyalty to the 'State', my Babsey".

As they approached the two 'Link' sheep, the flocks directly behind them parted, making a pathway; the more they parted, the longer it got until eventually a space appeared, very symbolically in the middle of the flock. In that space, a solitary sheep stood, looking directly at Donduce and Beauty. It was the little lamb's Mum. She walked slowly, but in a very dignified manner, as if to try and hide the trauma and emotion that she had gone through for days and days. As she got to the fence, the 'Link' sheep stood apart, as she came between them, but with a gap. With sheer joy at such a happy ending, Donduce and Beauty both had moist eyes, as together, the little lamb, they placed in the gap, beside Mum. They both crouched down, and Beauty put her hand on the Mum's head. A few moments later, Beauty said "It's a pleasure, and take care". Then, she turned to Donduce and said "Babsey, my Lovey, put your hand out a minute". Donduce did so, and the Ewe licked his hand three or four times, after which he stroked her head, and said to the Ewe "Don't worry, we are always here for you, take care".

Beauty then put her hand near the little lamb who had been nuzzling up to Mum and licked it, then whilst Mum nuzzled the little lamb, Beauty put her hands on the heads of the 'Link' sheep. Again a few minutes later, she said to them, "No problem, as Donduce has said, we are always here for you, you all, no matter what".

Beauty then stood up, her hair had been dangling between the grass and the sheep, and on the sheep; bits of grass were stuck in it and she brushed them off. Donduce stood up as well, and said "All's well that ends well, my Lovey, are we done now?". Before Beauty answered, Donduce suddenly became aware that during all of this time, every animal present had fallen silent and you could have heard a pin drop; there wasn't even a whisper of a breeze. The only reason why he had noticed this unusual quiet was that as he asked his beautiful Wifey if they were done, his own voice sounded deafening.

"We are, my Babsey", said Beauty, "I very much think it is home time now for a beer", she added.

"What did they say, Babsey, the sheep I mean?" asked Donduce. "I will tell you when we get back, my Lovey," replied Beauty.

A solitary 'Baah' attracted Donduce's and Beauty's attention back to the flock, and the Ewe, reunited with her little lamb started making her way back down the cleared path. Once she and the lamb reached the middle they turned and faced Donduce and Beauty. They both waved and blew kisses, and at that point, the entire presence of animals mooed, neighed, and baahed as the gap in the flock closed up. The two 'Link' sheep came forward and Donduce and Beauty crouched down and patted them both. They stood up again and the animals fell instantly silent once more. It was only when Donduce and Beauty both waved their hands, that the din started again before all the animals moved away from the fence and returned back into the fields.

"That was amazing my Babsey weren't it, and suce a happy ending", said Beauty as she, had in hand with her Husband returned to the jeep.

"Oh crumbs, yes, my Lovey" said Donduce as they reached it and he opened the passenger door for Beauty to get back in. "God, look Hun", she said brushing bits of the grass out of her hair with her hands, "I am still covered, turn round a minute, Babsey, I'll check yours.". She did, and several bits flew out as well, onto the grassy bank.

"I think a hot bath will be needed before we go to bed tonight, otherwise we will be itching like mad, my Angel".

When Beauty had got herself settled, Donduce shut the door and walked around to his side. Once in, he leaned over to Beauty and they kissed passionately.

"That, my Lovey, was a very happy ending. It's amazing what we have done this morning; I can't wait for you to tell me what them sheep said to you up there my Lovey", said Donduce as he started the jeep, and it moved forward.

"As soon as we settle again with our beers, my Babsey, I will tell you all about it, but obviously it's all very good, and the sheep absolutely adore us. 'State Crown' popularity, which was good is now almost worshipped", replied Beauty, and rested her hand in it's usual place on Donduce's knee.

Back down the farm track they went and round the right hand bend; and down the slight hill to the junction with 'Main Entrance Road'. Although the track sloped downhill, the tyres of the jeep made a slushy noise as the surface was still muddy and dewy, even though it was by now, virtually lunchtime.

Donduce signalled right; out of habit more than anything else, because there was never anything on the road to signal to. They pulled out and travelled the 700 yards or so the farmhouse. Very soon, they went past the back gate and then turned left into their driveway. Donduce parked, and said to his beautiful Wifey: "Shall we leave the jeep out, or put it away my beautiful Angel?"

"Babsey my Darling", said Beauty, with a big broad grin spreading across her beautiful pretty little face, or what you could see of it under her gorgeous floppy fringe: she loved her hair like that and so did her Husband; Beauty had a side parting and her hair flopped right down over her beautiful eyes. Well, not exactly a side parting, but it certainly wasn't in the middle – No, "Please could we leave the jeep out, my Babsey: I am absolutely sure that before the end of the day, we will be having a 'Dane and Freckles moment'. I know we will, I am sure we will, and if we don't, we will anyway Honey!".

"Of course we will my Babsey", laughed Donduce and leant over to give Beauty a kiss.

"I love you, my Babsey, I really do", he said looking deep into her loving brown eyes. She had a glint in them and he knew immediately what that was about; Donduce just simply said "Likewise, my Babsey", and Beauty replied "Likewise too my Lovey".

He got out of the jeep and after shutting the door let Beauty out of the passenger side. Then, they opened their front door for what seemed like the 100th time that morning (Babsey, what a milestone, 100 sides, I Isn't never written this much before and it's all thanks to you my gorgeous Angel; I love you my Sweetheart) and went back into the kitchen to check on Fang. He was sitting or rather lying is his usual place, and Donduce and Beauty let him out into the back yard to stretch his legs. They flopped down on the settee, and their beers, which they had put down on the side tables had gone warm and flat. Beauty took a slurp and pulled a face "Ugh my Babsey, them beers have gone flat, how appaulingly awful; I was really looking forwards to that", she said.

"Pass it here, my Babsey", said Donduce in a commanding voice. Beauty did so, and Donduce held the can in his left hand, and put his right hand over the top: then he shut his eyes. After about a minute, he opened them again, and passed the can back to Beauty. "Try that my Darling", he said lovingly.

"Bloody hell, Babsey", exclaimed Beauty as she took the can, "It's chilled, and "; she paused as she took a slurp, "It's fresh and fizzy!", she exclaimed. "How on Earth did you do that, my clever Husband?"

"The same way as I do this, my Lovey", said Donduce, as he took his own can, and the same thing was repeated: he passed it to Beauty for reassurance.

"O.K., my Lovey, I am mystified," said Beauty, "go on, how, Babsey?"

"Well," said Donduce, "My Babsey, many many years ago, I discovered I had these powers, my Angel, and it were when we were both much younger. You did know about them, but also you discovered, after I had installed your special way with animals, just how good you was. It was back in the times when the 'State' weren't as developed as it is now, and due to our various circumstances we had to move off the farm 'Estate'. Recent happenings suddenly triggered my memory, and consequently your brilliant actions as well promptly reminded me of what you did all them years ago. Now seems like a good time, the vibes are telling us, and I think that the 'State' needs our special powers now more than ever, my Lovey".

"I know what you mean, my Babsey", said Beauty, "and I agree whole heartedly with you. Just what exactly, between us, are we capable of, Honey", she asked.

Donduce took both of her hands and looked lovingly into her gorgeous brown eyes which were wide with curiosity and excitement.

"Anything". Donduce replied, with a broad, but serious smile on his face, "Absolutely anything, my Babsey", he added. His voice was very loving but also very reassuring, controlling and commanding. "You, my Darling, are gorgeous", continued Donduce, still looking directly into Beauty's eyes, "and", he added, "I love you completely and forever; we are beautiful, and the most perfect couple that has ever existed".

"Oh my Darling, Likewise, Babsey, I love you too completely and forever, and yes, we are the most perfect couple that ever lived or existed, Awww.", said Beauty happily.

They embraced passionately and kissed for ages. Then, after sitting up again, they continued to slurp the, now chilled, beers. "So, my Angel, what did the sheep say up in the field when we took the little lamb back?"

"Oh yes my Darling," said Beauty, "Them sheep were saying that they had known we would help them look for the little lamb, but had just not anticipated just how quickly things would happen. When we left, the two sheep, the two 'Link' sheep, I am going to call them 'Millie' and 'Lulu', went to the Ewe, who's name is now 'Mary'......" Donduce interrupted her quickly. "Sorry, my Babsey", he said laughing, "I just think it is so sweet all of them sheep you have named! I love them names, do they know, Babsey?" he asked.

"Of course they do, I told them, Babsey" she replied.

"Where on Earth did you get 'Mary' from Babsey?" asked Donduce, then added "This should be good".

Beauty looked surprised. "'Mary'? Babsey! 'Mary had a little lamb' except this 'Mary' lost her's".

Donduce absolutely fell about laughing. "So, what's the lamb's name then, 'Larry'?" he asked.

"Babsey, the lamb is female. It's 'Dolly', Beauty replied, laughing herself.

"Of course, stupid me, sorry Darling, Darling, please continue Darling." said Donduce.

"Darling", said Beauty, "Thank you Darling. Right, as I was saying, 'Milly' and 'Lulu' went to see 'Mary' and reassured her that we was going to do our best to find 'Molly' (Bleeding hell, Author is confused now my Lovey, your giggling, I just called 'Dolly' 'Molly', who is, of course, the cat – oops; read on my Babsey) wherever she might have been. 'Mary' had been off her food for them three days and she said she just hadn't slept a wink. Even the ram, her husband hadn't seen 'Dolly' but was keeping a lookout. So, when 'Millie' and 'Lulu' rushed to her and said that the 'Royal Jeep' was back, her heart was in her mouth. She hoped and prayed for her little 'Dolly' and all the sheep were with her giving much needed support and comfort. One of the taller horses came over to the other fence and called 'Millie', he said to tell 'Mary' the brilliant news that the 'Queen' had just emerged from the 'sacred barn' with 'Dolly', and they was bringing her back home to you. So, 'Millie' and 'Lulu' prepared the welcoming home ceremony, and the rest is history. 'Mary' said a very big 'Thank you' to both of us and was eternally grateful. She said that if there was anything she could do, she would and I said that from this day forth, she would be a 'Link' animal, and so would little 'Dolly', obviously, we had already bestowed the 'sacred privilege' of being a 'State Link' animal on 'Millie' and 'Lulu', as long with this honour comes 'Royal Estate Protection'. Also, because we rescued 'Dolly', and also so quickly, we are loved and now worshipped by all the farm animals, and have their complete loyalty to the 'State'. So much so, that the Crown State, and 'Millie' was very serious about this, that we could consider doing away with the farmhands and re- employ them elsewhere my Babsey. I did however point it out to Millie and Lulu that if we did, it would destroy the Link, and we need that as an essential communication tool in State security. Millie agreed, and I reassured her that herself, Lulu, Mary, and Dolly when she were older were Link spokesheep, my Lovey, that's about it", finished Beauty.

"About it? My Lovey, well done Ewe, (sorry Babsey, my Lovey, couldn't resist!), you have done so well with all your skills and it has given me an idea to test the absolute required loyalty to the Crown State", said Donduce, with a grin.

"The animals all are, Babsey", said Beauty, looking at her husband, rather confused.

"I wasn't talking about the animals", said Donduce. "Whilst I think of it, my Lovey, two things: firstly, I have got to phone Mac-Hastle to terminate the code one now that we have finished the Link tour, and nextly, do you still want to tour the farm animals here my Babsey?"

"Well, my Darling", said Beauty, "I wouldn't mind nattering about the palace design first to get some idea what you had in mind. Then, I would love you to take me to the 'Dane and Freckles', after all, it's just about after lunch. We could do the immediate animals when we get back, if it is still light, or even tomorrow morning if you like, my Babsey, your thoughts my Donduce?"

"Definitely the 'Dane and Freckles' and I will tell you the plans I have thought up after another beer and this call my Angel" said Donduce, happily.

He picked up the phone and dialled a number. After the usual short pause, he said "Mac-Hastle, hello, please terminate code one, thank you, out". Donduce replaced the phone back on the side table. "Done," he said "Come on my Babsey". They stood up and Beauty flicked her hair down her back and the rest flopped forward over her eye. She looked beautiful as ever, and customarily, as he always did, Donduce did the same. Then, they both went into the kitchen and took two more beers out of the fridge. After checking that Fang was O.K.; he was sitting outside the back door sunning himself. It had turned out really nice and the backyard was quite warm. The usual visitors were at the bird feeder, twittering away, and whilst they were there, Donduce and Beauty stuck their heads round the side of the coal bunker, and peered up the meadow. Sure enough, ELKY was there and munching away on his favourite bush. Donduce and Beauty kissed and then returned to the kitchen.

ELKY was aware that Donduce and Beauty was back. Although he had deliberately left his Master and Mistress to their tasks as he knew where they had gone, he chose not to do anything as he was picking an appropriate opportunity to tell Donduce and Beauty of his plight. It had to be sorted out sometime, but he just didn't know when. As they had left Fang out for a bit of exercise, he had gone round to ask him when they would be back. Fang said that they might be a while, but were looking for a lost lamb as he had heard Donduce telling Beauty that he knew of it's whereabouts. Fang also said to ELKY not to worry, he would get Donduce out with Beauty if need be, but they were a bit preoccupied at the moment. ELKY had said 'thanks' to Fang, who had wagged his tail and said 'We're all in this together and good friends, and ELKY had agreed, and returned to munch on his leafy lunch.

Chapter 7

Donduce and Beauty had returned to their beloved settee and sat down. Beauty look a slurp of her beer as she settled her feet on her husband's leg.

"So, my Angel", she said happily as she stretched her elbows up behind her neck, whilst carefully balancing her beer on her tummy, "What is the palace going to look like then?".

"Well, my Lovey, I will run the idea by you, and see what you think". Donduce started.

"Imagine the brown, gothic style cross, the 'medieval' one that appears on the front of our Crown State letter paper. If you place it face up on the ground, it will look just like it does on the paper, which technically is an aerial view. The 'front' of the palace is the upper most curved edge of the top of the cross, and this part of the building will become the most seen part of our residence. As you travel further back the edges of the building curve inwards towards a central point. The other three points will be just visible, but hidden by specially obscuring walls made of iron railings. We will use our powers to make the walls give off the effect of mirages and so onlookers will never be sure if that part of the large building actually exists. This is the part that houses all of the State departments, which we are resituating from the existing buildings. On arrival at the palace, the entrance area is inside a special courtyard, within the cross, as it is in fact hollow. On my reckoning the palace will be ready and fully operational in six months and will be enormous, self contained, secure, private and operate as a principality within a principality, complete with gardens, helipad and total access to the existing farmhouse and the immediate animals. Apart from the front and the sides of the visible sector, high walls in appropriate areas will secure the building from prying eyes, and total absolute control of the entire State Principality will be centralized and governed by me, with your invaluable essential assistance inside the Crown State. I haven't really thought of the official State title of the area within this 'forbidden' area, but I am sure that one of us will think of one, my Lovey" Donduce.

Other changes will take place, my Babsey" he continued. "Mac-Hastle will cease his job as Farmhand Foreman, and will take on a role as simply a farmhand like the others, my Lovey", said Donduce.

"He won't be happy", said Beauty "My Babsey, it is a demotion".

"He has no choice, my Lovey, said Donduce "It is against the 'E.F.C.' to disagree with State policy or change, and it will also test his absolute loyalty to the Crown".

"My Babsey, that was your idea earlier, conceived with the lamb fiasco, weren't it Honey?" chuckled Beauty.

"No, my Lovey, funnily enough, I will tell you about that later", said Donduce. "Anyway, like I said, Mac-Hastle will be replaced by a sophisticated computer system, operated from inside the palace, and with a handset that I have here, in replacement of the phone. If we require a code one, I will just press a button on wherever the destination we want it, and so, will eliminate direct conversation with anyone we don't want it with. This arrangement will also assist with helping your hatred of humans. It will boost your communications with animals ten fold. You never ever speak to humans, and, it eases the uneasy feeling that I know you have when we go on State visits. When I say that you never ever speak to humans, that is a very good thing, a compliment, because I know you naturally hate them, and quite rightly leave the entire running of the farm to me.

Every single aspect of the State system, legal, payroll, admin, communications, maintenance and the running of the Crown State principality will be run from inside the sacred area, solely by me, and you helping". Donduce finished and he smiled at Beauty lovingly. "What do you think, my Lovey", he asked. "Babsey, it sounds fantastic, and much more under your control. It, like you said will allow me to concentrate on the animals and the Link as well, my Babsey", said Beauty. She had a bit of a glazed expression in her eyes as she took all of this news on board.

"When does all this begin my Lovey?" she asked, taking another slurp of her beer.

"Well, my darling," said Donduce, "When we go to the 'Dane and Freckles' in a little while, I am going to shake his hand".

Donduce gave Beauty a knowing look, and she smiled. She knew exactly what he meant by that.

"Then, my Lovey," he continued, "I will ask him to recommend building companies in the outside area who are reliable. We cannot use any of our State companies as this building is completely sacred and no State human will ever set foot in it or know what happens inside, obviously except us. However, and one clever bit, all of the materials used in the construction of the building and the contents will be manufactured using State sourced products, the stone, glass, wiring, all of it, but, purchased from outside company retailers who have already bought it; that way, the palace will be made of State material and will not look out of place or different from existing buildings. This eliminates completely the problem of the building being made of material other than State products, as onlookers are going to wonder where it come from: don't forget, nothing 'apparently' exists apart from the farm State. I will then get the landlord to make some calls this afternoon and if all successful, which it will be, the large screens will start going up as soon as tomorrow afternoon, my Lovey". Donduce finished, and took a slurp of his beer.

"What do you think, my Babsey,?" asked Donduce, reaching out, and stroking her feet, still resting on his knees.

"Absolutely brilliant, my Babsey", said Beauty with a look of total admiration, "You have thought of absolutely everything. I can't think of anything that has been left out, Honey", she added, enjoying her husband stroking her feet. She took another slurp of beer.

"I can only think of one thing we haven't done my Babsey", said Donduce, "and that is, tell Mac-Dad", he finished.

"Didn't we tell him when we saw him in the town Honey?" asked Beauty, "I am sure we did Babsey", she added.

"I can't remember, my Babsey", Donduce replied "I remember we told him about the shopping, but I don't think anything about the palace was mentioned. It doesn't matter though because if we didn't we will just tell him next time we phone or see him my Lovey", said Donduce. "Right then, my Queen Beauty", said Donduce again, "Dane and Freckles time, come on, my Lovey".

"Wonderful, my Babsey", said Beauty, and got up. Donduce did too, and they both went together into the bedroom and did one another's sacred hair. Their hair was getting longer, and it was completely against Donduce and Beauty's extreme natural beliefs to cut or touch their hair in anyway ever. Their beliefs were actually truths, and they were both very aware, and very proud of their beloved roots and views, and they were also very proud of the way they ran their State farm. Beauty flicked her sacred hair back when Donduce had finished combing it, as did he when Beauty had finished. Jewellery in place, they kissed and embraced passionately, then, left the bedroom, and on the way out, called to Fang. He came running into the hallway and sat down before them. They both stroked his head, and Donduce said: "Fang, just going out, you're in charge, good boy mate".

Beauty did her usual and said "Look after ELKY, Fang please".

Fang said, "I will, he needs a chat my Queen, don't forget, Ma'am".

"O.K., Fang love, I'll tell Donduce", said Beauty. She patted his head again, and then held her husband's hand as they went out the front door.

"Oh yes, my Lovey", said Donduce, "That idea inspired by the missing lamb. What we are going to do is 'set up' one of the farmhands", said Donduce.

"That sounds really good and clever," said Beauty with a chuckle, then she added "What did you have in mind, my Angel?".

Donduce pressed the remote to the garage, and said "I will tell you in a munute my Babsey in the Jeep", he said. "This sort of subject is strictly State policy and not for prying ears in the Dane and Freckles". He opened the passenger side, and kissed Beauty as she climbed in. Then, he walked arould thejeep and climbed in himself.

"O.K., my Babsey", he said as he settled himself down, "We are going to set-up one of the farmhands at random to enable us to confirm an average test of absolute State loyalty. When I say an average, if one State-selected farmhand shows the required dedication to his duty on the Estate, I will accept that all the farmhands would, if put into this position, also demonstrate the same attitude. We, through the kindness of our hearts and our love of animals, together with our special powers, helped Mary get her sheep back, and of course, we are rightly worshipped by every Link, and normal farm animal," said Donduce. They were still sitting in the jeep, and hadn't actually moved anywhere yet. "What do you think so far, my Babsey?" Donduce asked.

"Fabulous, so far my Babsey," replied Beauty, and she put her hand in it''s usual place on Donduce's knee, "Carry on, my Babsey", she said.

"Well, my Lovey", said Donduce. "What we do is this; we select a farmhand, and radio to him that one of the animals has not been accounted for in the branding roll. Prior to this, we decide on which type of animal, whether it be a cow, horse or sheep is to 'go missing', and go to the selected herd. Through your powers of the vibe, you instruct the Link animals of the herd to spread the word that one of them is missing and to 'act agitated'. Of course, the farmhands are not aware of any of this, and even more importantly, no animal has actually gone missing. On the day we select, I will inform farmhand Mac-Hassle that I require the 'branding role' to do a 'spot check' on the herds for an Estate Audit. We then go and collect it, under a code one, and using our vibe, I will erase one of the brand numbers from the list, so the role becomes one short, and, leaving some of the vibe power on the brand role pad, the selected farmhand will leave off the same brand number, for as long as we decide this 'test' is going to last.

The farmhands will become aware that the animals are upset about something and should inform us immediately. They should then get very concerned that this random 'State spot check' has been requested by the King, and then really worried when the role is incorrect, and even more worried still when they do a 'head count' of the animals and they all appear to be accounted for visibly. This will cause maybe arguments and distrust within the farmhand community team, especially with the farmhand that 'made the error'. If he apologises straight away, via Mac-Hastle to us, ensuring that it was a one-off mistake by him and won't happen again, assuring us of his continued loyalty, then he has passed. If it is found that the farmhands have squabbled and argued amongst themselves, instead of showing a positive attitude and actually sorted out the problem, then all the farmhands will be in breach of the E.F.C., my Lovey" said Donduce.

"God, that would be a good test my Angel," said Beauty, and then she added, "What would happen if they did all fail, my Babsey, would they all be evicted?"

"It would solely depend on their reactions, my Honey", replied Donduce. "If one or two of them became really obnoxious, then yes, but don't forget, we would expect the loyal farmhands to either passify the more outspoken ones, or to warn them of the consequences of their actions. They should all conform and act as we would expect, and as they must, but it will be a good test, don't you think, my Sweetheart?" said Donduce.

"Oh, it's brilliant, my Babsey, yes. When are we going to carry out this State experiment; soon?" asked Beauty.

"Certainly within the next few days my Lovey", replied Donduce, and then added "We really want calm to return to the animals after the real life ordeal with Dolly first, Poppet".

"O.K. my Lovey, I can't wait" said Beauty "Come on, our beers and a certain Dane and Freckles are calling us my Sweetheart", said Beauty, as she reached over and gave her husband a kiss; "I love you my Angel," she added.

"I love you too my Babsey", said Donduce, kissing her passionately. He started the jeep, and they left the front driveway turning onto the 'Main Entrance Road'. As they approached the cattle grid, Donduce said to Beauty; "See that area between the grid and the front entrance my Babsey, on the left, just before the tall State boundary trees?".

"I certainly can my Angel," replied Beauty looking first at the area and then her husband. "It sort of runs next to or rather parallel with the trees, and then gets over grown" she added.

"Well, my Honey, that is where the outside contractors trucks and diggers are going to access the farm from. They will start by making a track from here, right around the farm house area and to the far end of the field we are going to build on. That way, no one but is will ever see them come and go, as they will be well hidden, my Lovey", explained Donduce. "Blimey, my Babsey, you do think of everything", she said.

They went over the cattle grid, past the 'soon to be site entrance', and then under the State farm sign. Donduce signalled left, and they were on AKKS Road once more.

It was a nice bright and sunny lunchtime or rather early afternoon, and there was nothing else on the Road. The field to the right was it's usual self, rather over grown with tall grass covering most of it.

"I wonder who actually owns that field, my Babsey?" said Donduce as they drove round. "We don't, although, of course, we should do, but I guess it is owned by the town council of 'EYOW'", Donduce added. The town of 'EE-I-OH', was pronounced 'EYOW', however The King and Queen insisted that their State farm was pronounced 'EE-I-O', and it was a breach of the E.F.C. to mispronounce the sacred name. "I honestly don't know my Angel", said Beauty, "You have got that look in your eyes my Babsey", she chuckled, "What have you got on your mind my Lovey?".

"To buy it of course, my Babsey", laughed Donduce. "I have no idea what we would do with it, but it would be useful to own; develop it into something, my Honey", he said.

"What like my Babsey?" enquired Beauty, looking at her husband with great curiosity.

"How about a massively enormous extension of the 'Dane and Freckles', my Babsey?" said Donduce, and they both burst into hysterical laughter.

They continued round the lane and then saw the familiar lamp post that marked the start of the town.

"OOOhhh, nearly there my Babsey", Donduce and Beauty said in unison.

After a few minutes they had pulled into the 'Dane and Freckles' car park, and as thy pulled up in a space, Donduce said: "Lunchtime, my Beauty, and what would the Queen of 'EE-I-OH' like, my Lovey?".

"You, my Lovey", replied Beauty, as her husband got out and then let Beauty out.

"You have already got me, my Lovey", laughed Donduce.

"O.K., then my Babsey, I will have a beer please".

After locking up the Jeep, they took each other's hand and walked round to the front entrance of the 'Dane and Freckles'. Donduce always went in first, and Beauty always followed.

Donduce turned to Beauty, "God, Babsey, I hope the landlord is in, I can't just talk to anyone behind the bar", said Donduce, as they walked into the bar area.

Thankfully, he was, and was serving someone at the other end, near where Donduce and Beauty's favourite seat was, which also thankfully was empty.

Donduce deliberately guided Beauty up to a gap in the bar where the staff could access the serving area. The landlord saw them and nodded. He finished serving, and walked over; and as he did, Donduce held out his right hand; and; without thinking, the landlord offered his and they shook hands.

"Good morning, sorry, afternoon, Sir", said the landlord, "Ma'am", he added, nodding to Beauty, who smiled. "The usual, Sir?" he asked.

"Of course, and good afternoon", replied Donduce. "I require as well, a private word with you; please would you join us for a minute?".

"Of course Sir", said the landlord, "I will bring the drinks over for you, just give me two minutes".

"Thank you", said Donduce, and, after he had paid, they walked to their favourite settee by the fire. Donduce took Beauty's coat, and she sat down, making sure that her hair was flicked forward, and flopping over her right eye as it had to be Donduce did the same and put the coats next to them. They usually went on the chair opposite, but this time, the landlord was going to sit there.

"I am going to enjoy this my Lovey", said Beauty eagerly, "I love listening in when you are doing your arranging over something for the State, something for us", she added. "It is really good as well, my Lovey", said Donduce, holding Beauty's hand, "that I am going to be talking to him, in our own territory, as in on our settee. I wouldn't have felt so at ease if we would have had to sit somewhere else, hang on my Babsey, he's coming over". Donduce fell silent as the landlord, armed with their drinks on a tray, and one presumably for him, came over to their table and, after her had placed the glasses on their relevant spots, he turned and put the tray on the bar behind him.

"Sorry, it took a bit longer than I thought Sir". He said, "Mind if I?" and he pointed at the spare chair.

"Of course", said Donduce, "please sit down". Donduce thought to himself, and also, with their 'private vibe' to let Beauty know, "I am letting the landlord, or rather giving him permission to sit down, and he's the landlord!". Donduce glanced quidkly at Beauty, who looked at him knowingly and gave him a broad smile: she had got the message.

"O.K.", said Donduce, picking up his drink, "Cheers, by the way.".He touched Beauty's glass with his own, and then the landlord's.

"I wanted your thoughts and ideas please", Donduce said to the landlord.

"I will do my best Sir", he replied, taking a slurp, and looking suitably businesslike, "What did you have in mind?".

"We are going to build a new construction on the farm, a large residential area, and we are looking for suitable contractors to carry out the work" said Donduce.

Beauty smiled to herself as she had noticed that her husband didn't use the word 'palace'; obviously them outside contractors Isn't going to know either.

"O.K. Sir," said the landlord looking interested but rather puzzled. "Where do I fit into all of this?" he asked.

"I wanted to know if you knew and could recommend anybody who is reliable and could take on the project," said Donduce, and added, "We want the work to start as soon as possible.".

"How soon is 'as soon as possible'?" the landlord asked, taking another slurp.

"Well", said Donduce "In the time it takes for you to recommend someone and give us a quote. As soon as that is done, they can start," said Donduce. "Once the cost is finalised, I can give them the plans, then arrange a payment, and work commences" he finished.

"Right you are Sir", said the landlord. I will make a couple of phone calls, because I do know of one particular company what is local, and they are large enough to take on that kind of project and quickly. They don't hang about either; very efficient and thorough they are too. May I be so impertinent and ask you a question please Sir?" he asked.

"Of course," said Donduce, "Fire away".

"Why don't you get your farmhands to do the building Sir? It would be cheaper?" said the landlord.

"Oh no", said Donduce, "The few that we have got are far too busy attending to the animals and helping us. It would be a lot quicker to do it this way. When you have made these calls, when will you let us know?" Donduce asked the landlord, deliberately as well; changing the subject quickly.

"Are you in tonight?" asked the landlord.

"We can be, if you have an answer by then", Donduce started, then he glanced at Beauty, who smiled, but said on the 'vibe', "Don't forget ELKY, my Lovey".

"......If not, then tomorrow lunchtime", Donduce said, whilst saying on the vibe to Beauty "I won't my Babsey, don't worry", "Will you be here then?" Donduce asked.

"Yes Sir, I will, both tonight and tomorrow. I will go, if that is O.K. with you, and make a call now. You are going to be in for a while Sir and Ma'am, are you not", said the landlord.

"Yes," replied Donduce, "We will be here for a little while".

"O.K., Sir," said the landlord, "If you would excuse me, I will get back and sort these phone calls out as soon as I am able".

"Of course," said Donduce, "One more thing, I require to know your name".

"It's Paul, Sir", replied the landlord with a smile, and then added,

"Yours is......." He stopped but had a look of expectancy about him.

"You may call me Duce", said Donduce.

"And your good lady, Duce?" Paul enquired, looking at Beauty's natural beauty.

"That will be all, thank you, Paul", said Donduce, abruptly. No one asks for the name of his beautiful Wife; it is sacred and the very question is forbidden.

Paul got up from the chair, however Donduce remained seated. "I will get back to you as soon as I can, Duce, Sir" he said.

153

"Of course, and thank you", replied Donduce.

Paul turned and headed back to the gap in the bar, holding his drink; he then disappeared through another door behind the bar area, and it swung shut in the slight breeze that Paul had made.

"Well, my Lovey, that was very productive", said Donduce, as he kissed her and then had another slurp.

"Yes, my Babsey", replied Beauty. "It did. He was very cooperative; do you think he will come up with anything forthcoming my Angel?".

"Oh yes, he will and he will have to. He Isn't got not choice, he won't stop until he gets what we want, my Lovey", said Donduce.

"You shook his hand; I remember now, Babsey, WOW!!" she said.

"If you noticed as well my Lovey, when he got up to go, I didn't shake it again, so he will be extremely cooperative" Donduce chuckled, slurping again.

"How long will he be like that for then, my Angel?" asked Beauty, with a satisfied and rather triumphant tone in her voice, she already knew the answer but was just waiting for her husband to confirm what she was thinking.

"Until he comes up with the goods, my Lovey, and or, as an when I decide otherwise".

"I love it, my Babsey," said Beauty, and took another slurp herself. "I do love it here my Darling", she said, looking around the bar area in general. They keep it so nice, and it is very relaxing, not like other establishments where you get them rowdy crowds You don't get no yobs in here neither, a very upmarket clientel, l like it" added Beauty happily.

"I do too my Babsey", replied Donduce, "And it will stay this way too. If you think about it, it has had a relaxed friendly atmosphere ever since we started coming, all them years ago my Lovey".

"It must be the effect we have on it, my Lovey", said Beauty chuckling.

Donduce laughed himself, "Babsey, my Lovey, you don't actually know just how true that is. Like another beer my Babsey?".

"Yes please, my Lovey", Beauty replied with a beaming smile.

Donduce and Beauty had their own unique language that only the two of them spoke, which made it so much easier to talk about literally everything and anything without the worry of being overheard. They were both incredibly private people and that was the way it stayed and would stay. Donduce however, used the vibes of his unique powers to make conversations spoken in their language understandable to you (Yes my Lovey, hello my gorgeous Angel, wakey wakey!! Hubby calling! That woke you up, didn't it? Your giggling! Carry on…)

They both got up, and after the ceremonial flicking (I very nearly wrote something else then by mistake! Oops) of their long hair, they walked over to the bar. A lady was serving and when she finished she came over.

"Same again?" she asked with a smile.

"Yes please" said Donduce, and then added "New face behind the bar?".

"No", she replied, pouring out their drinks, "We're short staffed tonight, and me and Paul are here all afternoon, and all tonight. I'm his wife, Yvonne, and I'm usually in the kitchen, but like I said, we're short staffed; the usual guy who does the afternoons has got the day off. He did ask for time off so we couldn't refuse. Made us short though, never mind eh?"

She finished pouring the drinks and placed them on the bar. Donduce took out his wallet and produced a tenner which she took saying "Thank you".

As she took the note to the cash till, she called "You run the farm down that weird road, don't you?"

Donduce and Beauty did their absolute best not to have total hysterics, and Donduce replied:

"That's right, we do, down Akks Lane. Why do you say the road is weird then?".

Yvonne was still pressing the buttons on the till. "Only because on the few occasions I have gone that way, it's always really foggy and I have had to turn back. I have never actually seen the farm entrance; I only know it exists because we get all our produce from there and beautiful it is too" she said; the last bit rather hurridly more out of courtesy then anything else. "Come to think of it, I need to put

155

another order in: we are nearly out of....oh, something or other", she stopped nattering as she had got their change, which she came back with. "There you are Sir," she said, and nodded at Beauty, who smiled, "Enjoy".

Donduce said "Thank you", and then they both returned to their settee. The fire was roaring away as they flopped back down again, arm in arm.

It was Beauty who let out a loud giggle. "We run the farm down that weird road?", she said, repeating what Yvonne had said. "We are the Queen and King of the Royal State Farm Principality of EE-I-O, actually", said Beauty, indignantly, "Run a farm! Can I go and say to her that I would like her or rather demand that she kisses my feet, please, my Lovey?" Beauty was giggling.

"No, my Angel", said Donduce firmly, "No, you can't, my Lovey. One will just have to put up with their obvious ignorance, just this once. Never mind my Babsey" he added, laughing. Donduce and Beauty were relaxed, and soaking up the general atmosphere of the bar. It was about two thirds full. But didn't look it, as most of the clientel were sitting at tables as well, or at the bar on wooden bar stools. Sometimes, Donduce and Beauty would sit on stools as well, but only if their favourite settee had been taken.

There was a sudden squeak, followed by a clunk as the door behing the bar swung ope and Paul reappeared. He looked around and smiled when he saw that Donduce and Beauty were still in.

Donduce said "Here we go, my Lovey, I wonder if he has come up with anything".

"We will soon find out my Lovey", she replied, and held her husbands hand very tightly.

Paul arrived at the table and said; "Duce, Sir, mind if I?"

"Of course" replied Duce, and pointed at the chair.

In her mind, Beauty was crying with laughter: she had suddenly thought how funny it would be if, as Paul went to sit down, Donduce used his magic power on the chair, so that it moved backwards and Paul finished up on his bum on the floor. Unfortunately, at this point, Donduce had picked up on Beauty's thought vibe, and was desperately, on so desperately trying to keep a straight face, and even more desperately trying NOT to use his power TO actually move the chair so Paul WOULD finish up on his bum. (NOW I am in hysterics, so are you aren't you!! – carry on, my Babsey…..).

Paul sat down, and (safely) said "Duce, Sir, we have a result, which I hope will be to your satisfaction".

"Of course", said Donduce, and added "What have you got?".

"I have been in touch with a local company based just outside EE-I-O to the north, a company that has been in the area for several hundred years. It is called 'New Foundation Construction', and they would like to meet with you tomorrow afternoon if that is convenient with you both. I have given them a rough idea of what you require, and they would like you to ring them to confirm that tomorrow afternoon is O.K.", said Paul. He hooked at his watch and said "It's 4:15 now and they shut their offices at 6:00pm". He handed Donduce a piece of paper with a roughly drawn map and a phone number at the bottom. "Here's where they are based with directions from the pub, and the name and phone number of the manager, a Mr Robert Cunningham. Does this all agree with your requirements, Sir?", Paul asked.

"Of course, thank you very much for your assistance, Paul," said Donduce, very officially.

"Now, sod off, Paul" thought Beauty, very officially.

"Shall I actually move the chair, with him on it?" thought Donduce, very temptedly.

Paul stood up, and said "Glad I could help Sir, and you will have to let me know how you got on." He nodded to Beauty, who smiled, and then after saying "See you later", to Donduce and Beauty together, he went back round to the bar area, having first put the chair back into its original position.

"Oh my God, that was funny, my Lovey, and I did pick up you saying 'Sod off'. We appear to have a result my Angel" said Donduce, looking at the piece of paper. "Right then, let's finish our drinks and then head back home. We have ELKY to sort out, plus ring this company. I love you my Honey" said Donduce.

"O.K., my gorgeous Lovey" said Beauty, "Two minutes to finish our drinks and…." Her voice trailed away as a loud tapping noise from a window to their right interrupted her. She looked up and said:

"Bloody hell, it's a carrier pigeon, actually, there are two, one slightly smaller", Beauty exclaimed excitedly.

"How can you tell it is a carrier one, the pigeon, I mean? Babsey", asked Donduce, looking and sounding really interested by the apparent interest of these birds in them.

"By their colours, my Babsey" replied Beauty, "Follow me", she added.

They both stood up and went over to the window. The pigeons did not move and the window was shut. They didn't want to open it for fear that the birds would come in and start flapping around the bar.

"It is definitely, or tather they are definitely father and son, my Lovey", said Beauty, very confidently, "It's the way they are sitting on the ledge outside. The smaller one has the same plumage as the bigger one and they are very close together. They are grey, and if you look closely, they both have a small green ring around their necks. Also, the tips of their wings are black with white speckles. The females are completely brown all over, but Mum Isn't here, I wonder where she is?"

"Don't know my Lovey", replied Donduce, "But I am just thinking that if no one owns them, they would make incredibly good 'Link' creatures as they can fly all over the State if we trained them. What do you reckon, my Lovey?"

Beauty was looking at the pigeons intently. "Yes, my Babsey, they are definitely Carrier Pigeons or incredibly similar. Although they have that green bit on their necks, their wings are more pointed than a standard pigeon or 'Stock Dove' as they are sometimes called. Not only that, but they, neither of them have any rings on them, so are presumably homeless", said Beauty, smiling.

"Bloody hell, my Sweetheart", exclaimed Donduce, "You certainly know your stuff about virtually any creature you come into contact with don't you, my Honey", then Donduce whispered in her ear,

"It's just humans you hate my Babsey!".

Beauty laughed "You are right there, my Angel, and thank you for the compliment. I don't know why we are whispering for anyway because no one can understand us!" she added.

Donduce laughed, and then Beauty started looking intently at the pigeons again. After a few minutes, she said:

"My Babsey, your wishes have just been answered. The Dad pigeon has a Mrs Pigeon and another sibling. They are currently nesting in the town but know of the Estate: they would very much like to nest with us and help us in anyway they can, how brilliant is that Honey? Also, it has just said that if it is O.K. with us, they will flap back home and tell Mrs Pigeon, and then the whoe family, four of them will flap to the farmhouse later on. Is that O.K., my Babsey?" asked Beauty, smiling.

"Of course it is my Lovey", said Donduce excitedly. "What I will do is build a special big nesting box in the back yard, so they can come and go as they please. It will be doubly useful as they will become the only Link creatures who are free to fly both on the Estate and in town, and indeed anywhere they choose. They can even monitor the contractors when they come and go building the palace, my Lovey. Go on, my Babsey, tell them, Lovey", said Donduce.

Beauty once more stared at the pigeons, and then they both started stretching their wings. Then, with a bit of a waddle, they turned on the ledge and with a glance back at Donduce and Beauty, they prepared for flight. Donduce and Beauty heard the muggled noise and a small ruch of air as they took off. High into the sky they went, and circled a couple of times before disappearing from view; Donduce and Beauty waved as they went.

"My God", said Beauty "Babsey, how brilliant was that, we have now got our own aerial messaging service!".

"Fantastic, my Sweetheart", replied Donduce, "Come on Babsey, lets sit down again and finish our drinks. Then we had better head home, because I have got to phone the contractor before 6.30pm and the time is getting on."

They left the window and returned to the settee, kissed passionately, flicked their hair forewards and sat down.

Donduce looked at his watch: "It's 5:15pm my Lovey, go in ten minutes my Babsey?"

"O.K., Sweetheart my Angel" said Beauty. They kissed passionately again and finished their drinks.

After their last slurp; they finished their drinks at the same time, Donduce said "My gorgeous Babsey, is one ready?"

Beauty laughed and said "One is my darling, shall we depart this lovely establishment, to return later; I have actually got something and somewhere on my mind my Lovey."

"Of course my Babsey," replied Donduce with a giggle, "I know exactly what you're thinking as well!"

They stood up, and flicked their hair back, kissed, and then hand in hand, they took their glasses back to the bar, where Yvonne was emptying a rather large dishwasher.

"Thanks for them" she said, "Are you back later?" she asked, almost sounding hopeful.

"Oh yes", replied Donduce, almost with an air of authority, "We will be back later on, thanks".

"O.K. then, bye for now", replied Yvonne, and carried on with the emptying. Beauty smiled and then, hand in hand with her adoring husband, they headed to the door.

"Oh crumbs, my Lovey", said Donduce, as the early evening chill hit them as thy got outside, "It's a bit bleeding cold, Isn't it, Sweetheart".

Beauty let go of her husband's hand, and instead wrapped herself completely round him. Burying her head under his chin, so her beautiful little face was virtually hidden under his beard.

"Oh, it's cold my Lovey", said a little voice from under Donduce's chin.

Donduce laughed as he held his gorgeous Wifey as they walked, "It's not **that** far to the car my Angel", he said, comfortingly. "No", said Beauty; and then added, chuckling: "I don't do cold, No, No, No, No, No, **NO.**"

Arriving at the jeep, and after having pressed the remote, Donduce opened the passenger side and let Beauty in. She flicked her hair forward, kissed her husband and settled in. Donduce shut the door and then walked round to his side where he let himself in and then leaned over and kissed Beauty.

"I will soon warm you up my Lovey. I'll put the heater on", he said as he started the jeep again and then flicked a switch on the dashboard. Soon there was a warm draught of air blowing around

Beauty's feet; she could feel her toes warming up, even though she had her fur lined boots on.

"Awwww, my Babsey, that's better", she said. "It is like bloody Siberia out there."

"You've got them boots on as well, and you're feet were still cold, my Babsey? Awww, sorry Sweetheart", said Donduce.

Beauty put her hand in it's usual place on his knee, and they drove out of the car park, turned right and were soon heading towards the lamp post as the road curved round that big field opposite. Dusk was approaching and although the sun was still up, just, it was obscured by patches of low cloud. After what seemed like no time at all, Donduce signalled right and they were back on the Estate, over the cattle grid and pulling into the front driveway.

"Home briefly my Angel," said Beauty, "I love you so much my Sweetheart. Then we are back out again, aren't we my Babsey?!!".

"Yes, my darling, don't worry, we are", said Donduce, giving Beauty a reassuring kiss. "I had better leave the jeep out then, hadn't I my Honey", he added with a smile.

"Yes pleeeeaaaseee my Angel" she replied happily.

Donduce turned the engine off and got out. He walked around the front and let Beauty out, and then they walked, hand in hand to the front door. Once inside, Donduce hung the door keys on a hook just to the right of the front door, and then they both went into the kitchen to check on Fang. He was lying by the back door, which was still open wide, and as soon as he heard Donduce and Beauty approaching, he sat up and started wagging his tail.

"Hello, Fang!" Donduce and Beauty said together, as they got to him, "Are you O.K.? Anything been happening", added Donduce as they took it in turns to rub his head and make a fuss of their gorgeous guard dog. Beauty looked into his eyes.

"Hello," said Fang, "You're back finally you stop-outs – only kidding", he said. "No, nothing to report, everything has been quiet, but ELKY needs to have a chat, he's concerned about something, although he hasn't said what. I am not sure whether or not he can talk to you as well as I can. Don't forget he left you clues and visual messages like pointing at the fridge when he said that the gorilla was back, and, no, before you two get worried, I haven't seen him. Go and see ELKY though, don't worry, he's O.K. but just concerned. O.K. my Queen and King?"

"Oh, Fang, you are just brilliant," said Beauty. "O.K., thanks for all them messages and I will relay it all to Donduce, lots of love and thanks." Beauty rubbed his head again and told Donduce all of what Fang had said.

"What a fantastic guard dog we have, my Angel," said Donduce after he had listened intently to what his beautiful Wifey had to say. He patted Fang on the head again to show his appreciation, and Fang wagged his tail. "Well done, you clever Fang", said Donduce, and Fang said to Beauty "Tell him, thanks, and it was nothing". Beauty relayed that too, and Donduce laughed. "Come on", he said to Beauty, we had better go and see if ELKY is O.K. my Darling". Hand in hand they crossed the yard and went through to the meadow. ELKY, who had his head stuck in the bush as usual, immediately turned his head and then came trotting over. He nuzzled Donduce's arm and then licked Beauty on the nose; his usual greeting. Beauty put her hand, she thought was for the first time on his nose, and stared into his eyes. It was the first time that ELKY had let her do this, and she was quiet for quite a bit longer than normal.

"Are you O.K., my Lovey?" asked Donduce after what seemed like a long time.

"Yes, my darling, I am, but ELKY is very stressed about something. He wants, I think to take us somewhere to show us something but I am not sure. I get the feeling that ELKY has got a 'vibe' communication problem; I put it down to the fact that with Fang, he is used to humans, as are the 'Link' animals. ELKS are solitary creatures and so are not. We will get round it though but it's going to take a while my Angel," said Beauty.

"O.K., my Angel", replied Donduce, "Ask ELKY where he wants to take us".

Before Beauty did anything, ELKY must have understood Donduce, because like Donduce's sudden previous realization with the fridge, ELKY licked his arm, turned, and walked to the start of his pathway.

"Bloody hell, my Babes", exclaimed Beauty, "That's what I dreamt about the other night. Blimey, I forgot it was there, it's so overgrown. Where does it lead to my Angel?" she asked.

"I don't really know, just around that massive field we are developing I think, which reminds me, I've got to phone that manager, my Lovey" said Donduce. "Tell ELKY that when we get back tonight, we will follow him my Lovey. Don't worry, we will take torches, and anyway, ELKY knows where he is going, and the way back, because he's here, my Lovey", said Donduce.

"O.K., my Babsey", said Beauty, and then used the Bibe to confirm to ELKY the plan. After a few pats, and a nuzzle from ELKY, they left him to his bush and went back inside the house, hand in hand, to the lounge. After flicking their hair, and kissing passionately, Donduce got the piece of paper out of his pocket that Paul had given him. "Here we go then, my Babsey, Oh, I forgot to pick the phone up! Sorry my Darling," said Donduce.

"That's O.K. my Angel", said Beauty.

They both got up, flicked their hair back, walked hand in hand to the other side of the lounge where the phone was resting on it's cradle.

There was a sideboard against the wall, and the phone rested or rather lived on this. Donduce picked it up, and they returned to the sofa, flicked hair, kissed passionately and then sat down.

"O.K., my Babsey, let's try again", said Donduce. "It's 5:45pm so we are well in time". Donduce had checked the wall-clock. It was a really nice old-fashioned styled one with Roman numerals on it, and crucially, it did not tick.

Donduce looked at the piece of paper and said to Beauty: "Do you know what, my Lovey? That name of the manager of 'New Foundation Contractors', Robert Cunningham; his name sounds vaguely familiar for some reason. I have heard, or I think I have heard that name before, but I just cannot place where".

"I don't think I have ever heard it before my Babsey", said Beauty, "I will have to keep my ears open".

Donduce smiled, and then, reading the number, he dialled and paused whilst the line connected.

Donduce jumped and then said "Is that Mr. Cunningham? Oh hello, my name is Donduce, and I believe that Paul from the 'Dane and Freckles' has recommended you to me, well actually, he has personally. He knows you very well, and has mentioned to you that we would like you to give us a quote for a major building project that we want started as soon as possible, please could you bear with me for a second? Thank you".

Donduce pressed the silent button on the phone and said to Beauty "I'll put it on speaker my Lovey, so that you can hear what he says too, otherwise you are going to feel left out and only hear my end of the conversation, Babsey".

"Awww, thank you, my darling", said Beauty, smiling and taking another slurp of her beer. Donduce did the same, and then pressed 'speaker'.

"Hello again, Mr Cunningham," said Donduce, "Sorry about that".

"Good evening, Sir", came this rather deep voice. "Yes, Mr Donduce, Paul has been in contact with me, and I suggested a meeting between ourselves at 3:00pm tomorrow afternoon at my office. Will that be suitable for you? Sir?" Mr Cunningham asked.

Donduce looked at Beauty, who nodded vigorously, her floppy fringe all over her pretty little face, and said "Yes, that will be fine, Mr Cunningham", with a smile as he was giggling at Beauty nodding.

"May I ask briefly what this project actually is", said Mr Cunningham.

"No", thought Beauty, "Wait until bloody tomorrow, you nosey sod".

"It involves the construction of a large new building on 'EE-I-OH' Farm" explained Donduce.

"Exactly how large are we talking about Sir", asked Mr Cunningham.

"Bloody enormous, does it really matter how bloody large it is; we're paying for it, just bloody get on and build the sodding thing you nosey idiot", thought Beauty. She was smiling at her gorgeous Hubby because she knew that Donduce had picked up everything that she thought, and also she had picked up the hysterics and the giggles in Donduce's thoughts as he was trying to keep a straight face and sound serious.

"Well", said Donduce, as calmly as he could, "The easiest thing I can do is to bring the plans tomorrow, as it is difficult to describe dimensions, but it is big."

"I should hope you **are** bringing the plans with you Sir," said Mr Cunningham. "A bit tricky without them, don't you think?".

Donduce and Beauty looked at each other with open mouths and thought "Sarcastic Bum!" Is he related to Mac-Stupid!!".

"O.K., Mr Cunningham," said Donduce, still calmly, "I suppose the length of the building would be the equivalent of four football pitches, and the width about two, but that is purely a guestimate, as I hate football and can only imagine this visually."

"No problem, Mr Duce," said Mr Cunningham, "It certainly sounds an enormous project, and you want us to start immediately Sir?".

"Well, as soon as we have accepted your quote, then yes" said Donduce.

"May I advise you Sir, that we are the only company around that can take on a job of that magnitude, and at such short notice, so, our quote will likely to be the only one you will obtain", said Mr. Cunningham.

"With all due respect Mr Cunningham, you are most certainly not the only company that can do the work, and so therefore we expect a competitive figure", said Donduce, looking at Beauty with a loving grin.

Beauty thought "Babsey, who else is there then? I'm intruigued!"

Donduce sent Beauty a thought back, "US, my Angel, our own company".

"Oh yes!", laughed Beauty in her thoughts, "I had forgotten about them, my Babsey.

"Who else is there then, Mr Donduce?" asked Mr. Cunningham.

"That is for me to know and you to ponder over, Mr. Cunningham", said Donduce firmly. "Now, please could you give me directions on how to get to your company?"

"Of course Sir", he said, "Do you have a fax machine?"

"We do," said Donduce, "I will give you the number", he added.

"Do we, Babsey?" thought Beauty to her husband.

"Yes, my darling, its in our office, next to the bedroom, my Sweetheart", thought Donduce, back to Beauty.

"Good, Sir, then I will fax a map to you, with directions. We are very easy to find. We are actually located on the 'Foundation Industrial Estate' to the north of the town, sort of near the foot of the hills. We have actually done a great deal of work for you in the past, Mr. Donduce. I believe we have built quite a few of the buildings on the farm, the relatively new ones; well, new in the last 50 to 100 years, anyway." said Mr Cunningham.

"Well, they have certainly lasted the test of time, and I am sure that everything will be fine and run smoothly to a satisfactory conclusion" said Donduce. He then added "We will expect the map any minute then?".

"Sending it through now Sir, and see you tomorrow, Mr Donduce?" said Mr Cunningham.

"Absolutely", said Donduce, and then he added, "It's not Mr Donduce, please, just Donduce. Do you have a first name I can call you", he looked at Beauty, waiting for a suitable answer from him.

"Yes, 'Mr'," said Mr. Cunningham, then he said "No, Donduce, I am only joking, please call me Bob".

"O.K., then Bob, see you tomorrow", said Donduce.

"Bye" said 'Bob', and the phone clicked off.

Donduce and Beauty both fell about in hysterics. "What a stupid, self opinionated, sanctimonious, pompous, cretinous idiot", my Babsey" exclaimed Beauty. "Oh my God, my Lovey, you have got to shake HIS hand tomorrow afternoon, so that he knows who's boss", she added.

"Oh, don't worry about that, my Lovey", replied Donduce. "By the time the meeting is over, he will be eating out of our hands".

"What building work has he done previously then my Babsey?" asked Beauty, I don't remember that at all my Lovey.

"Nor do I Sweetheart", said Donduce thinking carefully. "It must have been at the time when we were not living on the farm".

"Mr. Cunningham, or Bob, now, said they have been built recently, and then he said, between 50 and 100 years ago," said

Beauty, a thoughtful but curious expression spread over her face. "That's recent, my Lovey?" she asked.

"My Sweetheart, it is to us", replied Donduce, smiling.

Just then, their attention was interrupted by the sound of a beep, and then a churning noise, coming from near the bedroom.

"Ah-ha, my Sweetheart," said Donduce; "That will be the map coming through on the fax machine.

"Awww, let's go and see, my Lovey", said Beauty excitedly.

They got up, flicked their hair, kissed and embraced passionately, and went out of the lounge, down the hall where the office was, situated just before the bedroom. As if dutifully, the tray just under the mouth of the machine had two 'A4' sized printed pages: one was a confirmation that the fax had been sent, the other being a photocopy of a map of the town. The farm, or rather the 'Main Entrance' end of the Estate was in a valley, with hills and then mountains to the south, the Estate starting near the bottom of the valley. The town of 'EE-I-O' was roughly in the middle, and the large industrial estate was a bit further up, between the north end of the town and the hills to the north as well.

Donduce and Beauty peered at it, and then Donduce said, "Oh yes, my Angel, we won't have any problems finding him; it's very straight forward. Good".

"Oh, I am so glad, my Babsey" said Beauty, "I am looking forwards to tomorrow now, as well as tonight", she added, the last bit being a hint".

"I hadn't forgotten, my Lovey", reassured Donduce as they left the office. Donduce had picked up the faxed map, and put it, together with the other piece of paper with Bob's phone number on, next to the phone's cradle on the sideboard.

Donduce looked at the time. "It's 7pm my lovey. Lets go out the back and check on Fang, and also try and tell ELKY that we will be back tonight to follow him where he wants to take us. Then, my sweetheart, we will return to the Dane and Freckles. How does that suit one?" asked Donduce looking lovingly at Beauty and waiting for a suitable answer.

"That will suit one very nicely, my gorgeous husband", she said, rather regally, then added "Come on then, my lovey, chop chop!"

Hand in hand they left the lounge and went back outside via the kitchen. They patted Fang on the way, and told him they were going back out again, he was in charge, and when they got back, they would be going somewhere that ELKY wanted to take them, but didn't know where. All they knew was that wherever this place was, it was up the back pathway, the overgrown one that led away from ELKY's meadow. Fang said "Ok, and see you when you got back, and did they want him to guard the house or come with them for security". Donduce said that everything would be OK and they needed him to guard the house and Fang agreed. Of course, Donduce said all of this to Fang through Beauty's interpreting skills.

Beauty and Donduce then went to find ELKY, as they reached the meadow, he was in his usual place, and when he heard them, he looked at them, then in the direction of the pathway, and then straight at Donduce.

Donduce made a big gesture of pointing at his watch, and then at the sun, and then at the pathway.

"I wonder if ELKY understood that, my lovey", said Donduce, rather worried.

"Well Babsey, I did", said Beauty reassuringly, "We are going with him down the pathway later when it gets dark, and we're back from the Dane and Freckles", she laughed.

As she said that, ELKY wandered over and nuzzled Donduce's arms and then licked Beauty's face. Then, he turned and went back to his bush and started munching the leaves.

"He understood all right!" said Donduce and Beauty together, and with that, they walked back hand in hand, to the back door.

"Do you want to stay inside or out?" asked Donduce, looking at Fang. After a moment or two, Beauty said "Out please".

"Not, you, my lovey, Fang", said Donduce.

"That WAS Fang who answered, my darling", giggled Beauty.

"No, it wasn't, you answered", said Donduce, teasing her.

"No, I answered for...." started Beauty and suddenly cottoned on to Donduce's tease.

"Right", said Beauty, "A slappy wrist when we get to the Dane and Freckles for my Donduce".

"Only one?, my Babsey, Awww", said Donduce, and then said "See you later", to Fang, who wagged his tail.

"Ok", said Beauty, smiling.

"Now, who the bleeding hell was supposed to of said that? This is getting confusing: you or Fang?" Donduce said laughing again. "Neither of us, my Babsey", said Beauty in total hysterics, "Fang didn't say anything, and I was pretending that he did and answered you, my Honey! Oh, Fang really has just said "See you later", really, he has".

Donduce looked at Fang, then at his gorgeous Wifey, and then said,

"The Dane and Freckles, my lovey, Immo!".

They walked hand in hand through the kitchen and into the hallway. Donduce picked the keys up off the hook and they went out the front door. It was really getting dark now, and they could see that the security lights had come on in the Main Entrance Road, the lights just visible above the surrounding hedge.

The passenger door opened, Beauty flicked her beautiful hair forward, kissed her Husband and settled in. Donduce shut the door and did his usual walk round the front of the jeep and let himself in. Once he had settled in and reached over and kissed Beauty he asked: "Are you warm enough, my Babsey, or shall I put the heater on?".

"Could you put it on please, my lovey, because then it will be warm when we leave", Beauty replied.

"Of course I will", said Donduce, and flicked the switch as he started the jeep.

"I am sure that our Jeep knows it's own way to the Dane and Freckles now", he laughed, as they drove out and turned left, after having turned the jeep round.

"I am sure it does, bless it", replied Beauty, "Let's just hope that the jeep doesn't get bored and drive itself home and leave us there", laughed Beauty.

"That would be a bad thing would it?" laughed Donduce, and added "Stranded at the Dane and Freckles. How would we cope, my Babsey?".

"Very easily, my lovey", laughed Beauty.

They had just driven over the cattlegrid and were turning left onto AKKS Lane. It was really dark, and the lights of the jeep lit up the lane ahead, and also the bottoms of the trees that lined the lane. Soon they would reach the lamp post marking the start of the town. They did, and in the distance could see the Dane and Freckles sign sticking out up on the left hand side.

"Nearly there my lovey", said Donduce as they approached.

"Awww goody my sweetheart, I can't wait", replied Beauty eagerly.

They pulled into the car park for the second time that day. Donduce and Beauty especially loved going to the Dane and Freckles in the evening as it was quiet and cosy; and tonight would probably be no exception.

"We are here, my lovey", announced Donduce, stating the obvious, but with a very happy tone in his voice.

"We certainly are, my angel", said Beauty; her voice so high pitched with excitement, she almost squeaked what she had said. They kissed passionately and then Donduce got out, shut his door and walked round to Beauty's side; opened her door and Beauty got out and straight into Donduce's arms. He held her tight and she reciprocated: "I love you my darling", he said, looking into her gorgeous, soft and loving brown eyes.

"Likewise, my sweetheart", replied Beauty, and gazed into his soft ocean blue loving and commanding eyes, "Forever and ever", she added.

They both flicked their hair back, an essential practice that was a major aspect of their deep religion. It, and also their natural preferences, forbade them to ever cut their hair or get it dirty in any way. They only let each other even touch their hair and any external interference was strictly forbidden. It wasn't as cold as it had been when they left the pub earlier that day, but there was still a chill in the air as they rounded the corner and went through the entrance door. Down a very small corridor; more like a hallway, and through the bar door. A very pleasant smell of burnt wood, and the warmth of the bar hit them as they walked in; Paul was behind the bar, and as soon as he saw them, he got two glasses out and started to pour their drinks. "Now that's what I call service, my Babsey" whispered

Donduce, and got his wallet out ready as they got to the bar. Because they were in Paul's earshot, Beauty only looked at Donduce and smiled; her acknowledgement that she had heard, understood and agreed with what her Husband had said. She could have 'thought' to him, but sometimes she just felt too close, or was too close to a human; maybe she was being silly? Suddenly, Donduce's voice came into her head on the 'thought' vibe "Stop worrying my Babsey, you are right, sometimes it IS off putting to transmit a thought, due to whatever the situation".

Beauty also didn't like Donduce letting go of her hand when he reached into his pocket for the wallet. Beauty always walked on Donduce's right, and he was always on her left, which meant for that split second, they weren't touching. Again, Donduce's thought vibe came into Beauty's head "I hate that as well. What I will do is move my hand up on the inside of your arm and then reach for our wallet, so that we never, if we can help it, let go, my lovey, and, my Babsey, don't worry, he can't hear us".

"Ok, my angel, God I love you my sweetheart and thanks" thought Beauty to her Husband.

"There you are Duce, Ma'am", said Paul, "Nice to see you tonight", he said as he took the tenner that Donduce had just handed to him.

"Thank you", he said as he headed off to the till.

"How's you and Yvonne, OK?" asked Donduce, he thought to Beauty "I couldn't give a shit really, but one is always polite, eh? My darling".

"Oh yes, my lovey, politeness costs nothing, even if one doesn't give a flying fu..anyway, I quite agree", thought Beauty.

She smiled at Paul, as he returned with their change.

"Yes, fine thank you Duce" replied Paul, "Mustn't grumble, though, you too OK?"

"Yes, thank you, we are", said Donduce, and Beauty smiled at him again.

They walked, hand in hand over to their favourite settee and put their drinks down on the table. Then, they kissed, flicked their hair forward, and sat down. Donduce immediately put his hand in

Beauty's, and they touched glasses. "Bottom's up", they both said, and started slurping.

"Now then my Babsey", said Donduce, putting his glass down. "You know that the power that I showed you at home my lovey?"

"Yes, my darling, with that mist, it was incredible", said Beauty, "What have you got in mind, my Babsey?" she added, looking at her Husband intently and excitedly.

"Well, my lovey" said Donduce quietly, we can have some fun with what I can do, and, in time, you my lovey will be able to do things too".

"Wow, my Babsey, really?" she said, very excitedly. Her eyes were wide open now, and she held onto her husbands hand, very tightly.

"See that glass mat, over there on the bar my Babsey, right at the other end, where you can see the top of the bar. Not this end, because the bar is too high".

Beauty looked over and slightly to the right. Her beautiful head was right against Donduce's neck.

"Oh yes, my Babsey, that blue square one", she said.

"Watch, my Babsey", said Donduce. He put his left hand out and pointed at it. Then he moved his finger as if to tell someone to 'come here'. The mat, moved, all by itself towards them and when it got to the edge of the bar, fell off and dropped to the floor.

"BLOODY hell, Babsey", exclaimed Beauty; she was so surprised and amazed that she almost shouted the 'Bloody' and then, wondering if anyone had seen what had just happened, or heard her, whispered the 'hell, babsey'. "Did anyone see that my lovey?" she asked.

"I don't think so, my lovey, is anyone looking at the glass mat?" asked Donduce.

Beauty looked carefully around the bar. "No my Babsey, they are all just nattering between themselves. There's no one standing by the bar where the mat is either" said Beauty, "You are going to do something else now aren't you, my Lovey?" she added, absolutely enthralled.

"No one is looking, my Babsey?" Donduce asked.

172

"No, my Honey, they Isn't", Beauty replied, captivated, and staring at the innocent little glass mat that was on the floor, or rather carpet.

"Watch that mat, my Lovey", said Donduce, and put his hand out again, pointing at it.

The mat started moving slowly across the carpet until it hit the base of the bar. Beauty put her right hand to her mouth, as, to her utter amazement, the mat flipped up onto its edge and slowly started inching its way up the side. Higher and higher it got; Beauty glanced at her husband's hand, and as the mat moved upwards, so did his hand, with his finger pointing at it. Beauty looked back at the mat and saw it rise to where the lip of the bar stuck over the side by about a quarter of an inch. The mat got under the lip and the top edge literally followed the vertical edge, then under the bit that stuck out and then the edge of the top of the bar until half of the mat was actually higher than the bar surface. When it had risen enough, the top edge flipped back away from them and it was float on the bar top once more. It moved back into the middle, more or less exactly where it had been originally.

"Impressed, my Lovey?" asked Donduce, with an air of obvious understatement (Crumbs, my Babsey, I think you've got your mouth open wide as well, bless you).

"I am totally speechless, my darling", said Beauty, "That was bloody amazing. Can you do that with anything?" she asked.

"Yes, my Lovey, but one has to be careful with the power we both possess, and no one must know it is us", said Donduce.

"The possibilities are endless, and it is a very good way to get someone's attention", he added.

"Babsey, my Lovey", said Beauty suddenly, "We could actually use it on the farm, this magical power, for anything we choose, couldn't we my Lovey?"

"We already do, my sweetheart, to quite a large extent, but I will explain a bit more about that when we are back at home in private, my beautiful Babsey", said Donduce, and he kissed his gorgeous bride on the forehead.

"Wow, my Babsey", sighed Beauty, happily, "That was just amazing my Lovey" she added.

They both had a slurp of their drinks, and fell silent for a minute as they listened to other people chit-chatting about everything and nothing; the weather, someone's relative, the news; something about a poxy prince getting married; the price of cars these days; but at least a nice relaxing happy atmosphere.

The relative peace was abruptly broken by Paul's voice calling from the bar: "Duce, mind if I come over for a second please?"

"Yes, of course, please come", called Donduce in return.

"No, sod off", thought Beauty to Donduce.

"I know it's annoying Babsey my Lovey" thought Donduce to Beauty, "but we are going to have a real laugh now", he thought again.

"O.K.", thought Beauty, "I'm watching and listening, my angel, what are you going to do, my Babsey", she added.

"You'll see, my Lovey, watch" thought Donduce, and then he added, "For God's sake, my Babsey, don't laugh".

Beauty chuckled to herself and held her Husband's hand tightly. Paul, picked up his drink and walked down to the far end of the bar where the access gap was, and walked through, turning back on himself, he then walked towards them.

"Watch this, my Lovey" said Donduce, whispering.

"O.K.", my Babsey", said Beauty, whispering back.

Donduce moved his left hand so it was under the table top.

Suddenly, Paul's right leg shot backwards and he fell, flat on his face, in the middle of the floor carpet, with his arms spread out infront of him, and a now, empty glass, still in his hand.

"Bleeding hell!" shouted Paul, from the carpet.

Beauty just stared at Paul, and tried her hardest to keep as straight a face as humanly possible.

"Please, please, just don't say a word, my Babsey", thought Beauty to her Husband; inside, she was crying with laughter, and her right hand was covering her mouth, to appear shocked, but in reality to cover a very very broad grin.

"Well, my Lovey", thought Donduce to Beauty; "he found and tripped over the rabbit hole".

"Babsey! You are not helping!" thought Beauty, her thoughts were so high pitched she was squeaking again.

"If you think this keeping a straight face is hard, my Lovey" thought Donduce, "We've got to listen to what he wanted yet" he added.

"Oh God, no, my Babsey, help!!" laughed Beauty in her thoughts.

Paul picked himself up, as Donduce and Beauty watched, and said to them, "Bleeding hell, I don't know what happened there. I'm just going to pour another drink and I will return".

"Are you O.K.?" asked Donduce, sounding concerned.

"Yeah, I'll survive", Paul replied, and went back to the bar, rubbing his clothes, where they got wet with his spilled drink.

"That's a shame", thought Beauty.

"Now, now, my sweetheart", thought Donduce, chuckling.

Paul had poured a replacement and was returning again.

"Here we go, my Lovey, grit your teeth" Donduce thought.

"O.K., my Babsey" squeaked Beauty in hers.

Paul pulled out the spare chair without asking if he could sit down, and let out a deep sigh. "Ooohhhh", he said, "Right, where were we? Oh yeah, Sir, Duce, I was going to ask you if you had contacted that guy from the construction company yet?"

Paul appeared to have one of them really annoying penetrating voices, that no matter where you were, in the universe, you could hear him, and so indeed could everybody else.

"Blimey", thought Donduce to Beauty; "Blimey, my Babsey, tell the whole bar area, why don't you, bloody loud mouth. I'll soon put a stop to that my sweetheart".

"I know, my Lovey", thought Beauty back to Donduce, "Yes, my Babsey, do SOMETHING!"

Donduce, who's left hand was now by his side, moved it slowly, but not obviously, slowly across his front, and made out he was rubbing his right shoulder.

Paul, who had just paused, because he was waiting for Donduce to answer, suddenly said:

"I had better keep my voice down, Duce, Sir; we don't want people to hear, now, do we?"

In her mind, Beauty was in total hysterics, she thought to Donduce "Could you make him have a small stroke while you're at it as well please, my Angel?"

175

"Babsey, my Lovey," thought Donduce to Beauty, "Don't tempt me!".

"Of course, yes, this is private" said Donduce "I have rung the gentleman you recommended, and we are meeting him tomorrow, which is a result, so thank you for your kind help in finding him. One question for you; his name; Robert Cunningham, it sounds sort of familiar, have you ever heard of him before?".

"Yes, Sir, I have" replied Paul, taking a slurp from his glass, and then another two in quick succession, his full name is Robert Cunningham Junior, and obviously is the son of Robert Cunningham Senior, in fact I think he might even be the third one with that name. The company has been going for hundreds of years and so are well established and very reliable. They have done a lot of work in this area, and I believe that they have built a lot of this town. I am not sure, but I think they built this pub as well".

Donduce and Beauty had been slurping as Paul had been talking, and they had actually nearly finished.

"Watch this, my angel", thought Donduce to Beauty, "Finish your drink and put the glass down on the table: I will finish mine at the same time, my sweetheart".

"O.K., my angel", said Beauty and did just that. So did Donduce, and as he finished his glass, he put them both together, so that they were touching.

As they touched, Paul immediately said to Donduce, "I'll get them, I insist. Same again, Sir?".

"Oh, thank you very much, Paul", said Donduce, squeezing Beauty's hand "Yes, the company sounds O.K. , so we shall see. The proof will be in the pudding.

"Back in a moment Sir", said Paul, and picking up their empties, he went back to the bar.

"Oh my God, my Babsey, what a totally brilliant evening this is", said Beauty, as Paul was now well out of earshot.

"It's lovely, isn't it, my Babsey", he replied and kissed her lovingly on her forehead, "So relaxing".

"Oh my God!" exclaimed Beauty suddenly, "Them two pigeons, my Lovey. We didn't see them when we went back to the farmhouse, did we Babsey, my Lovey?".

"No we didn't, my sweetheart", said Donduce. "Don't worry though, my angel, they will arrive at the farmhouse when they are ready. They are probably there now, but making a new nest somewhere on the Estate. They had to go back to tell Mrs. Pigeon that they were all moving, and I can't remember if the pigeon said whether or not she was keen on moving in the first place, my Lovey".

"Oh blimey, my Babsey, said Beauty, "We have inadvertently started a 'pigeon domestic'". As Beauty said that, she glanced up at the window, half expecting them to be there, but they weren't, as it was pitch black outside. Beauty said this to Donduce.

"Well, my Babsey", he said, "Even though it is dark outside, we would have heard them tapping. They are probably moving as we speak; they are no doubt roosting by now; it is getting late".

As Donduce finished talking, Paul came back with their drinks, which he placed on the table.

"Good health to you both", he said; "Better get on though. Let me know how things turn out, Sir".

"Yes I will", said Donduce, "Thanks again for the drinks, see you later".

"Watch again, my Babsey", whispered Donduce to Beauty.

"O.K., my Honey", she whispered back, smiling.

Paul had got halfway back to the bar. He headed towards the access gap, and when he turned, his leg seemed to pull backwards and he fell, straight through the access gap, flat on his face again, behind the bar; a muffled but clearly heard yelp was heard when he landed.

Donduce and Beauty just could not look at each other for fear of erupting into total hysterics, and Donduce thought to Beauty, "That rabbit gets everywhere, ;my Babsey, don't it my Lovey?".

Beauty just couldn't think back to her husband. He looked at her; her hand was covering her beautiful little face and her whole body was shaking with silent hysterics. What made matters even worse, was the very loud "BLEEDING HELL, my bloody leg, what in god's name is the matter with the sodding thing?" voice that came somewhere from behind the bar.

Donduce and Beauty just stared as Paul got up, but because the bar was obscuring their view, it looked for all the world as if he had just ascended from the basement in an invisible lift. A customer then got up, and went over to the bar, with a couple of empty glasses.

"Same again?" asked Paul, as he finished dusting himself down.

"Yes please", said the customer. "You O.K.? That leg of yours. Having problems with it? Old war wound?" he asked.

"Old war wound?" exclaimed Paul, loudly and indignantly, "Old bleeding war wound? I'm only bleeding 40".

The customer couldn't help but laugh; he said "I didn't mean the 1st or 2nd ", he chuckled, "There is always a conflict going on somewhere", he said.

"Well, mate", said Paul, "I Isn't been in no bleeding conflict, O.K., apart from the conflict I may have with the bleeding doctor if he don't sort my bleeding leg out".

"He could sort out your bleeding brain while he's at it", thought Donduce to Beauty.

Poor Beauty had only just about recovered from what she had seen, and was still in complete hysterics.

"Oh my God", thought Beauty to Donduce. "I have had tears all evening; I wont forget tonight for a very long time, if not ever".

Donduce pointed at the floor with his left hand again, and a muffled but clearly audible crashing noise could be heard, coming from the basement. Several of the customers in the bar looked up from their conversations, to see if anyone else had heard it, and if so, ask what it was.

"What was that noise my Babsey?" whispered Beauty in her husband's right ear.

"Me, causing all the barrels down in the cellar to fall over, my darling", Donduce whispered back in Beauty's left ear.

"Oh, O.K., my Lovey", said Beauty, giggling, then added "Nothing to worry about then, my Babsey?"

"No, nothing to worry about, my sweetheart", whispered Donduce.

"What was that crashing noise, Paul?" asked one of the customers, standing by the bar.

"All the barrels in the cellar falling over", replied Paul. "I'll go and sort it out in a minute", he added. He also had an expression on his face that read "I really couldn't give a shit, either".

"Babsey my Lovey", asked Beauty suddenly, "What happens now if WE want another drink, my sweetheart?"

"Then we will have one my Lovey. I didn't make OUR barrels fall over; just everyone else's", replied her gorgeous husband.

"Well, how jolly considerate of you that was, my beautiful Babsey", laughed Beauty.

"I know, my Lovey, how can you ever thank me enough?" laughed Donduce.

"I can't, my Babsey; I love you my darling" she said.

"I love you too, with all of my heart and soul", replied Donduce, and they kissed passionately.

"Do you still want to go somewhere else after this, my Babsey?" asked Donduce, as he took another slurp of his drink. "Bearing in mind the time, and we want to be back for ELKY, don't forget, my sweetheart", he added, looking at his watch. "It's 10:30pm now, so maybe go after this one my darling?" Donduce suggested, they kissed passionately, and then Beauty added softly, "Or the next one, my Lovey?"

"Whatever you would like, my Babsey", whispered Donduce in her ear, "We have all the time in the world, my Babsey", he added, and they kissed passionately.

The bar returned to normality and the low hum of conversation resumed. Paul had returned to the bar after restoring the basement cellar to normal, but every so ofter he looked down and shook his right leg. All the tables were against the walls and there was actually nothing in the middle of the room which was just as well really, as Paul would have gone headlong into one of the tables.

Donduce took another couple of slurps from his drink "My gorgeous Babsey", he said, "When we get back home, I am going to show you something quite amazing, which you will learn as well. It is all to do with our meeting with Robert Cunningham tomorrow, my Lovey".

"Oh, O.K., my sweetheart", Beauty replied looking curious. "I know we are going to talk about the palace Honey, what did you have in mind, and what on Earth will you be able to teach me?" Beauty asked.

"All will be revealed at home, my Lovey", said Donduce firmly.

They finished slurping, and Donduce kissed Beauty on the forehead.

"Another, or head off, my angel?" he asked.

"Actually", said Beauty, "My Babsey, I am getting quite peckish now, can we…", Beauty's voice trailed away, as she looked lovingly at her husband, knowing he knew what she was about to say.

"Of course we can my Babsey" he said, smiling.

They got up, and Donduce picked up the coats which he had put next to him on his left, since Paul had been sitting on the spare one. He helped Beauty put hers on, and she flicked her hair back. Donduce made absolutely sure it was beautiful and exactly how they both wanted it. Then, Donduce did the same with his coat, Beauty did his hair, and they both made sure that his beard was neat too. Donduce's beard was really long too, nearly down to his waistline. Then, all done, they kissed passionately, then Donduce picked up the empty glasses, and hand in hand, put them on the bar. Paul looked over and said "Night Duce, Ma'am, thank you, back tomorrow?"

"Maybe, Paul; busy day, see you" said Donduce, Beauty smiled. "Seeing 'What not' tomorrow, aren't you, good luck, Sir" said Paul, in his usual, diplomatic, way.

"Of course", said Donduce, "Bye".

"Pillock", though Beauty to Donduce, "I wonder if that Dick-head is related to Mac-Stupid, my Babsey".

"Probably, my angel" thought Donduce to Beauty, and then added "However Dick head is less stupid than Mac Stupid is stupid, although Paul IS stupid.

"Yes, darling, come on darling, let's go Darling", said Beauty.

"O.K., my darling" said Donduce, and hand in hand they went to the door, Donduce opened it for Beauty, and they walked out into the cold night air.

The night definitely wasn't as cold as the late afternoon had been, but Beauty still wrapped herself tightly around her husband for extra love. He put his right arm around Beauty's shoulders, and her head nestled into Donduce's neck once more. They walked past the car park and turned left, then up the road. Beauty and Donduce's breath came out in little clouds of water vapour as they walked, and then Beauty said "Oh, brilliant, I can see it; the KFC; oh Babsey, Goody!".

Donduce and Beauty crossed over the road near the top and Donduce opened the door of the KFC for his gorgeous Wifey.

In they went. It was about half full and this time, there weren't no seats at the windows. "Sodd it!" thought Donduce to Beauty. "We will have to sit by the wall, Sorry my Babsey, what a bummer". Beauty looked lovingly at her gorgeous Husband and thought to him,

"It's no problem, my angel, we'll get a take away instead, after all, we have got to sort ELKY out later, my Babsey".

"O.K., sweetheart", said Donduce as they walked up to the counter.

"Good evening Sir, said a man who was serving, but dressed from head to foot as a chicken. "Ma'am", as the chicken nodded in her direction. "What can I get you?" it said. The chicken paused and looked at them expectantly.

Chapter 8

That was it. After the days events, neither Donduce or Beauty could control themselves any longer and both burst into hysterics. (I am too Babsey, how about you, my Lovey?!"). When they had composed themselves, the chicken said, "What is so funny? Haven't you ever seen a chicken before?".

"Erm yes, of course", said Donduce, holding Beauty's hand very tightly. "Erm, please could we have two portions of, erm, chicken portions, two portions of chips, two corn on the cobs and two drinks to take away, please".

"Certainly", said the chicken, and entered their order onto a computer screen, wearing yellow gloves. "That will be £15 exactly", said the chicken. Donduce reached for his wallet, using the new method, so that Beauty still remained with her hand under his arm and paid the chicken. Beauty smiled and thought to Donduce "I love you my Babsey, it could only happen to us".

"Using the power, my Babsey, I could always make that chicken fly", replied Donduce in his thought "Shall I, my angel?"

"No, my Lovey", thought Beauty "It will be too obvious!!"

"O.K., my Babsey" thought Donduce.

The chicken got some boxes ready, selected the portions, and picked two delicious looking cobs from the heated storage area. Then got two big boxes, and filled them both with chips. The whole lot then went into a big carrier bag.

"Have you noticed something, my Babsey", thought Beauty to Donduce,

"That chicken, my Babsey, It's got a name badge on it: Esmerelda!"

"Oh my God!" thought Beauty to Donduce, "A male chicken called 'Esmerelda', and he has, sorry 'it' has named itself or has the same name as our hen".

"To be fair" thought Donduce to Beauty, "I can't think of a name for a male chicken, and anyway, what am I talking about? All bloody chickens are male!" my Lovey".

The chicken handed the big carrier bag to Donduce, and said "Enjoy your meal, Sir, and please come again".

"Thank you, Mr. Chicken", said Donduce, "We will", then Donduce added, "Is this some sort of promotion, you being dressed like that" he asked.

"No, Sir, it's company policy" said Esmerelda.

Donduce and Beauty tried hard not to laugh. Donduce said:

"Even the name badge?"

Esmerelda looked at him, well, two eyes and a beak looked at him and said "Yes, even the name badge; 'Henrietta' is out the back".

Beauty's eyes opened wide: "They've stolen the name of our other hen, my Babsey", she thought to Donduce, "That's one hell of a coincidence my Babsey".

"I know, my Lovey" thought Donduce, and added, "Esmerelda will announce that the manager's name is 'Bleeding Doo' next, my darling, shall I ask?"

"Go on my angel, yes, just for fun" thought Beauty, smiling.

"Before we go, may I ask you what the manager's name is?" asked Donduce, and they both waited for the response.

"I am the manager", said Esmerelda, cheerfully.

"So what's your real name then?" asked Donduce.

"'Esmerelda', is what I have to be called; its company policy", said Esmerelda.

"O.K. then", said Donduce, and with that, they said their goodbyes and Donduce held the door open for Beauty as they went out into the night air.

"What a day, my Babsey", said Donduce, chuckling to himself, "That poor chap has got to spend his entire shift dressed like that, my darling", he said as they walked along the pavement towards the junction, heading back to the Dane and Freckles car park.

"I know, my Lovey", said Beauty. "There is no way in a million years that I would do that, my angel" She added firmly.

"There's no way I would let you, my Babsey", said Donduce, even more firmly, "No".

They rounded the corner, after crossing the road, and were relieved to see the car park appear on the right hand side. Beauty had wrapped herself around Donduce, and he had his arm in its usual place, around her upper body. As they got nearer the jeep, he moved his arm so that he could get the car remote up, and as he did, Beauty adjusted her collar so that the flaps on her fur lined coat went up even further to cover her ears.

"Brrr, my darling", she said, "When we got round that corner it turned really freezing, my Lovey. It's that poxy wind".

"I know, my Honey", said Donduce, "Don't worry, we will soon warm up when we get into the jeep" he added.

Pressing the button, there was a click as the jeep unlocked itself, and there was already a slight frost on the roof. Donduce opened the door, and Beauty flicked her hair forward, kissed her husband and got in., "Would you like me to take the bag, my Lovey while you get in my Babsey", she asked.l

"Oh, O.K. my Babsey, thanks darling", he replied, and then Beauty added "I have got to hold it anyway, my sweetheart, whilst you are driving".

"Oh yeah, my Babsey" said Donduce, with a giggle, "I hadn't even thought about that one: what it is to have a brain", he added, as he handed the bag to Beauty, and kissed her passionately at the same time. "I love you my gorgeous princess" he said, as he was about to close the door. "Likewise, my gorgeous prince" replied Beauty with a loving, caring smile.

Donduce shut the door and walked around to his side, where he also flicked his hair forward, opened the door and got in, kissing Beauty passionately before he started the jeep. The heater sprang into action, and a lovely draught of warm air started circulating around their feet; even though Beauty had boots on; she could feel them warming up.

"Aaahhh", they both said together, "That's better".

They drove out of the car park, after Donduce had turned the jeep round, and turned right.

"I bet that take away is stone cold now, my Babsey", said Donduce. Beauty leant forward and put her head in the bag. Her right hand had been in its usual place on Donduce's knee, but had to move it to stop the bag from tipping over. She felt the boxes. "They are sort of luke warm, my darling" she said. "It's O.K. though, I can put the whole lot in the microwave oven when we get in, my Lovey".

"No need, my angel", said Donduce with a smile, "I'll warm them up, my Babsey, remember?"

"Blimey, my darling, can you do that as well?" exclaimed Beauty, and added "Heat things up, I mean, my Babsey?"

"Yes, my Babsey, and cool things down. I'll show you when we get in", Donduce replied with a smile.

They were about half way round AKKS Lane now, and the frost was already beginning to form on the road. You could see it in the lights of the jeep; a sparkly glistening thin white film covering the lane. It was made from tarmac, but quite worn, and there didn't seem to be a definite join between the lane and the grassy verges that lined the lane either side. There were a lot of leaves as well that had blown down on both sides, despite the trees only being on the farm side: the other side had the hedge that surrounded the big field between the town and the farm Estate.

"Here we are, my Babsey, home at last", said Donduce as he signalled right and they turned onto the Main Entrance Road and under the big wooden 'EE-I-O' farm sign.

"Ooohhh, hot KFC in a minute, my angel", said Beauty licking her lips and smiling at her husband, "I am looking forward to this", she added happily.

Over the cattle grid they went and very soon were turning right into their front driveway.

"Do you know what, my angel?" said Donduce, "Apart from the fact that I love you so much, after all these years that we have lived here, I keep forgetting that our front drive way is the second right into the gap in our tall hedge that surrounds the front. The first gap being the track that leads to our back gate to the yard, my angel. Isn't it strange, don't you think my sweetheart?"

"I guess so, my gorgeous Hubby", replied Beauty. "When we have built the palace, we could always totally re-arrange the layout here, couldn't we, as well, my Lovey", she added.

"I hadn't actually thought of that, my darling, but yes we could, we would have to live in the palace whilst we carried out any alterations, if that was O.K. with you though, my sweetheart", said Donduce.

"Of course it would be O.K., my Babsey", she said, "I will leave all of that in your more than capable hands, my darling".

"O.K., my Babsey" replied Donduce. "Let's see what transpires, my Lovey, but, in the meantime, let's put the jeep away and get in the warm. We have ELKY to deal with yet, my Honey".

"Oh shit, yes my darling, we have and I love you" said Beauty.

"I love you too, my angel", said Donduce, and pressed the remote on the dashboard. They had just pulled in and the garage door started rolling up. Donduce manouevered the jeep so that they were pointing towards the front door, and then when the garage door was completely open, he reversed in and then switched the engine off very quickly as it made a hell of a din when it echoed around the garage walls. Once parked, Donduce and Beauty kissed passionately and said "I love you", to each other; then Donduce opened his side. Out he got and flicked his hair back. He shut the door, and the thud it made when he closed it echoed around the garage walls as well, but it wasn't loud and the air, out in the front drive was still.

Donduce walked round to Beauty's side and opened her door: she passed the carrier bag to her husband and then got out herself, flicking her beautiful hair back, so it cascaded down and now reached the backs of her knees. As she tilted her head to do her hair, Beauty's earrings made a chinking noise as they were shook. Beauty had the same number of earrings as her husband, which was essential: Eleven in her right ear and ten in her left, ten being a lucky number they both shared, and eleven, consisting of two ones: a symbol of their unity.

Beauty checked Donduce's hair as well, it was long and straight, reaching down to just below his bum. (I had to get that in, my angel, sorry!) Then, when they was both ready, hand in hand, they walked across the front driveway, opened the front door, and went in. Once inside, Donduce locked and bolted the front door, and pressed a button on a panel similar to the one by the back door, and this one also activated the security alarm system. It could be isolated as well, and as they were going to be going out the back later, Donduce set it for the front only. He would do the back when they departed.

"My Babsey", said Donduce, when everything was set, "We have got torches in the kitchen, Isn't we? I just suddenly thought that I didn't get any out of the garage and I just suddenly thought that I didn't get any out of the garage and I have just locked it all up! Help!"

"Don't worry, my angel", replied Beauty, in her gorgeous reassuring voice, we've got more than enough in the kitchen to support our pending expedition" she chuckled.

"Blimey my Lovey", exclaimed Donduce with a giggle, "We are going with ELKY up a farm track, and a little one at that, we Isn't going to conquer Mount Everest, well not tonight, anyway, and besides, Mount Everest has already been conquered", he laughed.

"Not unless we re-conquer it my Lovey" giggled Beauty.

Donduce hung the keys up on the hook, and then, putting the carrier bag down on the hall table for a minute took Beauty's coat off for her; then his own, and hung them both up in the cupboard, which was between the front door and the lounge.

Donduce picked up the carrier bag, they kissed passionately and hand in hand, walked through to the kitchen where Donduce put the bag down on the breakfast bar.

The back door was still open, and Fang was lying just to the left.

"My God, my Babsey", exclaimed Donduce, "Let's get Fang in now and shut the bleeding back door, it's freezing in here"

"Yes it is my Babsey", said Beauty, "We'll leave it shut next time, it's just that Fang wanted to stay out, didn't he, my Babsey" said Beauty.

"I'll give Fang a flaming key to the back door at this rate, my angel", laughed Donduce, "We Isn't leaving that door open anymore in this weather; God, it's cold" he added.

"Are you O.K., Fang", they both called together as they stood by the open back door, "We are back", added Beauty.

Fang got up and wagged his tail.

"Yes, hello, my Queen and King", said Fang. "I'm O.K., but ELKY is rather nervous about tonight", he said, and then added, "Is it O.K. to come in now please?".

Beauty relayed what he had said to Donduce, who said "Of course it is, and we had better go and see ELKY, my lovey, and tell him we will go on this trip when we have eaten".

Fang eagerly disappeared into the kitchen, while Donduce shut the back door from the outside. He and Beauty then walked across the backyard, past the coal bunker, and saw ELKY standing, waiting for them.

"Blimey, my Babsey", said Donduce, "ELKY looks well stressed. Even I can tell that".

"I know my darling" replied Beauty, as they walked up to him and stroked his nose, "What's the matter, ELKY", she asked.

ELKY nuzzled her arm, "If only you knew", thought ELKY "I just hope that..." his thought pattern abruptly stopped, as Donduce spoke, "It's O.K. ELKY", he said, also rubbing ELKY's nose, "We are just going to have a bite to eat indoors, and then we are coming out to come with you. We know that you want to take us down that pathway; it's O.K., really".

ELKY was relieved: he was or had been worried that it was getting too late in the evening, and this HAD to be sorted out. He could wait just a bit longer. He nuzzled Donduce's arm to acknowledge what he had said. Then he turned and went back to his favourite bush; he needed a snack and little did Donduce and Beauty know, but they were in for a long night.

"I think ELKY understood that we were going with him, my darling, don't you think, my angel?" asked Beauty, as they walked back hand in hand towards the back door. "He nuzzled your arm didn't he, when you said that we were going in for a bite to eat first, before joining him, my Babsey", Beauty added, partly to reassure herself as well.

"Yes, I think he did know, my Lovey, and he sort of looked a bit happier when he returned to his bush", replied Donduce, and then he added: "Why don't we put some of our takeaway into a bag, and bring it with us, my Babsey. I can always warm it up again".

"My darling, that would mean we would warm it up twice; No, my Babsey, only the once then we'll have it cold if there is any left", said Beauty firmly.

"Oohh my darling, O.K.", said Donduce, and then with a giggle added "I do love it when you get all forceful my angel".

Laughing, they opened the back door and went into the kitchen. Beauty went over to a cupboard and got some plates out. Everything was dished up and they sat down at the breakfast bar.

"This should do the trick my angel", said Donduce, and passed his hand over Beauty's plate and then his own. Within seconds, both plates had steam coming off them, piping hot. "Brilliant", exclaimed Beauty, "Babsey, that is fantastic" she added, and after a short pause whilst they put butter on the cobs, they started munching.

"That thing I was going to show you, my Babsey, to do with tomorrows meeting, I might have to leave it until the morning, if that's O.K. It's just that we need to sort ELKY out first", said Donduce, as he munched on a chicken leg.

"O.K., my darling, whatever you say, and this chicken is gorgeous Isn't it?".

"Delicious my angel, just like you sweetheart", replied Donduce, "I was bloody starving", he added.

They were putting their discarded bones on a plate for Fang to munch on, and Fang was getting more and more excited as the pile of bones grew.

Beauty sensed what Fang was thinking, and said to him:

"You will have a feast while we are out, eh Fang?"

"Too bloody right my Queen and King", he said, "It smells fabulous".

"It will certainly keep him quiet my Honey", chuckled Donduce.

They finished eating and were slurping their drinks: Beauty suddenly looked at hers and said "Babsey, is it wise to drink all this? I am just concerned that we might need the loo on the trip".

"We will be O.K. my lovey", said Donduce reassuringly, "It's our land and it's dark; we will find a convenient bush somewhere".

"Me?! The Queen! Behind a bush! In the dark! Babsey! No, No, No, No, NO!" exclaimed Beauty, shrieking with laughter.

"It's O.K., my lovey", said Donduce, even more reassuringly, "I wont look".

"No, darling, I don't mind if you did, but ELKY might!" said Beauty.

"Well, I will tell him not to my Babsey", said Donduce "Now, then, come on, we've got to get ready my Babsey".

"O.K., my Babsey, and I love you sweetheart" said Beauty. They both got up, held hands and kissed passionately. "I love you too my lovely", said Donduce, and then he put Fangs plate of bones down on the floor for him. Instantly, there was a noise of crunching bones, as the Fang waste disposal machine sprang into action.

They got the torches and flashlights out of one of the kitchen cupboards near the sink, and funnily enough, next to the cupboard where they had experienced the skunk problem. The flashlights and torches were put into a rucksack which they kept in the bedroom, and then they went to the cupboard in the hallway and got their coats out. Donduce helped (29/04/13 Oh My God) Beauty on with hers, and then she flicked her hair forward: Donduce make absolutely sure it was perfect; right down over her eyes as she loved it and it had to be, and cascading to it's beautiful length just below her knees. Then, in turn, Beauty did Donduce's hair after he had donned his jacket; he flicked his own hair forward, so that it was the same way as Beauty's falling down to just below his bum. This small ceremony was essential for their deeply religious beliefs and also their deep views. Once done, Donduce put the rucksack on, and kissed Beauty on the forehead. "We're ready", he said "Let's go my angel". "O.K., my gorgeous husband, I love you", replied Beauty, and picking up the mobile phone, just in case, plus their keys, said "See you later Fang", to Fang, rubbing his head. "See you, and good luck, my King and Queen, regards to ELKY", thought Fang to Beauty, who relayed it to Donduce, who said "Thanks Fang, back later". They let themselves out of the back door and locked it behind them.

"Here we go my angel", said Donduce as he held Beauty's hand walking across the backyard towards the meadow. "What are you expecting my Lovey?" he asked.

"I have not the faintest idea my Babsey", replied Beauty, "But I'll tell you what, I wish we were going back to the Dane and Freckles! What do YOU think is going to happen, my Lovey?" she asked.

"Well my sweetheart, one thing is for sure; it Isn't going to be a cave!" chuckled her husband.

ELKY heard them coming and was standing waiting for them. He started walking towards them, and Donduce said to Beauty "Babsey, he looks happier, but almost serious".

"I know, my Babsey", replied Beauty, and added "The thing is, to him, this is serious".

ELKY thought to himself after listening to Donduce and Beauty talking as they approached "This is also serious to you as well, not just me, in fact, it could affect, potentially the whole Estate".

Donduce and Suzi Beauty (Whoops – sorry Babsey, exciting, isn't it? Your head is nodding vigorously, and your thinking "I love you Babsey, but please sod off, I'm reading (only kidding)) reached ELKY and they both stroked him on the nose.

"We are here now ELKY, so don't worry about a thing, we are with you all the way", said Donduce, offering ELKY some comfort. "Anything you need, you can have", added Beauty: "We are here for you always", and she stroked his nose again. ELKY looked at Beauty and licked her hand and arm. Then he did the same with Donduce. ELKY then turned, and sniffed the air, for a moment.

"Keep very still my Babsey" said Donduce, "Wait until HE gives the word" he added.

"O.K. my lovey", said Beauty, holding onto her husband's hand for grim death.

ELKY stopped sniffing the air, turned his head, and looked directly at them. "We're off my lovey", said Donduce and added "Don't worry, my Babsey, I am right beside you.

They started to walk forward, and as soon as ELKY saw them do this, he turned his head back again and started walking. Donduce and Beauty followed behind at a small distance of about an ELK and a half. Soon (stop giggling) ELKY had crossed the meadow, and with a final glance back to make sure that Donduce and Beauty were still following, he started down the pathway. They reached it, and, with a quick glance behind from Donduce, who almost expected a 20ft carnivorous hungry bear to be following THEM, they too started down the pathway. It was overgrown, and they kept brushing past branches that stuck out from the hedgerows and over the old pathway. It wasn't so much a proper pathway as in made of Tarmac, but more like a track that had been worn into the ground after many years of usage. It was a clear night which was handy and moonlight gave some illumination in the darkness. Donduce had turned on a flashlight, and the beam from it bounced and swayed from side to side as they walked.

"Any idea where we are actually going or where we are my angel?" asked Beauty; her voice interrupted the dull thudding of ELKY's hooves.

"No idea where we are going, sweetheart, but we must be nearing the big field that is going to house the palace, I am sure", replied Donduce. "The trouble is, my Lovey, that the trees either side of this old pathway are so thick, that you can't see any further than up ahead, and even that is difficult when you have a bloody great ELK right in your field of vision" he added. Beauty absolutely howled with laughter; "Oh my God, my Lovey, don't please start me off! It's just the way you said it my Angel; oh dear". Beauty recovered herself and resumed her grip of Donduce's hand.

ELKY, a little further ahead suddenly turned right. Surprised by this change of direction, Donduce and Beauty approached with caution, got to where ELKY had turned, and discovered that the whole pathway turned right. "Oh", they both exclaimed, and carried on. ELKY plodded on, but he was walking at just below walking speed, a sort of fast stroll.

"I'll bet we have reached the big field, my Lovey, and are walking all the way round it, my Lovey" said Donduce., "If that is the case, then the pathway should turn left, eventually", he added.

"That is, my sweetheart, if we go that far, which I hope we don't, because I am getting bored, tired, I want a drink, I want to go to the Dane and Freckles, I want another KFC, and I also want to snuggle up to my beautiful husband in bed", said Beauty. "Immo!".

"I want all them things too, my Babsey, and we can certainly fulfil your last request, my Lovey, but unfortunately not yet" said Donduce.

After what seemed like ages, up ahead, ELKY DID turn left.

They saw him do it and Donduce groaned, "Oh shit, we are walking round that massive field. This is going to take hours; my Lovey".

"Awwww, shit my Lovey" whimpered Beauty and wrapped herself completely around her husband, placing her head against his neck, and pulling his beard down over her face. Donduce put his arm around the upper part of her body and held her close. They carried on walking and so did ELKY.

The left turn came, they turned left and saw ELKY. He had stopped, and was looking round. Donduce and Beauty were just about to let out whoops of delight that they had arrived, when ELKY looked at them, to make sure they had caught up, and carried on walking.

"AWWWWWWWW NOOOOOOOOO!!" groaned Donduce and Beauty together, but ELKY thought to himself, "We are there, just another...few...yards".

He plodded on for about one minute and then did stop. He looked around again and waited.

"He is just waiting for us, my Lovey", said Donduce as he and Beauty caught up with him.

"We must be nearly..." started Beauty.

"Sorry Babsey, my Lovey, wait a minute" exclaimed Donduce. He shone the torch towards the hedge like trees, "There's a sort of meadow, to the right, look!".

As Beauty looked, ELKY walked into the clearing between the trees on the right hand side of the track and into the meadow.

"Wow, my Babsey", said Beauty, you can see it in the moonlight. A bit dim though.

They walked into the clearing and stopped.

"What's ELKY doing, my Lovey", asked Beauty, "He seems to be nudging at something on the ground. He's stopped nudging and looked at Donduce and Beauty.

"Well, whatever it is, we have arrived, my Babsey" said Donduce, and he shone the torch at whatever it was that ELKY was nudging.

"OH MY GOD!" shrieked Beauty, "It's another ELK!!" she stopped, totally amazed.

"Bloody hell, my Babsey", exclaimed Donduce, and just stared transfixed.

The ELK had been lying down in the tallish grass, and now stood nose to nose with ELKY. They rubbed noses, and their heads nuzzled each other, as if they had met before.

"My God, my Babsey", exclaimed Beauty, clutching onto her husband, "That ELK is much thinner and doesn't have any horns; which can only mean that it is Mrs. ELKY".

"O.K., my Babsey, I can understand that, but what on Earth is she doing out here? Why didn't she come with ELKY to the farmhouse in the first place I wonder. No wonder ELKY wanted us to come with him; my angel, and it's no wonder that you dreamt that he had disappeared, but only at night. He was missing her desperately, but at the same time didn't want to upset us by making us think he had gone".

"Wait a minute, my lovely darling", said Beauty, ELKS like living in our meadows, but ELKY's meadow is not near a swamp or even a lake my Babsey. You see, ELKY loves the little roots and aquatic plants that grow there, and also likes a bit of a swim too. ELKY's favourite bush, I have noticed is willow, and there are poplar trees as will which ELKY likes, however, the nearest pond for him is on the other side of the Main Entrance Road, next to the sacred barn, which he cant get near to my Babsey. So I am wondering if this meadow has a pond which Mrs. ELKY prefers, which is why she is here? What do you think my angel?".

"Bloody hell", exclaimed Donduce for the second time, "Babsey, my Lovey, you know everything there is to know about every creature on the planet; you are a very talented and clever Lady, my Beauty, and I love you with all of my heart and soul".

They kissed passionately, and then Donduce said "O.K. my Babsey, let's see if there is a pond somewhere in this meadow. It isn't that big; I can see a line of trees which marks the end, even in this moonlight. Let's take a look".

They started walking forward, but stopped abruptly. ELKY and his wifey stopped nuzzling immediately and the female ELK moved so that she was standing directly in front of them, but about 40 yards back. ELKY was to her right.

"What's all that about my Babsey?" asked Donduce, looking puzzled.

"I really don't know", replied Beauty, a puzzled expression spreading across her beautiful little face. "Why don't we inch forward, very slowly, in front of her, and see what happens, my angel. If she doesn't let us pass, obviously it means that we are encroaching on her territory" added Beauty.

"Good idea, my sweetheart", replied Donduce, but then added, "I thought that protection was the males domain. If either of them were going to be protective, it would be ELKY, but then again, maybe not because he knows us and she doesn't yet. ELKY did talk to her when we all arrived, so surely he told her we were friends or even his new peers, what do you think, my poppet?".

"One way to find out my Babsey", said Donduce, with a smile.

"Oh God", said Beauty, "You aren't going to use our magic power and lift her out of the way are you my Lovey?" asked Beauty with a chuckle.

"Noooooo, my Lovey" laughed Donduce, "although that isn't a bad idea. No Honey, I am simply going to try and ask ELKY, if, that is, he is disturbable".

"O.K., my Babsey" replied Beauty, relaxing somewhat, "Good luck sweetheart".

With his right arm wrapped around Beauty, Donduce slapped his left arm against his thigh a couple of times and called, "ELKY, ELKY, here, a minute, yeah??".

To his surprise, ELKY turned, and started plodding towards Donduce and Beauty; as he went; in the moonlight, Mrs. ELKY was watching him intently, absolutely transfixed on her husband. ELKY arrived, and after having licked Beauty's face, and then, unfortunately, her hair he nuzzled Donduce's arm.

"Hello", said Donduce, stroking ELKY's nose, "Thanks for showing Beauty and I your secret meadow, and your lovely wife: she is terrific and a lovely surprise for us. We wanted to have a look around the meadow to see if there was a swamp or water supply near which we know you like, but your Mrs.l ELK doesn't seem to want us to come any further. Is there a reason? Please tell us, you know that there is no danger from us, and I hope you have told that to Mrs. ELKY?.

Beauty nodded in agreement and also stroked his nose "Yes, ELKY, that's right, and you are both welcome back to your meadow, you do know that don't you?" She said comfortingly, and she knew that the last bit about coming back, sounded like a plea. It was meant to. She knew that ELKY could decide to stay with his wife.

ELKY had turned to look at Beauty as she spoke; when she had finished, he turned back and looked at Donduce. Desperately, ELKY was trying to think how he was going to tell Donduce and Beauty, and decided, finally on a way. "Here we go", he thought; "This is going to take a while".

"You O.K., ELKY", asked Donduce, as he took a couple of paces back. ELKY turned his head, he looked as if he was sniffing the air. As Donduce and Beauty stared, Mrs. ELKY seemed to acknowledge this, and sniffed the air too. Then, she turned, and started to plod away.

"Oh my God no, she's leaving!" cried Donduce and Beauty together, then Donduce exclaimed "Babsey, wait, she's stopped, she only plodded about 20 feet. Look, she's doing something with her hoof".

"What do you think she's doing, my Babsey?" asked Beauty, staring at Mrs. ELKY.

"Search me, my angel" replied Donduce "It looks like she has got something stuck in her hoof, Babsey".

Abruptly she stopped, and, as Donduce and Beauty stared, two more ELKS stood up, out of the longish grass.

"Holy" exclaimed Donduce, "Shit, my Babsey", finished Beauty.

The other two ELKS, shook themselves, and plodded forward, up to Mrs. ELKY; they were much smaller than her, about two thirds the size, and they both had antlers, all be it, little ones.

"Well, my Lovey" said Donduce, holding Beauty even closer to him, "It looks as if we have now met the entire family".

"We certainly have, my Honey" Beauty replied, "And what a lovely surprise", she added.

"That's just it, my sweetheart", said Donduce, thoughtfully. Then he added, "My Babsey, I think there is far more to this than we know. For a start, ELKY turning up out of the blue on the Royal Estate, the passageway, the cave and now this, oh yes my lovey, and him befriending Fang; I know they are good friends now, bless them, but I was also thinking about how ELKY told us about the reappearance of the gorilla; that was him HINTING to me, whereas the other animals TALK to you. Nothing wrong with any of that so far, and I think it is because ELKS are such solitary animals, they just find it very hard to talk to anyone else apart from themselves. Even after he assured Mrs. ELKY that we were friends, she was very defensive over her family, my angel. What do you think my Babsey?".

Beauty was listening intently to her husband. "I agree with you completely", she said, and then went on "All this time, ELKY has been using to get to know us and gain our trust, and equally, us with him. Now, he has enough trust in us to introduce us to the rest of his family, and I can say, in front of ELKY and knowing that I have your full support, that we will and are inviting ELKY together with his family to live permanently in ELKY's meadow; we will even create a big new swamp, so they will really feel at home; that is on the obvious main condition that you agree and approve it, my Babsey; it is O.K., isn't it my Darling?" Beauty looked up at her husband for support.

"Of course it is O.K., my Babsey", replied Donduce, "In fact I insist on it. There is one thing though, my Babsey, that you have just said, which has been puzzling me for ages, and maybe ELKY…" Donduce reached over and rubbed his nose, may be able to explain", he said.

"Go on, my Babsey, I'm all ears…and antlers, if I had them", said Beauty.

"Well, it's what you said a moment ago, my sweetheart. You said that we would let them all live permanently in ELKS meadow and build or rather dig a new swamp, so that they will really feel at home. (01/05/13) That's just it! Where IS ELKY's home really; it must be hundreds if not thousands of miles away, and why have they come all this way, straight to the King and Queen? ELKY does not live on the wildlife reserve beyond the mountains. He prefers colder climates to that, where snowfall is quite regular. The plains and lakes way way beyond the mountains is more like ELKY's home territory and they must have taken several months to get here and also to survive that sort of a journey. My Babsey, do you mind if I ask ELKY?" asked Donduce, giving Beauty a kiss on her forehead.

"Of course not, my gorgeous Babsey", replied Beauty, "I hadn't actually thought of that, but yes, it is very curious, and I want to know too!" (Your nodding your head vigorously aren't you my Babsey; you are dying to know as well – your giggling…) she added.

The moonlight had now faded and it was a lot darker in the meadow. The stars were still glistening and shimmering in the night sky, and the longish grass, which came up about shin height started to glisten white as dew began to form. A slight breeze rustled the leaves of the tall bush like trees that surrounded the meadow, but, apart from these natural noises, the meadow and the immediate surrounding area was silent.

When Beauty had finished, they both looked at ELKY, and he thought to himself; "Right, I am going to need help with this, if it doesn't work, I will try another tack; there will be some way or another, and my peers have been exactly right so far. Here we go".

He nuzzled Donduce's arm again, then Beauty's ; they patted his nose in return, and then he plodded back to Mrs. ELKY. They rubbed noses again, and appeared to be in deep conference.

"Oh dear", said Beauty. "Babsey, we have an 'ELK's domestic'!"

"Oh dear", said Donduce, and then added "Babsey, my Honey, that was very apt weren't it?"

"What's that, my darling?" she asked curiously but smiling.

"You saying 'Oh dear', my lovey" he replied, chuckling.

"Why is it apt? Babsey?" she asked, puzzled.

"Because they ARE deer, my dear, aren't they dear?" laughed Donduce.

"Oh dear, yes dear, they are deer, aren't they dear, oh dear, sorry dear", said Beauty laughing.

"Oh dear oh dear oh dear", replied Donduce, and he cuddled his gorgeous bride, whilst they waited.

ELKY suddenly moved next to Mrs. ELKY, and the other two ELKS stood side by side next to her. Then, ELKY fell over, onto his side and lay still on the ground for a moment, before getting up again.

"Oh my god", cried Donduce and Beauty together. Before they had time to say anything else, Mrs. ELKY went down onto her front haunches and did the same thing, before getting up again. The other two ELKS did the same thing too, and then the whole process was repeated three or four times.

"What on Earth are they doing my Babsey?" asked Beauty, "Keeping falling over like that", she added.

Donduce was thinking hard, "I don't know, my Babsey", he said, "Falling over, lying down, it's as if....OH MY GOD, OH MY GOD are being shot!! By poachers!! Exclaimed Donduce.

"Oh my God!" exclaimed Beauty, clutching her husband tightly.

"Is that why they keep falling over Honey?" she asked.

"I think so, my Babsey, they are simulating what they have seen what happens to the other ELKS where they live. I am just going to try something, my angel, watch this, it might work, but sorry, my Babsey, I have to let you go; just for a second, but, you must hold on to me, my Lovey".

Beauty clung onto her loving husband. ELKY, Mrs. ELKY and the other two were all standing in a line, watching Donduce and Beauty intently. Then, Donduce, using both hands took an imaginary gun and made out to aim it straight at ELKY, even looking with his eye down an imaginary sight. Even in the night, the glow of the moonlight which seemed to have returned as the clouds that had temporarily blocked it, moved away. As soon as Donduce aimed this imaginary gun, ELKY fell over. Donduce aimed it at Mrs. ELKY, and, sure enough, she did too. ELKY got up again, so did Mrs. ELKY, and they both started nuzzling each other in conversation.

"I thought so, my sweetheart", said Donduce, as he put his arms around Beauty once more. "This is worse than poaching, although that is what's happening, it's mass culling, my Babsey", he added.

"How do you know that my angel?" asked Beauty, looking more and more shocked by the minute; "It is appallingly awful, my angel, whatever you call it my Babsey".

"Well, my Lovey", explained Donduce, a breeze rustled the trees as he spoke, letting out a small shiver; Beauty did the same, and cuddled up to her husband even more tightly.l

"When poachers go out, my Babsey", said Donduce, "There are usually between three and four of them, and they are usually only after one or two animals. They hide near the selected herd, and choose one animal that has been separated from the rest. One shoots it, and then the driver speeds in whilst the remaining two others man handle the carcass onto their jeep, or whatever they are using. If they are lucky, they will shoot another, but after that they won't have anymore room on board for a third or fourth carcass. They then make a very fast getaway before OUR game wardens catch them, or rather hear the gun shots. Although our farmhands do carry rifles, they are for the sole intension of shooting animals with tranquilizers, if they need medical treatment", said Donduce.

"O.K., my Babsey, I can understand that, and it's shocking, but how do you know they aren't tranquilizing the ELKS, and not shooting them dead?" asked Beauty.

"That is my second point, my Lovey", explained Donduce "ELKY and his family have just simulated a whole number of ELKS being shot at one time. Like I said, poaching is one or two animals, and tranquilizing is just the one. In this case it's poaching, but on a much larger scale".

"So, who is doing, or carrying out this awful poaching then, my Babsey, and, my Lovey, getting away with it?" asked Beauty, shocked by this awful news.

"It can only be one set of people that could get away with it, my Lovey", said Donduce, "The game wardens themselves!"

"Not farmhands then my Lovey?" asked Beauty, curiously.

"Well, on them parts of the Estate, due to the warmer, and colder climates, depending on where you are, the farmhands are called Game Wardens, my Babsey, he explained.

"Oh my God my lovey", said Beauty, "What on Earth are we going to do then?"

"We are going to have to have a really good think about this my Lovey", said Donduce. "Somehow, we are going to have to find out exactly what is going on there, or wherever it is that ELKY and his family have come from. We have got to find out just how widespread this is, as it could, potentially, affect the whole Estate. It might just be an isolated region, but as yet we don't know, as I don't think the link actually spreads that far, my angel. Also, and extremely worrying, is that the minds of these game wardens have been polluted somehow, as it is completely against the EFC. It won't be anything to do with the Network, as any Estate farm management methods have to be authorised by me, and I Isn't done any exercises like that, my Lovey. The only one, in the pipeline, so to speak was that idea I had about setting up a farmhand, after we rescued Dolly", said Donduce.

"How would the game wardens minds get polluted, my angel?" asked Beauty. "It Isn't possible is it?"

"It is impossible, my Darling" replied Donduce confidently, "There are only two ways that it could happen, firstly, their absolute loyalty to the Crown has been reduced due to the distance they are from the Estate, and complacency, and secondly the influences of an intruder or trespasser onto the Estate, however, neither of these instances are possible, but then thinking about it, my Lovey, the first one is, which is why we have this potential problem. I have just done a process of elimination, here and now, my Babsey". (02/05/13)

"O.K., my Darling", said Beauty, and then added, "How come the intruder situation is impossible then Honey?"

"Quite simply, my Babsey, due to 'the power' that I and we have, we would know about it, and the only way that situation would ever be possible is if I personally arranged it, as one of our Estate loyalty tests; so no, that situation is impossible, my Babsey. Like I said, we have got to find out somehow, my darling, a way of finding out exactly what is happening, and, it must be a major situation as ELKY and his family wouldn't have travelled all this way to tell us".

"I know, my angel", agreed Beauty, and hugged her husband tightly. He felt this, and said, "I love you my angel", and they kissed passionately. "I love you too my Darling", replied Beauty, and cuddled her husband tightly.

As Donduce and Beauty embraced in the moonlight; they were waiting to see what was going to happen next. Donduce moved his arm and looked at his watch, pressing the illumination button with his hand that was holding Beauty as well.

"Oh my God", he said "My Babsey, do you know it's 4:30 am! God, we have nearly been up all night, and we have got to go and see Bob this afternoon. Honey, when we get back, we really ought to get some sleep before we go, don't you think, my Angel?".

"Let's see how we feel then, my Babsey", said Beauty. "If we do go to bed, we'll never be up and ready in time; don't forget all the things what we have to do".

"Yes of course, my darling, said Donduce, and added "We ought to start heading back soon anyway, and poachers or not, we need to sit down and relax for a while. I will call ELKY and see what he and the family want to do; we don't yet know if he wants to remain here with his family; come back with us and return later or anything".

"O.K., my darling", said Beauty; she sounded really tired; Donduce noticed this and said "You are knackered, my angel, bless you; definitely bed when we get back".

"OOHH, sorry my sweetheart", exclaimed Donduce, "it is amazing what we have done in one day".

"A day and a night actually my Honey", laughed Beauty.

Donduce was just about to call ELKY over, when ELKY and Mrs. ELKY started plodding across the meadow, towards them.

"Blimey", they both exclaimed and waited patiently.

As they got closer, a female voice came into Beauty's head, "Hello, Queen Beauty; and King Donduce; I have heard so much about your kindness and everything; may I introduce myself please; I am the ELK's wife, and behind me are our family; I am so pleased to meet you both".

"Oh my God, my Babsey", as Mrs. ELKY and ELKY got closer, said Beauty, "Mrs. ELKY **CAN** talk. She has just introduced herself. Maybe she can tell us what has happened, and could be the link that we needed, my angel" she added, really excited now.

"That is fantastic, my angel" replied Donduce, feeling a renewed sense of hope, "See what you can find out, my sweetheart", he added. ELKY and his wife arrived, and ELKY did his usual nuzzling, and then let his wife do the same; she gave Beauty an extra lick on her beautiful face.

"I don't know if Mrs. ELKY will be able to understand me yet", said Beauty, "My angel, I really do hope so, because I could understand her. Here we go".

Beauty put her right hand on Mrs. ELKY's nose, and looked into her eyes; "Hello", she said, "Can you understand ME?"

"Loud and clear", said Mrs. ELKY, "Tell your husband the good news, go on", she said.

"My God, my Babsey", said Beauty, "She is coming through as clear as anything, just as good as Fang. What I will do, if it is O.K., my sweetheart, is amplify what the animals are saying to me, and simultaneously translate their words into our language so that you can hear them too. That way, I won't have to keep relaying what they say to me, to you. The only thing being is that I will always have to be right next to you when you want to talk to the animals, my Lovey", she said.

(03/05/13) "That's a problem, my Lovey?" laughed Donduce, and squeezed his gorgeous bride tight.

"I love you too", replied Beauty with a smile and a knowing look, "Right then; Mrs. ELKY", said Beauty, almost with a business like tone in her gorgeous voice: "Mrs. ELKY, please could you tell us all about your problems, and exactly what IS going on where you come from, and we will sort it all out".

"O.K.", said Mrs. ELKY, as ELKY, Donduce and Beauty listened, "I will do my best".

Dawn was beginning to break as Mrs. ELKY started talking: the sky above the trees, just above turned a pale blue, and the stars were no longer visible. The dew which had started to form on the longish grass made it really damp looking, and it was easier to see Mrs. ELKY, now that it was lighter. She, like her husband was also greyish-brown, about two thirds the height of ELKY, but did not have any horns, and her head towered above Beauty, and Donduce by almost 6 inches; water vapour which looked like steam rose from both the ELKS as their warm bodies heated up the dew that had formed on their backs.

"Your husband, King Donduce, is absolutely right about virtually all of what has happened, but I will explain it in more detail. We have indeed come from the forests of the colder parts of the Estate and have travelled a distance of around four thousand miles, with breaks on the way. It has been awful being subjected to what we have witnessed, and we have seen many of us ELKS slaughtered for our antlers and our fur. It's not just ELKS that have been suffering; Moose as well, and it has been going on for nearly a year. The game wardens, as your husband guessed are the culprits, and, if this continues for much longer, we, along with the mooses and other animals, bears as well, will be driven to the point of extinction. It has taken us roughly a year to walk the distance, and we are, absolutely, desperately tired. There isn't an actual herd of us ELKS; there are just separate families living quite close together, but in the same area; however, we did all get together to discuss what the best course of action was, and it was decided that one family should represent the whole ELK, indeed the whole endangered population, and make the pilgrimage to the very top of the Estate; the head person, and and so we formulated a plan. We know we would have to travel the distance to the source of the vibe which, obviously is you, Queen Beauty, and your Husband, King Donduce. It was going to be a long journey, and we followed out instincts as we only travelled in the directions where the vibe would become stronger. As we travelled, the vibe did indeed get stronger, however the vegetation changed, as did the scenery, some of which we had never seen before. The one major problem we had not envisaged or accounted for was the vast expanses of water that are in certain areas of the Estate. However being ELKS and used to swampy areas, we just literally swam and basically hoped for the best, and yes, swimming was certainly a challenge; it meant one of us having to stay awake, whilst the others just tried to doze and tread water. That lasted for weeks. There was one occasion when we were all discovered quite close to land by an Estate cargo boat. They picked us up, and as luck would have it, took us in the direction we wanted to go, however, we were stuck in the hold of this big ship, and when we eventually docked, the shipping hands put us in this sort of quarantine area, and then disappeared off to make their enquiries. Of course, whilst they were gone, somehow, we managed to break the door down, as animals of our size are not usually kept in areas like that and thankfully are not designed or built to hold ELKS, and so, we escaped, and carried on with our journey. After a few more months, the climate started to get warmer and the vegetation took on a greener appearance. The vibe was much stronger by now, and we knew that we had to be in, except of course, we had no idea as to what it was supposed to look like, suffice to say that the vibes would reassure us, in which of course, like animal instinct, we trust without question. Anyway over many hundreds of miles, we remained on this sort of track that we followed, we cannot remember exactly where it started, or indeed, for that matter, at which point we joined it, but it was the track that eventually was to lead to this meadow, so, in fact, it is many hundreds of miles long.

This place seemed as good as any to make our house, and so then we sat down and decided on just how we were going to make contact with you, get to know you, and I don't mean 'use you', we genuinely wanted to make friends, also with the knowledge that it would be very unlikely what we would ever return home, well, at least not on foot anyway, not unless we got transported back, but then, transport back to what? The threat of being shot again, no thank you.

So, once we had settled for a few days, ELKY and I sat down and discussed the next move, which was how to contact, and get to know you. We decided that the best option was for ELKY to suss out the immediate area, and to find some clues which proved that you and the king were who you were, because, don't forget, we had no clue as to what you looked like. So, ELKY set off one day down the pathway. Logic told us that because the pathway was so long, it had to lead to somewhere special and important; not only that, but the 'vibe' was incredibly strong, ELKY would return every night and report to us what he had seen", said Mrs ELKY.

The sun was up now, and the chill of the morning had gone a little. Every so often, ELKY nuzzled Donduce's arm, and, he knew what she was saying as when Mrs. ELKY got to a dramatic part, or something really significant; it all was, but a major part of their story, he nuzzled Donduce's arm, quite hard, as if to emphasize her point. Donduce acknowledged this by rubbing ELKY on his nose, as Beauty also did the same thing with Mrs. ELKY. Donduce also, every so often kept an eye on the other ELKS, to make sure they were O.K., and also to check on them as after all, Mr and Mrs. ELK's backs were turned. They were O.K. though, because they were standing together grazing, eating the longish grass.

Mrs. ELKY, was in the middle of her story, but had actually stopped to pause for a minute, and to acknowledge Beaty's rubbing of her nose, which she did with a nuzzle of Beauty's arm.

She continued: "The first time he came back, he told her with great delight that the end of the pathway came out in a meadow, similar to this one and there was a large farmhouse at the other end, which he just knew and could sense that it was where the King and Queen lived. He knew it was a farmhouse or as we ELKS say, a human lair, surrounded by animals, so safe, as we had seen them countless times before on our journey. We knew that this wasn't any old farmhouse, it was yours because, like I said, the vibe was massively strong and oozing out, and also that it was at the end of the path. We also know these places are called farmhouses because ELKY has heard you and the king call it that. We also know that you call my husband ELKY for the same reason, which I think is really sweet. Anyway from a discrete distance, ELKY saw you my Queen, attending to the various animals, always with the King, and you were talking to them, unlike any other human on the Estate. (05/05/13)

The next time ELKY reported back, he said that he had managed to plod, unseen over to the field where other animals existed and had also seen a barn and a pond. He had also laid down on this metal thing in the middle of this large road, but once he had sniffed the air he had moved on, back into the safety of the trees for camouflage.

On his last trip back, we both decided that ELKY should somehow establish a second base, much nearer, if not next to the farmhouse and really make himself known. We would stay here, with ELKY returning when he could, and eventually, with a bit of luck, destiny, if it was going to work out, would bring him back here, accompanied by you both. So, ELKY deliberately made a bit of a nuisance

of himself, and he came back, when he could and told me all about it; some of the things, one involving what I know now is called a coal bunker, as ELKY explained it, really made me laugh., What surprises me as well, is the speed in which ELKY managed to befriend you and the King, and now here you are; it's only a matter of about a week, and the things that have happened have only been in the last few days.

ELKY also told me of a passageway that he discovered quite by accident. He decided, no sorry, I got that wrong; the King discovered it, and after a slight accident, ELKY thought that going down this passageway; he had not got a clue where it would finish up, but it would cause you and the King to get to know you a bit more. So, he found that it led to a cave, and ELKY simply sat down, knowing that you both would come looking. He could sense that you were concerned, which boosted his confidence no end, and he heard you two talking, he couldn't understand what about, but sensed a lot of love between you, and for him; giving even more confidence to ELKY. (11/07/13). He sat on the beach in the cave and stared out to sea. He was remembering about all that swimming we had endured, and also the cargo ships they had seen, especially the one that had eventually picked them up. We realize now that we are in a valley, surrounded on three sides by hills and mountains, with the ocean at one end. The valley is actually horse shoe shaped, and the only way to get here is either by the Farmhand's cargo boats, or else over the mountains.

So, anyway, ELKY physically contacted you for the first time, deliberately in the cave, as it was actually on neutral territory, away from anywhere any of us had been. Then, he plodded back to the Farmhouse, knowing you would follow him back, and also hearing or assuming you were going to let him stay in the meadow. The first two stages of our plan were complete, the next stage, the third, was to ascertain if any sign of this poaching business was going on here as well, or just confined to our part of the Estate. Even this question was answered when, first of all ELKY said that you had rescued a dog from beyond the metal thing in some road, and you used one of them devices that you humans use to get round faster. I knew exactly what he meant as it is what them poachers were using, but they had more than one, and they were a sort of two tone colour, the same as the Earth. To take care of an animal like that proves there's no sign of poaching as the vibes are wrong. Then, ELKY told me something about all the animals being upset and worried because one of them had gone missing, and he heard all about it from the new dog, which ELKY really likes; and they both get on like anything. Then, ELKY got very concerned one night on his way back to report, because a gorilla, which had been hiding on the farm, but had been taken back to the sanctuary, which we went through on the way here, was coming the other way. ELKY did not want the gorilla to know that

ELKY was there, and so he hid in the bushes. He didn't want the gorilla to know either that we were here, obviously for our own safety, and he was obviously concerned.

However, ELKY has met the gorilla, and it was before the gorilla, started hiding in the farmhouse, and you and the king don't know this bit either. We first met the gorilla when we travelled through the 'Arc' sanctuary, and were in the rain forests at the time looking for food. The gorilla was feeding as well, and asked us what we were, what species, and why we were there, so far away from home. When we eventually disclosed to him our plight; we had to gain his trust first, and language, funnily enough wasn't a problem between us, he said that he was also concerned about this poaching business. He said that although he hadn't seen anything amiss, he also wanted to inform you of this impending possible problem, and though he would come on the same sort of mission. Unfortunately, he decided that the only way to contact you was to 'be caught' somewhere in or on the farmhouse area, but before he had time to get to know you, he was discovered and returned. He is however in the area, and will make contact with you at some point; obviously we will tell you if we see him first, and that is about it my Queen – here we are!" said Mrs ELKY.

Donduce and Beauty, tightly embraced, were lost for words. Silence fell in their thoughts for what seemed like ages, until finally, Beauty spoke.

"My God Mrs ELKY", she said in her mind "We cannot even begin to comprehend what you and your poor family have endured over them months. We find it hard to believe that you managed to survive the journey here and we think you have done brilliantly to get to where you are now. I must now allow my husband to speak to you as he has absolute control over me, and also the entire Estate. All decisions and arrangements are solely and completely for him to assess; however, he is so understanding and I am his sole advisor as well as his wife. I am also his translator, so he will have understood everything that has been said so far, as well as what I have just said to you now. My Babsey; your views please, my Darling."

Beauty, who had been keeping her beautiful little head warm tucked up under her husband's beard; which incidently Mrs ELKY found rather sweet, but amusing, looked up at her husband and awaited his response.

"Mrs ELKY", replied Donduce, after being deep in thought for a minute or two. "I can only echo Beauty's admiration and wonder at how you made it here through such unimaginable pain, suffering, endurance, perseverance, sheer determination, and a great deal of unbelievable luck. First of all, it would be an honour for you and your family to move onto the Private Royal Estate area, into ELKY's meadow, which soon is to become part of the exclusive and strictly private Royal grounds. As from this moment on, you, together with your family are to be known as the Royal ELKS, and will spend the rest of your days in happy retirement. You will however be required to perform Royal Duties, but from now on will have no need to fear anything or anyone. Obviously you and your family will be answerable to me and to Beauty, but, you will have freedom to roam wherever you want around the Estate if you require. Your knowledge of the ancient pathway is to remain Royal Estate knowledge only. Using specific powers, I am to make access to the Private grounds accessible to the Royal Household only. You can move to the other meadow, we now affectionately call ELKY's meadow, now officially named, whenever you like, but I think it would be better under your own steam; it depends on what you prefer.

I am sorry that I was proved right about the poaching problem, only proved right when you all demonstrated what you had seen and experienced, before that I had, and nor did Beauty, any idea that this catastrophe was happening. It concerns me gravely as well that the gorilla was independently aware of the problem too, over in the Arc sanctuary. That area covers many hundreds of square miles, and what is even more alarming is that it *is* an 'inside job', performed and carried out by Estate Wardens/farmhands, as you unknowingly revealed, Mrs ELKY, that the jeeps they used were 'the colour of the Earth'. That is brown and gold; brown with a gold stripe down the middle, horizontally, and are the Estate official colours, proving that Estate jeeps were being used.

In my view I think a plan is going to have to be devised as to ascertain the source of the problem, and then take whatever action is required. This plan will be formulated back at the farmhouse, between the Queen and I, and also after further consultation with yourself and ELKY. Does all of this meet with your approval?" he asked, smiling a little, because he and Beauty already knew the answer. They just needed it to be confirmed.

Mrs ELKY spoke "I can vouch for the whole family that it would indeed be an honour to live on the private part of the Estate, and thank you, my King and Queen for bestowing it on us. We will serve you both completely and with utter and absolute loyalty. With regards to your question about when we move onto the Estate, you are right in saying that it would be better under our own steam, but we will all be in this place, my husband knows where it is, this ELKY's MEADOW, watching the next sunset.

A question, if I may be so bold, and also an idea that I would like your opinion on, My King, please Sir".

"Fire away, Oh Shit!" exclaimed Donduce, "Bad choice of expression (That made you giggle, my Babsey; you *are* still awake aren't you…!) he added "I am all ears, Mrs ELKY, what is your idea, and also your question?"

"Well, my King", replied Mrs ELKY, "My question and idea both refer to the 'vibe'. The 'vibe', is of course a psychic means of communication that enables selected animals; selected by the Estate, in other words, the King, to communicate with humans properly. I do refer of course to the Royal vibe, which I am using now as you both automatically authorised it".

Beauty exclaimed "Babsey, I was surprised when I could understand Mrs ELKY instantly. Did you do that then my Lovey?"

"No, my Angel" replied Donduce looking puzzled: "I was honestly just as surprised as you, however I guess that some animals find it easier than others; for instance, I cannot hear them, I hear them through you, and it must stay that way because I promised you my Darling. Right then, Mrs ELKY, you were saying?"

"Well", she replied, "In order for us to monitor the remaining ELKS and other animals in the suspected poaching zone, it would be a good idea to establish a communications link with the other ELKS, and so would it be possible for you to increase my vibe power so that I am able to communicate over such a vast distance. It just seems logical to know at first hand if the poaching problem has been resolved from the animals who are actually being slaughtered; no, I phrased that badly, I meant hear from the animals who are witnessing their own kind being slaughtered, along with news of others who are under threat, what do you think, my King?"

"I think it is a good idea, and will certainly give us valuable information about who is to blame, where and when, and in what numbers; also it will ascertain why." Said Donduce, he then added, "Also, I am going to have a complete overhaul of the vibe, creating different levels, of strengths, as we could experience interference problems, with long distance signal strengths dominating local ones due to the sheer strength of the users, your thoughts, my Lovey" he asked Beauty.

Beauty thought for a minute and said "Leave that one with me and I will get back to you, if that's ok, my Angel?"

"No problem my Darling", he said, smiling, and kissing Beauty on the top of her head.

"One last question, please my King" requested Mrs ELKY

"Of course" replied Donduce.

"How would you and your Queen like to be addressed", she asked politely.

"I am to be referred to as King Donduce, or 'My King', and it's 'Queen Beauty' or 'My Queen' when addressing your Queen. You must without question use King or Queen, or My King or My Queen" announced Donduce, and then said "Your Queen and I really have to head back to the farmhouse, as we have a very busy schedule to attend to, and as it is we have been up all night. So, if you will exuse us, we will head off, and expect you all in the Royal Estate meadow later today or tonight?"

"Ok, My King and My Queen", replied Mrs ELKY, "We will see you there later, thank you so much for everything, and have a safe journey back".

After Donduce and Beauty had stroked each ELK's nose, Mr & Mrs ELK's, that is, and they had nuzzled Donduce and Beauty's arms, Donduce and Beauty turned and walked back through the gap in the tall trees lining the pathway, turned left, and started on the long walk back to the farmhouse. ELKY and his wife plodded over to their family and relayed to them what was going to happen, later that day.

Donduce had his right arm tightly around Beauty, and she was wrapped around him with her gorgeous head tucked under his chin, and behind his long beard.

"I love you my Angel", said Donduce yawning, "I didn't think we was going to be up all night Babsey", he looked at his watch, "Bloodly hell, it's 07:30am, good morning, my gorgeous Angel" he said, "and how are you on this bright and sunny, peaceful morning?"

"NOOOOOOOOOOOO!" exclaimed Beauty and then giggled from somewhere under the depths of Donduce's beard. "NO, NO, NO, NO, NO, NO, NO, NO, NNNOOOOO!!", she said again. The 'NO's echoed all round the pathway, all round the trees, and even the sheep in the fields miles away thought they heard her. Fang, their vicious, always on duty, who never ever took his eyes off the back door, even for a second when the King and Queen were out, was sound asleep, snoring his head off on the kitchen floor.

"It's going to take Bloody ages to bloody walk back, my Babsey", said Beauty. "It's bloody cold, and we're bloody knackered, and it's bloody morning, and later we have got to go and see bloody Mr Cunningham and we should be in bloody bed, bloody cuddled up, and instead we're bloody out here: bloody hell!" she added. (Your giggling Babsey).

"Don't worry my Babsey" said Donduce, trying to passify Beauty as best he could. "When we get back, we will have a coke, and then probably go to bed for a little while. We don't have to be at Mr Cunningham's Company until 3pm, so once we have recovered a bit, we'll decide what to do", he added.

"Ok, my Sweetheart" replied Beauty, as she held on tightly to her husband. They soon discovered though that as they were walking at a faster pace, they were covering the journey back a lot faster.

Before long, the right hand turn that the pathway took was visible, only because they could see trees directly in front of them. This was the first time they had actually seen the path in daylight: a soft of brownish colour to it, slightly muddy, and partially covered in leaves and twigs which had either blown off or broken off the trees and turned brown. Their boots make a crunching noise as they walked and the morning dew glistened in the rays of sunshine that penetrated the gaps in the branches.

"We are nearly at the bend, my Angel", said Donduce, trying to give Beauty some degree of reassurance.

"I know, my Babsey", said Beauty, "I am still toying with the idea of a nap before this afternoon".

"Whatever you like, my Sweetheart", said Donduce", and I can always wake you up in plenty of time before we go".

"I love your wake up calls", said Beauty fondly, "Let's see how we feel when we get back, my Darling".

They reached the right hand bend and carried on. They knew that they were actually walking around the edge of the big field where the palace was to be constructed, on the right, but due to the density of the trees, they couldn't see it at all.

"The palace is going to be well hidden, my Lovey" said Donduce, looking right, "And not only that, the rear of the building is going to be so secluded and hidden in the trees that, as planned, no one apart from us on the Estate will know that it is there".

"What was that thing you were going to show me, concerning our meeting, my Angel, you have just reminded me about that", asked Beauty, hugging her husband tightly. Her beautiful hair was still flopped forward, but at the bottom, it was blowing slightly out behind her knees.

"I will show you when we get in and sit down for a bit, my angel, you will be impressed, or at least I hope you will my Lovey", replied Donduce, and then added, "The speed at which we are walking, we will be back quite soon, my Honey".

"Ok, then, my Babsey" she replied, "Believe it or not, I am actually quite awake again now, but I bet I go flop into your gorgeous arms as soon as my bum hits that settee, my angel", she laughed.

"I am sure you will my Sweetheart", chuckled Donduce, but then added, "I think a coke is in order first", he looked again at his watch again, "It's 08:15am, my Babsey; let's say another half hour to get back and settle down, we could catch a couple of hours sleep over lunch if you like darling".

"Let's see what happens, my Angel", said Beauty, "I want a coke too and see this thing; I'm curious".

(09/09/13)

"Ok, then my Babsey, no problem" said Donduce.

It was only another ten minutes and then the left turn of the pathway came into view. After that, it was straight ahead and then finally back into ELKY's meadow, and then the farmhouse. Was Fang awake? Was he ok?

It was getting warmer as Donduce and Beauty rounded the left hand bend, and saw an arched shape of light signalling the end of the pathway, and the welcome knowledge of ELKY's meadow beyond.

"I feel like I have been away forever my Babsey", said Beauty from underneath Donduce's beard; her breath was warm, and Donduce could feel it underneath him.

"It certainly does seem like we have been away for ages my Lovey", agreed Donduce, as the archway of light got closer. From there, you could just make out the back of the coal bunker and the gap that led to the back yard. It was very bright in the meadow; it looked brighter than normal, but then again, they had both been in the forest for hours, and at night. "Don't forget also that we have been up since yesterday morning and on average, we have spent very little time at home, my Lovey" added Donduce, as they finally reached the end.

"Oh, at last, my Babsey!" exclaimed Beauty, as the curtain of trees gave way to ELKY's meadow, "Home at last".

"It didn't take us as long as I thought it would, my Honey", said Donduce, looking at his watch whilst still with his arms around Beauty, "It is 8:40am, and time to see if Fang is ok, maybe let him out, and then flop down with a couple of drinks and recover, my darling?" he added, the last part, seeking already known and expected approval.

"Oh God yes please, my King and Lord and Master and gorgeous Hubby", sighed Beauty happily.

"That's good then my Queen Beauty, gorgeous Angel and my perfect Wifey Lovey", said Donduce.

They had crossed the meadow, walked past the coal bunker, had crossed the back yard. Donduce got out their keys, whilst a very excited Fang was visible through the bottom half of the glass panel in the back door, wagging his tail. He had heard the coming, and was eager to know how they had got on. It must have been eventful as they had been out all night.

Donduce and Beauty kissed passionately just before he unlocked the back door.

"I love you my Sweetheart", said Donduce, looking into her loving, caring, but sleepy brown eyes.

"Likewise, my Angel", said Beauty, looking into his ocean blue eyes, lovingly.

"You've got that glint, my Babsey" whispered Donduce, into Beauty's ear, I think we are going to have to do something about that, my Honey".

Beauty smiled and with a quiet giggle in Donduce's ear, she whispered, "Yes please, my gorgeous Hubby, Immo!!"

Donduce smiled and whispered "Ok" in Beauty's ear, and then opened the back door.

"Oh my God, my Babsey, that's better, heat! Warmth, aahhh, you suddenly realize how cold it is out there when you come back in my Angel", exclaimed Beauty, once Donduce had shut the door behind them, "and how are you Fang? OK? Anything happened? Anything to report? She rubbed Fangs head, as Donduce put the keys on the side, and went to the stores cupboard. He got out a bag and filled up a breakfast bowl from another cupboard, which he then put down for him, also rubbing his head. "Go on then Fang", said Donduce, "Tell your Queen and I all", and he kissed Beauty on the forehead.

"Wait a minute Fang", said Donduce, "Before you do anything", and Donduce took Beauty's hand and they both went to the fridge. "Please could you give me a slapped wrist, my Babsey" he asked.

"What for my darling" asked Beauty, looking somewhat puzzled.

"For disappearing without you and going to the cupboard to get Fangs breakfast, my Babsey, am I forgiven?" he asked, quite seriously.

Donduce and Beauty literally did everything together and were never ever more than one millimetre apart. They took this way that they were very seriously, and couldn't bare anything else.

"Yes, my Lovey", replied Beauty, and then gave Donduce a small, loving slap on his right wrist; he had a tattoo on it bearing her name, and likewise did Beauty, bearing his.

The fridge door was opened and he got two drinks out. Fang had finished breakfast, and was sitting waiting expectantly for them to finish talking.

Donduce and Beauty went over to the breakfast bar and pulled two stools round.

"Ok then Fang", said Donduce, "What have we missed?" Now that Beauty automatically made it possible through her massive talent and translation for Donduce to be able to hear and talk to Fang, it now could be construed as a normal conversation.

"My King", said Fang "and my Queen" he added. "Since you have been gone, you have missed a grand total of absolutely sod all. Nothing. Zero. It has been very quiet; obviously, I haven't seen ELKY, nor have I seen the gorilla, no one, and

the phone hasn't rung either. However, I am certain that you have plenty to tell me, I am all ears, and nose, and tail, and I await your recollection of experiences, plus of course the juicy gossip, my Lord".

For the next ten minutes, Donduce and Beauty told Fang all of what they had discovered, and what Mrs ELKY had said, plus the new arrangements for the Private Royal Estate. When they had finished, Fang was quiet for a few moments before he spoke.

"So, my King", he said finally, pausing only briefly to have a scratch, "ELKY has a family, they are being poached, amongst others; the gorilla suspected it in his area too, they are moving permanently to the meadow and are now Royal ELKS, with a higher power of the vibe, to what degree remains to be decided by you, as does a plan of action, and a Royal Palace is to be built, and all of this area is to be shut off to the rest of the Estate, making it totally private, royal and exclusive completely ruled and controlled, obviously as well as the rest of the Estate, by you, the King. Ok, you have my absolute loyalty; that goes without saying, but one little question; does that make me a 'Royal, everything else thrown in' dog, my King?" Fang looked at Donduce and tilted his head to one side, in a playful plea "Ppleeeeaase" he added.

Donduce and Beauty both cracked up into hysterical laughter. (10/09/13)

"No" said Beauty.

"No?" exclaimed Fang, looking at her in disbelief.

"No" said Beauty, doing her absolute utmost to keep a straight face.

"No, My Queen", said Fang, "You didn't really mean 'NO' did you?".

"No", replied Beauty.

"Was that a 'No' you didn't really mean 'No' or a 'No' to your original answer to my question", asked Fang, and then added, "I am sure I have got that question wrong as well?" haven't I?"

"Ok, said Donduce, "Fang, listen. Queen Beauty is only teasing you, but she is right to a certain extent, although she is in total supreme control of the animal vibe, it is my decision as to what happens on the Royal Estate, and that means anywhere on it. Yes, Fang, you are from this moment on the only Royal dog, and you will have the same powers as ELKY but for different reasons. Like I said before, I am over hauling the way the animal side of the vibe works to create a 'super, more, much more powerful version' that will only be used by Royal Estate animals. This will be decided, along with the details, after the Queen and I have discussed and nattered about the workings of it first. All you need to know for now are two things; the first is that you are now the exclusive Royal Guard dog, answerable only to your King and Queen, the second being that the Queen and I are now going to flop down on the sofa and have five minutes recuperation , so, see you in a little while, oh, faithful Fang".

"Thank you King Donduce", said Fang and then added "That sounded very official, symbolic, and almost religious".

"It was supposed to be, my faithful Fang" replied Donduce, and, with that, Beauty and Donduce got up, stroked Fang on the head, and hand in hand, Donduce said to Beauty, "Office first, my glorious Babsey".

Chapter 9

To the office they went and Donduce picked up a couple of sheets of blank white paper. "We have to do something in a minute, my Angel", he said "But first, I am going to show you that thing which will prepare us for this afternoon", and he kissed Beauty on the forehead.

"I can't wait", replied Beauty, curiously, "My Babsey, I am intrigued", she added excitedly.

"You will be amazed I hope, my darling", he replied, and with that, they both disappeared into the lounge. Before they sat down, they made sure that their hair was properly flicked forward, they kissed passionately again, and then Donduce arranged Beauty's floppy fringe for her, just as she loved it, covering her right eye and flopping down to her knees. Beauty did the same with her Hubby's; their large earrings jangled in the romantic silence as they performed the sacred ritual; which was also a way when needed, of getting much closer, spiritually, with their powers.

They sat down and Donduce put one of the pieces of paper on the table in front of them longways. As Beauty looked on, Donduce rolled both of his sleeves up and put his left arm underneath his right and held Beauty's left hand.

"Ok, my Babsey", he said, "Watch".

"Of course, my Lovey" whispered Beauty; her eyes transfixed on the piece of paper.

With his right hand and forearm, he moved his hand and the top part of his forearm over the paper from left to right, once.

When he had done this he put his hand over his other, holding Beauty's left.

They both stared at the paper and after a few moments, Beauty yelled "Oh, my, God, look, Honey!!"

An image was slowly forming on the paper, getting clearer and clearer as it came into view. "It's a cross! Babsey!" exclaimed Beauty, absolutely transfixed with what was happening.

"Wait, my Lovey", said Donduce with a slight smile.

A greenish blur was coming around the edges of the cross which was taking up most of the page and also taking on a brownish yellow colour. "Bloody hell, my Lovey" exclaimed Beauty again, "All that green; they're trees, and the cross, my Babsey, it's…it's…the Palace! The palace we are having built, it's an aerial view, isn't it Honey!"

"That's right, my Angel", said Donduce, "And if you look on the other sheet of paper you will see printed every measurement, and every size of everything that is required, windows, doors, the styles, the lot, even the precise location of where

we want the palace in the field, my Babsey, what do you think?"

"It's incredible, and absolutely beautiful; in colour as well, my darling, that is just amazing, and I can see now, we are taking this along with us to Mr Cunningham this afternoon, so that he knows exactly what we want. One question though, my Babsey, blimey, I sound like Fang now", Beauty giggled, "You said you had the exact location of where we wanted the palace actually in the field, my Lovey. Is it significant then?" she asked.

"It's only significant in that it is located in the field at a point where each part of the building is as far away as possible from existing buildings of forest ensuring that it doesn't affect anything, and crucially looks as if it has always been there, my Angel. The only disruption will be to the sacred pathway, however I have a very special plan for access there", said Donduce, smiling again.

"How do you mean, my Lovey, as in access" asked Beauty.

"Well, my Babsey" said Donduce, "The contractors are accessing the field from the rear, not from the Main Entrance Road. So, they will need to travel straight across the sacred pathway However, how they achieve this, without going near the pathway or touching the forest trees, and keeping out of sight of the Main Entrance Road, will be revealed in the next day or two, or whenever Mr Cunningham can start building, my Babsey".

"My God, my Angel" said Beauty, "You have thought of everything, my Babsey, and I can really feel the beautiful force that you have over me so strongly, my darling; I am loving it, and it's irresistible, my Angel", said Beauty.

"That is because I am about to show you something else, my gorgeous Beautiful Wifey", announced her husband.

"Wow, my Lovey", exclaimed Beauty, happily, "What are you going to do now?" she asked.

"Close your eyes, and blank your mind completely my Babsey", said Donduce, "My Darling, I am going to do something now, and this involves us standing up, in the middle of the lounge", said Donduce.

"Oh my God, my Babsey OK", replied Beauty, and together, they got up and went to the middle. Donduce took both of her hands in his, and then said, "OK my Angel, now don't panic; just shut your eyes, gently".

"O.k., my Sweetheart", and did just that.

Beauty didn't feel anything at first, but then she became aware of a light; she wasn't sure whether it was in her mind, but it was almost as if she could see inside her feet. Along with this light; a very bright pinpoint, but with a white mist radiating from it and swirling round in the peaceful darkness of her mind. Along with all of this cam a very warm and tingly feeling; almost like the warmth you get when you stand next to a log or open fire.

This glow rose slowly and steadily up every part of her body until she could see the light properly inside her eyelids. Instead of the usual pinky brown darkness one usually sees when one's eyes are closed, and the white patches of images still remaining when one has just looked at something and then shut one's eyes quickly, like a camera. This light, along with the swirling mist and the warm feeling was rising past her eyes, like a dancing angel, darting about, and making weird patterns. As it did this, the mist was forming a line across her line of vision like a distant, foggy, blurred horizon. Beauty became aware woo of her ears burning, not painfully, but certainly warm and tingly, and the area affected seemed to form a line right around her head. It was like a planet had suddenly taken to orbiting around her at eye level. After a little while, the light rose again, and moved up past her forehead, until eventually, her whole head was tingling, then, she felt it move above her completely and stay hovering about a height of a foot.

Donduce's voice came into her ears: "Keep still, my Angel", he said, "We are about half way through, my Babsey, and don't worry about a thing".

"Ok, my Babsey", whispered Beauty, very nervously, and held even more tightly onto Donduce's warm but firm hands.

Her eyes were still tightly closed, and after a few moments the light returned into her field of vision, along with the swirling mist. (11/09/13)

This time, the light stayed still, but the mist started circulating around the central ball in a clockwise direction, a little like a very small but pleasant white Catherine wheel. As it spun slowly, the light got bigger and bigger until the brightness subsided and it became like a disc. An image was forming on the disc and to her total amazement, as this image (13/09/13) became clearer, she knew that the image was her beautiful husband. He was smiling at her and she whispered "Oh, my, God, my Babsey", to him, reassured that her hands were still firmly in his. The image, now complete, was of her husband's head and neck and the top part of his shoulders, on a light blue background, slightly lighter than his eyes. The disc had now formed into a sort of picture frame, circular and completely steady. Suddenly, the picture of her husband was replaced by one of Fang; so quickly, that it made her jump, and what made her jump even more was that to accompany Fang's image, she heard Fang's voice in her ears saying, "My Queen and King, through my King". Beauty was doing her best not to say anything, but was dying to, so all she did was to cling onto her husband's grip for grim death. It reassured her as well, that she also felt her husband clasping her hands even more tightly, as if he knew what was going on, and telling her that she was ok and that there was nothing to worry about.

Abruptly, the image of Fang changed into one of Dolly, the little lamb that was lost and she heard her voice, however she couldn't make it out, then this too was changed abruptly to one of Mary, with her voice, she could understand saying thank you in her ears.

Then images and sounds of other animals, the link sheep, amongst others, along with the sounds, and she then found that the images were changing, faster and faster, building up speed, and the audible and understandable sound of voices in her ears, just turned into a sort of drone. Eventually, the images were changing so fast in this disc frame that they just became a whiteish grey blur, and it started fading, although not completely. Beauty just watched this image in her mind for what seemed like ages, until eventually, it began to get brighter and the changing images began to slow down. Finally the drone in her ears faded and the image became her husband once more. A definitely familiar voice in her ears then said "This is the image in your vision nattering, my Babsey", and as she watched this image, with her eyes tightly shut, she could actually see her gorgeous husband mouthing these words. "We are nearly done, Babsey", said the image, and she really gripped on so tightly to her husband's hands, she really thought she was going to crush them. She felt him increase his grip too, firmly but gently, reassuring but not so that he was in any way hurting her at all.

"Ok my darling", she whispered in her mind, and waited. After a few moments, this image too disappeared into the disc, which became white again, and it too shrank into a pinpoint, before disappearing into the mist, which drifted off like smoke leaving a bonfire. Beauty just stood motionless, transfixed, waiting for what, if anything would happen next. She still had her eyes closed tight, but didn't dare open them until it was safe to do so.

It only seemed like a few moments later, that Beauty felt Donduce pull her hands towards him, and he said:

"It's ok, my sweetheart, we're finished now, you can open your eyes, my Babsey".

Beauty cautiously opened one, her right, and first of all made sure that her husband *was* on the end of his hands! Then she peered around the room to make sure she *was* still on planet Earth, in the lounge and there was nothing different. She half expected to see thousands of animal's faces staring back at her.

Thankfully not, just Donduce's her beautiful Husband. She pulled him to her and they kissed passionately.

"You ok, my Babsey?" asked Donduce, finally, with a little smile as what he had just asked her was a massive understatement.

"Oh my God, my Babsey" said Beauty, "That, that whole thing; that experience, from beginning to end. It was indescribable; fantastic, incredible; the light, the warm glow, then you! Bloody hell

Babsey, my Lovey, that was really you in my mind (14/09/13) weren't it? Then all of them animals; I know you are going to explain it all to me, but I do actually feel really good now: so relaxed, and contented. So, go on then my gorgeous Angel, what exactly did, you do, my Babsey?".

"Let's sit down first, my Angel" Donduce replied, "Then I will explain".

They returned back to the settee, and had a big slurp of coke each. Then, Donduce held Beauty's hand.

"What happened", my Lovey, said Donduce, "Was me installing the power of the 'Super animal vibe', from the energy of the Earth, and converting it to a proper power, if you like, that is only unique to me and you. Now, you, my Angel, through me, have complete control of every animal, indeed every living creature (including the Sow; sorry my Angel Babsey, I couldn't resist; that woke you up!! Your giggling! Continue...) that exists, did exist or will exist on the planet, that is non human. I deliberately did it, the installation that way, due to your total hatred of the human race, and that you never want contact with them.

The first thing to do was to summon the energy from the Earth, which is what the light and the warm glow was. The light then hovered in your eyes and ears, making them senses, ie sight and sound responsive to animals and their language, but crucially, even when they are not here or within earshot. That is why in part two; if you like you saw me. Two reasons for that; the first is that this power, this gift, if you like, is coming from the Earth, via me, to you, and the second, is an added thing, where I can now hear and *see* whoever is talking; which ever animal through you, so you don't use up excess energy doing your translations for me, anymore; it is coming directly from the Earth, my Babsey. Another aspect of your new power, and mine through you, although like I said, I remain obviously in ultimate control if it; is the ability to be able to talk to; let's say ELKY; even when he is miles away, a bit like using a mental video link. You will be able to understand what he says, and what he is thinking, and see what he is doing, and crucially, he does not have to know you are there in your mind monitoring him. I can do this too, and for me, it's a bit like using the same phone, but a different extension; so, my Babsey, that's why every image of every creature on Earth flashed through your mind as you were establishing the link. Like I said as well; this is only unique to me and you; no other creature knows about the super link, and no other creature will, either. You okay my Babsey?".

Donduce finished and took another slurp of his coke, kissing Beauty first.

"Babsey my Lovey", said Beauty, "It's amazing, totally brilliant, and you say that I can hear 'every' animal, see it in my mind, and understand what it is saying?".

"That's right, my Angel" replied Donduce, smiling at her look of wonder.

"The only thing is, my Honey", said Beauty, looking concerned, "Wont it interfere with my own thoughts: it will be a hell of a hullabaloo, all these noises in my head, and come to think of it, my Sweetheart, why can't I hear them now, my Angel?"

"Come here, my Babsey", chuckled Donduce, and held his arms up. Beauty wriggled her body, so that she was lying against his chest, with her head resting on his neck, and under his beard, which she put over her pretty little face for comfort. Donduce put his arms around her so that his hands held hers on her tummy.

"Babsey my Lovey", said Donduce reassuringly, "You will only hear the animal, whether it's Fang, Mary or who ever you choose if you summon them. All you have to do is shut your eyes and say in your mind, "I wish to speak or listen to, and then say their name if they have one, or just a description, like 'The chief link cow'. For security reasons, you always have to say the 'I wish to' bit, otherwise you have a connection every time the name was mentioned, and so you are quite safe. Also, it is possible to see the summoned image with your eyes open; it will just appear in your line of vision, but will be transparent, so you can still see what you were looking at, my Angel. Does any of that help or make sense, my Angel?"

"Yes, my gorgeous beautiful husband, it does", said Beauty, and added, "Please could you pass my coke?"

"Of course, my Babsey" Donduce replied and reached over to the can and passed it to her. He looked at his watch and said, "Babsey, it's now 10:30am, we are to leave for Mr. Cunningham by 2:30pm to give us half an hour to get to his 3 o'clock meeting. Shall we catch a couple of hours night nights, or stay up my Lovey? It's up to you, my Darling," said Donduce.

The glint in Beauty's eye abruptly returned, and the way Beauty eagerly said "Ooh, a couple of hours nite nites sounds brilliant, (Dad passed away 09:15am Bless you), my Honey", was decisive enough for him. Beauty then added, "Babsey, on the subject of Mr. Cunningham, and the palace building, you said that the equipment is going to be brought to the back of the field, along with the access for the construction workers, didn't you, my Lovey?"

"That's right my Angel", said Donduce, "Why Honey, is there a problem my Lovey?"

"I am curious", said Beauty, "My Lovey", she added, "Because that means that they are going to have to make a massive gap in the trees, and will ruin the ancient secret pathway; they are going to have to drive all their heavy gear straight across it and cut down all them lovely trees that are beautiful. We cannot disturb that area, my Babsey, what are we going to do?, my gorgeous Angel. That is worrying".

"Don't worry, my Angel", said Donduce, "I have already thought of a way that the contractors will be able to access the field, from the back, without disturbing the pathway, or even touching it in any way, and, without cutting any trees down, so we will finish up with the area as it always was and always will be, and the palace there as well, my Angel".

"How on Earth are you going to do that then my Angel?" asked Beauty curiously.

"Once the arrangements have been finalized with Mr. Cunningham later, my Babsey, and the finances and the start date has been agreed, I will show you, my gorgeous Angel", he replied.

"Ok then my Angel", replied Beauty, happily, and then added, "Come on then, my King gorgeous husband, nite nite time; our bed is calling us!".

Beauty got up first, and still holding her hand, Donduce followed and they disappeared into the bedroom. Then after they had got ready, they held each other in a tight embrace and kissed passionately. Then, climbing into bed, Donduce set the alarm clock for 1pm, "That will give us an hour and a half, my Angel" he said, "Plenty of time for us to get ready for this afternoon my Babsey".

"That's ok, my Sweetheart", said Beauty, "Now, come here you, I love you my darling", she added.

"I love you too my Angel" said Donduce, and with that, they both disappeared under the duvet.

ELKY and his wife were discussing their future as they munched on the poplar bushes in the meadow, as were the rest of the family next to them.

"This", said Mrs ELKY "is better than we could ever have hoped for; a new life of safety for us, and also a sense of purpose. Never having to worry about food, or danger again, and also the King and Queen promoting us to Royalty. I don't know about you, but I am going to love living on the private Royal Estate in total seclusion and privacy " she said, taking another bunch of leaves in her mouth.

"Yes, it was worth every inch of that gruelling journey", ELKY replied. "When are we going to make the final part then? To the meadow that the King has named after us I mean? After lunch?" he asked.

"Yes, when we have finished lunch", replied Mrs ELKY, then she turned to the others and said, "You two, does 'after lunch' suit for our last bit of the trip?"

"Fine with us", they said looking at each other, simultaneously, and then at her, "We could sleep for a week".

"So," said ELKY, addressing the other members of his family. "You or rather we are all agreed that we will not be returning to our own land of origin. We are going to stay permanently on the Royal Estate in a life of luxury, and serve the King and Queen from now on? It is absolutely fine with me, however I just wanted to make sure it was ok with all of you as well".

Mrs ELKY, and the other two ELKS all said "Yes, of course it's ok with us" simultaneously, and at this, ELKY said:

"Ok, then, shall we go home, to our new home, now?"

"Yes, please!" they all said, even ELKY himself, and, with a big ELKY smile, he said: "To ELKY's meadow, here we go, and here we come!".

ELKY and Mrs ELKY nuzzled, and then she said to him "You had better lead the way, don't forget, we've never been!"

"Oh yes" said ELKY "I hadn't thought of that". He nuzzled Mrs ELKY once more, and said "Right, you lot, follow me". ELKY started plodding forward to the gap in the line of trees that formed the edge of the ancient secret pathway. Mrs ELKY followed immediately behind him, and the other two followed one behind the other, and behind her. By the time they would get to ELKY's meadow, Donduce and Beauty would already be up and out; on their way to see Mr Cunningham.

The line of four ELKS made their way, slowly plodding down the pathway, and had no idea they were being watched! From a distance, crouching low in the dense undergrowth at the bottom of the trees, the gorilla was transfixed on every move the ELKS made. He had been in the forest, hidden for quite a while, and he had been monitoring what the ELK family had been doing. His sole intension, was actually to take up residence in the meadow that the ELKs had been occupying, but as he was a lone solitary animal, he wasn't going to share his home with anyone or anything. He had seen the King and Queen return with ELKY to the meadow, and he was counting on them to allow the ELKS to take up residence on that big bit of grassland behind the farmhouse. Obviously he had seen ELKY stay in it on numerous occasions, but always returning at night to his family, which although the gorilla respected because ELKY was bound to check on their welfare, and he obviously missed them, it was a disturbance for the gorilla as he was always wary it would be something else using the pathway. The gorilla also knew that ELKY was aware of the poaching problem, and had no doubt told the King and Queen; the gorilla would have to make himself known too, but in a different way. He had already failed miserably in gaining access to the farmhouse loft, but it was his natural arrogance that had let him down; not only that, but humans feared him, as did some of the animals. He also missed his own kind over on Noah's Sanctuary, but for now, he had to somehow make sure the King and Queen aware that it was not just ELKY's homeland that had the problem. He had heard of this poaching situation, but had never actually witnessed it; just the rumour of its existence was bad enough. Once his mission to tell the Estate was accomplished, and he had some sort of reassurance from the King and Queen that something was going to be done about it, and soon, he wanted to return back to the sanctuary, the wildlife reserve and live in peace.

Now, he thought, and decided, that once ELKY and his family was out of sight, he would break cover, bound very quickly through the trees, across the sacred pathway, and disappear into the meadow. From here, it was ideal. He could live in relative secrecy, monitor the comings and goings of whoever was using the sacred ancient pathway, and, best of all, he could use it himself to travel the brief distance to the back of ELKY's meadow, and befriend ELKY once more. That way, maybe, he could get a message to the King and Queen; or ELKY might tell the guard dog; he was supremely loyal, so, for that matter was ELKY: the gorilla did not want his presence known. Would ELKY tell the King he was here? Would his wife? Would they tell Fang? Would Fang tell the King and Queen?

Silence fell once again on the pathway, and only the wind rustling the tall trees could be heard. There was bird song too: little chirps and cheeps could be heard echoing in the trees as they foraged for their food in the branches or picked at the leafy ground searching for a meal.

The gorilla looked around the trees and surrounding area that was visible, and then made his move. He bounded, all be it as quietly as he could, making sure that he wouldn't tread on any twigs that would snap under his weight, and slowly made his way to the pathway. He stopped every so often behind a tree, and peered around it to check no one was coming. (You are giggling, aren't you, my Babsey?") He got to the pathway, and paused, very briefly at the edge of the line of trees. He was actually getting his bearings as well; looking round, he was about two thirds of the distance from the right hand bend to the meadow clearing, up on the right hand side of the pathway. No one was about, so, after checking once more, he broke cover, and bounded quickly up the path. He had done this once before a few nights ago, but wasn't quite so wary then, as he had just escaped from the reserve, and didn't care. It wasn't that he couldn't leave the reserve and *had* to 'escape', it was just that fear of being seen by hostile humans that worried him and not only that, he had to travel through human territory, to which he definitely wasn't accustomed. Up the path he bounded, and because he could move actually a lot quicker than either human, or ELK, using his strong arms as well, he covered the distance very quickly. He found the gap in the trees on the right hand side, and the small clearing, it was actually very secluded and any passer by would walk right past it if they didn't know it was there. In he bounded and paused, looking back one more time: no one around, so down the small clearing, only a matter of a few feet, and to the other side, in effect of the line of trees. Then he was in and bounded to the middle. The meadow was completely surrounded by trees except for the small gap he had just entered from. Through the trees, it was possible to just see a pathway traveller, however, the knee height long grass was more than adequate to hide him, and also the trees around. He could get well used to this, he thought as he sat down and had a scratch; maybe even bring the rest of the troop of his kind from the reserve, to live in secret in the Royal Estate Forest; gorillas would keep a watchful eye out for 'imposters' or strangers and report back, just depended on what the King would decide, having been asked the question. It didn't, however, solve the alleged poaching problem in the reserve area.

The gorilla stopped pondering and marked out his new territory. He walked on all fours to the trees and sat down again, surveying the meadow from a different angle. It was ideal: plenty of food; berries, insects, leaves and most importantly, plenty of cover, with the smaller trees and the longish grass, and total privacy, which he craved. The only major downfall, however, which the gorilla was absolutely sure he could sort out, was the total lack of bananas, but as for right now; since he didn't have to look over his shoulder for a while, and he could stop being quite so wary and nervous, it was time to have a well deserved nap. So, leaning up against the trunk of a tree, and putting his arms behind his head for comfort, the weary gorilla shut his eyes and dozed off.

"I can't wait to see what this meadow looks like", said Mrs ELKY as they approached the left hand bend of the pathway and turned to start the final, last little bit of their long journey. Although

ELKY had made the pathway trip on numerous occasions, this was the first time that, as a family, they had officially arrived at their final destination; their resting place, and they were all very excited.

"See that arched bit of light up ahead", said ELKY, turning his head to Mrs ELKY, who was plodding beside him but slightly behind, "That's the meadow, beyond".

"Oh I see", said Mrs ELKY, "It's no wonder that you said this had to be the source of the vibe and the Royal area, because after the hundreds of miles that the pathway goes, there is no other way to go, but to the meadow; it is like your journey's end, or destination has already been decided for you; for us".

As they got closer, the meadow became clearer, and Mrs ELKY could see the distant coal bunker as they neared the 'arched by the trees' end of the pathway and the end of foliage cover.

They entered the meadow in single file, and when they had all arrived, they stood in a line, similar to the one they formed when they were demonstrating being shot to the King and Queen.

"Well", said ELKY, to the others: "We have arrived; this is it – our new home, and that building there" he said pointing with his nose at the back of the farmhouse, "Is where the King and Queen reside. When they come to see us, they arrive through that little gap", and he pointed again with his nose, in the direction of the grassy bit, and the coal bunker. "Behind that, is a sort of outside area for humans; the King and Queen refer to it as their 'back yard', and it is where you will usually find Fang, who is really nice, and has already become a really good friend, and absolutely to be trusted. So, everyone, what do you think then? Do you like it?"

"It's really lovely" replied Mrs ELKY "It's a lot bigger than I thought it was going to be, in fact, it's more or less the same size as where we have just come from I think." She looked at the other two ELKS, "What do you think guys? Ok?, not bad?, shit?, brilliant? What?"

"It's fine, absolutely fine", they said together, "We will get well used to this".

"Good. Everyone is happy, and it will also be a nice surprise for the King and Queen, when they come here and find that we have all arrived, to see us and know that we are now here", said ELKY, happily and somewhat triumphantly too. It had been a long and dangerous ordeal, and, now, he felt that, because his whole family had arrived too, and were safe, he could also relax far more himself.

"Ok, then, everyone" said ELKY, "Just have a wander around and get the general feel of your new home. I am not sure if the King and Queen are in or out at the moment, but we will soon know when they appear, as it happens, the Queen, always seems to catch me eating, and they do laugh, because the King, who is always at her side, and she, always at his, does comment to the Queen that 'I have got my head stuck in my favourite tree scoffing'.

They all laughed, and then the other two ELKS wandered off round the meadow for an explore. ELKY took Mrs ELKY for a guided tour which also involved them entering the grassy bit by the coal bunker.

"Go on", said ELKY to his wife, "Stick your head around the coal bunker and you will see their back yard. You might even see Fang. I don't think he is out though, because he is usually wandering around. Go on" he said again, "Have a look, it's

ok; don't be scared – it's technically your home as well, now".

Mrs ELKY very cautiously plodded silently forward a few steps and peered gingerly round the bunker and to the right a bit

"Oh yes", she said softly, "I can see the yard and a back door; it's shut, and there's no sign of Fang. I can't see in either, because it's too far away, and all I can see in the windows are reflections of what is outside. There is no sign of life anywhere, it's dead peaceful.

"It always is", replied ELKY, speaking softly himself. "I think the only disturbance I heard was some idiot fat farmhand, who shouldn't have even been here, and annoyed the hell out of the King; he soon disappeared though, and I haven't heard him since. Come on then, let's go back and relax a bit now".

"Ok", said Mrs ELKY; she turned, and then they both plodded back to the meadow, where they sat down, and nuzzled one another, affectionately.

After a little while of just resting and surveying the surroundings ELKY became aware of a small flock of birds that were circling high above the farmhouse. As he watched they slowly got lower and lower until he could see them more clearly. There were four of them;

two large and two smaller ones; the smaller ones seem to be following the larger ones, two were greyish looking and two were brown. They disappeared from view after a few minutes below the farmhouse roof. They had obviously landed somewhere close by, probably looking for food, or so ELKY thought.

The alarm clock went off in the farmhouse bedroom, and a hand came out from underneath the duvet, switching it to snooze. The hand returned back under the warm folds, accompanied by a muffled, but audible "NOOOO!!"

The occupants of the space under the duvet disappeared further under it, until the alarm clock sounded, heralding the wonderful news that their five minutes snooze time was up.

Donduce reached out and turned the clock off completely and then wrapped his arms around his gorgeous Wifey, who had just finished a long stretch with a yawn.

"Hello, my Babsey", said Beauty, as she returned his wake up cuddle with a big kiss, "What time is it my Darling?"

"Nearly ten past one, my Honey", he replied, stretching himself, and after he had kissed, "It's time to get up in a minute, and then go and see Mr Cunningham, my Lovey".

"Five more minutes then, my Sweetheart", she replied, "Crumbs, I really needed that snooze".

"Well, my Babsey, we were up all night", said Donduce, "We have only had two hours sleep in the last 48, so we should sleep well tonight too", he added, putting his arm around her shoulders.

They were both now sitting up in bed, and slurping the drinks that they had started earlier, and had brought them in with them.

"Do you know where Mr Cunningham's place is, my Angel?" asked Beauty, having a slurp.

"Yes, roughly, my Darling", replied Donduce. "I had a look at the map that Mr Cunningham faxed us, and it's pretty straight forward", he added, having a slurp himself.

"The office is located on an industrial estate, also called 'Foundations' my Babsey" said Donduce. "If we drive round AKKS Lane as if we are going to the Dan and Freckles, and turn left, just past the car park where we found Fang, we will drive up that road to the crossroads, where we bumped into Mac Dad. This time, we will turn left there, go past the car park on the left, and we arrive at a roundabout. This roundabout we turn right, and it is actually the EE-I-O bypass. We follow that road which ends up quite a way behind the church in the middle of town to the north, take a left there, and the road heads off towards the other set of hills, then mountains which form the top prong, if you like of the horse shoe shape they form. The industrial estate is up there on the right hand side, or it should be, my Angel" finished Donduce.

"It sounds easy enough to find, my darling", said Beauty, "How long do you think it will take us to get there, my Angel?" asked Beauty, "Half an hour?"

"Oh crumbs, my Babsey, at the most, my Angel", replied Donduce, having another slurp of coke. He looked at the bedside clock and said, "It's 1:30 now, so we had better get ready, my Babsey; we are going in an hour".

"Ok, my Sweetheart", said Beauty, "I love you my Angel", she added.

"I love you too, my darling", Donduce replied, and they kissed passionately.

Once out of bed, Donduce and Beauty flicked their hair, and embraced, kissing passionately again. Then, holding hands, they gazed into each other's eyes, and felt the spirit of the Earth rise from their feet and pass through their bodies, before rising above their heads and dissipating; Donduce, and, passed on to Beauty, did have unique and special talents.

After they had been to the bathroom, they got dressed, and did each other's sacred beautiful hair, it did seem to be growing; Beauty's was now right down to her ankles, and looked stunning; black, with a hint of red and a little brown, and Donduce's was now down to the top of his legs. They could both sit on their hair and their appearance was very special to them;

Donduce and Beauty did not conform to society; they were society, and society had to conform to them; they were the supreme affectors, not the affected.

They had finished in the bedroom, and holding hands, walked down the hall to the kitchen.

"Oh my God Babsey, look!!" exclaimed Beauty, pointing at the window.

"Bloody hell, my Angel", exclaimed Donduce, "I had forgotten all about them!" he added.

Lined up, side by side on the outside kitchen window sill, stood four pigeons; one large grey, one slightly smaller and brown, one slightly smaller grey, and a smaller still brown one. They were all staring in expectantly as if they had just rung the doorbell, and had been waiting ages for a response.

"It's them pigeons we saw at the Dane & Freckles, my Babsey", exclaimed Beauty excitedly, "They have obviously gone home, told Mum, and now they are all here to stay", she added.

"That's brilliant, my Angel", replied Donduce, "I haven't even had time to build coup for them yet, what with ELKY's problems. We will open the window and let them in, my Lovey, just as long as they don't flap around the kitchen, they will hurt themselves otherwise".

"Ok, my Babsey" said Beauty, and as soon as she had spoken, the largest of the pigeons ruffled its feathers and said, "Hello, I told you we were arriving. Thank you for letting us live here. Don't worry, when you open the window, we will just sit inside, but if you could leave the window open, then we still have the freedom to flap around, until you very kindly build us a new home".

"No, problem" replied Donduce, "Your Queen and I welcome you to the Royal Estate, however you are going to have to roost in the kitchen until I have sorted out your new home. I will make arrangements for the window to open and shut, as an when you require, if that is ok. We cannot have it permanently open, as that will interfere with our heating system, and also give us too many security issues".

"You've got a bleeding guard dog, my King" said Fang, interrupting Donduce's train of thought.

"Of course, we *have* got a bleeding guard dog", continued Donduce, trying not to laugh, "Unfortunately he is usually asleep, and so wouldn't know a burglar was in, even if the intruder threw him a bone, so…."

"Well if the King and Queen didn't stay up out all night", interrupted Fang again, wagging his tail, because he was enjoying this conversation, "Then their bleeding guard dog wouldn't be so bleeding knackered, after having been up all bleeding night, bleeding worrying, and wouldn't be bleeding asleep so much, would he?" finished Fang.

"I am sorry about our overly lippy guard dog", said Donduce, "His name is 'Fang' by the way", he added, and then continued "You won't be seeing him for much longer though, as he obviously has never heard of the dog pound".

"I thought this was the dog pound", interrupted Fang yet again. (16/09/13)

"it was Beauty's turn to have hysterics "Oh my God, my Babsey", she laughed "Let's just get this bleeding window open and let them poor pigeons in, my Honey. I am sure the pigeons didn't understand what Fang said anyway".

"We did, my Queen", replied the largest one, "We did our best not to giggle, but don't worry, if Fang gives us any bother, we will fly over and shit on him from a great height; only joking Fang".

"I know", replied Fang, wagging his tail, "Welcome aboard, and my God bless her and all who sail in her".

Donduce and Beauty, still holding hands, waited for the pigeons to move up the sill, away from the window, and then Donduce opened it as wide as it would go. One by one, each pigeon moved along the window sill and hopped onto the work top; when they was all in, Donduce shut the window again, and then he and Beauty got a bowl out from one of their cupboards and filled it with water. Then placed the bowl on top, and all four birds crowded round and started drinking.

Donduce looked at his watch; "Babsey", he said, "It's 2:20. We really have got to get ready to go" put our coats on and everything".

"Ok, my Lovey", replied Beauty, and then she paused, and said to the big pigeon "Where were you roosting before you came here then?"

The pigeon looked up; "Oh, we were staying in the back garden of a really nice man. He had a friend with him too; a woman, I think her name was Naomi".

"Oh my God", exclaimed Beauty, her face a picture of total surprise, "You stayed at Mac Dad's; he's our other Dad, on my side; what a coincidence", she added.

"My goodness", exclaimed Donduce, surprised himself, "Out of the entire area of the town, you happened to stay with relations", he said, then he looked at Beauty and gave her a kiss on her forehead, "We must go", he said, looking at his watch again: "It's twenty five past two, and time we weren't here, my Lovey".

"Ok then my Sweetheart", replied Beauty with a smile, "Let's hit the road, my Lovey".

They popped into the lounge and picked up the two sheets of paper that Donduce had put on the sideboard; the aerial architect's plan of the palace with the dimensions and measurements, and also the faxed copy of the map showing how to get there.

Donduce showed Beauty this and said "See what I mean, my Lovey, it looks straight forward enough, don't it?"

"Yes, my Lovey", said Beauty peering at it curiously "It looks funny when you see all the roads like that, I can almost feel myself walking down them", she added, then they looked at one another and smiled;

"And finishing up at the Dane and Freckles!" they both said in unison.

They went out of the lounge, armed with the paperwork, and Donduce picked the keys up off the hook and set the front door alarm.

"See you later, Fang", they called, as they went out the front door.

They heard a rather muffled, but still audible "Bye, my King and Queen" from the kitchen, as Fang lay down again, and the pigeons just carried on nattering amongst themselves.

Donduce had opened the garage door, and when it had rolled up to just above head height, he opened Beauty's door, and said "Are you Ok, my Babsey?", as they kissed and she got in.

"Just a bit nervous my darling", she replied, "You know how much I hate going to see humans, and especially on an official basis, my Sweetheart. It's Ok talking about it, but when it comes to actually doing it, Ugh. I think we will definitely be coming back via the Dane and Freckles later my Lovey", she added, with a smile.

"Of course we can my Babsey", said Donduce, and then let out a giggle: "We can always go on the way there if you like".

"Ooh, yes please, my Sweetheart", said Beauty giggling, "And miss out the meeting bit?" she added in mock hope.

"Er, No, my Sweetheart", laughed Donduce, kissing her again, and then he asked "Are you settled in Ok, my Honey?"

"Oh yes, my Angel", she replied, and stuck her feet out in the well under the glove compartment. Just before Donduce shut the door, Beauty reached down and 'folded' her beautiful long hair onto her lap as it was trailing along the jeep's carpet. "I can't have that", she laughed, "We have only just washed it, my Angel".

"I have only just dried it as well", laughed Donduce, and he shut the door, walking round to his side. Once in, he kissed Beauty and then checked his own hair which settled comfortably on his knees. Beauty leaned across and they kissed passionately, before she rested her right arm in it's usual place on Donduce's left knee. She also made sure that her hand was under Donduce's long hair, as she liked to twiddle with it (his hair, my Babsey, your giggling aren't you?....) whilst he was driving.

The engine started, the heater blowing warm air around their feet, they pulled out of the garage and onto the front drive. It had turned into a nice sunny day after the cold start they experienced that morning, but there was still a bit of damp in the atmosphere, and everything had that moist soggy look to it. Even the roof of the farmhouse, a reddish brown tiled slope had a darker damp bit along by the guttering, but the top part up towards the apex was dry, and the sun was shining on it. Donduce turned left, and then drove the jeep through the gap in the front tree line, and then turned left onto the Main Entrance Road; across the cattle grid, past the bit of field that was going to be used for the construction worker's access, and then under the familiar farm sign.

"Here we go then, my Angel", said Donduce, as they turned left onto AKKS Lane, "To the Dane and Freckles; I mean, Mr Cunningham's!" he laughed.

"Babsey!", laughed Beauty, and held her gorgeous Hubby's knee, tightly.

Soon, the lamp post signalled the beginning of town came into view, and they left the trees and the field behind. Donduce slowed a bit, as the car park appeared on the left hand side. They could see the Dane and Freckles in front of them, and to the left; they glanced at each other, and both said "NO", again, simultaneously.

They turned left, and this time, got up to the crossroads where they met Mac Dad, by jeep. They turned left again, and were now in unknown territory. Past the 'Fang' car park, and onwards, past some more shops and then went past quite a few Victorian looking terraced houses on both sides of the road, the roundabout was straight in front of them about five hundred yards ahead.

"Well, my Babsey" said Donduce, "So far, so good. The map is right; it does exactly what it says on the tin".

"Are we nearly there yet? My Lovey", teased Beauty, knowing full well they weren't; "We are committing the ultimate sin, you know, driving *away* from the Dane and Freckles!"

"Oh, my God, we can't have that!" exclaimed Donduce, "We are just going to have to make amends later, aren't we, my Lovey", he added, giggling again.

"Yes, please, my Lovey" replied Beauty, and then added, "Like now!!"

They had turned right at the roundabout and were now heading north, but in a very wide right hand arc.

"There should be one more roundabout, which we turn left at, and then the Industrial Estate should be up on the right hand side, my Babsey", said Donduce as they drove along.

"Is there a Dane and Freckles on the Industrial Estate, my Lovey?" Asked Beauty, as the road continued it's long, slow curve to the right. That was it. Donduce and Beauty just broke down into fits of hysterical laughter, and he was laughing so much, that he had a job keeping the jeep in the direction of the road.

"At this rate; my Angel, I bloody hope so", laughed Donduce, and then added, "If there isn't, I will ask Mr Cunningham to build one whilst we are waiting, my Lovey".

Eventually, the next roundabout loomed, and Donduce slowed down signalling left.

"ELKNYAK? My Lovey?" asked Beauty, looking at a road sign, as they approached the roundabout, "What on Earth, and where on Earth is Elknyak?"

"Well, my Lovey", replied Donduce, "The sign said 'ELKNYAK left', so I can only assume it's the name of the town to the north of EE-I-O, and just before you get to the hills and mountains, but, I must say, my Lovey, I have never heard of it either. We must go there sometime to have a nose around. I wonder if ELKNYAK has a pub too?"

"Shall we go and find out, whilst we are there, my Angel?" giggled Beauty, looking lovingly at her husband.

Donduce roared with laughter, "We are not even going as far as this bleeding 'ELKNYAK' place, my Babsey, but we will go sometime, I promise".

"Ok, my Babsey," said Beauty, "I can't wait, my Lovey", she added with a giggle, "I'll bet that the coke is nice".

"We don't even know if ELKNYAK *has* a pub yet!" laughed Donduce; they had got to the roundabout, and, looking right, Donduce pulled out, and then they took the next left. "Ok, my Babsey" he said, "This pub, god, you've got me at it now, this place, 'The Foundations', should be sign posted, but it's somewhere up here on the right.

The roundabout had been located in an area that was at the back of some housing estates. As they took the ELKNYAK road, the houses got fewer in density, as they left EE-I-O behind. The surrounding area became fields again, and in front of them, in the distance were the base foothills of the northern most mountains. They drove past a road sign that said 'ELKNYAK' 6 miles.

"Blimey, my Babsey" said Donduce, as they drove along, ELKNYAK is further away than I thought. It must be at the foot of the hills or something".

"Yes, my Lovey", replied Beauty, "I thought it would be nearer than it actually is. I have got my eyes peeled, looking for this Estate place, but I haven't seen anything yet. Have you, my Lovey?" she asked.

"No, my Babsey, not yet', he said, and then glanced at the dashboard clock, "Ten to three, my Angel", added Donduce, "We are going to be more or less on time".

"Ah, Babsey, look up there!" exclaimed Beauty, pointing at a big brownish sign, up ahead on the left, 'Foundations', it said, with a big black arrow pointing right, underneath it.

"We have arrived, my Babsey, and well spotted you", said Donduce and signalled right onto a specially marked filter lane in the middle of the road. After a suitable gap, they turned right into a largish entrance which for all the world looked exactly the same as the front entrance of the Estate farm, except that a big brownish sign stood either side of the road saying 'THE FOUNDATIONS' on it.

Donduce and Beauty were quite surprised by the layout: it was almost bleak, and each company's building looked like it was isolated in the middle of it's own field. After a minute or two, a large stone coloured building loomed, and it did look quite similar to a cathedral, except that it didn't have a spire. Across the front in big gold letters the words 'New Foundation Construction' was written.

"We are here, my Angel", said Donduce, as he signalled left and pulled into a largish car park at the front.

"God, my Babsey," said Beauty, clutching tightly to Donduce's knee; "It looks very imposing, and sort of dominates all of the others; I think it looks quite scary".

"We'll be ok my Angel", said Donduce, reassuringly, as he parked the jeep.

There was two revolving doors, and a sign above saying 'Reception', so Donduce parked as close as he could. There were quite a few cars there, and beyond the car park, could be seen large designated areas where Mr Cunningham kept the large, earth moving machinery etc. It all looked very impressive, and on a very big scale as well.

Donduce turned off the engine, and leaned across to Beauty. "Are you ok? My Babsey", he asked. He could see the look of nervousness on her pretty little face and he knew she didn't like making these sort of journeys.

"Yes Darling, I will be fine", said Beauty; she was trying to reassure herself, more than her husband, and as she spoke, he noticed the slight squeak in her voice.

"You'll be fine", he said comfortingly, "Just hold on to me tight my Babsey".

"Oh, my Babsey, I will, don't you worry about that", she said, and they kissed passionately.

"Ok, my Babsey, here we go then" said Donduce, and he got out of the jeep. It was quite windy, and a fresh breeze caught his hair as he shut the door, causing it to blow across the jeep's bonnet.

Beauty saw this from looking out of the windscreen and gave Donduce an 'Oh my God' look. He opened her door, and she said, "Oh my God, my Babsey, I didn't know it was that windy". She got out, and held her hair, as Donduce shut the passenger door and locked the jeep with the remote.

They walked, somewhat apprehensively towards the revolving doors, and Donduce went in first, with Beauty, holding tightly to his hand right behind him. On the other side, they were pleasantly surprised by a big, warm and friendly lobby: in front of them were groups of what looked like leather lounging sofas, with glass tables in front of them on a white and grey marble floor. To the right, but still facing them was a very large reception desk, mahogany brown, and a couple of people dressed in suits sitting behind. The desk was quite high because only the heads of the people were visible; the whole room was not unlike a posh hotel lobby, and spotlessly clean.

"Come on then, my Angel", said Donduce, pointing at the nearest receptionist, "Let's go and wake up Mr Gormless". Beauty smiled at her husband and sent a thought to him: "Rather you than me my Sweetheart".

Arriving at the desk, Donduce was just about to announce their arrival, when to their surprise, the receptionist stood up, having glanced first at a computer screen which was hidden from view, and said "King Duce, and Queen Beauty; It is a pleasure", and shook Donduce's hand, at the same time nodding to Beauty, who smiled. "Mr Cunningham is expecting you: if you go round to the lifts on the left, you want floor 3, and the third door down the corridor on the right hand side. It will have his name on it, just go straight up, my Lord and Lady, thank you, and I will let him know, thank you".

Donduce looked somewhat startled by this unexpected efficiency and respect, and thought to Beauty "Bleeding hell, I wasn't expecting that, my Lovey, were you?"

"No" giggled Beauty in her thought back, "Oh my God, Babsey, what's HE going to be like? I dread to think!"

"Thank you very much", replied Donduce, and he and Beauty left the desk and found the lifts; one door was open, so they got straight in and pressed 'three' on the panel. The door swished shut, and they started ascending.

"I love you my darling, are you ok?" asked Donduce, as a 'One' appeared on the lift display. Beauty was just about to reply, when a loud woman's voice came over a speaker located just above the lift door. "YOU ARE NOW ON FLOOR ONE!!!"

She yelled.

"Bloody hell", exclaimed Beauty, as she recovered from jumping out of her skin, "Yes, darling, I love you too, with all of my heart and soul, by gorgeous husband, but...". Beauty was suddenly interrupted again by the woman: "YOU ARE NOW ON FLOOR TWO" she yelled again, (17/09/13) and that loud mouthed, sanctimonious, self opinionated, appallingly awful, hideous, bloody rude woman can go and..." "YOU ARE NOW ON FLOOR THREE" she yelled once more. "Boil her head," Beauty finished.

Donduce was giggling, as they waited for the lift doors to open, which they didn't.

"Oh," said Donduce, as he and Beauty stared at the still sealed door. "Babsey, what the bloody hell do we do now?" asked Donduce, and he looked at Beauty for inspiration. As he did, he said "Oh my God, Babsey, look behind you!"

Beauty who was looking worriedly at her husband, turned her head very slowly round, half expecting a 10 foot tall Frankenstein lookalike to be staring back at her with his arms outstretched. To her surprise she was greeted with the sight of the third floor corridor, visible, through the now open lift doors; doors that had been behind them, but they hadn't noticed. "Oh my God", they both exclaimed, kissed quickly, and left the lift hurriedly, just in case it decided to take them to the fourth floor. Down the corridor they went, and Donduce counted "One, two, here we are my Lovey, door three". A brown door, and sure enough, it had Mr Cunningham emblasened in gold at eye level height.

"You ok, my darling?" asked Donduce, before he knocked.

"Yes, my beautiful Angel", replied Beauty, and held her husband's hand very tightly.

"Ok then my Sweetheart, here goes", said Donduce, and knocked firmly on the door three times. After a short pause, they could hear footsteps, and quite a few of them, like someone, was running.

The door opened, and Donduce and Beauty were greeted by the sight of absolutely nothing, apart from a desk in the far left hand corner, a window, which had blinds, drawn horizontally, covering the glass, and a reddish brown carpet.

Donduce and Beauty looked at one another, and were just about to burst into hysterical laughter, when a voice said:

"Good afternoon, King Donduce, and Queen Beauty; I am so pleased to make with your acquaintance".

They both looked down and their eyes were greeted with the sight of Mr Cunningham. He was no more than four feet tall, was about late 50's, and had greyish short hair. He was smartly dressed in a dark suit.

Beauty sent a message to her husband: "How did he know we were Royalty, my Angel, I thought that we were only known as the King and Queen on the farm".

"I know my Angel" replied Donduce, in his thought back, "I was surprised too, especially how we were addressed by the receptionist as well my Babsey. I certainly haven't told him, or downstairs, and I would have told you if I had anyway; you would have been there and known. The only assumption I have is that Paul must have said it when he set up the initial meeting, as in this one, but must have heard it from someone in the pub. I certainly haven't picked up anything on my human vibe, so a bit of investigating to do, I think, my Lovey, anyway, to matters in hand, and you are going to love this, watch and enjoy, my beautiful Angel.

"I am all eyes and ears, my Sweetheart", replied Beauty in her thoughts, but kept a straight face; then forgot that Mr Cunningham had just greeted them, and smiled down at him.

"Good afternoon, Mr Cunningham", replied Donduce, and shook his hand so firmly that Beauty thought he would bounce up and down, as if he was on a trampoline.

"Please", said Mr Cunningham and stood to one side waving his arm towards two chairs facing his desk. "Thank you, said Donduce, and he put his arm round Beauty as they swept regally past Mr Cunningham, Beauty's long beautiful hair nearly smothering him on the way past.

As Donduce guided his beautiful bride to the seat on the right of the desk, he thought to her "Babsey, my Lovey, how would you feel if we bought his entire company from him, this afternoon as well? That would mean sole charge of all building operations both inside and outside the Farm Estate?"

"That would be fantastic, my Lovey", she thought back, as Donduce pulled the chair out for her. She flicked her hair forward and sat down, then added "Can we afford it though my Angel? You are talking millions there my Angel".

"Of course we can my darling", her husband replied, confidently, "So I take that as a 'yes' then my Babsey?"

"Of course, yes, my Honey", she replied, "I can't wait for this".

Chapter 10

All of this was obviously done in their thought vibe to each other, and they waited for Mr Cunningham to shut the door and return.

"Have you noticed something my Babsey?" giggled Donduce after looking around his desk.

"Nothing obvious, my Lovey", she thought back: she knew something funny was coming, but she did her best to keep a straight face. "What is it, my Angel?" she added with a giggle.

"Well, my Angel", he thought back, "Where is his chair? I can't see it, can you my Sweetheart?"

"NO! Babsey, where is it?" Beauty laughed back in her thoughts. "I don't know my Angel, but we are about to find out!" he replied.

Mr Cunningham walked over to them, behind Donduce and disappeared behind his desk, so that only his head, and the top part of his shoulders was showing. Then he disappeared completely for a minute, before rising into view, as if he was coming up in an invisible lift. His chair was the same as the other two, except that every time he wanted to get up, he had to lower it first.

"God," he said, cheerfully, "The things you have to do when you are short. Now then, this project, my Lord. Did you bring any details?"

"Of course", said Donduce. He reached with has left hand sweeping across his body in the upper chest area and went to his right hand inside pocket; whilst still holding Beauty's left hand in his right. "Oh," he said, "Sorry", quickly swapped hands with Beauty, retrieving the documents. Beauty knew exactly what was going on, as he had done the same thing, only in different circumstances in the Dane and Freckles with Paul. She just hoped and prayed that he wouldn't fall off his chair, luckily, he didn't.

Donduce handed the documents to Mr Cunningham, and whilst he studied them closely, Donduce swapped his hands back with Beauty. "The magic has been cast, my Lovey", he thought to her. "I know, and I love it my Angel", she replied, happily in her thoughts.

After a few minutes, Mr Cunningham looked up and said:

"This will be an honour to undertake. There is no problem at all, and from start to finish will take a maximum of four months to complete, with crews working twenty four hours a day. There will be daily progress reports, covering any problems we might encounter, and of course, you both are free to inspect the site at any time. Should you decide to make any alterations, we will be more than happy to cater for them, even if this requires a rebuilding of some, part or all of the original design. The total cost of this project will be a fixed sum of five hundred million pounds, which includes all fixtures and fittings, installations and services. We would like ten per cent of the total cost as a deposit, payable when you decide that it is our company that you would like to carry out the construction, and of course when you have signed the contract. How do you feel about this, my Lord and Lady?"

"Completely satisfied, thank you, Mr Cunningham", replied Donduce, and then added "If we pay you thirty per cent up front, right now, in other words one hundred and fifty million, would you be able to commence the work tomorrow morning?"

"Of course, Sir", said Mr Cunningham confidently, but then looked again at the aerial view. "Just one problem I can see straight away, that makes your request impossible, or at the very least very difficult to overcome in that sort of time scale, is the access to the rear of the site: it is lined with dense trees, they will never be…"

Donduce interrupted him, "Don't worry about that", he said, "I had to use an old plan of the Estate to draw the palace plan on. When you arrive at the site in the morning, you will see the access area, it has changed slightly from how it appears on the plan, Mr Cunningham".

"Has it? My Sweetheart?" thought Beauty to her husband.

"It will have, my Lovey!" thought Donduce back to Beauty."Ok then, Sir, that is totally brilliant", said Mr Cunningham, smiling. He had a very thoughtful expression, and an almost wistful look spread across his face.

"You know what, Sir", he said, "Winning this contract will provide a massive boost to this company. We are doing very well, of course, but it will give us plenty more room for expansion, and, with any luck, one more deal like that, and I can seriously start thinking about retiring, but of course, not yet. What I really want is absolute guaranteed contracts for the next five to ten years at least, which will then finish my pension off nicely."

"Of course, you are or were thinking of selling the company anyway, weren't you, Mr Cunningham?" asked Donduce, looking at him straight in the eye. He also held Beauty's hand tightly, and she responded by squeezing his.

"Well, yes, Sir", he said, "You are thinking of buying it, Sir, of course", his question came over more like a foregone conclusion than a question or statement.

"Of course," said Donduce. "Please give me the details of exactly how much the company is worth; it's assets, liabilities, opening and closing stock, contracts up to the next five years that are outstanding, your profit and loss figures, and from the computer screen on your left, where all this information is to be obtained, I will take a printout, and then phone our bank, and do an instant credit transfer for the amount, plus half of the amount again, securing the company's existence. You will stay on for now as the General Manager, and when the transfer is complete, we will both sign the two copies, there by me and the Queen, taking sole charge of our new company. Of course, I will add the Farm construction fees to the balance of this transfer, but no doubt you will be aware that as from us signing the transfer it will state on a second sheet that we will take over the company's bank account also; so in effect, we will just simply be transferring capital from one to another. None of this part will affect you though, as you are now, or will be in a minute, working for us. I will wait here whilst you start the proceedings, Mr Cunningham".

"Of course, at once, Sir." He replied, and immediately started tapping away on his keyboard.

Beauty just stared, transfixed. "Blimey, my Lovey", she thought to her husband, "Soon, we will own all of this; Babsey, we really will need to go to the Dane and Freckles after this, please Sweetheart?"

"Of course we will my Lovey" thought Donduce back, "This wont take too long my Honey".

The printer had already sprung into action, and very soon they had two copies of everything they needed. The total figure to be transferred worked out to be just under twenty billion, a good healthy figure for a very profitable company.

"You have the bank details on screen, Mr Cunningham", prompted Donduce, looking himself. "Oh, that is handy, he said, 'New Foundation Construction' uses the same bank as us, which will make the transfer that much easier. Just to let you know, I am about to transfer 30.5 billion into that account which will produce the name transfer documents as well".

"Of course, Sir", replied a very relaxed Mr Cunningham.

Donduce reached into his left hand jacket pocket, and produced their mobile phone. He pressed a number, and then waited, looking at Beauty. "Won't be long now, My Angel, I love you", he thought to her.

"It's ok, my Sweetheart", she thought back, smiling.

"Hello, yes", said Donduce on the phone, "I would like to arrange an immediate transfer of 30.5 billion into" he started, and gave them all the details they needed, including authorization codes, some given by Mr Cunningham. Then he said "Please could you send immediately two faxed copies of all transactions plus the change of name of 'New Foundation Construction' ownership to" he said, and picking up the faxed copy of the map they had of how to get there, which had the number automatically printed on it, gave it to them. "Thank you very much" he said, and hung up.

Mr Cunningham's fax machine was on a longish table against the wall which separated the office from the corridor.

"Look at the screen, Mr Cunningham, and watch closely", said Donduce, and as he, Beauty and Mr Cunningham looked on, the account details changed to display Donduce and Beauty's name under 'New Foundation Construction', and a credit of the transferred capital appeared under the last entry.

Then, three heads suddenly turned as the fax machine sprang into life.

"Allow us", said Donduce, as he and Beauty went over to it and watched, as the requested documents started falling into the tray by it's output slot.

"That is all in order, my sweet Angel", thought Donduce to Beauty, and added "All we need now is his signature, plus mine, of course, then, my Lovey, we are done".

"Wow, my Babsey, it's fantastic Isn't it", Beauty thought back.

"Sure is , my Lovey", thought Donduce, as they returned with the Documents; as they sat down again, he passed Mr Cunningham the paperwork and said "Your signature please, wherever there is a dotted line".

Mr Cunningham read through all the documentation, very carefully, and after saying that everything appeared to be in order, signed and dated each piece. Then he passed them to Donduce, who signed them all, and then Donduce passed them to Beauty, who completed the required set. Finally, Donduce gave Mr Cunningham the bottom three documents, which were the copies of the top three, and the deal was completed. Donduce and Mr Cunningham shook hands and Mr Cunningham said "Congratulations, you have bought a very good quality reliable company, and, with me as your now General Manager, you have my absolute word that I wont let you down".

"Of course, Mr Cunningham", replied Donduce. "A couple of questions for you now: Firstly, am I correct in assuming that the company is responsible for the construction of virtually every building in both EE-I-O and ELKNYAK, that is of course including every house?"

"Yes, Sir, that is absolutely correct, and we are, sorry, you as well now, should be extremely proud of that fact", he replied.

"I am, we are all," replied Donduce. "Am I also correct in assuming that all of these properties are leasehold, and not freehold contracts?"

"Some are, and some are not", Mr Cunningham replied. "All the commercial enterprises are leased from the council, and I would estimate that seventy per cent of private dwellings are freehold, the remaining thirty per cent are leasehold and consist mostly of flats, and houses that have been converted, of course, by us."

"All of these private contracts, leasehold or freehold", Donduce continued, "Are nominated by local Estate agents and arranged by the various banks of this area then? It's just that I have seen from the company records that all of the property contracts appear to go through our bank: I am of course referring to their monthly mortgage or leasehold repayments. This, I take it is due to the company's obligatory duty, to ensure regular maintenance on all of our constructions as part of the company's guarantee arrangements".

"That is correct Sir", said Mr Cunningham, "Setting all the contracts up to go through our bank makes it much easier for monitoring financial operations."

"That is good, and thank you, Mr Cunningham, I will leave all that as it is, however I will be changing one aspect of that operation, which I will notify you of in due course. Apart from that it has been a pleasure doing business with you, and we will expect to see our men on the farm tomorrow morning", said Donduce.

"Thank you, Sir, it has been a pleasure", said Mr Cunningham, and they all stood up. Donduce and Mr Cunningham shook hands, "Thank you, Sir", he said again, and then looked at Beauty, "Ma'am", he said, and Beauty smiled.

"Don't get up again", said Donduce, helpfully; every time they had, Mr Cunningham had had to lower his chair, and Donduce was fed up with having to lean over. He was however now seated. "We will show ourselves out" he added.

Donduce and Beauty left the office and as soon as they had shut the door, Beauty said "That was brilliant, my Angel, and we own this whole company, what was all that business about freehold and leasehold about though, my Lovey?"

"Yes, my Angel, and I know where I have heard the name Robert Cunningham from now, so I wanted to keep the company in the family", said Donduce. "In our family, my Babsey, what do you mean?" asked Beauty.

"Because, my Babsey, Mr Cunningham, is your half nephew in Law, my Lovey!" said Donduce, and held Beauty's hand tightly.

"Oh my God!" exclaimed Beauty, looking visibly shocked, as they walked back towards the lift. "Please could you tell me all about it, my Angel" said Beauty, as Donduce pressed the lift button, and they waited.

"Of course I will, my Lovey," he replied, "And all about them questions I was asking him about the properties in the area being freehold and leasehold as well; there is a major point to all of this, my Lovey, but all will be revealed in the jeep on the way to the Dane and Freckles; is that ok? It's just that we can't talk about it in here, it's too personal and private. It is also a strange feeling, don't you think, my Sweetheart, that we now own all of this, lock, stock and barrel, and, nobody here knows either. That's the way it is going to stay for now, but the staff here will soon notice subtle changes that occur in their normal working environment, my Babsey".

"Ok my Sweetheart", replied Beauty, "I can't wait to get into the jeep and hear all about it, and especially the history behind Mr Cunningham, my Lovey".

There was a 'bing', and the lift doors swept open with just a very soft whoosh,. Hand in hand, they stepped in, the doors closed; Donduce pressed the 'G' for ground on the panel. A red '4' was lit up on the screen above.

"Oh crumbs, my Babsey", chuckled Beauty; "Don't forget that we leave by the doors on the.."

"WELCOME TO FLOOR THREE", shouted the female voice on the speaker above the door.

"And don't forget the interruptions from that bloody woman either, my Angel" laughed Donduce, as they both turned to face the doors opposite.

"Now that we own the company, my Angel", said Beauty, "One of the first changes that I am going to oversee personally, Is the…"

"WELCOME TO FLOOR TWO", shouted the woman's voice yet again.

"Removal of that bloody awful, loud mouthed, self opinionated, condescending, stuck up, toffy nosed bitche's voice, out of that sodding" continued Beauty.

"WELCOME TO THE GROUND FLOOR", the woman's voice interrupted again.

"Bloody speaker!" said Beauty. "Babsey, seriously, I never want to hear that appallingly awful voice again as long as I continue to draw breath. (18/09/13) I hate, loathe, despise, dislike, can't stand, and detest that voice. Who does she bleeding well think she is; Lady sodding Kidiver? The sodding Countess big nose of Sodbury – Ugh, and NO, NO, NO, NO, NO, NO, NO. She can go and boil her head, Immo, My Babsey".

"My darling Angel", said Donduce, in the most calming relaxing voice that he could muster, without bursting into complete hysterics,

"YES? My Sweetheart?" replied Beauty, and then added, "Sorry, Honey, I didn't mean to shout".

"Babsey, the lift doors are open, and everyone can hear you shouting; they think we are having a domestic" whispered Donduce into Beauty's ear.

"Oh shit, I mean 'oh dear', Sorry Babsey", said Beauty and chuckled, giving her husband a big kiss on his cheek.

Still as always, holding hands, they left the lift behind them, turned left, and walked back towards the revolving doors of the main entrance.

"Anyway my Lovey", Donduce added, "That wretched voice was actually computer generated and can easily be erased from the system. When we return, I will make sure that it is erased. For now, my Babsey, it's Dane and Freckles time".

Donduce looked left, towards the reception desk, but no one actually looked up to see them go: they all appeared too busy, on the phone, or concentrating on the computer screen in front of them.

Donduce reverted his gaze to Beauty and said:

"Darling, I love you so much, my Angel, just in case you weren't sure", he said, lovingly.

"Oh my God, I love you too my gorgeous Angel, and oh, yes, I am sure, Honey", Beauty replied lovingly. "Are you sure you love me, my Sweetheart?" Beauty asked softly.

"More than anything else in the world, my Angel" replied Donduce, equally as softly, and they wrapped their loving arms tightly around each other, as they went out through the revolving doors.

A cold breeze caught their hair slightly, as they returned to the outside world, and Beauty had to hold her hair from blowing across her pretty little face. "You know what, my Angel", she said, "I felt so chlosterophobic in there: the lobby was big and open; spacious once we got into that bloody lift, it felt like everything closed in on us. I think it was them corridors, and the lack of height of Mr

Cunningham didn't help either: I felt we were towering above him. What do you think my Babsey?"

"I couldn't agree more, my Sweetheart", said Donduce, holding Beauty even closer. "We are going to have to redesign the inside of that company to make it open plan. Mr Cunningham can for now, keep his office, but I am going to have an office next door; if there isn't one, I will build one. We'll finish up with two main areas for 'New Foundation Construction'; one here, and the other within the palace, on the 'Estate Operations Wing'".

Donduce got the jeep remote out and unlocked the doors. He held Beauty's door open and they kissed passionately. "That sounds interesting and a good idea, my Babsey" she said as she flicked her hair forward and got in. Once she was settled, they kissed again, before Donduce shut her door, and then walked around the front to open his. Once in, he leaned across to Beauty; they kissed passionately, and then putting the keys in the ignition, started the engine. The heater started blowing warm air around their feet, and then Donduce said:

"Ok, my gorgeous Sweetheart, I will explain all of this as best I can; first of all, Mr Cunningham being you're half nephew in law and so technically being family".

"I am all ears, my darling", said Beauty happily, and rested her hand on Donduce's knee, as usual, and started playing with his hair.

"Well, my Lovey" began Donduce, "As you know, Grandma Tilly, or Mathilda, to use her proper name, is your Grandmother in law, and obviously my Grandmother. Well as you may or may not know, only because the subject has never come up, possibly, is that Tilly had a brief unmarried relationship with a man, who's name was Robert Cunningham. They produced a daughter, your Mother in Law, but because of the then strict laws of the land, she had to be adopted. Tilly then married properly, and produced another daughter, who is Mum's half sister. Anyway this Mr Cunningham married, produced a son, another Robert Cunningham who would be you half Uncle in Law, and his family produced a third Robert Cunningham, who's name actually appears on our documentation as Mr Robert Cunningham 3rd, and is the very same person who we have just bought the company from. I said when we were in the building that

253

we wanted to keep the company in the family; what I meant was return it to it's rightful place on our side of the family. What do you think so far my Babsey?"

Since Donduce had started explaining these various situations to Beauty, they had started on their journey to the Dane and Freckles, and were on the road heading back to EE-I-O and the roundabout, heralding the start of the bypass.

"Well, I am amazed, my Angel", said Beauty, "I had forgotten about all of the details of the family tree, but how did you, or what prompted you, or even what made you discover that it was indeed that Mr Cunningham, and not someone else, my Babsey?" Beauty asked curiously.

"I had a sort of hunch in the back of my mind, My Lovey", said Donduce, as they continued along the road. "However, it was really confirmed when we first met him; didn't you notice that he was virtually the same height as Mum, and has a vague family resemblance; although, as we both know, you and I are very unique, and stand very separately from our families for one major reason, my Lovey?" he asked.

"Oh yes, my Babsey, I know all of that, and also our very special and personal circumstances too my Sweetheart. Don't worry, my Darling, I am more than aware of our unique circumstances; however, I was so nervous, and you know that I am proud to be homophobic, that apart from his height, or should I say lack of; I didn't notice, or even gave it a thought that he resembled Mum, or for that matter, you, my Angel; Babsey, should have I noticed? Was it something that you *wanted* me to notice, my Lovey?" asked Beauty, sounded very concerned now.

"Oh, no! My Lovey, of course not, no. It was probably the last thing I thought you would have had on your mind, and to be honest, I would have been surprised if you had pointed out in our vibe chats to each other. No, my Babsey, don't worry about that, but it's interesting though isn't it, don't you think?" he asked.

"Oh crumbs, yes, my Babsey", said Beauty, "Like you said, it's great that the company is back in Royal hands now, where it belongs. It's like that age old saying: 'What goes around comes around' my Angel".

They were making good progress on their journey home as they nattered away. Donduce and Beauty had reached the roundabout and turned right, taking them nearer to the point where they turned left, and then back into the centre of town at the 2nd roundabout. Donduce noticed that the urban side of the landscape had increased with the number of housing Estates that they were going past on this return journey. He said to Beauty "The increasing volume of these various housing estates, my Lovey, and the Victorian styled terraced houses that we have returned to, and saw on our journey out, brings me to the other point I was asking Mr Cunningham, my Sweetheart".

"Oh, Babsey, you do sound so businesslike; Aww, I love it", exclaimed Beauty, and continued to fiddle with her husband's hair, "I am all ears", she added, "Please explain, oh clever hubby of mine".

"Well, my Sweetheart", said Donduce, as they approached the last roundabout and he started to signal left, "As you know, the difference between freehold and leasehold is that with a freeholding, after you have paid all of your mortgage, which is a massive bank loan that you take out to pay for your property, once it is paid off, it becomes yours outright; and with a leasehold agreement, you are paying the Leasor a fixed amount per month, via a similar mortgage arrangement, but after a period which is usually 99 years, the property you have paid the lease on, reverts back to the ownership of the original owner. The major advantages to the lease are that all the maintenance must be paid by the leasor, and not the lease, and also the monthly repayments are usually less, and don't vary with interest rates. In other words Freehold mortgages enable the buyer to own their property outright, but have to fork out all the costs in the process, whereas Leasehold mortgages, are cheaper, last a lifetime anyway and have the bonuses of no maintenance costs, my Darling. Are you with me so far My Babsey?"

"Yes, I am my Sweetheart, totally", she said, "Carry on Lovey, my Angel".

"Well", said Donduce, "My Lovey, by us, or rather as a result of us buying 'New Foundation Construction', we have also succeeded in owning outright, because our name is on the bank accounts, all of the leasehold establishments in EE-I-O, and indeed, ELKNYAK without the residents actually knowing; so we have literally taken over absolute control and ownership of half or maybe two thirds of two entire towns. The next stage is that as we are in control and own the bank accounts of all the freehold mortgages we will send out a notification to the relevant residents of them properties, offering them the chance to simply convert their existing arrangement to a leasehold one, which is cheaper, and we then take over the maintenance of them too, thereby owning the remaining third, and ultimately taking absolute control of not only our beloved Farm Estate Principality, but also all the immediate 'outside' residency as well, including the land, thereby conforming them to the way that 'we operate'. It also gives us the power of eviction both inside and outside the Farm Estate, which also my gorgeous beautiful Angel Babsey, means that, if further enquiries prove positive, we will finish up owning, if we don't already, the certain establishment that we have just parked in the car park of, my Angel".

"The Dane and Freckles! My Babsey" exclaimed Beauty, really excited now, "Babsey, do we now actually own the 'Dane and Freckles'?" she asked.

"Well, my Lovey" said Donduce, "It is going to be 'owned' one of three ways; firstly, it could be owned completely by Paul, lock, stock and barrel; quite likely actually, because he does introduce 'guest beers', making it a 'Free House', but, then guest beers could be simply different beers, supplied by the brewery, as indeed we do, obviously from the Farm Estate.

Nextly, Paul could be leasing the building from the brewery, who did own the leasehold, but as it was arranged with 'New Foundation Construction', we do now, or lastly, the Pub is completely leased from 'N.F.C.', in which case, we still do. I am pretty sure though, my Angel, that Paul said when he first recommended Mr Cunningham to us, that the recommendation was on the strength that 'N.F.C." *had* built it, and from the quality of the building, and it's endurance over the years, the recommendation was good, my Angel."

"Oh my God, my Lovey, that is fantastic, and I take it we will, or rather you will find out when we go in, shortly", said Beauty.

"Of course, my Lovey", replied Donduce, and they leaned towards each other and kissed passionately.

"One question though, my Babsey", said Beauty, as they prepared to go for a well earned coke, "What about all the leaseholds, like maybe this one that are owned by the brewery and not 'N.F.C.', which you said was the first option? What happens then my Angel, where do we stand my Babsey?"

"Simple, my darling" replied Donduce "Mr Cunningham stated, and it is proved on our documentation that all buildings, both in EE-I-O, and ELKNYAK were built by them; in fact he said we should all be proud of that, including us now".

"That's right, my Sweetheart", said Beauty, smiling, "I remember him saying now, sorry Honey, carry on".

"Well, my Babsey", said Donduce, "When and if Paul says that the Brewery own the leasehold, they don't; they didn't build the Dane and Freckles, N.F.C. did. The brewery pay the monthly lease, out of Pauls income to N.F.C. who *did* own it, but we do now. All we have to do is to ask Paul if the Dane and Freckles is leasehold or freehold, if it is freehold, it won't be eventually if it is, actually because that would mean that Paul, in effect would be buying it from us, to own outright, we just tell him we are changing it, and, my Babsey, Guess What? If he doesn't like or agree with the new arrangements, what happens, my perfect Angel?"

"We evict him!" exclaimed Beauty. "My Babsey, how lovely!" she added.

"My Honey", laughed Donduce, "That will happen after we have tripped him up again, my Sweetheart", he added.

They both dissolved into total hysterics, and then kissed passionately. The journey back had gone in an instant, as they had talked for the whole journey, and were actually still in the jeep.

"Oh, Babsey", said Donduce, "It's Paul! He's walking up to our Jeep, my Babsey".

Donduce had noticed Paul approaching, because, kissing Beauty, he happened to glance out of her passenger window and saw him.

Beauty, looking rather startled, didn't look round, but just kept her eyes transfixed on her gorgeous husband, both hands now placed on his knee.

"Is he really coming here, my Babsey?" she asked, nervously.

"Yes, my Lovey, but don't worry about a thing", said Donduce, as Paul walked round the front of the jeep, and motioned Donduce to wind the window down, which he did.

"Hello, Sir", he said, with his head tilted down slightly, so that he could look in, "Ma'am", he added, acknowledging Beauty, who smiled, but only briefly.

"I am sorry to disturb you", he started.

"So are we, sod off", thought Beauty.

"I wanted to catch you before you came in, and I saw you arrive", he said.

"Blimey Paul, were you standing by the front door looking out then or something; you can't see the outside world from behind the bar" said Donduce; he had a rather quizzical and sarcastic tone to his voice, as the one thing that both Donduce and Beauty hated was being watched, or just plain nosey people.

"Oh no, Sir", replied Paul, detecting the venom in Donduce's tone, I was actually just finishing off writing on the board outside; you know, the one that has the menu's written on it", he said, "I saw you coming down the road, correctly assumed you were coming here, went in and came out again. Anyway", he said, "I wanted to ask you something, but off the pub premises, and out of earshot of the customers. Is that ok Sir?"

"Yes", replied Donduce, "But please make it quick, because it is bloody cold out here, and we want to come in".

"Of course Sir", said Paul, "I will be as quick as I can, and your first drink is on me. Right, what I was going to say was this. I have just had a call from Mr Cunningham in the last quarter of an hour, and he tells me that you have just bought his entire company, New Foundation Construction. Is this true?" he asked.

"What the bleeding hell is Mr Cunningham phoning Paul and telling him that for? It Isn't got nothing to do with him", thought Beauty.

"Hang on a minute, my Lovey", thought Donduce back, "This could be the answer we wanted, and there must be a reason *why* Mr Cunningham has phoned him my Angel", he added, "Don't worry, my Babsey".

"True or not, Paul, why did Mr Cunningham phone to tell you this alleged news", asked Donduce, carefully, and then he reached with his left hand and swept it across his chest, making out he was fiddling with the seat belt roll, above the driver's chair.

"Well, because this place; the pub; I mean, is owned by 'New Foundation Construction', but is leased to the Brewery, who in turn, get their monthly repayments from us. It is also the same arrangement with the ELKNYAK Arms, over in ELKNYAK, Mr Cunningham was simply giving me the news that you are now the new owners of the Dane and Freckles, which means that you, Sir, and Ma'am, are the new landlord and landlady. I have been acting as landlord, but I'm really just the manager, and Yvonne is the manageress, obviously.

"Of course, Paul", replied Donduce, carefully. He squeezed Beauty's hand and thought to her "This couldn't have worked out better, my Lovey, now, my Angel, let's test his reaction to the news".

"I know, my Sweetheart," she replied excitedly, "This should be good, my Angel".

"So," began Donduce "How do you feel about this new arrangement, Paul? Are you happy with it?" Donduce asked.

"Oh yes, Sir, Ma'am" replied Paul, with an unexpected air of confidence and relief in his voice. "Now, that I know it *is* true, I am more than happy with the new arrangement, Sir. It Isn't going to affect me, is it? I am just going to continue running the place, send the brewery their money, and then they pay you, under the N.F.C. name, so nothing has changed, except that you are now the owners and the landlord".

"What do you mean, it's not going to affect you, Paul?" Donduce asked rather puzzled, interested in his answer; "Of course it is, isn't it".

"How come, Sir?" asked Paul, suddenly looking worried.

"Because we have the power to sack you" replied Donduce.

"And right now, you big headed idiot", thought Beauty.

"You can't, Sir, with all due respect, you can't. Although you are the owners and the landlord; by the right of that ownership; I work for the Brewery, and it is only them that can sack me Sir" he said.

"Who owns the Dane and Freckles, Paul?" asked Donduce.

"You do, Sir" replied Paul, looking puzzled.

"Who is in charge of the Brewery's Franchise, Paul?" asked Donduce.

"You are, Sir" replied Paul, still looking puzzled.

"So who then tells the Brewery the requirements of what is needed in the pub, as well as the supply of employees, Paul?" asked Donduce, trying not to grin.

"You do, Sir", replied Paul, he still looked puzzled.

"So, because I employ, sorry we employ the brewery here, we select the employees who work here, who are supplied by the brewery, which means you, Paul. So, Paul, yes, we can sack you if we want, and, carry on with that sort of belligerent arrogance, we will and soon, if you are not careful!". Said Donduce.

Paul gave Donduce a very startled look, and then composed himself.

"I am sorry Sir, Ma'am", he said "I appear to have completely misunderstood the implications of my manner and comments, if you would be so kind as to forgive me and accept my sincere apologies, I would be most grateful, and please accept the offer of free drinks, for you and your good lady for the remainder of the afternoon, with mine and Yvonne's compliments".

"Firstly, my wife is not just my good lady, she is Queen Beauty, and I am King Donduce; we will be treated as such by you and everyone else, and nextly, as we own the Dane and Freckles, lock stock and barrel, how on Earth can we accept free drinks from you and your wife, when they are ours anyway, bought and paid for as part of the stock? We expect waiter service from you as from now, and if you don't mind, the Queen and I would like to come in to our establishment, as of now, so if you would be so kind as to return to your duties, it would be appreciated". Said Donduce, and wound the window up.

Donduce and Beauty watched as a very flustered Paul hurried back around the jeep and disappeared from sight round the corner.

Donduce and Beauty waited until he was completely out of sight and then burst into total hysterics.

"Oh my God, the look on his face, my Babsey, when you finished that speech was a picture", shrieked Beauty with laughter, "He really is a self opinionated total idiot; Babsey, we are not really keeping him on are we?" she asked.

"Babsey, please could we actually go to the pub now, and warm up, my Babsey? I am absolutely gasping for a coke", asked Donduce.

"Of course, my Darling, come on then Honey", and they kissed passionately.

Donduce got out and shut the door behind him, before walking round the bonnet of the jeep and making Beauty laugh, as he pretended to wipe some stains off, that Paul had left. He opened Beauty's side, she got out, and as he shut the door, he held her hands and said, "I love you beyond love itself my Angel Queen Beauty", and after Beauty had kissed him on the cheek, she said "I love you beyond love itself my handsome Angel King Donduce", and they kissed passionately. The warm glow rose from their feet and began to surround them until they were warm from head to toe; the dim circle of light orbited their bodies as well, before rising to a point about a foot above their heads; the power was strong in them, and they knew it, they had always known it, and they also knew that they were unique and the chosen ones to possess it; and, for only their private knowledge did it exist.

"Is the Queen ready to sample a royal drink?" asked Donduce.

"Yes", replied Beauty, "My Babsey, the Queen is always ready to sample several Royal drinks, as is the King, and could the King get a bleeding move on and take the Queen indoors, as it is getting awfully dry in the Queen's juices", she replied, with a giggle.

Hand in hand, and after they had flicked their hair back, making two huge sets of hooped earrings jangle, they walked to the front door of what was now their own pub, and went in to the front hallway part. They half expected it to have changed somehow, but were pleasantly surprised that everything was exactly the same as it was when they had left the previous evening. Paul was standing at the bar, talking to a customer, and Yvonne was cleaning one of the tables of glasses. She took the pile of empties on a tray to the bar, and said "Hello, how are you, Sir and Ma'am?" as she returned across their path to collect the rest.

"Absolutely fine, thank you", said Donduce, as they approached the bar, "And yourself?"

"Oh, we are fine, thanks", said Yvonne, as she put the remaining glasses on the tray, "Has Paul sp...." She was interrupted by Paul, who had come over to serve them.

"Yes, Paul has spoken to them, thanks", said Paul, very dominatory, and with a very officious tone to his voice.

"Heelllowww Again, Sir, Ma'am", said Paul, with such a massively false cheesy smile on his face, it looked as if he had slept all night with a coat hanger in his mouth: "How are you this afternoon ? " he asked, bowing to Donduce, and then to Beauty.

"For god's sake, DON'T laugh, Babsey", thought Donduce to Beauty, "You'll just start me off".

"I just cannot look at you, my Lovey, for a minute", squeaked Beauty in her thoughts; she could feel the tears of laughter beginning to well up inside her.

"We are just as fine as we were when Yvonne asked us" replied Donduce, "and that was at least ten seconds ago", he added, then he asked Paul, "How are you Paul, since I gave you that bollocking, less than ten minutes ago" have you packed your bags yet? No sign of this waiter service yet either. I don't know: just can't get the staff these days".

"Oh, how very droll Sir, ha haa!! Your drinks are coming right over Sir, and I'm sorry again for any upset I may have caused to you, King Donduce, and you Queen Beauty; your wish is my command".

Queen Beauty smiled and thought "Good, sod off then".

"Your apologies are accepted, Paul", replied Donduce, and quickly swapped hands with Beauty, he shook hands with Paul, using his right, and Paul's left.

"I will bring your drinks over", he called, as Donduce and Beauty went over to their table by the fire. Donduce took Beauty's coat and put it on the spare chair. Then he took off his own and did the same, then, flicking their hair forward, sat down in the body swallowing settee style seats.

"Awwww, that's better, my Babsey," said Beauty as she made herself comfortable, sticking her feet out so they were just under the table.

"It is, my Lovey", replied Donduce, and added "Here come the drinks, right on cue".

Paul was approaching with two glasses of coke on a silver tray. He got to the table, and placed one glass in front of Beauty, and the other in front of Donduce.

"Would either of you like any nuts in a bowl?" he asked politely.

"Er, no thank you" replied Donduce and thought to Beauty "Nuts! Nuts! Oh my God, my Babsey, but it has given me an idea, shall we have some fun, my Angel?"

"Oh, darling" said Beauty in her thoughts "This just couldn't get any funnier....could it? Yes please for some fun my Sweetheart, what do you have in mind, my Babsey?" she thought, smiling.

"Watch, and enjoy, my darling" thought Donduce, with a grin.

"Ok, my Lord, enjoy," replied Paul. He turned and headed back to the access gap.

Donduce moved his left hand and pointed discretely across at a couple who were sitting on a similar seat against the left hand wall of the room.

"Excuse me", said the man, beckoning Paul to them, "We are feeling a bit peckish. Do you have a menu available please?"

"Of course Sir", said Paul and detoured to a pile on the bar. Picking one up, he went over and handed it to them.

"When you have made your choice, let me know and we will sort it for you, ok, sir?" he said. (20/09/13)

"Thank you", said the man, and he and his wife looked at it and started nattering. Paul turned and headed towards the bar. Just as he was about to reach it, the man said "Excuse me please".

Paul made a ballet style mini 'U' turn without stopping, and returned to their table.

"A problem sir?" he asked politely.

"The choice: 'Coq Isles St. Jaques'; please could you (Oh my God, Babsey, I am crying with laughter here, and I think you are giggling too aren't you...continue...) explain to us what it is? It does sound nice", said the man.

"It really does", added his wife, and then she said "Please could you tell us what the dish 'Coq Isle St. Jaques', consists of? What it is, it does sound nice".

"Oh my God, Babsey, No!" thought Beauty to Donduce, she was keeping a straight face, but inside was in hysterics.

"Keep watching, my Lovey", thought Donduce to Beauty.

"Certainly Sir, Madam" replied Paul, patiently. "That particular dish is originally from France. It consists of a scallop shell, shaped like a small plate, and on it, various types of sea food, prawns, mussels etc, with a cheese and parsley sauce as a topping".

"Ok, it sounds lovely", said the man, "We'll let you know when we want to order, thank you".

"Certainly Sir", replied Paul, and returned on his trip to the bar, he nearly made it this time, except that the man said "Excuse me" again, and Paul raised his eyes to the ceiling, before making another mini 'U' turn, and returning to their table once more, looking rather red faced.

"We are ready to order now please", said the man.

"Of course sir, what would you like, the…" started Paul.

"The plaice and chips with peas please, twice, and an extra portion of onion rings please", said the man.

"Yes", added his wife, "The plaice and chips with peas please, twice, and an extra portion of onion rings" she said.

"Ok, ok", said Paul, writing it all down. "Thank you sir", he said, and jokingly added, "I nearly wrote it down twice then sir".

"Why's that, waiter?" asked the man.

"Oh, no reason, Sir", replied Paul, and said "Your order will be ready as soon as possible sir, thank you". With that, Paul nearly ran towards the kitchen doors, out of sight, round the corner.

Donduce took a slurp of his coke as the quiet murmur of conversation resumed once more. "What do you think of the show so far, my Lovey?" he asked Beauty with a giggle.

"Oh my God, my Babsey", replied Beauty, wiping her eyes. "That's all I can say, my Honey at the moment. My stomach completely aches with all the laughing, and trying to keep a straight face whilst all that was being said was even funnier, my Lovey".

"Well Sweetheart", said Donduce, "You do realise that it is going to get worse, don't you?" he added giggling.

"It CAN'T get any worse, my Honey…..can it?" exclaimed Beauty, and had several large slurps of her beer, whilst half of her attention obviously being with her husband, the other half on events happening with this apparently mad couple seated half way up the room.

"You just watch and enjoy, my Babsey" said Donduce. "Anyway, it appears that we do indeed own the Dane and Freckles, and also this other pub called the ELKNYAK Arms, my darling. We will have to go there sometime, but , unannounced. That way, we can see and experience at first hand, the vibe of the place, what the staff are like, and the kind of clientele that the pub attracts. I haven't yet looked at any of the sales returns for either here or there yet, but then again, we have only just come from the meeting, my Angel. What made me laugh was how fast news travels, as we came in here originally to recover, and to find out if we really did own the place, only to find out everything before we had even put one foot through the door. I am however very glad, my Lovey, that it worked out the way it did, as we have already put Paul in his place over his rudeness, especially with his apparent total lack of respect for us. He is a borrowed time, but we will keep him on for the time being my Lovey".

"Yes, my Babsey, it is amazing how fast the jungle drums work here" said Beauty, and added "I am so glad that you deal with all the business side of things. I can also see as well, how our views are going to influence things like you said, my Babsey, both on and off the Estate. Oh yes, my Babsey, when we get back, somehow, we are going to have to clear a path to the back of the field, how are we going to do that, by tomorrow morning, my Babsey?"

"Don't worry, my Angel" said Donduce, as he finished his coke; "All will be revealed when we get back home after we have had another one" he said, and looked at Beauty's glass. "Still a bit left my Babsey" he chuckled, "Come on my Lovey, chop, chop!"

Beauty slurped the rest of her coke, and then put her glass down. "I love you my Darling", she said, "And yes please to one more, and then we had better be going my Angel".

Donduce was looking around for Paul or Yvonne to summon up a refill, but they had both disappeared, he assumed into the kitchen.

"Coming up, my Babsey" he said, "And yes, we will go after we have had this one. I would go and get the drinks myself, with you, but I don't want it known that we are the owners, well, not yet, anyway".

Just then, Yvonne appeared behind the bar, and Donduce called her, and asked for another two drinks.

"Coming up", she called back and in next to no time, she had brought them over and put them down on the table.

"There you are my King and Queen", she said, "Enjoy".

"Thank you very much" said Donduce, and Yvonne called, "You're welcome" as she returned to the bar.

Donduce and Beauty kissed, raised their glasses and said "Cheers, here's to us", and took a slurp. Just then they heard a thud, as the kitchen doors thudded shut which heralded the return of Paul.

"Right, watch this, my Angel" said Donduce with a chuckle.

"I can't wait, my Sweetheart", said Beauty, and looked on.

Paul came into view, carrying two large plates, each with a large piece of breaded plaice, steaming, a pile of chips and loads of peas. He walked over to within three feet of the couple's table, and then Donduce pointed to a chair just in front of the man and woman on the opposite side of the table. It moved, directly in front of Paul, who instantly tripped over it, and each plate flew out of his hands and landed, food side first on the faces of the man and woman. The plates, slid down onto their laps, closely followed by the food. Paul dived, rather like he had just come off a board, across the table and finished face down, his head between them; his left arm across the man, his right arm across the woman, and the rest of his body, stomach down, on the table. His upper legs were dangling over the edge of the table, and his lower legs and feet were resting on the seat of the chair, that Donduce, had, very quickly and discretly moved back to its original position.

The room fell silent, as everyone had their eyes just transfixed on the scene: everyone was motionless; customers who were just about to take a slurp, sat with their glasses held in mid air, as they just stared. The silence was broken, briefly by a piece of plaice, which had been lying on the man's knee, falling onto the floor carpet, making a flopping thuddy sound.

The man turned to his wife; and as he did, a couple of chips dropped off his head and landed on the carpet. "When the waiter recovers, shall we ask him, if he could replace our order with that 'Coq Isle St. Jaques' thing: it did actually look nice".

His wife turned her head, and a whole load of peas rolled down the back of her shoulders and onto the settee seat next to her. "Yes, we could do", she said, "We could ask the waiter when he recovers, if he could replace our order with that 'Coq Isle St Jaques' thing; it did actually look nice".

Paul's arms started flapping, one over the belt line of the man, and the other one over the waist line of the woman; he looked like he was trying to take off, but with a muffled sound, as his head and face were still pressed against the cushioned back of the settee.

Donduce and Beauty were just watching in silent fascination, and then a couple of the regulars, went over, one each side of the table. Supporting one arm and with a hand around his back, they each pulled Paul into an upright position.

"Thank you", said Paul, and eventually climbed off the chair.

"I am dreadfully sorry about that", said Paul to the couple, as he dusted himself down. "The washrooms are just round the corner, if you want to freshen up. I really don't know what happened there: I was just about to tell you that I was going to return to the kitchens to get your extra portions of onion rings, but I don't think they really matter now, do they; my apologies again; I just didn't see that chair, Sir".

"Which one?" asked the man, puzzled.

"Which one?" asked his wife, also puzzled.

Paul looked around and said, "The one I bleeding tripped over, which one did you think?" Paul was now really irritated by these two parrot like idiots, and was just about to return to the staff area and change into something else, when the man said "Ok, waiter, we can't resist it, we simply must try the 'Coq Isle St Jaques', except we would like to eat it and not wear it, thank you. Please also don't forget the portions of onion rings that we ordered as extra, don't you agree, my dear?"

"Oh yes", replied his wife "Waiter, we can't resist it, we simply must try the 'Coq Isle St Jaques', except we would like to eat it and not wear it thank you. Please also don't forget the portions of onion rings that we ordered as extra".

Without a word, Paul turned and walked stiffly back towards the kitchen doors, looking straight ahead, just like the man in the top hat who carries a cane, leading a wake.

Beauty looked at her husband, at the same time as he looked at Beauty.

"That was brilliant, my Lovey", she thought "You orchestrated all of that my Babsey?"

"The whole lot, my Lovey", thought Donduce back to her. "Even down to their mind bendingly irritating repeating conversation" he thought. "That is the power I have, and you can use through me, whenever you want my Angel".

"Wow...my Babsey" thought Beauty, and they carried on slurping their drinks.

The regulars who had helped Paul up had returned to the bar. A normal buzz of conversation resumed, and the lady had gone off to survey the damage she had experienced, in the Lady's bathroom.

The man remained and he was quietly slurping, and looking around generally. Yvonne was nowhere to be seen, and Donduce and Beauty assumed she was in the kitchen helping Paul prepare that bloody dish. They kissed passionately, and just as they finished, Yvonne reappeared and came over to their table. "King Donduce, and my Queen Beauty" she said with a very timid and apologetic voice. "Please would you mind at all if I disturbed you for a minute and asked you something?"

"Of course not", said Donduce, and thought to Beauty "This should be good, maybe even sack Paul and keep Yvonne employed; now how interesting would that be, my Angel?"

"Yes, it should, my Babsey", thought Beauty "Let's see what she has to say".

"You carry on, Yvonne", said Donduce, in a very business like manner.

"Thank you, my Lord", she started. "I will ask you straight out, after Paul's attitude with you outside earlier, and the accident he has just told me about, which happened in front of you, is he going to be sacked?" Yvonne had the expression on her face of someone who is praying that the answer was 'no', but waiting with a sort of distant hope and awkwardness that she might be greatly relieved with a more positive answer. Donduce saw all of this written all over her face and in her body language; normally, when someone is having an argument or negative conversation, they have at least one hand on their hips, or arms folded. Yvonne had both hands crossed in front of her, over her stomach, and her head was bowed slightly, as if she was standing in front of her old headmistress.

"No, Yvonne, he isn't", said Donduce firmly, but added, "However, he does need to buck his ideas up somewhat drastically; especially with that brash, sarcastic attitude, not to mention his pompous and parsimonious manner. He has got to remember that them people, well in fact everyone in here, apart from the Queen and I, are paying his wages. Does he know that you have come out to ask me what you did ask, Yvonne?"

"No", she replied. "I just said that I was popping back to the bar to check if anyone needed serving whilst he was busy".

"Ok", said Donduce "Just do me one favour, don't tell him that we have had this conversation Yvonne. Do I have your word?"

"Yes, you do, and thank you", she replied, and then returned back to the bar, disappearing from view out the back through the door marked private.

"That was interesting, my Lovey", said Donduce, when Yvonne had gone, and this will be a very good test of his managerial skills too" he said, having a very large slurp of his coke.

"I know why as well, Babsey", said Beauty, "It will test I guess Yvonne, as well as Paul, but as you will explain it a lot better than I could, I'll tell you, my Angel", said Beauty again, but with a giggle. "Well, my Angel", said Donduce, "There are many issues that will be addressed, simply when Yvonne gets back to Paul. If she keeps her promise and doesn't tell him anything about our conversation, it will be solely down to his own choice to change his attitude, as he won't know that the King and Queen are reviewing his position. Of course Yvonne knows, but will she just keep quiet and maybe watch him dig an impossibly deep hole for himself? She has promised the King that she will keep quiet; where do her loyalties lie? with the King, who has supreme control, or with her husband who she loves and obeys, in theory. What happens if I do sack him and she tells him that he *was* under review; or if I keep him on, and she confesses anyway? How will he react? a secret between them, and over such an important issue. His temper; her timidness, and all because she promised me she would keep quiet! How exciting, eh? My Angel?" said Donduce.

"Absolutely brilliant, my Lovey", she replied "I know you would explain it better. Now then, my gorgeous husband; we had better depart and sort out what we are going to do about this site access".

"When we get back, my Babsey", said Donduce, "You are going to be astonished; astounded, because you will see the largest demonstration of power yet" said Donduce. He looked at Beauty's glass, and it was still quite full, as, Donduce had forgotten, with his power, he had topped both of them up full.

"Yes, my Babsey, still some left", said Beauty happily, "What time is it, anyway, it must be quite late now, I noticed it was sort of approaching dusk when Paul collared us in the car park".

Donduce looked at his watch: "Crikey, my Babsey, it's eight fifteen, we do want to get back really by nine thirty, as we have to go for a little walk".

"A walk, my Lovey, at this time of night?" Beauty exclaimed. "Do we really have to, my Sweetheart, it's dark!"

"Believe me, my Angel", said Donduce, with a very dramatic and reassuring tone to his voice, "You won't be cold, it won't be dark, and it will be worth the trip just to see the look on your face when I show you something; trust me Babsey", he added.

"Ok then, my Sweetheart", said Beauty, and then added "Babsey, can I ask you something?"

"Of course you can, my Angel", Donduce replied, looking puzzled; "What's up? What's on your mind, Honey?"

"If we have enough time, my gorgeous Hubby, after this marvellous trip, dearest, beloved, wonderful, gorgeous, my King Donduce", Beauty started, but then her Husband finished off her question for her.

"Yes, of course we will be coming back here after we have done what we have to do, my Lovey, I think we will need to anyway" said Donduce.

"Awww, thank you my Lovey", said Beauty, giggling, and then asked, "Babsey, when you just said 'we will need to anyway', why?"

"To recover, my darling", laughed Donduce, kissing her on the forehead.

"Babsey, recover from what?" asked Beauty, a very curious expression came over her pretty little face.

"Ah, you will find out my gorgeous Angel", said Donduce, being deliberately mysterious; "Dun, Du-Dun, Dun, Duuunnn", he added, giggling. (No, Sweetheart, that was Donduce saying the Dun, Dun, bit, not me! Don't panic! Well, not yet anyway..You're giggling aren't you! Carry on.....)

As Donduce and Beauty continued to slurp their drinks, a few more customers came in and a few left. It was a sort of switch over really; the people coming in were there for the evening, after they had finished their dinner, whereas the people going were either returning for their dinner, or just going home for the night.

The lady had now returned from cleaning herself up; she didn't look any different: about seventy-ish, greyish white hair, well it was until it got covered in chip oil, a thick jumper sort of creation with a huge pearl necklace, and a tweed skirt, which did look truly appallingly awful. The man had a suit on and remained unchanged; neither Donduce or Beauty knew if he had actually gone to the gents to clean up: they hadn't seen him go, but he was just sitting on his part of the settee looking very pensive. Donduce said to Beauty as they both looked at him "Babsey, that man looks as if he is sitting in a doctor's surgery waiting to be called; I would love to go over to him and say "Hello, Mr Whatever, the doctor *will* see you now, and yes, it is terminal".

Beauty, who was, just then, slurping on her coke, and had just swallowed, coughed violently, and put her glass down again rather quickly. "Oh my God, my Lovey", she giggled, "Coke everywhere again", she wiped her mouth, and then cleared her throat, "God, I love you my Babsey", she said passionately.

"I love you too, my Lovey", said Donduce, and they kissed passionately again.

"I wonder what sort of nice little catastrophe we can create before we go, my Babsey?" said Donduce, looking thoughtful.

At that point, the kitchen doors thudded again, and Paul returned carrying two more steaming plates, with the couple's replacement order steaming away. Yvonne followed him with the long lost, but now re saved extra portions of onion rings. This time, they both made it to the couple's table, and Paul very carefully placed each plate in front of them.

"With the compliments of the manager", announced Paul, and fiddled with the white towel he had draped over his right shoulder.

"We do hope you enjoy your meal Sir, Madam" he added, as Yvonne placed the onion rings on the table, each one next to the larger plate.

"Thank you very much, waiter", said the man, looking pleasantly surprised with the inviting plate of steaming food sitting under his nose, "This looks delicious, and please could you convey our thanks to the management please, waiter" he added.

"Thank you very much, waiter", said his wife, also looking pleasantly surprised. She looked at hers, and then at his plate, "and, this looks delicious", she continued predictably, "Please could you convey our thanks to the management please, waiter", she said.

"Erm, well actually", said Paul, standing to his full height, "I am the manager, not actually a waiter, and your thanks are gratefully received".

Yvonne, who had finished serving and was now standing next to Paul, had heard the way these two spoke and couldn't resist a comment. "Yes, actually", she said, "He is the manager, and not actually a waiter, and I am actually the manageress, and not actually a waitress; and yes, your thanks are gratefully received".

Before the couple had time to comment further, Paul and Yvonne turned, and made a bee line for the kitchen doors again. They weren't exactly running, but they both made it to the doors together, and there was a very loud thud as the doors shut behind them.

"That's it! Babsey!" exclaimed Beauty, "I have just thought of a brilliant finale to all of this, my Lovey" she said.

"Ok, my Babsey, go on then", said Donduce, looking excited now. "Right, my Sweetheart", Beauty said and made sure she was holding both of Donduce's hands. She shut her eyes, and went into spiritual meditation for several minutes, before resuming her normal position. As Beauty used the power of the vibe, even on her side of things via her Husband, he could see exactly what she had in mind, and what had organised. When Beauty had finished, and opened her beautiful eyes, he said to her "Brilliant, my Sweetheart, I cannot wait myself now".

It was Beauty's turn to look at her husband and say "My Babsey, now you watch and enjoy, my darling".

Beauty and Donduce continued slurping the rest of their drinks, and watched. After a minute or two, the door to the bar opened and a couple walked in. As the door slowly swung shut again; sometimes, it was attached to one of them closing arm contraptions, and this was one of those occasions, a cat wandered in and stood somewhat discretely but attentively on the other side of the door. It started down the length of the room and looked directly at Beauty. From that distance, even, you could see it was black, and you could also see it's pale green eyes.

Beauty stared back at the cat and then passed her right hand, from right to left, across the table, before replacing it back on top of Donduce's.

Silently, and without hesitation, the cat walked very quickly, straight over to the couple's table, jumped up onto it, walked straight into their dinner, and lay down, with it's head and front paws in the middle of the man's plate, and it's bum and back paws in the middle of the womans.

"Mission accomplished, my Babsey", thought Beauty, as the cat discretely looked over at her, and at Beauty's nod, started eating the man's dinner, between it's paws.

"Absolutely brilliant, my Lovey", thought Donduce, giggling, "Well done you, my Babsey", he added, trying hard to ignore the hullaballoo, coming from the table. The couple had shot up, and had started dancing round the table, yelling "Shoo, shoo", to try and remove their unwanted guest. They both sat down again, and just stared at the cat, who by now had finished what it wanted on the man's plate, had got up and done a small pirouette to turn round, then started on the woman's.

It did look up briefly at Beauty, who had to smile, as it had sauce all round it's little mouth.

Donduce and Beauty finished the last of their drinks, and Donduce said, "Well, my Lovey, I think it's time to make a move, wouldn't you agree, my Queen?"

"Yes, my Lovey, it is, until later", she replied, then added, "What *is* the time, my Sweetheart?"

Donduce looked at his watch "8:45pm, my Babsey, plenty of time to go and come back again", he said.

They kissed passionately and then both stood up. Donduce helped Beauty on with her coat and flicked her hair back for her, making sure it was straight, dangling down to her ankles. Then Beauty did the same to her husband's hair, once he had put his coat on, and his hair was now just below his bum.

Just as they were about to leave, Paul appeared again at the bar, and saw Donduce and Beauty standing up. "Coming back later, my Lord? Ma'am?" he asked.

"Oh yes, Paul", replied Donduce, as he took Beauty's hand and they started to make their way towards the door.

"That's good, see you later then Sir, Ma'am" he called after them, and then he glanced over at the couple.

As Donduce and Beauty opened the bar door to go out, they heard Paul's dulcet tones from within, "What the bleeding hell is that bleeding cat doing on a customer's bleeding table, in my bleeding pub? Who the bleeding hell let the bleeding thing in, in the bleeding first place, bleeding hell, that's all I bleeding need, I bleeding.....", the door had shut and so they didn't hear the rest of Paul's reaction to the situation; as they went through the open outer door and into the night air. Donduce said "Peace resumes again, my Lovey, situation normal, and I love you; God that was funny, what an evening, and it's not over yet!"

"I know, my Babsey", said Beauty, "It was another hilarious evening, but I will have to explain to the cat that on this occasion it was a one off; and is not usually allowed to jump up on tables, eating the customer's dinner. Although them too will definitely never be back in again, which is no great loss, pair of idiots, we cannot allow animals into the bar area, (21/09/13) because of the food: I don't mean family ones, they are on leads, they are fine, I mean stray ones off the street, my Lovey", said Beauty. They had already got to the jeep, and Donduce had already unlocked it. He was holding the passenger door open for Beauty, and they kissed passionately before she flicked her hair.

"God, l love you my Angel", said Donduce, as Beauty settled into her seat; she made sure that her beautiful long hair didn't touch the floor of the jeep, by folding it, ever so slightly, so that it fell just over her knees. It was dark outside and as Beauty sat back up again, leaning her beautiful head against the rest, Donduce noticed how visible the golden aurora of the vibe was, that surrounded her whole body, but especially around her head.

"My Babsey, the power in you is really strong tonight, I can see you glowing; it always does when you have been using it more than usual, especially with that cat, my Angel", said Donduce.

"It's funny you should say that, my Babsey, and my God, I love you too: I was just going to say that I noticed the glow around you increase dramatically as well, after all them happenings in the Dane and Freckles, my Angel", replied Beauty, and then added "The power of the vibe is so strong in both of us, and we both know who to thank for that, my Angel".

"We certainly do, my Babsey", said Donduce, and added "Is one comfy?"

"Very", replied Beauty, "I love you my Angel, now chop chop and in you get".

"I love you too, my Sweetheart", replied Donduce, and after kissing passionately, he shut Beauty's door and walked round the front and got in his side.

Once he had settled in, and they had kissed once more, Beauty's hand rested in it's usual place on Donduce's knee. He started the engine, and instantly the heater came on, blowing warm air all round their feet and legs.

"Well, my Angel, what an afternoon that turned out to be", said Donduce, as they pulled out of the car park and turned right. "Very soon, my Sweetheart", he continued, "We will be home, and then we can have our short walk, get back, and then come straight back to the Dane and Freckles, if you so desire. During our short walk, I am going to completely blow your mind, but, my Angel, I will need your help: is that ok, my Lovey?"

"Of course it is my Darling", replied Beauty, excitedly, "but what are you going to do? How are you going to blow my mind? Babsey, my Lovey, I really can't wait".

"Don't worry, my Babsey, all will be revealed", teased Donduce giving Beauty a loving smile, he loved keeping his beautiful bride in suspense. ("Don't I bloody know it!!" I can hear you shouting my Angel. I love you Babsey – you're giggling – carry on….)

They were just over half way down AKKS Lane now, and not far away from home.

"Oh crumbs, Honey, I wonder how them pigeons are, in the kitchen", exclaimed Beauty, "And Fang; in all the excitement of this afternoon, I had forgotten all about them", she added.

"I am sure they are all just fine, my Angel", reassured Donduce, "The pigeons are probably roosting on the worktop, and Fang is probably asleep on the floor as usual, my Babsey, which reminds me actually, Honey, now them pigeons are part of the family, they need names. Any ideas as to what we are going to call them, my Sweetheart?"

"I hadn't given it a thought, my Lovey", replied Beauty, looking thoughtful, then added "What do you think, my Babsey?"

"Don't know yet, my Lovey" he replied "But we will think of something that sounds right, my poppet".

They pulled into their front driveway after what seemed like no time at all, and Donduce left the jeep close to the front door.

"We are going back out soon, so we might as well leave it here, my Babsey", he said, taking the keys back out of the ignition.

"Ok, my Darling", said Beauty, and they kissed passionately.

Donduce got out, and shut the door, walked around to Beauty's side, blowing a kiss through the windscreen on the way. Opening her door, he leant in and they kissed passionately, before Beauty got out, and Donduce shut the door behind her, making sure that her hair wasn't caught anywhere.

"Awww, I love you, my Angel", said Beauty, as they held hands, even on the short distance to the front door.

"I love you too, my Babsey" replied Donduce, as he got their keys out. "Right, my Babsey", he said. "We'll go in, and check on

Fang, he should be ok, so should the pigeons. Then we'll pick up the flash lights, and go straight out again; is that ok, my Angel?"

"Of course it is, my Lovey", replied Beauty, "Them lights are still in the bag in the kitchen from this morning, I think, my Lovey" she added. "Oh crumbs, Honey", Beauty said again, as they walked through the front door entrance, "I wonder if ELKY and his family are in their meadow yet, my Angel. They said that they were moving to it this afternoon; I wonder if they arrived in the end".

"We will soon find out, my Honey", said Donduce as he shut the front door, locked it and set the alarm.

"My Babsey", said Beauty as she watched him, "Don't forget that we are going out again later, my Lovey".

"Oh shit yes", laughed Donduce, "Babsey, that is pure habit for you, Don't worry, I will just reset it when we go out, my Angel", he added.

They walked through to the kitchen, and, as predicted, all four pigeons were in a line, under the window sill, on the worktop, with their heads tucked under their wings, fast asleep. Their ferocious guard dog was also curled up by the breakfast bar sound asleep too. Donduce and Beauty gave each other a knowing look, and tiptoed over to the bar and picked up the bag. Then, very quickly, they both opened the back door, and closed it very quietly behind them, locking it securely.

"Ok, then my Angel, let's go", said Donduce, excitedly, and put his arm round Beauty.

"Yes please, my Babsey", said Beauty, and they headed off across the back yard. It was dark, but like the previous evening, when they had gone with ELKY to find out about his hidden family, the moon was shining down on the yard causing the usual shadows to be cast across the slabs of the yard floor. Even the shadow of the rotary looked elongated and a bit like a giant sundial, as they walked towards the gap next to the coal bunker and on to ELKY's meadow.

"My Babsey", said Beauty, holding her husband's hand tightly. "I wonder if he and his family are in the meadow? If they are, we had better sneak past them as they will want to know where we are going, and maybe come with us; that is, if they are all awake. Come to think of it, my Angel, where ARE we going?" Beauty finished the last part of what she was saying with a giggle.

"We had better walk through the meadow quietly, just in case they ARE here, my Angel", replied Donduce in an audible whisper, and then, still whispering he added, "I can tell you though, that we are going down the pathway, my Babsey".

"Well, I sort of gathered THAT, my Angel", said Beauty, in a mocking but loving whisper, "Der! I just don't know how far down the pathway we are going to get, my Babsey. Are we going back to where we found ELKY's family then?" she asked.

They had stopped for a minute as they had got as far as the other end of the green entrance, where the short grass finished and the long grass started, right by the back of the coal bunker.

"No, my Lovey", replied Donduce, still whispering, "Not that far, but a little way, you'll soon see, my Babsey".

At the back of the bunker, they both peered around it like two fugitives, escaped convicts, wondering how they were going to make the dash across this meadow, without disturbing anyone or anything or without a big search light suddenly turning on them and a booming voice yelling "Halt, who goes there?"

The moonlight caused the longish grass in the meadow to take on a misty silvery look, and the trees at the back took on a black appearance against a slightly lighter night sky. The trees, silhouetted against this starry backdrop almost looked menacing, especially to the casual observer, but it didn't phase Donduce or Beauty as the area was home.

"There they are, my Babsey, far left, over there, four grey lumps. They *are* all here, but together, and, they are all asleep. That's handy. All we have to do then is just walk, very quietly, straight ahead to the tree line, and then we should find the ancient pathway, my Lovey".

"Oh, bless them, my Angel, don't they look sweet, all together, and at peace, knowing that they are safe and secure", said Beauty happily, "How any bloody human could shoot even one of them, let alone a whole family or even an entire herd come to that is totally beyond me; it's hideous; appallingly awful, Babsey" she whispered.

"I know, my Angel" replied Donduce comfortingly, and added "Rest assured, my Lovey, that I will sort that poaching problem out as one of our top priorities.

Hand in hand, Donduce and Beauty started to cross ELKY's meadow. It was the first time that they had gone to the meadow not wanting to disturb ELKY or his family, and also the first time that they would have to find the entrance to, or rather the start of the ancient pathway on their own. They walked almost on tiptoe, and they could feel the dew of the long grass dampening their jeans, just below their knees. Their boots started to take on a wet appearance, and even though their feet and lower legs were warm, they still felt wet.

"When we left the pathway this morning coming back, my Angel", whispered Donduce as they walked, "The coal bunker was directly in front of us; you could see it in the distance, my Babsey". He looked back, sure enough, it *was* directly behind them. "Good, my Angel", he whispered, "All we have to do is walk straight ahead, my Babsey, and we should find it very easily".

"That's brilliant, Babsey my Lovey", whispered Beauty, peering round herself and automatically holding her hair with her right hand, and added "Of course, my Lovey, we can't use the floodlights yet, because ELKY and his family might spot them".

"Exactly, my Princess", whispered Donduce, "We are nearly at the tree line now, and, my Babsey, the moonlight is making it easier to make them out better: we might not actually need the flashlights anyway, well, not yet, but later on the path".

"Babsey my Lovey", whispered Beauty, "I don't know if it is any help", as they approached the thick line of trees, "But you know the pathway was all sort of muddy and certainly well trodden, well it had a sort of brown look to it, and so did the ground surrounding the entrance. There wasn't any tall grass there my Babsey".

"Yes, my Lovey", whispered Donduce, "That is a good point, so when we get really close, if we are on the right track, pardon the pun, the tall grass we are walking on should give way to a flatter surface, my Darling".

"Yes, darling", Beauty giggled.

"What Darling?" Donduce asked, giggling himself, "What's so funny, darling?"

"Well darling", giggled Beauty in a whisper "You did state the obvious; of course the grass will give way to a flatter surface if we get to the pathway.....darling".

"Oh Kay, clever clogs", giggled Donduce, and he kissed Beauty on the forehead.

They looked back once more, and could just see the bunker in the distance, directly behind them still. On they went and about two minutes later, sure enough, the long grass flattened out. They could see the trees fairly clearly now with branches hiding virtually everything beyond. Straight ahead they looked, and, yes, they could see the beginning of the pathway.

"There it is, my Lovey" said Donduce excitedly, "I remember that tallish tree just to the right of it; we had to walk round that bit of branch sticking out, and ELKY made a great point last night of walking round it. He was obviously telling us that he used it as a marker, the clever thing".

"Brilliant, my Lovey", whispered Beauty once more, and added "I guess that this is where our walk really starts, my Angel".

"Yes, my Lovey", said Donduce", "But", he added, "We Isn't going far my Babsey".

The arched gap that marked the start of the pathway entrance was pitch black, and so Beauty got a couple of flash lights out of the bag that Donduce had on his back. Then, handing her husband one, they turned them on and shone them forward.

The pathway almost now seemed familiar, just a grey, ghostly strip of ground disappearing off in a straight line into the distance.

"Come on then, my Lovey", declared Donduce "Let's begin".

"Aye aye Sir, my Babsey", giggled Beauty, and gave her husband a salute; they both fell about in fits of giggles; before they even started their walk.

The chlostrophobic feeling of the enclosed space started coming back to them after a few minutes of their trek. They were walking quite quickly; Donduce knew what he wanted to do, and he knew Beauty would be totally amazed, and he was also aware of the time and wanted to be back in the Dane and Freckles for a well earned night cap.

"Blimey, my Angel", said Donduce, after what only seemed a few minutes, "Here's the right turn already; that didn't take long at all, did it, my Angel".

"No it didn't, my Lovey", replied Beauty, thoughtfully, "Babsey", she said as they rounded the bend and carried on; the beams of the flashlights dancing from side to side as they went, "We are now walking roughly round the side of that big field where the palace is going, aren't we, my Honey?" she asked.

"That's right, my Sweetheart", replied Donduce, and added "Soon, my Lovey, we will get to the left hand turn of the pathway, my Babsey, where the big site field stops".

"So, my Lovey, what happens after that then, my Angel" asked Beauty, sounding very curious, and dying to know what was going to happen, when they arrived at wherever they were going "Don't worry, my Babsey", reassured Donduce, "All will be revealed very soon", he added, and held Beauty's hand tightly.

After about fifteen minutes of walking, at quite a brisk pace, Donduce and Beauty arrived at the left hand bend, walked round and went a few yards along, and then Donduce said "Ok, my Lovey, I think we are here".

He looked behind them and they were about sixty to seventy feet from the bend. He looked up the path, and knew that in the distance, on the right, was ELKY's wife's old meadow; he shone the flashlight, just to get some idea of distance. He gave Beauty a kiss on her forehead, and said "I'm sorry, my Lovey, but we have got to go on ahead, but only by another ten yards; is that alright, my Angel? Do you mind my Babsey?, he asked.

"Of course it's ok, my Babsey, but, I am dying to know; where exactly *is* 'here', and what is it that you are going to show me that will totally blow me away; amaze me, my Angel? This is just the ancient pathway; and we have been here before", said Beauty; she sounded both really, and curious.

"Here, my Babsey", said Donduce, "Is not an object, it's a position".

They walked up the remaining ten yards, and then Donduce said. "Right, my Lovey, we have now arrived". He shone the flashlight back down the pathway, and the bend was now virtually out of sight. He shone it up the path, and the other meadow was even further away than that.

"This is the perfect position, my Babsey" said Donduce, "And I now need your help, my Lovey", he added, smiling.

"Ok, my beautiful Hubby", said Beauty, full of excitement, "Is this where you are going to completely amaze me, my Lovey" she asked, curiously.

"I do hope so, my Sweetheart", he said, "Now, stand next to me, just here, in the middle of the pathway, and look straight ahead, my Lovey. What do you see my Babsey?" Donduce asked her.

"Well, Honey", replied Beauty, looking very puzzled, "Apart from the pathway, disappearing off into the distance, and the trees lining it either side, oh, and the other meadow, right up there on the right hand side, which we can't see from here, nothing, my Babsey".

"Good", said Donduce. "Take my right hand in your left, and hold your right arm out straight next to you, as if you are trying to reach the right hand side trees my Angel".

Beauty, who did have both hands wrapped around her husband, as did he with her, did just that, and as she put her right arm out, Donduce did the same with his left; his right hand held Beauty's left hand tightly.

"Ok,......My Babsey", he said, "Watch".

Donduce and Beauty stood in this position, in the middle of the sacred pathway. Nothing happened for a couple of moments, and then a very faint rumbling sound could be heard. It got louder and louder, and Beauty asked, "My God, my Lovey, what's that?"

"Don't worry, my Angel" he said, "Just watch, my Babsey".

The rumbling didn't get any louder, but just remained at a constant level, like the sound of distant horses. A mist quickly began to form around Donduce and Beauty, and indeed quite a lot of the immediate pathway area.

"Oh my God!" exclaimed Beauty; her eyes wide open in disbelief, "That tree, up there, on the left, it's moving backwards!" As Beauty stared transfixed, the tree, that had been with the others about ten yards up the pathway, was moving backwards, and as it did, the trees either side of it started doing the same; more and more followed suit, and on the other side of the original tree as well, until the last tree to move was just to the left of them. Then, Beauty turned her head slightly to the right, as the trees on the other side of the pathway started doing the same thing.

"Oh my God! Oh my God!" exclaimed Beauty "Babsey, Babsey, the trees are doing the same thing as the sheep did, when we returned Dolly back to her Mum, they cleared a path through the flock, so that Mary the Ewe could get through, my Babsey, bloody hell, this is amazing, my Lovey" exclaimed Beauty.

Further and further the trees moved back until the field beyond the trees was revealed, and they didn't stop moving until a big oblong of forest floor now linked the ancient pathway, with the field behind. The same had happened on the other side, so what existed now was in effect a crossroads.

"Ok, my Babsey", said Donduce, "Now, keeping your hands in the same position, step backwards with me, my Babsey, until I say stop".

"Ok, Honey", she squeaked, still absolutely awestruck at this truly magical and amazing event she had just witnessed, and copied Donduce, stepping backwards, but still looking straight ahead, until they had moved about twenty yards.

"Ok, my Babsey", said Donduce, "Stop, and watch again, my Angel". Nothing happened again for a minute or two, but then the rumbling noise started once more, and in her excitement, Beauty hadn't noticed it had stopped. It got louder again, and Beauty was looking all round to see what was changing this time, from first glance, nothing, nothing at all, then she shrieked "Oh my God! The pathway itself! Babsey, Babsey, it's sinking!" Indeed, the surface of the pathway started to develop a dip, as if someone had put their finger on a sponge and made a dent it it's flat surface. The dent increased in depth, and width until it reached about twenty feet, at the lowest part. At it's lowest point, the dip was directly in the middle of the new pathway that had been formed either side.

At that moment the mist, which had just been swirling in the air like the evaporation of early morning dew, suddenly got really thick and dense. The dip in the pathway disappeared from view, as did all of the trees; Beauty glanced left, and to her great relief, could still see her gorgeous beautiful Hubby. He was looking at her too "I love you, Babsey", he said "Are you Ok?", "Oh God, yes my Sweetheart", exclaimed Beauty,

I just wanted to make sure you were still there, my Lovey" she said, and added "I love you too, my Angel".

"Won't be long now, my Babsey", said Donduce, "And we can go and have a look", he added.

"Ok, my Babsey, God, isn't it brilliant!" said Beauty, and then added, "I'm still not actually sure what we are doing here, and how you knew this was going to happen, and what it is all for, my Lovey".

"Don't worry, my Honey" Donduce replied, "All will be revealed in a little while,…..Beauty, my Lovey, the fog is beginning to clear!"

They both watched, as the thick fog around them started to develop patches of clear spaces. They began to see the trees, or rather the outlines of the trees as they came back into view, and more and more of the pathway.

As Beauty stared into the slowly clearing fog, she became aware of a sort of big rectangular horizontal lump right in front of her. Massive, and it certainly wasn't there five minutes before. The fog cleared a bit more, the pathway came into view a bit further, and the big rectangular horizontal lump became clearer. "OH MY GOD!" exclaimed Beauty, for the third time, I don't believe it! A bridge! Over the ancient pathway! Babsey! Wow!"

The fog had completely cleared now and everything was visible. The pathway now sloped into a gradual descent and up the other side, untouched. The bridge crossed the gap with a wide arch. It was made of stone, and actually had a silvery grey appearance to it and looked as if it had been there since time began. The tree line stopped, just before the walls of the bridge where it's structure came well above the surface of the new clearing at a height of up to one's chest, and it was only possible to access this new clearing from the wood, as the tree line was so thick and dense.

"Let's go and take a close look, my Babsey" said Donduce, "There is enough moonlight to see most of it my darling" he added.

"Oh my God, yes my Babsey" said Beauty, "I just can't believe it's there; it's hard to believe any of it; come on, my Darling, let's go and look".

The only access was through the trees, so, hand in hand, they entered the dense line, and had to put the flash lights on, as within the trees it was much, much darker. There wasn't a sound in the dense forest; only the sound of Donduce and Beauty's boots making a scrunching noise as they trod on old leaves and twigs that covered the forest floor.

It didn't take them long before they broke cover, and walked out onto the new clearing. They stood roughly in the middle, and now back in the moonlight, could see more clearly. The new area was about four times the width of the ancient pathway and stretched into the big field. As it was still dark, it wasn't possible to see any further than the clearing that led into it, but it was definitely cleared, and so the field now had a main entrance of hard, solid earth and this extended across the bridge and away on the other side, through the other trees; at least, they assumed it did, for the darkness of the night restricted the view to nothing beyond the gap on the other side.

Donduce and Beauty surveyed the scene, and then walked to the bridge, leaning against the solid stone wall, just taking in the view.

"So, my Angel", said Donduce, kissing Beauty on the forehead, "What do you think of it all then", he asked.

"I just think it is amazing, my Lovey", she said, "But, my Honey, how did you know it was going to happen, and what is it all for exactly" she asked, wrapping both her arms around her gorgeous Hubby, and putting her head in it's usual place, under Donduce's chin, with his beard falling down over her pretty little face; she started fiddling with it.

"Well, my Lovey", said Donduce, "This is now the main entrance, in fact, the only entrance to the construction site, and it is going to be used for bringing in the heavy machinery that we are going to use building the palace. We did not want the forest, or indeed the ancient pathway ruined or harmed in any way whilst the construction workers travelled to and from the site. Also, we did not want the ancient pathway to be ruined by the heavy machinery that will be, in theory, spending many months crossing it, bringing in the

285

raw materials. All of that stuff would have ruined the forest, the pathway, and would have made and left an appallingly awful scar on this beautiful area which would have been impossible to remove, so, the only way to avoid all of this equipment and traffic from even touching the ancient pathway or the trees was to do two things; firstly, literally 'move' the trees out of the way, so we still haven't touched them or even chopped them down, which would have been inconceivable; they now, as a result haven't been touched or tampered with by human hands, and then nextly, build a bridge over the pathway so that it remains untouched, just, 'relocated', lower than it was. The bridge had to have a flat surface, to enable easy access for heavy construction vehicles, they don't usually cope very well with slopes or inclines, and so rather than build a curved bridge over a flat path, it was better to build a flat bridge, straddling a dipped path. The beauty of this 'arrangement' as well, is that we can restore it all, how it was, once the palace has been completed, if we so desire my gorgeous Babsey. Your final question, my beautiful bride, asking how I knew this event was going to happen, so that I could bring you and show you; we didn't come to witness it; we actually created it all when we stood with our hands out in the middle of the pathway. When I was looking up and down, sussing out a suitable spot, I was simply choosing a place that was far enough away from the start of the field, ie, the right hand bend of the pathway where it starts running along the longest edge of the field, and also, far enough away from the other meadow, as we did not want that area changed in any way. It's special, and where we met the rest of ELKY's family. Also, the bridge now, if we decide it should remain after everything is completed, will serve as a kind of official 'boundary', signalling to any would be traveller, that they are most definitely in a Royal secluded area, and to be wary that they are not meant to be this close to us, my Sweetheart. Are you ok, my Babsey,?, I will stop rabbiting now, oh yes, my Babsey, before I forget, we had come tonight to carry out this 'alteration', because Mr Cunningham's men, or rather ours now, arrive tomorrow morning, so we had to do it tonight, before *they* ruined it in the morning. Right then, my Babsey, I will now shut up, sorry my Sweetheart".

"Babsey, my Lovey", said Beauty, "I am just astounded; astonished; flabberghasted; amazed; I just can't think of a word that describes just how impressed with all of this I am, the whole thing even takes into account the conservation issues that all our animals would have had problems with, and, everything that has been altered here, whether it be temporary or not, is an area that we have not been in, and so wouldn't affect *us*. I have got to ask, my Lovey, but did our power really do all of this?"

"Yes, my Angel", replied Donduce, "Every last bit was done by the power we have, using energy transmitted through the vibe from the Earth, through us, and distributed wherever it is needed, my gorgeous Lovey".

"My goodness, my Lovey", said Beauty, dreamily, "You will be telling me that we can fly next, my Angel".

"We can, my Angel", replied Donduce, tightly hugging his beautiful Bride, and then added, "The trouble with flying, my Babsey, is that we cannot fly together. One of us must remain on the ground at all times".

"Why is that, my Darling?" asked Beauty, curiously.

"Simple, my Lovey, replied Donduce, "The Earth is our energy source. One of us has to have contact with the ground; well within, half and inch anyway. Either direct skin contact with the Earth, or no more than half an inch away, anyway. That minimum distance allows us to wear boots and still make contact, hence tonights ability; we could still do it, even with boots on. With flying, like our ability with communication, we can transmit power between us: I can stand on the ground, and enable you to 'float' as high as you would like, however, there are grave dangers with that; for instance, unexpected power losses, bad vibes; things that can cause the power to go suddenly and without warning. It would then cause one of us to fall, which would be very distressing; not only that, but we can't fly as we would not be together, and so impossible to achieve anyway." Donduce looked down at Beauty's pretty little face; she had his beard all over it, but what he could see of her, she was looking lovingly back at him. The same thought crossed their minds simultaneously and they started giggling again and said in unison "Dane and Freckles!"

"Will it still be open my Lovey?" asked Beauty, suddenly thinking of how late it was now, and the time it was going to take them to return. Donduce looked at his watch, "It's only actually ten fifteen, my Babsey", he said, "If we literally jog back, rush through the house, into the jeep that is still by the front door, my Babsey we can still make last orders. Anyway, my Lovey, you have got a completely daft husband – Of course we will make it in time; we own it!!"

"Oh my God yes, my Lovey, I just keep forgetting", said Beauty, "Anyway", she added, "We have only owned it since this afternoon, so I am allowed a mistake or two, aren't I my Angel?"

She looked at Donduce for reassurance, and they kissed passionately.

"Of course, you are my Angel", he said lovingly, then added, "Come on then, my Angel, let's start the journey back".

They left the wall of the bridge and crossing the new track started on their journey, briefly passing back through the forest, before rejoining the pathway at it's original height. There were also new fences by the edge of the trees to prevent falling from the original forest edge; the height of the bridge, to the new depth of the pathway; it was a sheer drop now, and not just a steep embankment.

In the other meadow, leaning seated against what was now his favourite tree, the gorilla was listening intently for any more signs of noise. He had been dozing, but the distant rumbling had disturbed his snooze and of course he had wondered what it was. Ambling on all fours to the clearing at the entrance to his meadow, he had peered up and down the pathway, but hadn't seen anyone or anything, and, he hadn't spotted Donduce or Beauty, despite the late evening being quite bright due to the moonlight. Then, that bloody mist, and the subsequent fog that followed rendered any chance of finding out anything impossible; in fact the fog was so thick, that he had a hard job to return to his meadow, even from the entrance, let alone his tree; he could hardly even see his paws. The gorilla had a good sense of direction though, and he did, eventually make it back, and sat down; and; just as he was congratulating himself that he *had* made it, the fog and mist had cleared completely. What the gorilla was completely unaware of, apart from obviously the new layout and the bridge, was that the fog and mist sound proofed everything, which is why the gorilla was unable to hear Donduce and Beauty, but then, they were out of ear shot anyway, so it didn't matter.

The ELKS back in their meadow were fine as well, sound asleep and oblivious to what had been going on.

Donduce and Beauty were half speed walking, in parts jogging, and often giggling in their haste to get back for orders in the 'Dane and Freckles', which didn't affect them anyway. It was just that they hadn't yet come to terms with being the new owners, and so at the moment, they both treated it all as a bit of a novelty. They had made good progress though, had come to the entrance or rather the passageway, and were doing a sort of 'quiet sneak', through ELKY's meadow, and were very close to the coal bunker once more.

"I could bloody murder a coke and a sit down, my Angel", said Donduce, rather out of breath as they got to the coal bunker clearing.

"Oh, God, yes, my, Babsey", panted Beauty and added, "It's the thought of sitting next to my beautiful Husband, in that beautiful settee, with a beautiful coke, in our own beautiful Dane and Freckles that is keeping me going".

"Me as well, my Lovey", said Donduce "And it won't be long now, my Sweetheart", he added.

They got to the farmhouse and opened the back door. They could not wait to see Fang and tell him that he was in charge *again*, and that they were going to the 'Dane and Freckles to celebrate the start of the palace, the start of running their new company 'New Foundation Construction, the start of running their own pub or even chain of pubs, helping ELKY and indeed themselves with the poaching problem, finding the gorilla, Donduce telling Beauty the horrific secret of the old empty barn and running the Royal Farm Estate Principality.

END OF PART 1

Look out for Farm News Part 2

Printed in Great Britain
by Amazon